I0651385

Henry Bascom Ridgaway

The Life of the Rev. Alfred Cookman

With a Brief Account of his Father, the Rev. George Grimston Cookman

Henry Bascom Ridgaway

The Life of the Rev. Alfred Cookman
With a Brief Account of his Father, the Rev. George Grimston Cookman

ISBN/EAN: 9783744772266

Printed in Europe, USA, Canada, Australia, Japan

Cover: Foto ©Raphael Reischuk / pixelio.de

More available books at **www.hansebooks.com**

THE LIFE OF

THE

REV. ALFRED COOKMAN;

WITH A BRIEF ACCOUNT OF HIS FATHER,

THE REV. GEORGE GRIMSTON COOKMAN.

BY

HENRY B. RIDGAWAY, D.D.

WITH A PREFACE BY THE

REV. W. MORLEY PUNSHON, LL.D.

" Suffer me to imitate the Passion of my God. My Love is crucified ; there is no fire n me desiring earthly fuel; that which lives and speaks within me says—' Home to the Father.' '
St. Ignatius yearning for Martyrdom.

Toronto :

COPP, CLARK AND CO.

—

1874.

PREFACE.

I HAVE been asked to write a few words by way of preface to an abridged edition of the "Life of Alfred Cookman," commending it to English readers. I comply cheerfully; and there is a fitness in my compliance, arising out of the fact that during my residence in Canada, I had opportunities—alas! only too few—of personal acquaintance and intercourse with that holy man, and out of the further fact that Dr. Ridgaway, the accomplished biographer, who has wrought his task of love in a way which leaves nothing to be desired, allows me to call him my friend.

If I would write down my impressions of Alfred Cookman's character, I find myself at a loss, for I can scarcely convey my lofty estimate of him in sober words. I have been privileged to meet with many gifted and godly men in various lands, and in various branches of the Catholic Church. I speak advisedly when I say that I never met with one who so well realized my ideal of *complete devotedness*. He was a separated man, thoroughly human, free from

b

asceticism and censoriousness,—the extremes into which high religious life is wont, if unwatched, to stray—and yet lifted above common cares and aims by the grandeur of his entire consecration. When some Pagan questioners asked a Christian of old about the religion of Jesus, and were disposed to ascribe its spread to its loftier thought and purer truth, the Christian made for answer, "We do not speak greater things, *but we live.*" This life, wherever it is embodied, is the highest Power. And it was felt to be so in the wide sphere in which Alfred Cookman was permitted to testify for the Master whom he loved. There are men of sterling worth who manage to hide their excellences from their fellows, living amongst men unappreciated, because they have no witness ; like some bird of rare plumage, of whose beauty the world knew not until they caught the lustre which flashed from its parting wing. He was not one of these. His life was a perpetual testimony that God can come down to man, and that man can be lifted up to God. It was impossible to doubt that "swift-like, he lived in heaven." There were many who objected to his doctrine. There were none within the range of his acquaintance who failed to be impressed, and few who failed to be influenced, by his life.

Neither apology nor introduction are needed for the issue of this book. There are some lives of godly men which belong to the Church universal in a sense so special that for any to be deprived of the teaching they bring is like the infliction of a personal wrong. Of such is the life, in my judgment, which these pages portray. It is not surpassingly interesting, considered as a story. It contains little romantic incident, and no prurient sensationalism. It is not even the record of brilliant genius, though the preacher was, like Apollos, eloquent and mighty in the Scriptures ; but it is the unfolding of the growth of a character which was perfect and beautiful as a star. It is a record of triumphs won for Christ by one who had given Him all. It is an illustration of the power of goodness. It shows how God honours on earth, and crowns at last, those who give themselves to His service with a full trust and a complete self-surrender.

May the Giver of good gifts multiply "some evangelists" of this type and pattern. If they abound—and surely some who read may catch the mantle—we will not despair of seeing a converted world.

W. MORLEY PUNSHON.

Kensington, *January*, 1874.

CONTENTS.

CHAPTER XVI.

CHAPTER XVII.

CHAPTER XVIII.

CHAPTER XIX.

CHAPTER XX.

CHAPTER XXI.

CHAPTER XXII.

CHAPTER XXIII.

CHAPTER XXIV.

CHAPTER XXV.

LIFE OF ALFRED COOKMAN.

CHAPTER I.

THE COOKMAN FAMILY.—GEORGE GRIMSTON COOKMAN.

THE REV. ALFRED COOKMAN was descended from a
worthy ancestry. His father, the Rev. George Grimston
Cookman, was a man of such powers and fame ; his talents
and reputation became, by so remarkable a providence, the
inheritance of his son ; his influence upon the son was so
direct and continuous, that I find, in the absence of any
adequate account of the father, it is quite impossible to do
justice to either without dwelling more fully on the career
of the father than a biography of the son would seem to
allow. While it might be honour enough for George G.
Cookman to be remembered as the father of Alfred, yet
there was that in him—in what he was and did—which
makes it proper that no extended memoir be given of the
son without such a portraiture of the father as shall be in
some degree worthy of his distinguished character and
services.

My apology for dwelling longer on the annals of the
father than is customary in such cases, is the simple desire
to so present the name of Cookman, made illustrious first
in the father, and maintained afterward in the son, as that

I

it shall be transmitted an unbroken name, suggestive of sanctity, eloquence, and usefulness wherever known and pronounced.

George Grimston Cookman was born in the town of Kingston-upon-Hull, Yorkshire, England, October 21, 1800. His parents were George and Mary Cookman. Of these parents George himself wrote in 1825 to Miss Mary Barton, who was then his betrothed, and afterward became his wife: " My father is the younger brother of an old English family who, as sturdy yeomanry, had resided upon their family estates in the east end of Holderness for five generations back. My father left home early in life, and at eighteen years of age became serious, and a member and local preacher in the Methodist Society. He is constant in all his purposes, and unwavering in all his attachments—a judicious rather than a romantic husband, a kind rather than a fond father. He is independent in his principles even to the verge of republicanism ; what the world terms a downright honest man. Yet there are perplexing paradoxes in his character. Possessing genuine, active courage, he hides it under a natural diffidence and modesty; with deep and strong feeling, he will generally pass for what Alfred calls a phlegmatic melancholic. Indeed, he has brought himself under so severe mental discipline and such habitual caution, that he represses all that gives a glow to feeling or a brilliance to thought under the fear of committing himself. But when you can draw him out of his shell, you find he can conceive and feel and speak with both brilliance and power. As a Christian, he is eminently consistent, liberal, and unwavering. I have sometimes thought that his habitual judgment has induced a want of faith in temporal matters, but I have met with few men so even and constant in their religious walk. Now my mother is almost the reverse of all this. She was the daughter of a retired and wounded officer of the Royal Navy ; was left an orphan in early life, and was educated in the same house with her cousin, Mr. John Bell, of Portington. She became pious in early life, and endured much persecution from her uncle with unflinching courage. She enjoyed the blessing of perfect love for many years, and when in health was eminent for activity and good works. She possesses a much higher range of talent than my father—has more genius and less judgment—romantic in all her feelings, ardent in her attachments and resentments. She has ten times as much faith as my father. She has a keen, ready mind, but wants comparison and discrimination. She has a vehemency of impulse, and a strength and decision of will, and a power of faith which, if it had been united with a strong frame in the other sex, would have made her an eminent missionary. Now my father professes little, but feels a great deal ; my mother feels deeply, and tells you of it too." He had a brother, Alfred, younger than himself by four years, and a sister, Mary Ann. Of them he also wrote, in order to complete the picture of the family : " Alfred is the finest youth I have ever met with—high in all his notions, lofty and liberal in his principles. Pride and ambition are his ruling passions. Of lion-like spirit, headstrong self-will, and a most vehement and over-bearing temper, the world will see in him a second Brougham. And yet I know no one to whom you might commit your-self for candid judgment with greater confidence than our Alfred. Mary Ann, my beloved Mary Ann, is a most affectionate and amiable girl. I thought two years ago she would be a tame, passive character ; but she is developing striking and spirited traits. She has more perseverance and judgment for her years than either I or Alfred. I think she will not be behind either in intellect, and before both in prudence."

What is here said of his brother Alfred is not too strongly put. From the testimony of friends, and the proofs given in his letters, essays, and speeches, he must have been a youth of unusual promise. He early devoted himself to God, and became one of the most exemplary Christians. His tastes and convictions led him to choose the law for his profession. When this preference was expressed, the judicious father laid before him all the difficulties which would lie in his path: the long and expensive process of college and professional education; the still longer period which must elapse before he could reasonably expect to get into practice; the want of patronage; the envy of the aristocracy, ever manifested to aspirants at the bar springing from the middle classes of society; and concluded by saying, "Remember, Alfred, if you insist on this course, the whole of your patrimonial fortune will be expended on your education;" to which Alfred fearlessly and magnanimously replied, "I care not when I enter the bar if I have not a shilling. I will make my own fortune, you may depend upon it." His facility of speech, readiness in debate, quickness of perception, wit —his striking person, and deep-toned and melodious voice —made him from boyhood "one of nature's orators." On one occasion, in the debating society of which he was a member, a gentleman of the bar from London chanced to hear him, and remarked afterward, "I would give my library, and all I am worth in the world, to have the amazing power of reply exhibited by that boy." He passed successfully through the course at Glasgow University, where he had the most capable of instructors, and listened on Sundays to such preachers as Chalmers and Wardlaw.

After his graduation at the University, he went up to London and entered a law-office. While engaged in his studies there, he became convinced of his duty to preach the Gospel. He determined to enter the ministry; and accordingly returned home, and began to apply himself unremittingly to a course of reading preparatory to admission into the Wesleyan Conference. His application was too close, his vigils too protracted ; his health failed, and he speedily fell into a pulmonary consumption from which he died.

Mr. Cookman, the father, was one of the best representatives of the English middle class. By success in trade he rose to that degree of affluence which enabled him to live in a style of great comfort and quiet dignity ; by his reputation for sound judgment and probity, he acquired the respect and confidence of his fellow-citizens, and was elected mayor of Hull, a position which he retained for many years; and by his earnest and consistent devotion to the doctrines and usages of Wesleyan Methodism, he enjoyed the loyal affection of both the preachers and laymen of his denomination throughout his neighbourhood. His good sense, genial piety, and generous hospitality made his house a centre of Methodist influence. In politics he sympathized with the more advanced men and measures of his times.

It is evident, however, that the mother, from the brief description already given, was the inspiration of the Cookman home. Her ardent temperament, vivid imagination, active faith, and courage, imparted to the sons the living spark which kindled in them a genius for speech and for the heroic in action. She was one of the women of gentle birth who became a Methodist when it was a reproach to be one ; and, persecuted for her faith by her own family,

she knew what it was to hold to convictions when it required
the keenest suffering to do so.   At the altar of her self-
denying piety was lighted the flame of the future missionary's zeal—a zeal which burned in him resistlessly till
quenched in death.   Thus we see that the parent stock
from which the Cookmans of this and a former generation
were derived was one combining in the father and the
mother that happy union of qualities which usually gives
rise in the offspring to distinguished powers and successes.

George Grimston, as the eldest born of his parents, very
naturally received a large share of their attention.   In an
account of himself written in 1826, before entering the
regular ministry, with a view to his own improvement, he
records, "Never was a child more carefully instructed, more
carefully watched over, or more earnestly exhorted by
Christian parents to love and serve God than myself.   And
perhaps up to my eighth year the influence of these gracious
instructions so far operated as to preserve me from the guilt
of actual sin."   At this time he was sent away to school ;
where, through evil associations, he was led astray and fell
into some sinful habits.   He was, however, at this early
period the subject of keen convictions of conscience.   He
lived with the fear that every night would be the end of the
world.   While the other boys of the school were sleeping
quietly, he would be standing at the chamber window,
"momentarily expecting the Judge to descend and the
trumpet to blow."   His views of sin and of personal guilt
were not such as to lead to repentance.   He was soon after
removed to another school at a fashionable watering-place,
where he began "a career of more decided sin and folly."
At fourteen he returned home a different being, changed in
principle and purpose—far astray from the simplicity with
which at eight he had left the parental roof.   His father

took him promptly under his care, and through his guidance
he imbibed a taste for books, and became a reader
especially of history. He was put to business, kept diligently at work, but was encouraged to read in all his leisure
hours. He became a member of a public library association, and formed, with several other intelligent young men,
a debating club, thus finding in literary pursuits a wholesome diversion for his active nature, and also a means of
stimulating and training his intellect. In contact with
Grecian and Roman characters and institutions, he acquired the lofty notions of freedom and the rights of man
which marked his subsequent career. Literature, though
attractive, did not reform him ; business was incapable of
it : he gave the reins to passion, and plunged into the
stream of worldliness.

When about eighteen years old he became a teacher in a
Methodist Sunday School. He was impelled by motives
which he could not regard as genuine : " I approved of the
design theoretically ; besides, my parents being Methodists,
I thought I should assist in their Sabbath School ; but I
had no more knowledge or regard for the religious duty or
responsibility of a teacher than the babe unborn." He was
convicted of sin through the questioning of his scholars as
to the meaning of God's Word. " I began seriously to
think and reason about the matter in the following way :
Why, I have come forward to instruct these children, and I
am ignorant myself. I, who talk to them about serving
God, am serving the devil, and on the road to hell—yea,
every boy in my class might turn round and say, 'Physician,
heal thyself.'"

I cannot give the story of his conversion more succinctly
than he has done it : " These goadings and lashings of a
condemning conscience made me miserable, and compelled

me to a more close examination of my condition; and soon
I saw that I was miserable and helpless and blind and
naked; that I stood obnoxious to God's holy law, was
under the Almighty's curse, and each moment in danger of
everlasting ruin.   Still, however, I was rather convicted in
judgment than broken in heart, and it is probable that these
gracious impressions would have been overwhelmed by the
strong bias of my mind to evil; but the good Lord added
one or two other circumstances to aid and quicken the
spiritual conviction.   Just at that time I was disappointed
in a particular friendship, which sickened and soured my
mind to this world's enjoyments; and immediately upon
this, the dearest friend I had in the world, after an illness of
three days, died.   This was the consummation of my
misery; it seemed the final blow.   I was tired of life, yet
afraid to die; I was indulging in the world, yet sick of its
pleasures; amid society, I was solitary; while within my
own heart I carried the alarm-bell of a guilty conscience—in
short, I hated life, I hated myself, I was miserable; this
misery was not repentance; it was misanthropy, not contri-
tion.   And, indeed, so well convinced was I of this, that
when the pious Methodists kindly invited me to partake of
the blessings of Christian communion, I told them that I
was totally unfit to be a member of their society, as I had
not a desire to flee from the wrath to come.   I had no soft
compunctions on account of sin, no realization of guilt
toward God; but the obdurate misery and wretchedness of
a disappointed votary of pleasure.   Thus I continued as
miserable as I could be.   Yet I did reform my outward
conduct; I did forsake my gay and frivolous companions;
nay, more, I acted diligently as secretary in a large Sabbath
School, and endeavoured, amid a multiplicity of business,
to bury all knowledge and memory of myself.   But this

arose not from any clear sense of duty, or any love to God or men, but simply because I was sick and tired of the world; and, as I could not enjoy it, I forsook it. At length, however, the day-spring arose in my benighted soul; the light of grace showed me more perspicuously my real condition. I saw that I had lost the image of God—bore the image of the Evil One; that I was ignorant in understanding, corrupt and deceitful in heart, polluted in body, and desperately wicked in conduct. I saw that in my present state it was impossible I could be saved, for 'without holiness no man can see the Lord.' I saw clearly that I must be eternally lost; for already I was under sentence of death, and God was bound by His immutable word to punish all transgression.

"Under these gracious convictions, having fully resolved to seek salvation, to renounce the world, and to serve God, I joined the Methodist Society in February, 1820, and soon I found the blessings of Christian fellowship. Under the fatherly instruction and care of my excellent leader, light beamed brighter into my soul; I was called to see deeper into my own depravity, and finally I clearly apprehended that salvation was only to be obtained by faith in a crucified Redeemer. Nine months did I seek the blessing of justification earnestly and with many tears. Often in secret places, in garrets, in the open fields, or under hedges, I have poured forth my requests with strong cries, but still the day of liberty seemed at a distance, until I had well-nigh despaired. One Saturday night I had retired to rest under considerable condemnation for having indulged in an acrimonious spirit toward a near relative. I recollect, before I fell asleep, this passage gave me considerable trouble: 'Let not the sun go down upon thy wrath.' I awoke (I believe by the providence of God) about two o'clock in the morning, and my misery and horror of mind were indescribable. All the weight of my sins seemed now bearing down upon my wretched soul, and ready to force me down to that bottomless pit which appeared just yawning ; in this situation I cried mightily to God for deliverance and pardon, but the heavens were as brass to my prayers, and the storm of Almighty wrath increased apace. My agony of mind was now wrought up to its highest pitch, when suddenly I caught a glimpse of Christ on Calvary ; then I cried with the desperation of a drowning man, ' Lord, I believe; help Thou my unbelief !' 'Lord, save, or I perish !' 'Though Thou slay me, yet will I believe in Thee !' And suddenly there was a great calm—the storm was hushed—the burden was gone—and I felt that God, for Christ's sake, had forgiven me all my sins. Being justified by faith, I had peace with God through my Lord Jesus Christ. It is true I had not that rapturous joy which some testify ; but I had the peace which passeth all understanding. Oh yes ! the Spirit did bear witness with my spirit that I was a child of God. I lay me down, and sweetly fell asleep; and in the morning, when I awoke, I asked, Is this a dream ? And I felt it was indeed a truth that I was justified freely through the blood of Christ."

The young believer now found a great difference in his experience, not only in the comfort which arose from a sense of acceptance with God, but also in the easy victory over sin which his spiritual renewal had bestowed. Nor was he content to rest in the experience of Divine favour : he at once gave himself to religious works in various plans of benevolence, such as the Young Men's Visiting Society and the Juvenile Branch Missionary Society. Yearning for the salvation of souls, he began very soon to feel the desire "for a broader field of labour as a preacher of righteous-

ness." His views of a call to the ministry were so positive
as not to allow him to go forward hurriedly. "Indeed, so
jealous was I of my own heart, and so severe in my notions
upon this subject, that I was resolved, if this call was not
unanswerably given from God to my soul, I would for ever
remain silent."

In keeping with this purpose, not to run before he was
called, Mr. Cookman kept steadily on his way, following
closely the indications of Providence and of the Spirit as he
could discern them. In 1821 he visited America on business
for his father; and returning, was as deeply engrossed as
any other young man of business, doing with diligence the
duty which lay next to him. After a lapse of over two
years I find him breathing the same devout and evangelical
spirit, with a persuasion that God, amid severe trials and
with great opportunities, was grounding him in the truth,
and conforming his heart more and more to His own will.
January 22, 1823, he writes: "I have been composing the
skeleton of my first sermon, from 1 Cor. ii. 2. Sunday
fortnight I am to preach at St. Paul's.* When I consider
my unworthiness, I am ready to sink into the dust. Lord,
prepare me." A week before preaching he asks, "Have I
a clear call to preach the Gospel?" and upon examining
himself by five tests, concludes "that a dispensation of
grace is committed to me, and woe be to me if I preach
not the Gospel!" In addition to the usual tests which
occurred to him, was the impression received while in
America, and while on shipboard, that he must preach the
Gospel, "and that too in America." He had gone to
America for secular ends, but God had already decreed his
return to America on a higher errand. His first pulpit

* Hull.

efforts were well received. He preached quite regularly,
and showed from the first the elements óf power. The
missionary ardour was kindling in his soul. His father
proposed to establish him in business ; but he wished to cut
loose from all such entanglements, and enter himself forth-
with at an American college for a course of preparation for
the ministry. He yielded, however, to the dissuasions of
his father and friends, who thought him already in the best
possible school of preparation and in the path of duty.
Without abandoning his purpose to preach, he waited upon
God, resolving to do his duty, and leave consequences with
God.

After a sermon preached at the Scott Street Chapel, he
was greatly depressed. " I had entered the pulpit with a
comfortable assurance of the Divine favour, when, strange
to tell, all upon a sudden my mind was beclouded; and,
although I was perfectly master of the subject, I was yet
bound in spirit." " I expected no one could profit; but, to
my amazement, almost all expressed themselves as being
much edified." He could not fail of a valuable lesson from
this experience. Within a short time he made his first
platform address, and achieved, in this maiden effort, that
marked success which, so often repeated in after years, constituted him a prince among platform speakers. "When I
ascended the platform my soul seemed weighed down with
a sense of my unfitness. 'Oh my God !' I could not help
crying, 'why am I here ? These poor heathen never trifled
away privileges as I have done.' When my name was
called from the chair, I was in this low state. I thought at
first (owing to a violent hoarseness) that I should have to
sit down ; but just at this instant Divine light broke in upon
my soul, my voice cleared, my heart filled with holy love
and fire, and I was enabled to speak with a force unknown

before. The place was filled with the heavenly influence, and the loud, silvery, and hearty amens were affecting and cheering. Nothing afflicted me so much as the compliments of my friends. It seemed dishonouring God; because I am convinced He gave the power and sent the influence. The Lord shall have all the glory." It is not difficult for those who subsequently heard Mr. Cookman in this peculiar realm, at the zenith of his popularity, to imagine the utter wonder and pleasure which this beginning of surprises must have occasioned to those who were present.

The purpose of God with His young servant was now fast showing itself. The apple was well-nigh ripe, when it either would fall of itself or could be easily plucked. Mr. Joshua Marsden strongly recommended him to offer himself to the American (Methodist) bishops, to take a circuit in the first instance; afterwards, if Providence opened the way, he could enter upon the missionary work. But he had engaged in business with his father for the term of three years, after which time he proposed to turn his attention more decidedly to the ministry, with the intention of going to America. His diary bears evidence at this period of the closest heart searchings; of the deepest and most unaffected devotion to the service of Christ. The prayer is constantly on his lips, "What wilt Thou have me do?" There is no duty which he does not discharge, no self-sacrifice from which he shrinks: he is ready to do any work—to go, if needs be, to the ends of the earth to preach the Gospel.

While his mind was particularly exercised in regard to an immediate entrance upon the ministry, he was appointed to drive Mr. Clough (one of the circuit preachers of Hull) to Partington. Mr. Clough impressed upon him the duty of present action, if he would not grieve the Holy Spirit; another young friend, and to his surprise the Rev. Mr. W.

Entwistle, on whom he shortly after called, expressed the same view. Considerably agitated by such a concurrence of opinions, he laid the whole matter before his father, fully anticipating his decided negative for the present, when, to his great surprise, his father frankly told him that he had long been of the opinion that he was called to the ministry ; and that, although his immediate departure might cause inconvenience, yet he would not throw one stumbling-block in the way, but rather further the ordinations of Providence by every prudent arrangement. As might have been anticipated, his mother fully coincided with this judgment, and " was perfectly willing to give him up to the Lord." Thus every obstacle to his full devotion to the ministry, and to his going to America as the field of its exercise, was removed, and his decision was accordingly made to emigrate at the earliest opportunity.

Happy in the decision which freed him from suspense, and introduced him into the definite course of his life, he was all aflame with zeal for the work which lay before him. " My peace flows as a river, and my heart exults to reflect that in a few months I may be permitted to preach Christ crucified to the poor blacks of Maryland." He could find no figures so adequate to express his ardour as that of the racer restless for the course, or the soldier in the battle eager for the conflict. This ardour, while it may not have been wholly void of the adventurous element which springs from the prospect of strange and hazardous enterprise, was nourished by the closest contact with the great heart of the Redeemer, and in the one simple purpose to save perishing men. He breathed constantly for entire deadness to the world and the spirit of true holiness, evidently regarding his mission as one of utter self-renunciation in the pursuit of the Divine glory. " Although privations and persecutions or shipwreck may await me, I feel strong in the Lord, determined to obey His will at all hazards." Such a young man was fit to follow a Coke, an Asbury, and even a Paul, over the sea in the sublime work of bringing continents to God. " I must be a man of one work—dead to the world, and alive to Christ."

The 28th of March, 1825, was finally definitely fixed upon as the day of departure for America. The last days and hours were spent in preaching, visits, farewells, and preparations. The little brig *Orient* weighed anchor at the time appointed, and bore away westward with her devout and expectant passenger. The long voyage was not idle or irksome ; the whole of its time was diligently consumed in close study and multifarious reading ; in meditating and maturing plans of usefulness. He thoroughly digested such works as Bishop Watson's Apologies, Mason on Self-Knowledge, Jenyn's Views of the Internal Evidences of Christianity, Lord Lyttleton's Arguments for Christianity, Baxter's Gildas Salvianus and Saint's Rest, and Butler's Analogy. He preached to the seamen as occasion offered, distributed tracts, and otherwise laboured among them. What is most striking, however, was the constancy of his devotions, and the watchfulness he exercised over his own spirit. " I have been reflecting upon Baxter's warning of settling anywhere short of heaven, or reposing our souls to rest on anything below God. Ah! how little do I think of this. This deceitful heart would fain set up its rest—not, indeed, in riches, honours, etc., but in creature love, a Gospel Church, gracious ordinances. This will not do. They are the means, not the rest itself. This is the ingenious device of Satan, by which we are seduced into a species of spiritual idolatry. Strive, O my soul, to consider thyself as a pilgrim in this wilderness, and rest in nought but God!"

Just before landing, retarded by calms, he took advantage of the smooth sea and quiet waiting to re-examine the motives which led him to America. "This is no womanish employ ; this ministerial work is no fine theory of fancy. It requires all the firmness, courage, perseverance, zeal, faith of the veteran soldier. Therefore I must fix my principles, and draw them from the fountain of all wisdom. I bless God my soul can calmly rejoice in the prospect, and yield all up to the will and direction of God." "Now, then, in the strength of the Lord, I will go forth to the Lord's work in this my adopted country." Would that more young men entering upon the Divine apostleship could have an "Arabia" of three or more months, or even years, on shipboard or elsewhere such as he had!

On Sunday, May 16, 1825, the "Orient" sailed up the Delaware Bay and River. Mr. Cookman was sorry to fall short of reaching Philadelphia in time for the services of the sanctuary ; but he had so drilled himself to make the best of circumstances, that he found compensation in secret communion with God and in thoughts of friends afar. He wrote to a friend : "This voyage has been profitable, both in an intellectual and spiritual point of view. I have been grounding myself in the grand principles of the Gospel. . . . I have preached several times to this most wicked crew, and I have been blessed to the captain's good, who is resolved to turn over a new leaf. Patience has had its perfect work. . . . I have found it good to lay my will at the Redeemer's feet. . . . I have had painful views of the depravity of this corrupt heart, and this has stimulated me particularly to plead for the whole image and purity of Christ, so that the fire of Divine love might devour all the grossness of sense and sin. . . . Here then we are on the Delaware. I regret that I cannot assemble the crew and passengers for public worship, as the pilot keeps all the former in working the vessel up the river. I felt melancholy this morning in looking on shore and beholding nature in all its bloom, the sun careering in the firmament, and then thinking, ' Ah! the people of God are now repairing to His holy temple to worship at His feet.' Nevertheless, I retired to my little cabin, and the Lord visited the temple of my heart, and spoke graciously and comfortably to His poor servant. I have renewed my missionary covenant. I am the Lord's: the same great principles which called me forth remain with augmented force; I go wherever He commands."

CHAPTER II.

MR. COOKMAN was cordially received by the Methodists
of Philadelphia, among whom he lived and laboured as a
local preacher, in connection with St. George's Church,
until the following spring. He was incessant in labours,
not only in preaching as opportunity offered, but visiting
the sick, the prisons, and hospitals. He also organized a
class of young persons, which included among its members John McClintock, Charles Whitacre, and William and
Leonard Gilder, all of whom subsequently became ministers
of the Gospel. During a protracted sickness of Mr. William
Barnes, the preacher in charge, he supplied the pulpit of
St. George's.

At the session of the Philadelphia Conference of the
Methodist Episcopal Church in 1826, he was appointed to
Kensington and St. John's churches, Philadelphia. Falling
thus softly into the regular ministry did not suit either the
design or the wishes of the young hero, whose soul was
burning for its mission to the Africans. He had left
England to convert the negroes, and it was not to his mind
to become a pastor amid the ease and refinements of
civilized life. He was patient, however, and sought constantly, in the utmost self-denial, the guidance of God's
Spirit and of His Church.

His cherished desire was doomed to disappointment. God had other work for him to do. As the sequel proved, instead of going as a missionary to convert the heathen —possibly to leave his bones after a few months on the sands of Africa—he was, by his advanced ideas and persuasive eloquence, to plant the seeds of missionary labours which were destined to spring up in ever-widening harvests to the end of time.

In February, 1827, Mr. Cookman returned to England on a brief visit. He was married to Miss Mary Barton, Doncaster, Yorkshire, on the 2nd of April, 1827, and immediately left with his bride for America. Miss Barton was a young lady of excellent family, of superior personal endowments, and of exemplary piety. In marrying Mr. Cookman she not only wedded him as her husband, but also as God's minister, and devoted herself, with the utmost simplicity and in entire sympathy with him, to the work which absorbed his soul and was to employ his life. The comforts and luxuries of an affluent English home were abandoned with the pure intent of becoming a true helpmeet to the man of her heart, the accredited ambassador of Christ in bringing the world a conquest to redeeming love. Mrs. Cookman still lives at an advanced age, a witness to the power of the same self-sacrificing zeal with which she originally left her father's house.

In the spring of 1827 Mr. Cookman was appointed to the Lancaster Circuit. This charge embraced Lancaster, Columbia, and Reading, three of the most important towns in Pennsylvania. It was a large and laborious charge, being what was called a six weeks' circuit, in the arrangement of which he preached at each church in the circuit but once in six weeks. His residence was at Columbia, situated on the Susquehanna River.

Here Alfred was born, January 4th, 1828. He was physically a healthful and remarkably well-proportioned child. With the persuasion that he was given to her of God, his mother consecrated him from birth to the sacred ministry, to be a builder of God's Temple. All her thoughts, feelings, and plans for the child grouped about this central idea, and the idea in turn stamped its character and complexion on all she did. She had talents and graces which would have made her useful and famous in any sphere; but she saw with womanly instinct and true maternal feeling that her greatest usefulness and utmost fame—as far as she could consider fame—would be found in losing herself in her son, in spending her time and energies upon him, in fashioning the man who was to stand a man among men.

She says of him at this very early age: "The tone of his mind had always a religious tendency, and before he was four years of age he imitated all the services of the Church. He would sometimes collect a crowd of coloured children around him, and in his childish way preach to them about the necessity of being good."

It is not uncommon for boys, who never become preachers or much of anything, to do just what Alfred did; and yet there is that in the ways of every child which shows the natural bent, and to some degree forecasts the after life. Goethe's painful sensitiveness to the presence of ugliness or deformity while quite a baby was indicative of that fine, delicate organization which is the constitutional basis of the poet. His mother had the eye to see it, and with skilful hand she guided the divine instinct by bringing to its nurture agreeable objects, and gently inciting it with narratives of the wondrous and beautiful; otherwise Germany had not had her greatest poet, nor the world one of its greatest educators. To every mother her child has an individuality, and she can discern in it the hidden germ which in the flower is to render its maturity distinct and beautiful. The difference in mothers is the power properly to direct this original faculty. Fewer children would perish in the promise if there were more mothers who knew how to cherish and train the natural and gracious endowment. Mrs. Cookman had one desire for her boy, and she sedulously watched every hint in his childhood which pointed in the direction of its fulfilment. She hailed every such indication as a precursor of his future, since it had been impressed on her mind from his birth that he was to do the work that was in her heart to do for the Lord. But she was a wise mother, looking for results, however good and desirable, to follow only upon the use of the proper means. She did not expect devout wishes and devout prayers to mould the character of Alfred without corresponding effort to rear him aright. Great and good men do not grow, like the rank weeds, untended, but, like the lovely and fragrant flowers, by culture. Here is a memorandum from the mother on this point : "Alfred was very correct in all his deportment, obedient to his parents, very truthful, and conscientious. He was, of course, watched over with more than ordinary care. Parental vigilance was ever on the alert to detect and correct anything that might mar the little tender plant." Yet there was not excess of training, nor morbid stimulating. "His father early impressed him with the idea, 'Play when you play, and work when you work.'"

It was hardly to be expected that the social scenes by which this child was surrounded at that period could permanently affect his disposition ; yet he ever after loved this country and its people, and to this day there is no name fuller of sweet odour in the whole region than that of Alfred Cookman. It is well known, too, that he cherished

throughout life a great love for the black race. He had
romped, wept, and laughed—nay, even prayed—with the
coloured boys ; and a common feeling, so self-asserting in
children, had taught him in the simple and innocent sports
of childhood the great truth of the oneness of humanity.
In the very lap of the warm, unselfish nursing of which the
negro woman is capable, associated with the strange and
weird stories, and the low, soft melodies, the earnest and
implicit trustfulness with which she mingles all her work,
he received impressions at this susceptible age which ever
endeared the coloured people to him.

CHAPTER III.

How far Mr. Cookman felt himself successful in his mission
to the coloured people does not appear. He found obstacles in promoting their liberation. He was useful to them,
as he was also to the white population ; but his talents were
soon in demand in the great city, and he was accordingly at
his next appointment assigned to St. George's, Philadelphia.
It showed the confidence of the bishop, and of the people
of St. George's, that he was sent so soon to the charge
where on his first arrival he had joined and laboured as a
local preacher. On the removal of the family to the city,
Alfred, with his brother George, was placed at school under
the care of Miss Ann Thomas, a member of the Society of
Friends, who was quite celebrated for her skill in teaching.
He remained two years under her care, and made rapid
progress in the elementary branches of education. She took
very special interest both in him and his little brother, and
expressed great sorrow when they left her.

Subsequently to the two years at St. George's, Philadelphia, Mr. Cookman spent one year at Newark, N.J.

On one Sabbath evening, Mr. Cookman was preaching to
a dense audience at Light Street, and, as sometimes hap-

pened with him, and happens to all men, however able, if
they are extemporaneous speakers, he had no freedom in
his sermon, and evidently did not succeed as he wished ;
but, with a fertility of resource which seldom failed him, he
began an exhortation as he proceeded to the consciences of
his hearers, which was so effective for direct and fiery appeal
as to subdue all hearts. A prominent citizen, who had been
attracted by his fame, but was about to leave the building
disappointed at his sermon, was so wrought upon by the
exhortation as to be awakened and converted.

Among the vast multitudes who hung upon the eloquent
lips of Mr. Cookman at this time, was a little boy of seven
years of age, not unknown to him. Alfred was no indifferent hearer to such lifelike expositions and delineations
as the father gave from Sunday to Sunday. The intelligence
of the lad had sufficiently dawned to appreciate a method
of teaching which was so well suited to awaken and chain
the attention of the young. His conscience was growing
with his other faculties, and now began to assert itself. The
seeds of truth cast into the soil of his heart were beginning
to swell, though the full time for them to burst into a definitive new life had not yet come. Referring to his early
experience, he has himself recorded : "I shall never cease
to be grateful for the instruction and example of a faithful
father and an affectionate mother. At this moment I cannot call up a period in my life, even in my earliest childhood, when I had not the fear of God before my eyes.
When about seven years of age, I persuaded my parents to
let me attend a watch-night service. It was held in Old
Exeter Street Church, in the city of Baltimore. My father
preached on the second coming of Christ. Thinking that
perhaps the end of the world was just at hand, I realized
for the first time my unpreparedness for the trying scenes of

the Judgment, and trembled in the prospect. I date my awakenings from that time."

The time had now come when Alfred's academic training was fairly to begin. Since leaving the charge of the gentle Friend in Philadelphia, he had been mainly dependent upon home instruction; but now, in the providence of God, he was to be placed in the most favourable circumstances for a boy's education. Mr. Cookman, for reasons which were sufficient to the authorities of the Church, was removed in 1836 from Baltimore to the town of Carlisle.

There was reason enough for Mr. Cookman's removal to Carlisle. The Methodists of the Baltimore and Philadelphia Conferences had recently purchased from the Presbyterians Dickinson College, located at that borough, and had made it their educational centre.

Mr. Cookman was accordingly sent to take the charge of the Church, composed of both town and college people. He was still a young man, in all the glow of youthful zeal, in the full force of rapidly culminating talents, and with all the earnestness of an absorbing devotion to the single work of a Christian pastor. His task as a preacher was a most difficult and delicate one—to stand before a congregation constituted as congregations are in a college town. He must satisfy professors, entertain students, and edify tradespeople. Could any position require more genuine ability?

But I must not forget our boy of nine summers, whose eyes opened upon these scenes in which his worthy father was so distinguished an actor. He also had come to college. Under such circumstances, in this focus of knowledge and piety, an impulse was to be imparted to him which was to determine his whole after-life. I know of few spots upon which Alfred could have fallen at this impressible age more suitable in all its adjuncts for his first formal entrance into school. Of the place and its environs much can be said. Carlisle has but little attractiveness in its immediate topography or in its artificial structure—a plain town, its only importance is as the civil and natural centre of a thrifty agricultural county, without any objects of taste whatever; the outlying country is very beautiful. The Cumberland Valley, in which it lies, is broad and undulating, abounding in springs and streams; its soil rich and productive, its whole bosom covered with fertile farms or luxuriant forests; while in the distance on either side the North and South Mountains, spurs of the Alleghanies, rise into prominence and sweep along in unbroken succession, save here and there a gentle gap, and form, in their continuous wavy outlines, one of the most agreeable prospects which can be offered to the eye. I doubt if old Carlisle, in England, after which it is named, possesses a more charming situation.

It cannot be supposed that this physical beauty was without educational effect upon the ardent temperament of the boy, inclined as he was by his healthful nature to relish all sensuous delights. Indeed, the æsthetical sense born in him, and afterwards so strongly marked in his intellectual development, and the devout reverence for God in works of nature always so prominent through his whole life, must have received from it an exciting and durable effect. A lad so reflective as he is represented from the very dawn of thought, could not have been otherwise than most favourably influenced by habitual contact with scenes so simple and pleasing.

> " Not seldom from the uproar I retired
> Into a silent bay, or sportively
> Glanced sideway, leaving the tumultuous throng,"

might doubtless be said of him at this as well as later periods of his youth, and that not so much to elude his companions in play, as to gain for himself the quiet communion for which his thoughtful soul thirsted.

But enough of my fancy, and a little of fact from Alfred's own hand. Fortunately one of his earliest letters has been preserved, and lies before me in his own handwriting. The composition must be regarded as creditable for a boy of ten years; not surprising, however, when the exercises he was then having in school and the constant care his mother gave him are taken into account. The penmanship already shows indications of the beautiful chirography for which his later manuscripts are noted. It is to his grandfather Cookman :—

"CARLISLE, *January* 27, 1838.

"MY DEAR GRANDFATHER,—I have long been thinking that it was my duty to write a letter to one for whom I desire to cherish the warmest affection, and to whom we are already under very great obligations. * * *

"First of all I must congratulate you on your very honourable election to the high office of mayor to the important and flourishing town of Kingston-upon-Hull. Although we boys are Americans and Republicans in our feelings, yet we are not insensible to the honour attached to offices conferred by the votes of the people. * * *

"I am very happy to say that dear mother's health continues very good. Fortunately for her, the winter up to this time has been unusually mild ; indeed, the last week has rather resembled the month of April than January, so that she has been able to go out three or four times a week in the middle of the day and see her friends. Indeed, ever since she was in Baltimore her health has been gradually improving, and long may she live to be what she has truly been, the best of mothers.

"About Christmas we had a slight fall of snow, which rendered the roads for a few days in good condition for sleighing, which is the favourite winter pastime in these parts. Almost every farmer has a good sleigh, and when you have a couple of stout horses and a plentiful supply of thick buffalo skins to keep out the frost, it is the finest riding in the world. Sometimes the citizens will put a great Pennsylvania wagon on runners, and yoke four or five good horses, and then thirty or forty ladies and gentlemen can enjoy themselves right well. Even we boys have our little sleigh, and it would amuse you to see myself and

George going at full speed, with Frank on the sleigh, holding little John on his knee.

"It becomes my duty to give some account of our progress at the Grammar School. This is a large, elegant square building, three stories high, opposite the front gate of the college. The basement floor is occupied by the steward's apartments, the second by two spacious, lofty rooms, above fifty feet square, and divided by two folding-doors into the English and Classical departments. Mr. Roszell has the superintendence, and is a very strict man indeed. Mr. Hey is an Englishman, and is said to be one of the best grammarians in the country. Mr. Cary and Mr. Bunting, under whose care I am at present, are the assistants. Since I entered the school I have gone four or five times through the English grammar, and twice through the Latin, having committed all the rules to memory. George has gone twice through his English grammar, and is now beginning Latin. I have been twice through Tytler's Universal History; I am nearly through my Latin reader and geography, and have drawn a few maps. In arithmetic I am as far as the last section of discount. Besides all this, I have constant exercises in parsing, composition, and elocution. I have written four or five original essays, and declaimed before the school three times, and frequently, besides three or four other tasks, have to write out an entire Latin verb in an evening. So you may believe we are not idle. Indeed, they work us very hard. Mr. Roszell says it will keep us out of mischief, and father says it is the very thing ; but, indeed, I really do not know how I should have got along if it had not been for the help of my dear mother, who usually gives her evenings to the purpose.

"In conclusion, allow me to say that we hope the deep interest and liberality you have manifested for our education will be met by a corresponding application and improvement on our part, so that you will not have cause to be ashamed of us.

"Father, mother, George, Francis, William Wilberforce, and John Emory all unite in great affection to yourself, uncles, aunts, and cousins Robinson and Holmes, for whose welfare, present and eternal, we are taught daily to pray to Almighty God.

" Your affectionate grandson,
"ALFRED COOKMAN."

Alfred's " first effort at epistolary writing" certainly needs no apology. It gives indications of the future man. He was studious and obedient ; but it must not be supposed he was a saint from the cradle. The moral heroism of his character was not without its physical and mental basis; and possibly, but for the timely training of judicious parents, the metal of his disposition would have betrayed him into many of the rudenesses of other boys. Twice in his life he was whipped—when four years old, for throwing a book at his mother, and, when seven or eight, for fighting with his brother George. Was there ever a boy who didn't enjoy once in a while the exercise of a little power over his younger and weaker brother? How else can he show his muscle? And who so fair a subject for Alfred's muscle as little George? It was a good thing in the mother that she flogged the darling even at four and seven, otherwise "her Solomon" would probably never have been, and her temple to God never have been reared. But how like a sweet melody breathes the testimony of the dear mother to the fidelity of her boy, even thus young in years: "His boyhood was spent pretty much like that of other boys, in the sports and occupations of that period of his young life. Obedience to parental authority was a prominent characteristic from his earliest years. Promptness in the performance of duty was another beautiful trait. Industry, patience, and perseverance were very early brought into requisition, and served a good purpose in laying a foundation for the successive periods of after life." In this letter, too, is seen already the dawn of his thorough Americanism, and of his faculty for description. The sleighs and sleigh-rides of a Pennsylvania winter—the sled, with himself and George in the harness, "going at full speed, with Frank on the sleigh holding little John on his knee"—are not these to the life? This first letter also shows us Alfred among his brothers. Alas! too soon the buoyant lad, whose heart knew no thrill except of gladness as he guided the sports of his glee-

ful brothers, was to stand among them an elder brother and
a thoughtful counsellor.   But let the veil rest, for we are
yet some way from the awful darkness, and have many
important and pleasant steps to take before we reach it.

In this winter of 1838 Alfred made another first effort, of
greater moment than his first essay at " epistolary writing."
The deep religious seriousness which he had felt in Baltimore had not at any time wholly subsided, and now, under
the power of the Holy Spirit, was vividly renewed.   " There
(at Carlisle) I became," he has recorded, " the subject of
powerful conviction.   Often I have risen from my meal and
sought some lonely place where I might weep on account of
sin.   Frequently I have lain awake on my bed, fearing to
sleep, lest I might wake up amid the darkness and horrors of
an eternal Hell.   Sin became a burden too intolerable to be
borne."   This is strong language for a youth of ten years, and
for one who had been uniformly affectionate and obedient ;
and yet such an experience even for a youth in those days
was hardly exceptional ; but though it might have been, in
his case it is not surprising in view of the sharp and definite
features his religious character always assumed.   Here, in
the beginning of the spiritual life, is the same positiveness
which afterward characterized his maturity.   " Sin is real,
Hell is real ; I am a sinner ; I am in danger of its punish-
ment."   Such was the revelation of the Holy Ghost made
in his conscience, and he felt and acted accordingly.   It
may not be necessary that every youth should feel thus
deeply in order to become regenerate, but for Alfred Cookman it was the very best preparation he could have had for
that clear and definite religious experience which subsequently distinguished him.   Fortunately he has left a narra-
tion of his conversion, which I give entire :—

" During the month of February, 1838, while a protracted meeting was in progress in Carlisle, I concluded 'Now is the accepted time,' 'now is the day of salvation.' One night, when a social meeting was held at the house of a friend, I struggled with my feelings, and, although it was a fearful cross, I urged my way to a bench which was specially appropriated for penitents. My heart convulsed with penitential sorrow, tears streaming down my cheeks, I said, 'Jesus, Jesus, I give myself away; 'tis all that I can do.' For some hours I sought, without, however, realizing the desire of my heart. The next evening I renewed the effort. The evening after that the service was held in the church; the altar was crowded with seeking souls, principally students of Dickinson College; there seemed to be no place for me, an agonized child. I remember I found my way into one corner of the church. Kneeling all alone, I said. 'Precious Saviour, Thou are saving others; oh, wilt Thou not save me?' As I wept and prayed and struggled, a kind hand was laid on my head. I opened my eyes and found it was a Mr. James Hamilton, a prominent member and an elder in the Presbyterian Church in Carlisle. He had observed my interest, and obeying the promptings of a kind, sympathizing Christian heart, he came to encourage and help me. I remember how sweetly he unfolded the nature of faith and the plan of salvation. I said, 'I will believe—I do believe; I now believe that Jesus is my Saviour; that He saves me—yes, even now'; and immediately

> " 'The opening heavens did round me shine
>   With beams of sacred bliss;
>   And Jesus showed His mercy mine,
>   And whispered I am His.'

" I love to think of it now; it fills my heart unutterably full of gratitude, love, and joy. 'Happy day; oh, happy day, when Jesus washed my sins away!' "

It will thus be seen that the great change wrought in his heart, as presented in his own language in mature life, was as decided in the evidences of its thoroughness as were his convictions for sin.

The altar was thronged with older persons, mostly students, whose presence and importance very naturally engrossed attention : he was only a little boy ; his feelings might be regarded as the result of a sympathetic excitement, and not worthy of especial notice ; but he understood himself, and oppressed with sin and bent upon relief, "he found himself in one corner of the church, all alone." Ah ! my little brother, God's Spirit was doing a genuine work in your young heart. Your great Creator had also put iron in your "make-up" when He formed you. There were hours coming when again "all alone with your Saviour" you must stand ; hours so bitter in their loneliness that only Jesus and self-reliance can keep you firm to duty and give you victory. Although Alfred was off in the corner, God sent him a kind friend who opened the kingdom of God to him. There are always some great souls who can understand the hearts of little children, and have faith enough to anticipate the harvests which will come of tiny seeds. But Alfred had good companionship among the youths brought to God in this revival. The great Head of the Church was electing others who, like himself, were to be marked and useful men.

CHAPTER IV.

THE time had come—spring of 1838—when Mr. Cookman must again remove, and go he knew not whither. Philadelphia, Charleston, and Washington wished his services. To the latter city, the national capital, he was sent, and the cozy college town was exchanged for the political centre of the nation ; and now upon a broader scene the eloquent and devout preacher was to make his appearance. Two more years, and four or six more, at Carlisle, would have been valuable to Alfred. It was hard for him to leave the " stately grammar school," with its " strict discipline," and to give up the prospect of a speedy entrance into the walls of the college ; but when the itinerant wheel rolls, the schools of boys must stand out of the way, and so Alfred must go with father and mother and brothers ; he is too young to be left behind, and he must do the best he can in the pursuit of "literature" in Washington. Mr. Cookman was stationed at Wesley Chapel, then a new charge, comprising in its membership many of the most cultivated and progressive Methodists of the city.

The proximity of his church to the Capitol rendered it convenient of access to the members of Congress and to

3

strangers visiting Washington during the sessions. His
ministry began at once to excite attention; soon the chapel
was thronged with hearers from all sections of the country,
irrespective of denominational connections, and his reputation was promptly established as a first-class pulpit orator.
It may be safely affirmed that no minister ever entered
Washington who maintained from first to last a greater ascendency over the popular heart. Men and women of every
grade of society, of every station in the government, were
equally charmed by his forcible and beautiful eloquence.
Senators, heads of Departments and their clerks, rich and
poor, the *littérateur* and the illiterate man, the slaveholder
and the slave, all alike were captured by his magical tongue,
and he swayed their hearts as with the wand of a magician
—with "a warrior's eye beneath a philosopher's brow" his
spell was irresistible.

It was Mr. Cookman's habit to make a companion of
Alfred. Frequently he took him to the Senate Chamber,
where he received the attentions of Senators in the genial
greetings which occurred. He was just then as handsome,
well-formed, and engaging a boy of eleven years as could
be found. He could appreciate, if not the intrinsic worth,
the manifest popularity of his father, as evinced in the position to which he was chosen, in the crowds that thronged
to his ministry, and in the compliments bestowed on his
preaching; and it is not to be supposed he was indifferent
to it all. His young heart swelled, no doubt, with emotions
of pride for his father, and for himself as the son of such a
father, and the consequent partner in his fame. The outside
world of men and things into which Alfred was thus introduced, differed vastly from the simple surroundings of
Carlisle : great men, great buildings, great measures, great
pageants—these now crowded the thoughts that so re-

cently were taken up and satisfied with books, play, and prayers.

I spoke of the disadvantage his education must suffer by his removal from the grammar school at Carlisle just as he was getting into thorough drill ; equally it should not surprise us if his religious life, when removed from familiar and genial friendships into new and strange associations, were to meet with a chill which would abate its warmth, if not stop its growth. The first few days and nights of a plant's transfer from the nursery to the open air are always days and nights of peril to its opening buds. How many young Christians, who commence with vigorous promise, fall away and perish because of a too sudden change of place or of pastors ! Alfred did not lose his religious faith ; but, by his own acknowledgment, his experience declined in vitality —he was not the same joyous little Christian for some months that he had been soon after being "all alone with Jesus" in the corner of the church.

In the autumn (1838) he united with the Church. His father had thought it best to keep him on "probation" until he gave satisfactory proofs of a stable piety. Soon after his removal to Washington he commenced to exercise himself on the platform as a speaker, and at that early age received much commendation and evinced great promise, so that "predictions were freely made of what the future of this young speaker might be, to which the father readily assented." It was no little credit to the youthful " Cicero " that his father readily assented ; for, whether for banter or not, Mr. Cookman used to rouse the mother's jealousy for her little " Temple builder " by intimating, "Your Solomon is rather a dull boy ! " I doubt if he was even then so noted for quickness of perception as for tenacity in sticking to a lesson until he had mastered it, and then

holding it fast. What is of most interest at this particular
point is—he appears before us at twelve years of age a
decidedly religious lad in experience and action, and a
speaker, thus affording us a clear view of the dawn of that
personal career which was eventually to open into full-orbed
day.

In the spring of 1840 Mr. Cookman was appointed to the
charge of the Church in Alexandria. He still retained his
Chaplaincy, and regularly fulfilled its duties until the expiration of the Congress of the fourth of March, 1841. His
pastorate in Alexandria was attended with all the marks of
public favour and of ministerial usefulness which had accompanied him in other communities. There occurred nothing
to the father to which any special significance can be attached; but with Alfred it was quite different. He had seen
but little of slavery since he lived a child on the eastern
shore of Maryland. In Pennsylvania and New Jersey the
coloured race was free; in Baltimore the free blacks were
more numerous than the slaves, and this was true also of
Washington. He had seen few, if any, of the more painful
aspects of the institution; and, young as he was, it had
seemed to him only a form of domestic servitude, relieved
by the kind relationships often subsisting between masters
and slaves. In Alexandria a free black was rather an exception. If, however, he had seen slavery even here only
as he had been accustomed to it, there is no likelihood that
any impression would have been made upon his mind of
decided aversion to it.

Near his father's residence was one of those painful features of the domestic slave-trade—a slave-pen or jail—which
the boy used often to pass, and where he saw poor men,
women, and children confined behind iron grates, sometimes
manacled, for no other crime than that they were owned as

property, and could be sold hither and thither by their owners
at pleasure. Alexandria was a depôt, to which the slaves
purchased in Maryland and the district of Columbia were
brought, and where they were lodged before being sent to
supply the cotton-growing states. Sometimes at the very
doors of the jail would happen those scenes which were well
fitted to rend a stouter heart than that of our sensitive young
friend. The husband would be rudely separated from the
wife, and parents from their helpless children ; and these
poor creatures, with all the instincts of human nature,
strengthened by tender associations, would vent their sorrow
in bitter cries, which gathered around them a sympathizing
crowd. How could Alfred look on without emotion, and
without forming a deep hatred to laws which sanctioned
such occurrences? Such sights were enough to wound the
heart of a boy born in the midst of slavery : how could they
do otherwise than curdle the blood of a youth born of
English parents, on free soil, and with such a soul as Alfred
Cookman possessed? The iron then went deep into his
heart, and for ever after he was the enemy of slavery, and
steadfastly did what he could consistently to abate and
destroy it. This is the only scrap of Alfred's education or
history in Alexandria of which I have any information.

The disaster which removed Mr. Cookman from the scene
of his usefulness and from the world was fast approaching.
In the spring of 1841 he determined to visit England, and
all his plans were accordingly made to sail from New York
early in March. He had been appointed by the American
Bible Society a fraternal delegate to represent it at the anniversary of the British and Foreign Bible Society to be held
at Exeter Hall, London, and was to be made bearer of the
first despatches to the British Government from the incoming
Administration of General Harrison. His main object, how-

ever, in going over, was to see again his venerable father,
and "to drop a tear on the grave of his mother." It was
fitting, in view of his position and popularity, that his farewell sermon should be preached in the Capitol. He was
regarded as a pastor not only by the Alexandria Church,
but by the Senate of the United States and large numbers
of the floating and unchurched population. A well-nigh
romantic interest centred in him. The spell of his eloquence
and the aroma of his character had completely fascinated
the people.

Never were there circumstances attending the delivery of
a sermon more fully adapted to awaken in the preacher all
his capacity of thought and emotion, or to render it more
thrilling and abiding in the minds of the hearers. Washington was literally thronged with strangers from all parts of the
country. General Harrison had been elected President by
an overwhelming majority, and his inauguration was about
to take place in the presence of crowds the like of which for
numbers and refinement the metropolis of the nation had
never before seen. Mr. Cookman's fame was now com-
mensurate with the American public : though no politician,
he was known to be in quiet sympathy with the dominant
party ; his piety was universally conceded ; his oratorical
supremacy none disputed ; expectation was on tip-toe. It
may be safely affirmed that never had sacred orator more
conditions in his favour. Added to all this was his speedy
departure for a foreign land, to encounter the perils of a
voyage from which he might never return—which consideration helped further to deepen in the popular heart the sense
of his value, and to intensify in his own heart the conviction
of his religious and ministerial responsibility. But he rose
with the occasion. The external excitement infected him ;
the grandeur of his spirit never before attained to such pro-

portions, nor shone with such effective light.   The account
given by eye-witnesses can best convey some true notion of
the man, the hour, and the place :—

" The session of Congress was about to close upon the administration
of Mr. Van Buren.   The inauguration of General Harrison was soon
to take place.   Mr. Cookman had all his arrangements made to visit
England on the steamer 'President.'   The first despatch from the new
Administration was to be confided to his charge.   The next Sabbath he
was to take leave of the members of Congress in his farewell sermon.
The day came.   An hour before the usual time the crowd was seen
filling the pavement of the avenue, and passing up the hill to Representative Hall, which was soon filled to overflowing, and hundreds,
unable to get seats, went away disappointed.   I obtained a seat
early in front of the Clerk's desk.   John Quincy Adams sat in the
Speaker's chair, facing Mr. Cookman.   The whole space on the
rostrum and steps was filled with Senators and Representatives.   The
moment had come.   Mr. Cookman, evidently much affected, kneeled in
a thrilling prayer, and rose with his eyes blinded with tears.   His voice
faltered with suppressed emotion as he gave out the hymn,—

> " ' When marshalled on the mighty plain,
>   The glittering hosts bestud the sky,
> One star alone of all the train
>   Can fix the sinner's wandering eye.

> " ' Hark ! hark ! to God the chorus breaks,
>   From every host, from every gem ;
> But one alone the Saviour speaks,
>   It is the star of Bethlehem.

> " ' Once on the raging seas I rode,
>   The storm was loud, the night was dark—
> The ocean yawned, and rudely blowed
>   The wind that tossed my foundering bark.'

" The hymn was sung by Mr. Cookman alone.   I can yet, in
imagination, hear his voice, as it filled the large hall, and the last sounds,
with their echoes, died away in the dome.

" ' And I saw a great white throne, and Him that sat on it, from
whose face the earth and the heaven fled away, and there was found no
place for them.

" ' And I saw the dead, small and great, stand before God, and the books were opened : and another book was opened, which is *the book* of life, and the dead were judged out of those things which were written in the books, according to their works.'

"Mr. Cookman was more affected when he gave us the text than I had ever seen him before. He several times passed his handkerchief over his eyes before he began. The first sentences are fresh in my recollection : 'When Massillon, one of the greatest divines that France ever knew, was called to preach the funeral service of the departed king, in the Cathedral at Paris, before the reigning king, the royal family, the chambers, and the grandees of France, he took with him to the sacred desk a little golden urn, containing a lock of hair of the late king. The immense congregation was seated, and the silence of death reigned. Massillon arose, held the little urn in his fingers, his hand resting upon the sacred cushion. All eyes were intently fixed upon him. Moments, minutes passed—Massillon stood motionless, pale as a statue : the feeling became intense ; many believed he was struck dumb before the august assembly ; many sighed and groaned aloud ; many eyes were suffused with tears, when the hand of Massillon was seen slowly raising the little golden urn, his eyes fixed upon the king. As his hand returned again to the cushion, the loud and solemn voice of Massillon was heard in every part of the Cathedral, ' God alone is great !' So I say to you to-day, my beloved hearers, there is no human great-ness—' *God alone is great !*'

"The subject was on the Day of Judgment. I had heard it preached before many times, but never as I heard it then. The immense congre: gation was held almost breathless with the most beautiful and powerful sermon I ever heard. He spoke of the final separation on the great Day of Judgment, and fancied the anger of the Lord locking the door that led to the bottomless pit, stepping upon the ramparts, letting fall the key into the abyss below, and dropping the last tear over fallen and condemned man. He closed—'I go to the land of my birth, to press once more to my heart my aged father, and drop a tear on the grave of my sainted mother : farewell !—farewell !' and he sank down over-powered to his seat, while the whole congregation responded with sympathizing tears."

A correspondent of the *National Intelligencer*, describing the same scene, after quoting Mr. Cookman's closing words, says :—"There was something prophetic, solemn, and deeply affecting in the tones and manner of the preacher. . . . All who had known him, or who had listened with wrapt attention to the eloquence which gushed from his lips, touched as with a living coal from the altar, were moved to tears, and seemed to feel as if they were taking in reality a last farewell of one who had given a new ardour to their piety, and thrown an additional interest into the sanctuary. The whole scene was in no ordinary degree grand, imposing, and affecting. The magnificent hall, a fit temple for the worship of the living God; the crowd that had assembled to hear the last sermon of the minister whose eloquence they so much admired; the attitude of the preacher, and the solemn and prophetic farewell, all conspired to excite feelings of the deepest solemnity and of the most intense interest."

CHAPTER V

MR. COOKMAN spent a few weeks about Washington, completing his arrangements and taking leave of friends, and
immediately after the first despatch of the new Administration was prepared by Mr. Webster and committed to him,
he left for New York. His last words to the gentleman
so freely quoted from were—" May heaven bless you, Mr.
Smith; if ever I return you shall see me in the West." He
spent Sunday, 7th of March, in Philadelphia, worshipping
with and taking the communion at the hands of his friend,
the Rev. Dr. Suddards, rector of Grace Protestant Episcopal
Church. On Monday he went to New York, and on Tuesday evening preached his last sermon in the Vestry Street
Methodist Episcopal Church, of which he was to become
the pastor after his return from England. He had intended
to go to Boston and there take one of the Cunard steamers,
but at the solicitation of friends changed his mind, and
embarked on the steam-ship " President," at New York, on
the 11th, for Liverpool. He left amid the tears and con-
gratulations of friends. Neither the vessel nor any of her
company were ever after heard of.

Mr. Cookman wished and intended to take Alfred with
him to England. He thought it would be gratifying to the
grandfather to see him; and the son had attained an age
at which he could be a companion to his father, and also

derive much improvement from travel. I can imagine how strong the paternal instinct was in him, and how he must have yearned to have his first-born accompany him in so long an absence from home, and under circumstances so suited to render them both entirely happy. There is nothing upon which a child can depend for safety more than this same paternal instinct. Ulysses was consistent in his feigned madness—ploughing the seashore with a horse and bull yoked together, and sowing salt instead of grain—until his little son Telemachus was placed in the way, when his deception was betrayed by his showing sufficient foresight to turn away the plough from killing the child. Mr. Cookman could not but feel what a privation it would be to his wife to have Alfred leave her for so long a time, and what an additional affliction it would be should neither the husband nor the son be permitted to return. The lad, also, was of sufficient maturity in years and character to be of great assistance to the mother in her care of the younger children. And so, finally, Mr. Cookman yielded his preference, and it was left to the boy himself to elect—to go with his father or to stay with his mother.

It is difficult to see how anything could have been more attractive to a youth of his age, tastes, and habits, than this trip homeward to England with his devoted father. He had heard the old country, grandfather, uncles, aunts, and cousins talked of, till his boyish fancy revelled in the thought of seeing them and their beautiful homes. But Alfred Cookman loved his mother as few boys ever did, he loved his brothers and sister as few elder brothers have ever done, his loyalty to duty had already become a passion, and his decision was given accordingly : "I will stay with mother, and help her take care of the children." These words give the key-note of his character. They not only preserved his life, but became the warp across which the web and woof of that life were woven into a fabric so strong and beautiful. He would do his duty first, and standing by his duty brought him into responsibilities which, under the Divine blessing, made him what he was—a prince among God's spiritual Israel. The father then had to go alone. He went off cheerfully. Among the last words he spoke as the family sat before the open fire, were these : " Now, boys, if your father sinks in the ocean, his soul will go direct to God, and you must meet him in heaven."

How like an angel of light Alfred now came to the side of his mother ! He restrained his own grief, and always appeared before her calm and cheerful. With the utmost delicacy he watched over her, anticipating all her wants with a foresight beyond his years, and exhibiting for her most hidden feelings a feminine tenderness of which she scarcely supposed him possessed. Mrs. Cookman, from revelling in the brilliance of her husband's fame and usefulness, found herself all at once in such utter darkness that her mind from the shock sank into the deepest gloom. So overwhelmed was she, that for two years she did not recover her cheerfulness. The name of her husband could not be pronounced in her presence without unnerving her, and so the mention of the father was studiously avoided by the children. All the while Alfred was preserving such a composed demeanour in the presence of his mother, he would lie awake nights thinking of his father. It was some distance from the quiet home in which the family were entertained to the nearest post-office, and as he often went for the mail, his heart would sink within him when no letter came from father, or from any one giving tidings of the ill-fated steamer. " How I did dread," he said in after years, " to return home, and meet my dear mother without a letter, and see her disappointment !"

Thus at thirteen years of age, when the thought of play is uppermost with most boys, was our young friend abruptly forced by the providence of God into a trying and important relation to the family. He must be a husband as well as son to his mother; he must be father as well as eldest brother to the children. It is easy to conjecture, but impossible to know, what would have been the course of Alfred's life, what the influence upon his character, what different impress he might have received, had his father lived. His training thus far, under the joint and harmonious direction of father and mother, was entirely judicious; he was as promising as the parents could wish; and, in all probability, had the father been spared to guide his studies as he grew to manhood, he might, in some respects, have been a more thoroughly cultured and intellectually a stronger man. What God's purpose was for the lad it is not for us even now to say; yet, permitted as we are to know the facts of his subsequent career, and to understand the distinctive nature of his mission as it afterward unfolded, I must certainly regard the great bereavement he sustained in the loss of his father as the crucial point of his history, in which the elements of character hitherto prominent were fixed, and also the lines of action which afterward distinguished him took their rise. Alfred Cookman was endowed from a child with a religious tendency. His anointing was that of a spiritual seer—to see with the spirit into the innermost heart of spiritual Christianity, and from such seeing to lead men's minds into depths of a vital and blessed experience of the things of God, to which mere reason and even ordinary piety has no access. As the poet, by an endowment which transcends cold logic, pierces the core of things and opens their realities to the untutored mind—makes the blind to see, the deaf to hear, and the dull to feel beauties otherwise hidden—so he, by a Divine gift above the processes of the understanding, was to know the truths of the great Teacher, perceive their highest religious relations, and then to stand as interpreter of God's work in the soul, so that multitudes, blinded by the dust and engrossed with the cares of the world, might come to perceptions and attainments to which but for such an interpreter they must for ever have remained ignorant.

I look upon this great trial, therefore, as beginning at once the special work of which he was to be a pre-eminent example and instrument. He was to be an unworldly, sacred man, and God commenced with the stroke which cut him away from the strongest earthly support he had. Accustomed hitherto to lean on his father—now mother, brothers, sister, all lean on him; and he, poor boy, has none to lean on but God! Once again he was "all alone with Jesus." He had been taught that God is the only sure foundation of His children, and now he must prove it for himself by experience or perish. He did prove it; and at that early age began to show a ripeness of wisdom, a steadiness of purpose, an unselfishness, a goodness, faith, courage, which were far beyond his years. His mother testifies beautifully to his conduct at this period :—

" He was only thirteen years old when his dear father left us on a visit to his native land, the sequel of which proved so disastrous to a large, helpless family; but which, notwithstanding, brought out in all their force and power what had been until now the germs of Alfred's character. He realized his position as the oldest of six children, and faithfully tried to fill up the chasm made by a wise, though inscrutable Providence. Eternity alone will unfold all he was to his family as a son and as a brother in the years of his minority."

There is an old story told of a runaway Indian slave in Peru, who, in his escape, fleeing up the mountains from his pursuers, grasped a young sapling, and, clinging to it, tore it from the ground—when lo ! he saw adhering to its roots the silver globules which revealed the precious metals of Potosi. That sapling was never planted again. It might have become a great tree, its branches a roost for the birds of the air, and its leaves a shade for man and beast ; but in its destruction the untold wealth of Peru had been discovered. The rude hand of disappointment tore from Alfred Cookman's heart the support of a father's love, and the tender leaves and flowers of hope which clustered around it ; but in doing so discovered to him a wealth of love far richer than silver and gold. His hold on the earthly father was broken, but his hold on the heavenly Father was made firm and indissoluble. In the wealth he gained, and the world through him, who shall mourn if the flowers, which might have been so fair, lie withered at the feet of his youth ?

Soon after her husband's departure for England, Mrs. Cookman had gone, by invitation, with her children to the eastern shore of Maryland, where they were all to remain the guests of Mr. Samuel Harrison, until the husband's return in June, when they were to remove to New York. Her stay was prolonged till the month of August. Since up to this time no information was received as to the fate of Mr. Cookman, and the prospect of his return was well-nigh abandoned, she began to cast about for the best thing to be done for the immediate future. From the grandfather and kindred in England the most urgent requests were received that she should at once take her children to England. Indeed, they wrote as though there could be no other course open to her. They were well able to provide for them, and her pecuniary means were exceedingly limited. Nothing would have been more natural than for Mrs. Cookman to accept this offer—alone as she was among comparative strangers, with no relatives near, and knowing, as she did, that the resources at Hull were so ample ; but she decided not to go.   She had left home for life ; her children had been born in America, and Americans they should be reared.   "She would take two small rooms, and keep them all together around her, rather than all or any part of them should return to England."   Such was the language this heroic lady held to her friends across the water, and nothing could move her from her purpose.   Mr. John Plaskitt, an Englishman residing in Baltimore City, and long known as the head of the firm of Plaskitt and Armstrong, booksellers and stationers, a prominent Methodist, and an intimate friend of the husband, with other gentlemen, rented a small house on Mulberry Street, near the Eutaw Street Methodist Church ; and to it the family removed in the autumn.

Mrs. Cookman and Alfred united with the Eutaw Street Church.   The children who were old enough were entered at the Eutaw Street Sunday School, and also at day schools. Alfred, at different times for the next few years, was under the instruction of Messrs. Robert H. Pattison, Perley R. Lovejoy, and John H. Dashiell—all recently students of Dickinson College—and of a Mr. Burleigh.   At Mr. Burleigh's school on one occasion he took several prizes—for elocution, an essay on simplicity, exercises in Latin, etc. He began thus early to attract attention as a speaker and writer.   Mr. Robert Armstrong, then superintendent of the Eutaw Street Sunday School, noticed his aptitude for public speaking, and was accustomed to put him up to address the boys' department of the school.   His first original declamation was on the American Indian, in which the richness of his fancy and the force and gracefulness of his elocution were already apparent.

The following letter from the grandfather shows the truly parental solicitude with which he regarded the widow and the children of his late son ; and the reply from Alfred affords us an example of his dutifulness, and some account of his doings and progress.

From Mr. George Cookman, of Hull, to Alfred, his grandson :—

"HULL, *April* 5, 1842.

"MY DEAR ALFRED,— I received three days ago the letter of your dear mother, sent off in February, and had a fearful presentiment of her recent affliction, as her letter of the 27th of December never came to hand. I am, however, very thankful that she is so much recovered ; and I trust, as the spring advances, she will regain her wonted health. I am quite as well as I can expect to be at my advanced age, and feel a most lively interest in the comfort and happiness of your dear family. I look to you, my dear Alfred, as an important coadjutor with your dear mother in forming the habits and character of your family ; and it gives me inexpressible pleasure to learn, from your dear mother's letter, that there is every reason to hope that my expectations in this respect will be fully realized. Rest assured that you will be looked up to by the younger branches of the family, and in setting them a good example—in cheerfully obliging your dear mother, in promptly and affectionately obeying her commands, and in sympathising with her under the pressure of family trials and bereavements—you will greatly lighten her burdens, alleviate her sufferings, and minister, in no inconsiderable degree, to her peace, comfort, and happiness.

"I hope you pay unremitting attention to your education. Your dear father, when about your age, was very attentive and diligent in the cultivation of his mind ; he read much, and kept a commonplace-book, into which he copied from the authors which he read such passages as he thought the most striking, either as to sentiment or language ; and by adopting this plan he very much improved his style in composition and his taste. He also began at the same time to write short essays on different subjects, as trials of his intellectual strength ; and resolutely struggled with and overcame those difficulties which, if not mastered, are often fatal to mental improvement. It was by his

4

unremitting perseverance in these pursuits that he formed his graceful and chaste style of composition, and which in after-life enabled him to write with such facility and dispatch.

"Allow me, my dear grandson, to urge you to follow the example of your dear departed father in the cultivation of your mind at this period of your life, for your future acquirements will very much depend upon an early development of your mental faculties. It was by adopting this course that your dear Uncle Alfred became so distinguished, both at home among his friends, as well as when he was a student at the University. I trust their mantle will fall upon you, my dear boy, and that you will emulate their talents and virtues—and like them secure the respect and admiration of your friends, and largely contribute to the happiness of mankind. I am glad to find that the portrait of your dear father is, upon the whole, as good as could be expected under all the circumstances in which we were placed ; we did our best to get it as faithful and correct a likeness as we possibly could ; and many of his friends here, judging of him by what he was when he left England, think it a striking likeness. We should, however, have been better pleased if the portrait had been more perfect. The Rev. Mr. Suddards dined with me on the 31st of March, and has been most obligingly kind in giving us every important information in his power, both with regard to your dear father, and all the members of your dear family. I feel under great obligations to him for the sympathy and affectionate regard which he has so uniformly and generously manifested, both to the memory of my late dear son and also to his family. I owe him a debt of gratitude which I can never pay—but our good Lord, I trust, will reward him a hundred-fold for his work of faith and labour of love in behalf of our family.

"You will please to give my kind love to your dear mother, to George, and all the younger branches of your family ; give dear little Mary a kiss for her grandfather."

From Alfred to his grandfather :—

"BALTIMORE, *August* 27, 1842.

"MY DEAR GRANDFATHER,—Your letter has remained unanswered longer than I had intended when it was first received. The reason why I did not answer it sooner was because I was very much engaged with my school duties ; and during my vacation, when I might have written, I was in Washington. I hope you will excuse me.

"Mother has been improving in her health since last March. She has not been as well as usual for two weeks past. She is quite a miracle to herself and to all of her friends, to be able to do what she does, considering how feeble she was. The warm weather always agrees better with her than the cold.

"I thank you for the kind advice which you give me in your letter. Rest assured, my dear grandfather, that it shall always be my first aim to comply with the wishes of dear mother, and in every way in my power to make her happy, for I deeply appreciate the obligations I am under to her: in sickness and health, she is always the same tender, kind, and affectionate mother. I am very much pleased with the plan you gave me of my dear father's method of improvement. I shall try to pursue it, but with how much success I know not. I have been in the habit of writing short essays on different subjects, and have found it very improving. I have been spending my vacation in Washington, and had an opportunity of attending the debates of Congress. I also attended a camp-meeting about sixteen miles from Washington. There were about one hundred and thirty tents on the ground, and about one hundred persons professed to be converted. We had a delightful time. I enjoyed myself very much.

"The treaty with Lord Ashburton has been amicably settled, and the people generally seem pleased. I got a sight of him one day in his carriage.

"I am connected here with the Sabbath School. I have a class of eight small boys, whom I take a great delight in teaching. I am also connected with the McKendrean Juvenile Missionary Society, who have appointed me secretary. I am also secretary of the Ashbury Juvenile Temperance Society of Baltimore. So you see I have plenty to do.

"The temperance cause is making rapid strides in this city and elsewhere. The Hon. T. F. Marshall, who is a reformed drunkard, has become one of its most powerful advocates. He is a man of fine talents, and excels as a public speaker. My brothers are all well. I wish, my dear grandfather, we could all see you and you could see us, and give us your valuable advice in person. We often look at your likeness hanging on the wall, and try to bring you before us. I hope you will continue your correspondence with me occasionally, and suggest plans that I may profit by. I resume my school duties to-morrow, for which I am very glad. I shall try to make the best of my time now, for I suppose I shall soon have to turn my attention to business. Mother says the next year will probably be my last for regular study. * * *"

I have before me a copy of the Fourth of July oration. It is creditable alike to the head and the heart of its youth-

ful author.   It is well conceived and well expressed, showing the elevation of thought and principle, the patriotic
and religious fire which thus early animated him.   In the
same composition-book, in his neat handwriting, are trans-
lations from the Greek and Latin, and original essays, which
give evidence of a vigorous intellect already well advanced
in culture.

CHAPTER VI.

HARMONIOUSLY with his intellectual progress, Alfred's moral and spiritual character was also growing. Mrs. Cookman, to satisfy her own yearnings for usefulness, to gratify the incessant demands for her counsel and society, and to obtain relief for her mind by activity, was much from home. She literally went about doing good—visiting the sick, needy, and penitent, attending social and religious meetings; and thus her heart was diverted, in a measure, from her great sorrow, and she was able to maintain a degree of health and cheerfulness. All this while Alfred was a keeper at home. He would urge her out, and volunteer to remain and take care of the children. Of an evening he could be seen, with his little brothers surrounding a large table, superintending their studies, helping them forward in their next day's tasks. Oftentimes the mother would return home weary, and she would say, "Come, children, we must have prayers before we go to bed;" and the quick response would be, "Mother, we have had prayers; Alfred has held prayers with us." At this age he showed habits of system and neatness which always followed him. His little room was a pink of tidiness; his bed, his books, his table, his clothes, all were kept in the nicest order, and he punctually observed the hours of coming and going assigned him by his mother.

Could a better testimony be given to a son than the following from the pen of his mother?

"There are very few who could fully estimate the love
and sympathy of such a mere youth as Alfred was when I
was left without the strong arm I had been accustomed to
lean upon. He turned at once into the path of a wise and
steady counsellor, to myself as well as to his brothers.
He tried to share every burden and supply every loss which
an apparent adverse Providence had laid upon us. In the
deep anguish of a stricken heart, he would say, 'Dear
mother, let the event be as it may, it is all right, and will
turn out for the best; our heavenly Father disposes of all
events, and He cannot err in any of His dealings with His
children.' Alfred did almost exclusively direct and control
the studies of his brothers, unite with them in their various
pursuits, and guard them from influences that might have
been prejudicial but for his timely warnings; and yet there
was no austerity in his admonitions; a spirit of consideration and kindness ever marked his efforts. He was remarkably constant in the path of obedience both toward God and
in his Church relations. His class-meeting was never neglected. His attendance at the Sabbath School, first as a
scholar and then as a teacher, was constant; and so marked
was his conduct as to induce the superintendent to request
him to address his youthful companions on the importance
of yielding their hearts to the blessed Saviour, and this before
he was fifteen years of age."

Although he was naturally thoughtful, and the care pre-
maturely devolved upon him tended to sadden his spirits, it
must not be inferred that he was at all gloomy or despondent.
On the contrary, he was one of the liveliest of boys, full of
fun and cheerful gaiety; he was always ready for a gambol
with his brothers and his neighbours. He was a great

favourite with his young companions. Known to be a ready writer, nothing was more common than for all the girls around to wish him to write their valentines.

The first public religious exercise which Alfred conducted was "to lead a class-meeting," when about sixteen years of age. A Mr. Childs had requested him to lead his class. The class met in a private house. The mother, in her great desire to hear him conduct it without embarrassing him by her presence, concealed herself behind a side stairway, and so listened to all the exercises.

Early in the year 1844, Alfred and George received a letter from their grandfather. It is so good that I cannot refrain from inserting it entire.

"HULL, STEPNEY LODGE, *January* 27, 1844.

"MY DEAR ALFRED AND GEORGE,—I received with more than ordinary pleasure your letters of the 27th of July, and in reading them I could scarcely persuade myself but that time, by some mysterious revolution, had thrown back my life for at least five-and-twenty years, and that I was again reading the pleasing letters of dear Alfred and George, my beloved sons. But, alas! the spell was soon broken by the painful recollections of the past. I am, however, delighted with your letters. The handwriting is very good; the composition, for your ages, is of a superior order; and, if you continue to prosecute your studies and exercises with unremitting perseverance, I have no doubt but you will, in your day, be the fac-similes of those whose endearing names you bear. * * * Let me entreat you, my dear grandchildren, to minister in every way in your power to the tranquillity, comfort, and happiness of a mother whose maternal care and solicitude for the welfare of her family have been as unremitting as her love has been pure and ardent. I was delighted to hear of your attainments as scholars, and of the very handsome manner in which your exercises were received by the audience at your public exhibition. You have, by these successful efforts, secured a prominent position in the estimation of the public; and if you should conclude from this circumstance that you may now relax your efforts in the prosecution of your studies, this elevation will be but the precursor of your fall. It is not enough to be considered the first among boys: you must look forward and aspire to be the first among your citizens.

But this cannot be attained but by unremitting industry. Decision of character is therefore indispensable in all important undertakings, and I have no doubt of your ultimate success if you are determined to excel. You are, I hope, proceeding with your learning in a systematic and methodical order, and making yourselves thoroughly masters of one branch of science before you enter upon another. This is indispensable, as this is the basis of all after-improvements in learning.

" I am glad to find that you have become members of a literary society, and have no doubt but it will be of great service to you. Your dear father and uncle had the same privilege, and they often surprised me by the papers they produced and the speeches they delivered on the questions discussed at their weekly meetings. Mixing with members of superior acquirements, they obtained a great increase of knowledge, and also obtained an easy and graceful mode of public speaking. There is, however, *some danger* growing out of these institutions, against which I would most urgently caution you. The questions for discussion have seldom any connection with each other, and this necessarily induces a desultory and careless course of reading and of thought. Now the danger to be apprehended is this : that you will seek applause in the forum rather than in the academy, and fall into a dislike of the study of those dryer branches of learning which require greater mental application and labour, and the mastery of which is essential to your becoming proficients in sound learning. Above all things of this life, seek first the kingdom of God and His righteousness, and leave the rest to the good pleasure of your Heavenly Father." * * *

From Alfred to his grandfather Cookman :—

"BALTIMORE, *March* 22, 1845.

" MY DEAR GRANDFATHER,—This day's mail has brought to hand a letter from Aunt Mary Ann, which has been the first to break the long-continued silence which has reigned for some months. In the perusal of her letter we were not a little gratified to learn that you still enjoy your accustomed health, and are able to attend to all the concerns of domestic life. Believing that it would afford you pleasure to hear from us, I have sat down and will write a few lines on what we would call the leading topics of the day.

" Well, in what condition are we as a country ? What have we done, and what are we doing ? I think we may with propriety be compared to the ocean : we have had the storm, and now the calm is beginning to succeed. For the last few months we have as a nation been torn with party strife ; for from the tiny school-boy as well as the gray-headed old man have been heard sentiments, together with enthu-siastic shouts, in honour of some favourite partisan. Meetings have been held frequently, at which vast concourses of people have assembled, and where the talent of the country have been present to display their forensic powers. However, although I am favourable to party spirit where it can be kept within bounds, believing that it tends to keep alive a spirit of inquiry in the minds of the people in regard to those subjects connected with their country's welfare, yet when it reaches the height which it has here, and is productive of the same direful results, I, for one, would say, ' Subdue, and silence it.' It has been prostituted to the worst purposes. Men who have stood in our council chambers, ever ready to second any effort that would conduce to the prosperity of the nation, and who, in very many instances, have been the originators of noble and useful measures, have had their characters defamed and their spotless reputations sullied and disgraced. But the evils of party spirit have not ended here. There has been the greatest amount of betting : thousands have been swallowed up in this greedy vortex, and, among a certain class of our citizens, that man who would bet the greatest amount has been considered a noble-hearted, generous fellow. At the large meetings of which I have spoken, liquor has been used, occasioning drunkenness and riot. All these evils combined have presented to the virtuous and patriotic mind a sad and mournful picture.

" But the contest is over ; the combatants have withdrawn from the field of party strife, and the champion of the victorious party has been awarded the title of the President of the United States. All the various portions of society are beginning to turn their attention again to their daily avocations, and are bending all the energies of their minds towards amassing money or something else.

" The main question which now agitates our country is the subject of slavery. Not content with harassing us in our civil institutions, it has entered the borders of our Zion, and will, in all probability, effect a division. At our late session of Congress it was decreed to annex Texas to our Union. This lying to the south of our Republic, and being itself a slave country, will be connected with Southern interests, who (the South) may insist on measures which may prove detrimental to the North, who, in turn, retaliating, may bring on that most-to-be-dreaded of all evils—civil war. Oh, grandfather, I regard the measure of Congress, in this point of view, as highly reprehensible. I believe that it will cast a dark stain on the fair escutcheon of our liberties, and that

eventually it may prove the breaker on which the proud ship of State
may be wrecked.

"In the Church a difficulty has arisen—whether it is in harmony with
the spirit of Methodism for a bishop, who is called to all parts of the
Union, to be the possessor of human property ; and at the late session
of the General Conference much time was spent on this question, which
was finally decided in the negative. This decision has so enraged the
Southern portion of the Church that they have declared that they
will not submit to this (as they would term it) arbitrary measure,
and they have called a General Conference, to be held in May next, to
take steps toward division. What it will end in is for the future to
develop. I trust that the Great Head of the Church will rule all things
well; that He will adjust these difficulties, and bring all things to a
happy termination. I had intended when I commenced my letter to be
rather egotistic ; but ideas on the subjects which I have alluded to have
multiplied, and I have just recorded them. My next shall be more
about myself and family. As we boys are accustomed to say, ' *tempus
et spatium*' fail me, and I must close."

The reader of these pages will readily forgive our young
friend for his want of "egotism" in this letter, since more
of him, as an observer of his times, is seen that any merely
personal narrative could have given. It is evident that he
was thoroughly alive to the stirring events of those days, in
which party strife, both in State and Church, had reached
the pitch that already foreboded the calamities into which
the whole country was soon precipitated.

Thus at the age of seventeen he evinced a familiarity
with public movements, a close sympathy with the welfare
of the nation, and of the Church to which he belonged,
which never forsook him. From this time onward he could
be no indifferent citizen of the State or member of the
Church. It was not in the nature of a soul so thoroughly
human, and so richly imbued with the Master's spirit, to be
a passive cipher in the midst of such active forces as those
into which he was born and in which he grew up. It has
been conjectured, in a most graphic delineation of his father,

that the stirring, warlike spirit of Europe in the beginning of
the nineteenth century, at the period of the father's birth,
had much to do with his martial spirit as an orator. A
heart more responsive to the weal of the nation and to the
weal of the Church never throbbed than beat in the breast
of Alfred Cookman ; nor has there arisen among us a
public man, whether in the pulpit or out of it, whose character was more affected by the reflected influence of these
two objects. To those who knew so well the genuineness
of his patriotism, and the unselfish zeal of his Methodism
in later years, it is no unpleasant matter to get a peep at the
early dawn of these two great passions which is afforded us
by this letter. How like the temper of the perfected man,
the sentiment, " I trust that the Great Head of the Church
will rule all things well ; that He will adjust these difficulties,
and bring all things to a happy termination " !

About this time—the year 1845—Alfred entered distinc-
tively upon his evangelistic career ; not, however, as a
preacher, but as an earnest worker in Sabbath-school
and missionary effort. A band of young men, most of
whom were connected with the Charles Street Church,
formed a mission to the seamen and poor children who frequented the upper docks of the harbour in Baltimore. Their
hearts were touched with pity as they saw the large number
of sailors, most of whom were confined to vessels doing business wholly in the waters of Chesapeake Bay, and were entirely
destitute of the means of religious improvement. They first
rented a small room at the head of Frederick Street Dock.
This proving too limited, they removed to a more commodious and eligibly located one in Pratt Street, at the head of
the Upper Basin. It was not the first time that Methodism
began a good work in a " Sail Loft." The old Sail Loft,
christened " The City Bethel," was the scene of the zealous

labours of these devout young men on Sundays and week-day evenings. Alfred was the youngest among them, but not least in graces and gifts. He was so powerfully affected by the " Bethel Fraternity," then and always, for the shape and for the friendships it gave him, and those who constituted this band of generous youths have since come to such repute, and the immediate object for which they laboured has come to such stability, that I offer from the pen of the Rev. T. H. Switzer, the first pastor of the City Bethel, a circumstantial account of the matter :—

" The Baltimore Bethel was the second organization of the kind in the city; its object was to reach sailors, watermen, and neglected children, who loitered about the wharfs on the Sabbath-day. It was called City Bethel to distinguish it from the Sailors' Union Bethel, of Fell's Point, Baltimore.

"Brother Alfred Cookman, although the youngest, was one of the most active and efficient members of the society; at our regularly monthly meetings to devise ways and means of advancing the interests of the association, he was always present, and took part in our deliberations and discussions. In the Sabbath-school, the experience meetings, and in the preaching of the Word, he manifested a lively interest. Soon after my appointment to the charge, an incident occurred which brought him particularly under my notice. Thomas Dryden, son of Joshua Dryden, after a protracted illness, fell asleep in Jesus. His death was deeply lamented by the society. His example was bright while he lived, and his death was signally triumphant. The friends of the deceased and members of the organization requested Brother Cookman to prepare a funeral discourse, which he did, and delivered in the lecture-room of the Charles Street Church.

This was Alfred's first sermon, then in his seventeenth year. The discourse made a strong impression on the audience, and those present who are now living remember it to the present day. His call to the ministry was undoubted by those who heard him on that occasion.

"The sermon was delivered with much feeling, his enunciation was distinct, his language chaste and impressive, his illustrations forcible and appropriate; his pathetic allusions to the deceased touched the tender chords of the hearts of many present. Those who were familiar with his father's method, and the character of his preaching, could not fail to discover in the younger Cookman traits that reminded them of that eminent minister of Christ, George G. Cookman.

"Alfred Cookman was as that time modest and unobtrusive in manner, ardent in his feelings. His judgment was in advance of his years, his imagination was vivid, and illustration was successfully employed in his themes. In person he was slender, and his genial countenance wore the cheerful glow of sunshine."

The communication of Mr. Switzer has anticipated a little the fact which was to give direction to Alfred's future calling. From the incident of the funeral sermon, it is evident that an impression was already prevailing among his associates that he was "called to preach." His selection by those who knew him most intimately for so important a service for their departed associate, shows that they not only believed him called of God to preach, but also the high estimation in which they held both his talents and his piety. It was a great mark of respect to be put upon a youth of seventeen years. His text on the occasion was, "To die is gain." The general style and effect of the treatment have been described. The mind of the Church now distinctly

pointed to him as a suitable person to preach the Gospel of
Christ.   The call to preach, among the Methodists, is
regarded as a twofold and simultaneous movement of the
Holy Ghost upon the heart of the individual and upon the
heart of the Church with which he is connected.   However
reserved the person thus moved may be in withholding
his impressions, the Church will be led, independently
of any communication from him, to feel that he ought to
take upon himself the office and work of the ministry.
Many a young man who, in his modesty, has tried like
Saul to hide himself among the stuff, ignorant that any
one suspected his struggles of soul, has been drawn out of
his hiding-place and thrust forth into the work.   Such, too,
has not unfrequently stood head and shoulders above his
brethren.

The initial steps were taken in designating Alfred Cookman for the ministry, November 1st, 1845, when he was
licensed as an exhorter in the Methodist Episcopal Church
by the official meeting of the Charles Street Station, Baltimore
Conference, Edwin Dorsey preacher in charge.   In less
than a year from this time, on July 7th, 1846, he received
from the Quarterly Conference of the same charge a license
to preach, signed by the Rev. John A. Collins, as presiding
elder.   The preparation for the examination which he had
to undergo before the Quarterly Conference was made
wholly by himself.   It was conducted very thoroughly by
Mr. Collins, who, at its close, pronounced Alfred more
proficient in the subjects comprised in the examination than
any young man who had ever come before him for license.
He was at this time an assistant teacher in a private
academy ; his work was arduous and confining, his social
and religious engagements numerous, so that he must
have studied diligently to attain such a clear understanding

of the Scriptural proofs of the fundamental doctrines of Christianity.

George G. Cookman had thus early a successor in the ministry. Five years only had gone since the great light was quenched in the sea, and now in the person and office of the eldest born the work of illumination was to be continued. The deep emotions of the mother may be better imagined than expressed, as she saw her little Solomon recognised as God's chosen one, and designated by the Church to the great building to which she had so sincerely consecrated him in childhood. To such a mother this hour for her first-born was cause for richer joy and juster pride than if she had seen him selected for an earthly throne, or as the heir of the wealthiest man in the land. Of Alfred's own feelings at this important period of his career but a limited statement is at command. In after years he made this reference to it: "At the age of eighteen I took up the silver trumpet which had fallen from the hand of my faithful father, and began to preach, in a very humble way, the everlasting Gospel." This allusion, and that found in the following letter to his grandfather, are enough to show the humility and earnestness with which he received the great commission. The letter also lets us into his anxious questionings as to his immediate future course. Its references to the late Rev. George C. M. Roberts, M.D., D.D., cannot fail of grateful interest to the host of friends, in Baltimore and elsewhere, who cherish with such affection and reverence the memory of that able and devout man. At once physician and local preacher, he ministered to the bodies and souls of thousands, and for the space of a quarter of a century wielded an influence in the community second to no other citizen.

To his grandfather Cookman he writes,—

"BALTIMORE, *July* 7, 1846.

"A favourable opportunity for transmitting you a few lines has presented itself, inasmuch as Dr. Roberts, one of the most respected and esteemed members of our community, is about to depart for England with the design of attending the World's Convention. This gentleman is a member of the medical profession in our city; in connection with this he is an official member in the Methodist Church, and has always evinced great zeal and energy in the promotion of every good and benevolent enterprise. I am sure that Baltimore possesses no son more highly esteemed and more generally loved than this brother, and it is on account of his noble and excellent qualities that he was unhesitatingly selected to represent the interests of what is termed 'the city station' in this coming convention. He is a man of the deepest and most devoted piety, and an earnest anxiety for the prosperity of Zion has prompted him to establish a Saturday-evening prayer-meeting, where Christians are accustomed to meet and pray, more especially for the sanctifying influences of God's Spirit. At these meetings I have frequently been found, and have there eminently realized the presence of the King of kings and Lord of lords. I am sure you will be pleased with him. Possessed of a sweet, Christian-like spirit, affable and winning manners, and no small share of intellect, he secures for himself the affection and good-will of all with whom he is called to associate.

"As you are aware, I have been engaged in teaching for the last twelve months. I have not realized those sanguine expectations that I indulged when I entered upon this arduous employment; for I confidently hoped to do more in the improvement of my mind, while engaged in teaching, than I could possibly if my entire time were devoted to literary pursuits. I thought that, while instructing youths, I should effect a review of old studies, and that between schools I could devote myself to mental labour or literary acquisition; but, alas! alas! my hopes have proved vain, and I have not reached that point in the hill of science whither my aspirations would have led me. The school in which I am engaged as assistant has been small, and made up principally of boys who were in the very first rudiments of science; and day after day my duties have been to hear the little urchin repeat his task either in spelling, geography, arithmetic, or some other minor branch, all of which it would be almost impossible to forget; and thus I, of course, have not realized my first expectation. Although these my scholars had progressed but little, though their attainments were but limited, I felt it to be my duty to devote myself with as much assiduity and energy to their improvement as if I had heard them every day recite an ode of Horace or a section of Homer. The consequence has been that, when after having performed my duties I have returned home and retired to my own study, I have experienced a general prostration of my entire system. My nerves have been unstrung, my energies paralyzed, and I have had no spirit to proceed with study. I must not, I cannot consistently say, that I have made no additions to my stock during the year. Many theological works I have carefully perused, and think that I am pretty well grounded in the fundamentals of divinity. During the year I felt it to be my duty to assume a more responsible station—namely, that of a minister of the everlasting Gospel. Frequently I have stood up in the sacred desk to expound the oracles of God; and, in declaring the unsearchable riches of Christ, in dwelling upon the amazing love and infinite condescension of the Saviour in redemption, my own soul has been warmed, and I have realized that in dispensing the Gospel I receive much of heaven's comfort.

"I have been seriously considering which would be the best course for me to pursue in the future. My engagements with Mr. L. will terminate in a few days, and I do not feel disposed to shackle myself for the coming year as I certainly have during the past. I have sought the counsel of some of my father's tried friends, as, for instance, Messrs. Hodgson, Durbin, Thompson, and others, and they advise me to enter the itinerant field, assuring me that I shall not only have more time, but more disposition to study. I have calmly and dispassionately weighed this advice, and think it is good; that perhaps it would be to my advantage, in an intellectual point of view, as well as the consideration that, in the hands of God, I might be made useful."

Alfred's mother, in referring to his habits at this date of his life, says, "He very early threw in his efforts (with others) to work among a class of degraded human beings, who were drunkards, and were almost taken out of the gutters. His young voice was often heard in denunciation and earnest entreaties for them to turn from sin and become new men in Christ Jesus. With what zeal and earnestness did he follow these poor outcasts! Alfred was very exact in the distribution of his time. He had to depend, in a great measure, on his own efforts. He felt himself a fatherless youth, and had very ardent yearnings to acquire knowledge, and to prepare himself to fill a useful and honourable position in life. Thus he became a very diligent student in the various departments constituting a thorough scholar. In Latin, Greek, German, and French, he was very proficient, and his knowledge in the arts and sciences was considerable. Even at the age of twelve his father acknowledged he was farther advanced in those branches than he was himself at the age of eighteen. Humility and timidity were two of his peculiar characteristics, which kept him from anything like display or assumption."

Subsequently to his license to preach, and before leaving Baltimore, he preached frequently. His friend, Mr. Samuel Kramer, a local preacher, would take him to his country appointments contiguous to the city, and would have him supply for him. All the opportunities he could desire, and more perhaps than was prudent for so young a beginner, were opened to him. His engagements were constantly up to the full measure of his strength and his time. In the best pulpits of the city his services were accepted, and in the best society of the city his company was eagerly sought. The name he bore was hallowed to the people. They were prepared, for his father's and mother's sake, to listen to his words and to love his character. But he was everything in himself that was attractive—one of the most engaging youths who ever stood in a sacred desk or moved among a circle of friends. There was a freshness and healthfulness of physique, an openness of physiognomy, a spiritual beauty, a ripeness of culture, a manifest piety, a gracefulness of movement, and a native eloquence which won all hearts ; and from this early day until his death there was no minister of the Methodist Episcopal Church who could draw together a larger crowd of ardent, admiring hearers in the city of Baltimore than Alfred Cookman. A halo invested him from the beginning to the end of his career.

CHAPTER VII.

BUT the time had now come when plans for the more regular and permanent exercise of his ministry began seriously to agitate him. We have already seen from his last letter that thoughts of a collegiate course had been entertained and discussed. It appears that the counsels of his father's closest friends were adverse to this, and favourable to an immediate entrance upon the itinerant ministry.

Certainly the results of his ministry are not such as to leave room for many regrets on the ground of greater possible usefulness. What he was we know; what he might have been with the influences of the broader culture which comes of the studies and associations of the college we cannot fully conjecture. A more liberal education, prosecuted at greater length, would probably have rendered him different, in some respects, from what he was as a man and as a preacher, but it is extremely doubtful if it could have rendered him more intense in his personal and ministerial influence. In the cry for scholars, we are too apt to forget that it is not so much ideas as their application; not so much new truths as the practice of old truths; not so much thinkers as actors—men of deeds—that the great world needs. A man to move and mould the people must be a man of positive convictions, be the circle of his knowledge never so small, rather than a critical investigator.

Alfred Cookman was capable of becoming a scholar of a high order, but he chose to narrow the sphere of his studies to the subjects which nourished his own soul satisfactorily, which he felt would make him most useful as a pastor; and it was the thoroughness with which his intellect grasped these, and the heartiness with which he believed them, that gave him in his domain so marked an ascendency over the minds of the people. So that I am frank to acknowledge that if a collegiate education (taking education in its multiplex sense) would have made his ministry different from what it was, I can scarcely see how it could have made it more useful. I fear the contrary might have been the result. Upon the whole, it is quite safe to assume, where the sincerest efforts are made by those who have the shaping of Christ's chosen instruments, that their course is about such as God orders, and in the outcome is the best for them and for His Church.

The point being settled that the young evangelist should at once make full proof of his ministry by entering the regular pastorate, the next question for decision was, " What conference shall he join ? " Some of his friends urged him strongly to seek admission into the Baltimore Conference, while others as strongly urged the advantages of the Philadelphia. It would have been natural for him to remain where he was, but the reasons for going to Philadelphia were controlling. His former and much beloved teacher, the Rev. Robert Pattison, had joined that conference; several of his young associates, such as Charles J. Thompson and Adam Wallace, preferred it; his father had first united with it, and he wished, as far as possible, to follow in his footsteps.

But, as usual, the mother's judgment turned the scales. There were better schools and better opportunities of business in Philadelphia, and Pennsylvania was a free state. Her repugnance to slavery made her adverse to rearing her children in contact with it. There was another consideration which weighed with her possibly more than all others: she felt the time had come when she must give herself more fully to the care of her children. While, therefore, her heart was deeply attached to Baltimore and to its loving, noble Christians, she determined that, for her family's sake, she must cut herself loose from their companionship, and seek, in another city and amid new scenes, to enter upon a course of more exclusive devotion to home nurture.

Early in the autumn of 1846 the household goods were stowed in a canal-boat and shipped to Philadelphia. The family soon followed. Alfred had already been requested by the Rev. James McFarland, presiding elder of one of the Philadelphia districts, to supply the place of Rev. D. D. Lore, who had been appointed missionary to Buenos Ayres, on Attleboro Circuit, Bucks County, under the charge of the Rev. James Hand. He accepted the invitation, and so soon as the family were settled, and he had procured the necessary outfit, he started for the "appointment." His horse he named "Gery," in honour of his friend Gershom Broadbent of Baltimore. Gery became a great pet with him and with all the brothers and the little sister. Alfred and Gery were much talked about at home, and their joint arrival on a visit was henceforth hailed as the brightest day which could dawn on Philadelphia.

It was a proud hour when the young preacher, leaving his mother's door, with her blessing on his head and her warm kiss upon his lips, springing into his saddle, hied away over the hills to his first pastoral charge. What a pang it must have cost him to part with that loving parent, to leave brothers and sister, who had clung to him as a father, and to

go off among total strangers ! But though young, and sensitive even to feminine delicacy, he had the hopes of youth
to cheer him. His heart was full of zeal for the Master's
glory, and the romantic interest which belongs to an earnest
nature in the first commencement of a chosen and chivalrous
career. On the mother's part, his devotement to the work
was one of pure self-sacrifice ; and as she saw him ride away,
in the first act which was for ever to take him from her roof,
the light went out of her eyes and the joy from her heart.
But she made the surrender cheerfully, thanking God that
He had "counted him worthy—putting him into the ministry." She could not, however, let him go without salutary
advice—advice which he never forgot, and which became a
watch-cry in his ministry. Here is his reference to the occasion : "Quitting about this time one of the happiest of homes
to enter the itinerant work, my excellent mother remarked
just upon the threshold of my departure, ' My son, if you
would be supremely happy or extremely useful in your work,
you must be an entirely sanctified servant of Jesus.' It was
a cursory suggestion, perhaps forgotten almost as soon as
expressed ; nevertheless, applied by the Spirit, it made the
profoundest impression upon my mind and heart. Oh the
value of single sentences which any one may utter in the
ordinary intercourse of life ! Sermons and exhortations are
frequently forgotten, while the wish or counsel simply and
precisely expressed will abide, to lead us into clearer light.
Let this fact, which will find an illustration in many experiences, serve to stimulate and encourage even the feeblest to
speak for Jesus. My mother's passing but pointed remark
followed me like a good angel as I moved to and fro in my
first sphere of itinerant life."

Attleboro Circuit lay among the hills of Bucks County,
and embraced in its territory a fine rural district. It obliged

a good deal of travelling and much hard work from the youthful minister. The social status of Methodism was not so high as he had been accustomed to in the cities, and, although he met with great kindness from the people, he missed many comforts which he had hitherto deemed quite necessary to his well-being. But he shrank from no duty, however hard, and no work which lay in his way. Among the youths whom he had found on removing to Philadelphia was Andrew Longacre, now the Rev. Andrew Longacre, of the New York Conference. They soon felt themselves to be kindred spirits, and very speedily there sprang up between them a friendship which grew closer with maturing years, and has constituted one of the most profitable and lovely of human attachments. Andrew was younger by three years, but Alfred gave him his whole heart. The following letter is a proof of this affection, and also a fair exhibit of the circuit life. It discloses to us the dutiful service he was ready to render as a "junior preacher," the fidelity with which amid bodily ailments he stood to his post, and also the zest with which, though now a grave minister, he could enter into the pleasantries of his young friend :—

NEW TOWN, *February* 22, 1847.

"MY DEAR FRIEND ANDREW,—I had intended to reply to your interesting and affectionate letter some days since, but circumstances have been of a character to prevent me. Not only have I had the duties of a protracted meeting devolving upon me, but within the last few days I have necessarily been obliged to travel a good deal, in compliance with the wishes of my colleague. On Friday last, in conjunction with his expressed desire, I procured a covered wagon and a pair of horses, and, assisted by a teamster, proceeded to bring a table that had been constructed in New Hope to this village, the place of its destination. The distance is about twelve miles, and the road being exceedingly bad, owing to the continued wet weather, we were about three hours in accomplishing the journey. During the day I got my feet very wet, and on my return was so thoroughly chilled that I apprehended a severe cold. My surmises proved but too true, for after passing a rather disagreeable night—my slumbers being disturbed—I rose in the morning threatened with my old complaint. I had promised the day previous that I would return to New Town, and, if necessary, would endeavour to preach on Saturday evening in Attleboro. Not willing to sacrifice my word, I very imprudently again left New Hope in an open sulky, and with great difficulty reached New Town, when I was obliged to alight and lie down. I found, from the state of my feelings, that it would be impracticable and impossible for me to proceed any farther. Debility and pain seemed to have seized my entire system, and I was sick—*very sick*. My colleague came in, and very kindly consented to put away and take charge of my horse, and thought, from my symptoms, that I should at once see a doctor. He soon arrived, dosed me with laudanum and castor-oil, said he would call again, and hoped that I would soon be better. In the unbounded mercy and undeserved goodness of my Heavenly Father, I have been almost entirely restored; and though I feel a little debilitated and suffer a little pain, yet still I hope very soon again to plunge into the battle and fight valiantly for my God.

"But what am I doing? Here I have filled up a page and a half with an account of the state of my physical system: something that must be as uninteresting as unprofitable to you. Since I left my Philadelphia friends (friends that I regard with feelings of peculiar tenderness), I have almost constantly been engaged in active service for my Master. Almost every evening has found me upon the battle-plain, surrounded by a devoted few, and arrayed against the armies of the aliens. My ear has been saluted, not by the clash of arms, the roar of cannon, the shrieks of the wounded and dying, but, thank God, by something infinitely sweeter, nobler, and more delightful. Night after night I have heard the sweet hymn of praise gushing warm from the Christian's grateful heart; the fervent and importunate prayer from him hungering and thirsting after righteousness; the hearty exclamation, 'God be merciful to me, a sinner!' from him who regarded sin as a burden too intolerable to be borne; the transporting accent trembling upon the lips of the newly-regenerated creature, 'Glory! glory! I *do* love Jesus, for He has taken my feet from the mire and the clay, and He has planted them on the rock of ages.' I praise the Lord for what I have enjoyed in my own soul; the flame of heaven's love has been burning brightly upon the altar of my heart, and these circumstances to which I have made allusion, viz., the conversion of my fellow-mortals, have been like fuel thrown upon the fire to add to the power and bril-

liancy of the flame. I often look at myself, Andrew, and when I call
to mind my manifold shortcomings and repeated backslidings, when I
remember my constant wanderings, both to the right hand and to the
left, I am lost in wonder and astonishment that my Saviour should be
so kind and good as to lavish upon me such unnumbered and undeserved
blessings, that He should choose me as one of His creature-instruments
to extend the honour of the Redeemer's name. I need and earnestly
desire to love Him more and serve Him better, to have every power of
my nature consecrated upon the altar of His cause,—in a word, to be
sanctified throughout, soul, body, and spirit ; for I verily believe that,
if we would be eminently useful as well as supremely happy, we must
love God with all our soul, mind, and strength. I certainly should feel
very happy if I thought I had so secured your confidence as to prompt
you feelingly and conscientiously to array my poor unworthy self with
so many noble and excellent qualities. Perhaps that sentence was
penned, like many of my own, from impulse, for I am sure that were
you to bestow upon me the least scrutiny, my deformities, physical,
mental, and moral, would induce you to start back astonished. One
thing, though, is perfectly certain. I love my friends, and I covet their
esteem and regard."

All who remember the expression of genuine modesty
which Alfred Cookman's face always wore, will appreciate
the self-deprecating reference with which he meets his
friend's tribute to his personal qualities. I can almost see
the girlish blush which mantles his youthful brow at the
mention of these excellences. But the feature of this first
letter in his ministerial life which is most significant is the
ardent breathings which it manifests for entire consecration
to God. The leaven of his mother's advice was already
working. Circumstances were close at hand which were
distinctly to impress his whole subsequent career. In the
providence of God he was thus early brought into contact
with influences which gave definitive shape to his views and
experiences on the great doctrine which was henceforth to
occupy so much of his thoughts, and to the maintenance
and propagation of which his talents and time were to be

so signally and so successfully devoted.   He shall speak for himself :—

"Frequently I felt to yield myself to God, and pray for the grace of entire sanctification; but then this experience would lift itself in my view as a mountain of glory, and I would say, It is not for me,—I could not possibly scale that shining summit; and if I could, my besetments and trials are such, I could not successfully maintain so lofty a position.   While thus exercised in mind, Bishop Hamline, accompanied by his devoted wife, came to New Town, one of the principal appointments on the circuit, that he might dedicate a church which we had been erecting for the worship of God.   Remaining about a week, he not only preached again and again, and always with the unction of the Holy One, but took occasion to converse with me pointedly respecting my religious experience.   His gentle and yet dignified bearing, devotional spirit, beautiful Christian example, unctuous manner, divinely illuminated face, apostolic labour and fatherly counsels, made the profoundest impression on my mind and heart.   I heard him as one sent from God, and certainly he was ; his influence, so hallowed and blessed, has not only remained with me ever since, but even seems to increase as I pass along in my sublunary pilgrimage.   Oh how I bless and praise God for the life and labours of the beloved Bishop Hamline !

"One week-day afternoon, after a most delightful dis. course, he urged us to seize the opportunity, and *do* what we had often desired and resolved and promised to do—viz., 'as believers yield ourselves to God as those who were alive from the dead, and from that hour trust in Jesus as our Saviour from all sin.'   Kneeling by myself, I brought an entire consecration to the altar.   But some one will say, 'Had you not done that at the time of your conversion ? '

I answer, Yes! but with this difference : then I brought
powers dead in trespasses and sins, now I would consecrate
powers permeated with the new life of regeneration, I would
offer myself a living sacrifice ; then I gave myself away, but
now, with the increased illumination of the Spirit, I felt that
my surrender was more intelligent and specific and careful,
—it was my hands, my feet, my senses, my attributes of
mind and heart, my hours, my energies, my reputation, my
worldly substance, my everything, without reservation or
limitation. Then I was anxious for pardon, but now my
desire and faith compassed something more—I wanted the
conscious presence of the Sanctifier in my heart. Carefully
consecrating everything, I covenanted with my own heart
and with my heavenly Father that this entire but unworthy
offering should remain upon the altar, and henceforth I would
please God by believing that the altar (Spirit) sanctifieth the
gift. Do you ask what was the immediate effect? I answer
peace—a broad, deep, full, satisfying, and sacred peace.
This proceeded not only from the testimony of a good conscience before God, but likewise from the presence and
operation of the Spirit in my heart. Still I could not say
that I was entirely sanctified, except as I had sanctified
myself to God."

CHAPTER VIII.

THE annual session of the Philadelphia Conference was held in the spring of 1847, at Wilmington, Delaware. Bishop Hamline presided. Alfred Cookman, having finished up his work, repaired to the seat of the Conference. He was an applicant for admission into the Conference, in company with a large number of young men, most of whom were his personal friends. The Conference was very full, it being found difficult to station all the preachers, and so, at the advice of the presiding bishop, it was voted to receive none "on trial." This was a sore disappointment to our young friend, as it was to others applying. He had preached at least a half-year under the presiding elder, and now to be obliged to do so an additional year was somewhat grievous. The policy of such a procedure on the part of a Conference is always of doubtful expediency, and sometimes may be very unjust and injurious to the parties and to the work. The young minister, however, had consecrated himself to the Master's cause, according to the order of the Methodist Episcopal Church, the Church of his father ; and so, bowing gracefully to the decision of the Conference, he accepted again a position under the presiding elder, and entered cheerfully upon it. He was appointed by the Rev. Daniel Lambdin to the Delaware City Circuit, in the State of Delaware, with the Rev. Robert McNarmee for his preacher in charge.

Before I follow him to his new circuit, an important fact
in his inward life must be stated. It will be remembered
that his early religious experience received a check upon the
occasion of his removal from Carlisle to Washington. His
later experience received a similar but a more prolonged
check during this session of the Conference. The explanation is best given in his own words. They are a continuation of the published narrative before quoted from : " Oh
that I could conclude just here these allusions to personal
experience with· the simple addition that my life to the
present has answered to the description of endless progress
regulated by endless peace ! Fidelity to truth, however,
with a solicitude that others may profit by my errors, constrains me to add another paragraph of my personal testimony. Have you ever known a sky full of sunshine—the
power of a beautiful day subsequently obscured by lowering
clouds ? Have you ever known a jewel of incalculable
value to its owner lost through culpable carlessness ? Alas
that so bright a morning in my spiritual history should not
have shone more and more unto the perfect day—that I
should, under any circumstances, have carelessly parted
with this pearl of personal experience ! Eight weeks transpired—weeks of light, strength, love, and blessing ; Conference came on ; I found myself in the midst of beloved
brethren ; forgetting how easily the infinitely Holy Spirit
might be grieved, I allowed myself to drift into the spirit of
the hour ; and, after an indulgence in foolish joking and
story-telling, realized that I had suffered serious loss. To
my next field of labour I proceeded with consciously
diminished spiritual power."

The new circuit was found to be very congenial. From
a lady who knew him well, and between whom and himself
there was a pleasant friendship—Mrs. L. A. Battershall, of

New York—I have received the following reference to his character and work at this time :—

"Numbered with the most pleasant memories of the bygone are my recollections of the Rev. Alfred Cookman. After his appointment to Delaware City Circuit, he was a frequent guest at the hospitable home of a relative, whom I was then visiting. Domiciled beneath the same roof, ample opportunity was thus afforded me of observing his habitual deportment in the daily amenities of life. He was richly endowed by nature with a genial spirit, and an ease and grace of manner which eminently fitted him to shine as the centre of the social circle, and yet I never knew him betrayed into a levity unbecoming a minister of the Gospel of Christ.

"Delaware City Circuit at that time embraced a considerable portion of the wealthy agricultural district of Newcastle County, Delaware, and was populated by a people of more than ordinary intelligence. To all classes of this population young Cookman came as the messenger of life. His young heart burned with love for souls. He went from his closet to the pulpit, and, thus panoplied with power, it is no marvel that the multitudes which from Sabbath to Sabbath hung upon the earnest pleadings of his eloquent lips for their salvation, regarded him as a royal ambassador from the Court of the Most High."

The year, according to this testimony, passed profitably and pleasantly, as he glided about from village to village and home to home among a devout and hospitable people. In those days it was not customary for the young preacher to have any fixed boarding-place on the circuit. No appropriation was made to pay his board, but he was expected to "stay around" among the families, remaining longest where it was most congenial, or where, from the means and kindness of the families, he could be rendered most comfortable, and found the greatest facilities for reading and study. Sometimes the young preacher would be so fortunate as to have one or more such homes at each of the churches. Occasionally he would arrange to spend most of his time at one central home, where his books and wardrobe—if he were rich beyond the contents of his saddle-bags—could remain, and where he was always made heartily welcome. Nothing could exceed the cordiality with which the families at these homes greeted and entertained their young minister. The best room was at his disposal, the richest products of farm and garden, the choicest poultry from the swarming broods, were put before him. At the protracted and quarterly meetings these homes became the gathering-points of the ministers and official members of the circuit, occasions of happy reunions, and of deep spiritual as well as social enjoyment.

At the session of the Conference in the spring of 1848, Alfred Cookman was again an applicant for admission, and was received. His first appointment in the minutes occurs this year, to Germantown Circuit, which included German-town and Chestnut Hill. The Rev. James A. Massey was his presiding elder. The circuit comprised a very beautiful suburban region of Philadelphia. Germantown and Chest-nut Hill have grown into important stations. His labours were marked by fidelity to duty, and all his exercises were indications of the future successes which were destined to crown his ministry.

Large cities have a wondrous attractive power for all the forces which can augment their greatness. It is not sur-prising to find Philadelphia Methodism speedily demanding Alfred Cookman for its service. In the spring of 1849 he was appointed as junior preacher, under the Rev. David

Dailey, to Kensington and Port Richmond, with the Rev. John P. Durbin, D.D., as the presiding elder. He was now following closely in the footsteps of his father, this having been the first appointment of that godly man ; and the brick church of Kensington, that was so often vocal to the eloquence of the father in his youth, was again vocal with the fervent and persuasive tones of the son. The veneration of the young minister for his father was an absorbing passion ; consequently there could be no motive, next to his reverence for the Divine Master and the sense of responsibility to Him, so powerful as the consideration that he was standing directly where his father had stood, and was ministering to the very people who had listened to his burning and instructive words. But little record remains to us of the exercises of his mind or of the character and effect of his preaching.

One of the best proofs of his success is that he was re- turned a second year to the same station, with the privilege of supplying his work for a part of the year and making a visit to Europe. It was about this time that I first saw Alfred Cookman. Although he and I lived as boys in Baltimore through some of the years, yet he was so far my senior, and the charges to which we severally belonged were so wide apart, that it happened we had never met. I had heard so much of him, that when I learned he was to preach at the Charles Street Church, I hastened thither, and found myself a curious hearer amid the crowd which thronged the building. Many of those present had been his father's friends ; they had known him from boyhood, they comprised very many of the most highly cultured Methodists of the city—all facts not little adapted to embarrass the young preacher. His theme was the " Resurrection of Christ." His action is distinctly before me now, as he described

Peter and John in their eager race to reach the tomb
of Jesus, after they had heard the announcement of
Mary that " He had risen from the dead." The preacher
was then just past twenty-two years of age, of very
handsome, pleasing personal appearance—slight, erect,
with a most engaging countenance, rendered doubly
attractive by the massy black hair which fell upon his
neck and shoulders.

A letter to his grandfather Cookman immediately preceding the Conference of 1850 gives some insight to his
feelings. It breathes the tenderest pathos, and shows how
well prepared he was already to fill the highly important
office of comforter to the afflicted :—

" PHILADELPHIA, *March* 16, 1850.

"I find by a reference to the newspaper that a steamer will leave
New York for Liverpool next Wednesday, and although the near
approach of Conference gives me an abundance to do, yet I have
managed to economize an hour, which I most joyfully devote to the
delightful exercise of English correspondence. Though old ocean's
waters serve to separate us, yet frequently thought and affection, hand
in hand, defying space and distance, wing their way to your sea-girt
isle, and by the eye of fancy I can see you moving from place to place
or attending to your daily duties. How much I wish at such times
that flesh and blood could travel with the rapidity of thought. Often
would you find me lingering near, eager to pay you those attentions
which not only old age but your recent heavy afflictions so imperatively
require. Believe me, dear grandfather, when I assure you that I think
of and deeply sympathize with you, and when I kneel down before Him
who can be touched with a feeling of our infirmities, I endeavour as
best I can to bear you up upon the wings of faith and prayer. The
trials which in the mysterious providence of an all-wise God have come
upon you are indeed distressing—aye, almost overwhelming. To bid
farewell to those as dear to you as life itself, to gaze upon their countenances for the last time, not knowing that you will ever again meet
with them in the flesh, to be left alone with no relative to offer his
tender sympathies or kind attentions—all this certainly must have been
agonizing in the extreme. At such a period, when the vanity of every-

6

thing sublunary must be seen and felt, how comforting and encouraging
to remember that in the blessed Saviour we have 'a Friend that sticketh
closer than a brother'—One that will never leave nor forsake us, who
will stand by us in six trials, and not forsake us in the seventh ! I
have no doubt but that you have personally experienced the preciousness of these Scriptural assurances.   Under the shadow of His wing
you have found a covert from the stormy blast ; and not only so, but
perhaps with holy triumph are able to affirm that 'tribulation worketh
patience; and patience, experience; and experience, hope : and hope
maketh not ashamed, because the love of God is shed abroad in my
heart by the Holy Ghost given unto me.'   These light afflictions, which
are but for a moment, are intended to work out for you a far more
exceeding and eternal weight of glory.   I would gladly, if possible,
pour the balm of Christian consolation into your bruised and bleeding
heart.   But I rejoice to remember that there is One who regards you
with more than a mother's love ; who behind a frowning providence is
hiding a smiling face ; who encouragingly whispers, all things shall
work together for good to those who put their trust in God.   May His
richest blessing rest abundantly upon you, and although you are descending the hill of life, yet with the everlasting arms beneath and
around you, may you realize that your path shineth brighter and brighter
unto the perfect day.

"In a little more than a week the Philadelphia Conference will
assemble in our city.   If all should be well, I expect during the session
to be admitted to the order of deacon in the Methodist Episcopal
Church.   I have been endeavouring to preach Christ and Him crucified
for upward of three years, and realize an increasing love for my work.
Now that I am to be received into full connection, I would dedicate
myself more unreservedly to God, and in the strength of grace resolve
to spend and be spent more fully in the service of my Heavenly Master.
Oh that with the laying on of hands there may be a special anointing
of the Holy Spirit, that I may indeed become a flaming herald of the
King of kings and Lord of lords l

"My studies occupy much of my time and attention.   Watson's
Institutes (with which you are quite familiar) is perhaps the most difficult work we have to digest preparatory to examination.   There is such
a number of points and multiplicity of theories to treasure up that I find
it requires a little extra attention.   As a production I regard it as
a masterpiece, an enduring monument to the cherished memory of its
distinguished author.   Our examiners have, by the direction of the
bishops, put into our hands a volume entitled the Principles of Morality,
by Jonathan Dymond, who, if I mistake not, is an English Quaker.

The work, though embodying some excellent truths, contains much that is unquestionably heterodox. The author argues strongly in advocacy of the doctrines peculiar to the Society of Friends—such as quiet worship, absence of all excitement, unpaid ministry, etc., etc. I acknowledge that I have been considerably astonished during its perusal that it should have received the sanction of our Episcopacy, and can only account for it on the ground of inadvertence. I had intended to give you some account in this letter of the slavery excitement, which has been shaking the temple of our liberties to its very foundations, but will be obliged, from the want of time and space, to defer it until a more convenient season. After the adjournment of Conference I shall be more disengaged, and will embrace an early opportunity to pen with more care another, and, I trust, more interesting letter than this. Mother, brother, and little sister were all well when I saw them a day or two since, and join me, I am sure, in the tenderest love to yourself and all other English friends."

Fortunately the student of Watson's Institutes in this instance had had a training at school which qualified him to grapple with its "number of points and multiplicity of theories." The examinations of the second year all satisfactorily passed, the probationer was admitted to the Conference and elected to deacon's orders. Together with all the members of his class (except one, whose place was supplied by the addition of Henry Hurn), he was ordained deacon by Bishop Waugh. There subsisted between Alfred Cookman and the members of his class a close and loving devotion through his whole career.

To young Methodist ministers, the companionship of the four years' course in the Conference has much the same influence on after-life as that of the college or theological seminary has upon those who are students in such institutions. This " course," with its associations and its drill, however imperfect, is a feature of Methodism not understood by many who have wondered at the slowness of the Methodists to adopt theological schools, and their readiness admit to the pastorate young men of comparatively little learning. Young preachers can be continued indefinitely on trial, till voted to deacon's orders, or they can be discontinued before this, if in the judgment of the Conference they do not give proofs of original capacity and of proficiency in study. So that it is a fair inference that by the time a licentiate is voted to orders he has become a well-informed minister.

As I have already intimated, Mr. Cookman was returned this year to Kensington and Port Richmond. There awaited him now one of the most delightful episodes of his life. It was determined that he should visit his aged grandfather in England. The veteran himself strongly urged the visit, and it was thought the visit would be not only a gratification to him in his advanced years, but also that at this period of the young minister's life it would be of incalculable advantage to his future career. There is an education, a breadth and definiteness of view, a knowledge of the world, which can be obtained in travel which is possible in no other way. The preparations for the voyage were rapidly hurried forward, and in the month of July Mr. Cookman sailed in the steamer "Europa" from New York for Liverpool. It was with no little trepidation that the good mother risked her dearest treasure once more on the uncertain deep, and that the son launched upon the waste of waters which had engulfed his beloved father; but it was deemed the order of God, and so both took courage, as only thus filial duty could be discharged. It was hard to leave friends behind, but grandfather, the best friend next to mother since the father's loss, and old England, the "sea-girt isle," were beyond.

To his mother he writes :—

"STEAMER EUROPA, *Friday morn, July* 19, 1850.

"Thinking that you will feel interested in hearing of my progress, I avail myself of the present opportunity to pen a few lines, expecting to mail my letter this afternoon in Halifax. Concerning my movements up to twelve o'clock on Wednesday, George can give you all possible information. At that hour I bade him farewell, and with my fellow-passengers started on my voyage across the blue Atlantic. As we passed down New York Bay, I was much interested in viewing different objects upon the shore. Here was a magnificent edifice, with its solid and majestic columns, its symmetrical and beautiful proportions; there an angry-looking fort, with its gaping iron mouths, ready to roar at the presumptuous invader of the land of the free and the home of the brave. As we passed Sandy Hook, we parted with our pilot (the last link that seemed to bind us to the shore), and put out fairly to sea. By this time I had formed an acquaintance with one or two of the passengers, and had already enjoyed much pleasant conversation. The wind being pretty fresh, occasioned some roughness of the water, and this, together with the combined influence of our sails and engine, caused the boat to roll considerably.

"Now, then, for the tug of war. As the ship would rise, I would not suffer the least inconvenience, but when, immediately after, she would make a lurch, there seemed to be a strange nervousness of feeling in the region of digestion. After a while a disagreeable dimness began to steal over my vision. I fought like a lion. At four o'clock the dinner-bell rang, and thinking that perhaps a little food would serve as a barricade on the field of battle, behind which I might ensconce myself from the attack of the foe, I ventured to eat a little. A very few mouthfuls served to suffice, for, finding myself driven from my position, I resolved on retreat. Down I went to my state-room, the enemy following me. First he got me on my back, then he seemed to turn everything round within me, then he commanded me to restore what I had so insultingly swallowed at dinner-time, and, will you believe me? I felt obliged to yield. Up it came, with a good deal more, and I left the *treasure* at his feet. After so fierce a contest and so signal a defeat, I thought I might lie down. As seven o'clock (supper-time), however, rolled round, I inscribed on my banner, 'Often beaten, but still unconquered,' and staggered up again to the charge. A little toast and tea was all I ventured to take, and yet the enemy, as if maddened by my obstinate resistance, laid upon me a heavier hand than ever, and down I went a second time. What a trouncing I got! I gave him back all—aye, more than all. I shed tears, I groaned, I rolled, and at last, with some difficulty, got to bed—not to sleep, however. During the night, with the motion of the boat, I pitched from side to side, and as morning dawned rose and went forth to walk the deck. During yesterday, although feeling somewhat squeamish, I concluded myself decidedly better, and ventured to partake very moderately of food. Last night I slept gloriously, and this morning began to feel like myself again. I can now just perceive the aforementioned foe in the distance, almost out of sight, but now and then turning round to know whether it would not be well to return. From suffering experience, I think I know something respecting sea-sickness, and feel it in my heart to say that hereafter I will cheerfully relinquish my share to any other for a very trifling consideration.

"Our boat is a splendid one. Her officers are gentlemanly and skilful, her crew is orderly and obedient, the servants are attentive and obliging, and our accommodations are all that could be desired. At half-past eight we breakfast, at half-past twelve enjoy lunch, at four sit down to dinner, and at seven drink our tea. The dinner service is certainly splendid, and the food unexceptionable. We have every variety and any quantity. My state-room is not quite as far forward as I should like, and yet its situation back is not without advantage, since there is an absence from noise and a retirement which is very desirable and delightful on shipboard; besides, I have it all to myself, and you know from experience that this is a desideratum. Our passengers, though mostly foreigners, are very kind and gentlemanly. Perhaps there is a little too much liquor drank, and last night I observed some card-playing. With two or three I have formed rather an intimate acquaintance, and find them to be gentlemanly, communicative, and affectionate.

"Our noble steamer has been urging on her course steadily since our departure from New York. Yesterday, notwithstanding rather unfavourable weather, she accomplished about two hundred and fifty miles. After we leave Halifax, and become a little lighter by the consumption of coal, I apprehend her speed will be very considerably increased. Though sailing on the vast ocean, with nought but sky above and sea around, I rejoice to say I realize the presence of my Heavenly Father. Indeed, I think I feel, as I never felt before, my dependence upon Him for life and everything else. I desire to remain momentarily beneath the shadow of His almighty wing, for there I am sure nothing wrong can befall me. Thus far I have accomplished but little in the way of reading and writing; indeed, my sea-sickness would not allow of it. I hope, at least, to keep up a short diary, or, as the sailors say, *log*.

The weather in this latitude is foggy and cold. Last night I wrapped myself in a blanket, and during the day find my overcoat no encumbrance. I spend much of my time thinking of you ; you are as dear to me as my own life. May God bless and mercifully preserve you all ! Pray for me. My sheet is full, and I must close my letter, written with some difficulty, owing to the motion of the boat and the noise of the machinery. Give my best love to brothers, little sister, and all friends."

CHAPTER IX.

On Sunday, July 29th, he arrived at Liverpool. His own descriptions are so full and vivid as to supersede any efforts of mine to describe the delight with which he set foot on English soil. He had been educated all his life to believe everything was grand and beautiful in England, the home of his ancestors; he had been taught so to revere his kindred, had been told so many noble things of them, that it was natural he should expect much, and hence should be correspondingly gratified if his ardent expectations were more than fulfilled. Though accustomed to the thought of the genuine worth of his kindred at Hull, the social and material elegance in which they lived, yet reared, as he had been, in the modest surroundings of a Methodist preacher's son, he was hardly prepared for all the refinement which was to greet him. Nothing could be more pleasing than the letters so artlessly detailing his observations and impressions.

To the mother and family at home :—

> "STEPNEY LODGE, HULL, YORKSHIRE,
> *Monday evening, July* 29, 1850.

"I am in a perfect ecstasy! my joy is unbounded and uncontrollable! my only fear is that I will wake up and find it all a dream. *I am in Hull;* nay, more,—I am at my dear grandfather's residence. Would you believe it? I can scarce realize it myself. And now I shall endeavour to conquer emotion a little, and, as calmly as I can, go back and detail my progress since my departure from Halifax, for in that town I mailed a letter for you written upon the ocean after we left New York. I will not advert to the routine of our proceedings on shipboard ; if you should feel interested in anything of that nature, have recourse to my excellent friend and host, viz., Brother J. Baily, and you can readily obtain the desired information in a letter which I shall mail in the same steamer which will convey this. Suffice it to say that, after a prosperous and most delightful voyage of not quite eleven days, no storm having occurred and the wind having continued favourable nearly all the way, we reached Liverpool on Sunday a little after two o'clock. I immediately proceeded to the *George Hotel*, a magnif.• cent establishment ; when, having adjusted matters a little, I sallied forth, sighing most for religious privileges, for Christian communion. As I passed up the street, I providentially met with a gentleman whom I took to be a Wesleyan from his plain and neat costume. Addressing him, I inquired if he could direct me in my search for a Wesleyan chapel. Immediately informing me that he was connected with that excellent body, he kindly proposed to conduct me to the place of my pursuit. Arm-in-arm we passed up the street, enjoying pleasant conversation, and came to Mount Pleasant Chapel, one of the oldest churches in Liverpool. The Sabbath School was about to close, and, by request, I united with them in prayer, and felt, indeed, access to our Father through our Lord and Saviour Jesus Christ.

" Yielding to a most urgent and importunate invitation to accompany this brother home to tea, at six I went with him to Stanhope Chapel, when a brother Roebuck preached a most capital sermon. More of this anon. The service charmed me, but about this we will have one of our old-fashioned *tête-à-têtes* upon my return. After the benediction I went to Dr. Raffles's church, and after this to a Mr. Fallows's, a most evangelical and excellent member of the Establishment. Having accomplished as much and endured more than I anticipated in the way of church-going, I returned to my hotel, and about ten retired—not, however, to sleep. The circumstances of the evening as well as the prospects of the morrow drove slumber from my eyes. However, not to linger by the way, morning dawned, and an early hour found me at the custom-house, where the delay and tardiness of the government officers greatly provoked me. Stating my situation, and manifesting much anxiety, I secured my trunks, and drove with all possible speed for the railway-station, and got there just fourteen minutes past nine o'clock, one minute too soon for the Hull train. Off we flew at the rate of thirty miles an hour, through first a manufacturing and afterward an

agricultural district, through tunnels—one of them *four* miles long—
under and over noble bridges, until at about three o'clock we entered the
station-house at Hull.

" I ascertained by inquiry as well as by reference to the directory that
Mr. Holmes's residence was quite near. Taking my carpet-bag in my
hand, I went round and found a double mansion, elegantly furnished,
with handsome park and garden, and immediately rang the bell. A
servant appeared. I inquired for Mrs. Holmes, ascertained she was in,
was asked for my name, I replied a 'stranger'; the maid disappearing,
my *own aunt* made her appearance. I observed, 'An unexpected visit
from a stranger; look at me, and tell me if you know me.' She looked,
and immediately replied, 'Cookman!' I was then introduced into the
drawing-room, and cousin after cousin came in—among the rest two of
aunt Smith's daughters: all fine, noble-looking girls. Shall I say I
spent a pleasant hour with them? It was more—infinitely more; no
adjective is strong enough to express the joy I realized. We sat around
the tea-table, and conversed about the past and the present; and oh, it
was glorious! There are many little facts and circumstances I could
detail, but I must forbear. After an early tea I ordered a cab, and,
after kissing one of my fair cousins who leaves in the morning for
boarding-school in London, I proceeded to Stepney Lodge, where
dear grandfather, I am most happy to say, still resides.

" As I approached the mansion my feelings were indescribable—a
thousand reminiscences rushed irresistibly upon my mind and heart. I
rang the bell, and immediately the housekeeper made her appearance,
and told me that grandfather had gone to town to meet the property
committee. I then resolved I would fill up the interim with the scrawl
which I very much fear you will be unable to read. I am now waiting
for him. Stepney Lodge is a lovely spot; I glance out of the window,
and there is a small park, bounded by a beautiful hedge; to the left is
an artificial pond, surrounded on my right by a series of walks through
noble trees and luxuriant shrubbery; and behind, a garden abounding
with all kinds of fruit. I went out a little while ago and *tasted* gooseberries the size of a walnut, ripe raspberries, the largest strawberries I
ever saw without exception, red and black currants, and saw pears,
apples, and any quantity of ripe grapes in his summer-house. It is a
paradise—glorious, enchanting. The house is old-fashioned and exceedingly comfortable, containing everything that heart could wish. Over
the mantelpiece of the room in which I am writing hangs a likeness of
dear father—excellent, decidedly the best I have seen. Before me is
the portrait of uncle Alfred, from which the picture we have is taken.
*   *   *   *

"The Conference commences on Wednesday in *London.* Just think of it; how fortunate! Thus I can attend its sessions, and at the same time visit the lions of this world-renowned city. Thus far Providence has smiled upon me, and everything has turned out just as my wishes would dictate. Shall I be ungrateful? Rather let me, by a renewal of my spiritual covenant, prove that I am not insensible to the thousand blessings which my Heavenly Father so indulgently lavishes upon unworthy me. Oh, I feel I cannot be thankful enough! My cup runneth over with mingled happiness and gratitude. John Holmes, the oldest son, is a fine fellow—tall, with rather an intelligent face, and certainly very affectionate; but, indeed, I cannot talk about my cousins now; my feelings will not permit.

"Grandfather has not yet arrived. After an interview with him I will close this sheet and immediately mail it for Liverpool, in order that it may be in time for the 'Pacific's' mail, which steamer sails on Wednesday. Let me just now say I am *delighted* with England. My expectations were exalted, and they certainly have been more than realized. Grandfather is coming; I see his tall, erect, and commanding figure. He has an umbrella under his arm, and walks both firmly and fast. He enters, but does not know me. Gradually I reveal the fact that his grandson stands before him. He manifests the greatest delight. During the evening, until about half-past ten, we sat together conversing about persons and things; when, taking my candle in my hand, I retired to my room, and received from him a most affectionate good-night. He still dresses in the old English costume—short clothes, white cravat—and is altogether the finest-looking old gentleman that I have seen in England, or that I have ever met with. He is splendid; oh, how happy I am in his society! This morning he goes to perform his duties upon the bench. He has a charming residence. * * * I have entered into particulars, because I know that they will interest you. Much more I have to say, but I must close. I have seen Mr. Henwood, a noble old gentleman, so kind and affectionate. He sends his affectionate regards, as do all the others."

The following letter from a niece of Mrs. Cookman will be read with interest :—

"HULL, *August* 2, 1850.

"Your son tells me that you are expecting a letter by the mail which leaves this afternoon, and will be very much disappointed if you do not hear from or of him, so he has deputed me to be his secretary. I wish

his choice had fallen on a more able person, for I am not much accustomed to or fond of letter-writing; but I doubt not any news of your
son will be to you most acceptable, so I will do my best to tell you his
present whereabouts and future course.   He and my uncle Holmes went
this morning to Sheffield, where they will spend a few hours; thence
going to Doncaster, will stay all night there.   Poor mamma will, I
know, be very much dissatisfied that *only one* night is allotted to her,
but my cousin has promised to preach in Thornton Street Chapel twice
next Sunday, so he is obliged to return to Hull on Saturday afternoon;
he leaves here again on Tuesday for London, visiting Birmingham,
Bristol, and Oxford on his way.   He will, of course, stay a night in
Bristol to see my aunt Hannah and her family.   From London he is
going to Paris, Brussels, and Antwerp, returning about next Saturday
fortnight to Hull, where he will preach on the following day in Waltham
Street and George Street Chapels.   I do not think he has yet made up
his mind whether or not to visit Scotland.   I wish you could see our
family party gathered around the table, endeavouring to fix his tour,
with maps and railway guides before us; you would be quite amused to
hear first one proposing one plan, then a second another; one says he
ought to see this town, another, that is the best route; while my cousin
Alfred sits quietly looking on, and listens to all in turn.

  "Now I have told you what I know about my cousin's proceedings,
I must tell you how delighted we all are to have him among us; our
only regret is that our eyes behold *one* and not *all* our cousins, with
their dear mother, but we are at present satisfied with what we have,
and hope at a future day to see some, if not all, of your family in
England.   As we cannot know them personally, we have endeavoured
to do so by report.   Alfred yesterday morning brought their portraits
from Mr. Cookman's, so we all tried to judge their characters by their
faces, and made Alfred tell us their several characteristics, till I could
almost fancy I know my hitherto stranger cousins.   As for John Holmes,
he has taken such a fancy to little Mary, that he proposes sending me
his own sister Annie and exchanging me for his cousin; but that I suppose you will hardly agree to.   I asked Alfred yesterday if he had any
message to send to you, and his answer was, 'Tell my mother that my
cup of happiness is overflowing'; indeed, he receives so many attentions, and is so much thought of by his father's friends, that it will be a
wonder if he is not quite spoiled before he returns to Philadelphia.
Mr. Cookman and he dined with us last Wednesday; the old gentleman
seems quite pleased with and proud of his grandson.   He went with us
in the evening to hear him preach in Thornton Street Chapel, and
appeared quite delighted with his sermon.   And now, my dear aunt, I

must draw my letter to a close ; in order it make it *valuable*, my aunt has half promised to cross it, so on her return from the town, if she has time before the post leaves, I shall request her to do so.

"My aunt Holmes has just come in from the town, but says it is impossible for her to find time to write even a few lines this afternoon, but I am to tell you that she is quite charmed with her nephew."

It seems, then, that grandfather, aunts, and cousins were all "charmed" with the American cousin. Such a picture of him and his surroundings from the pen of a maiden cousin must have been very grateful to the mother's feelings. His visit was not only busy with sight-seeing and social joys, but also with engagements to preach. In the very chapels where his father, when but a year or two older than he, first thrilled the hearts of his neighbours, the son now preached to the delight of grandfather and all. To the noble parent it must have been as though his own son were alive from the dead.

To his mother :—

"STEPNEY LODGE, HULL, *August* 5, 1850.

" I should have written to you the latter part of last week but for the multiplicity and urgency of my engagements. The Hull people have made quite a lion of me, and hence I am expected to exhibit myself on all convenient occasions, and occasionally interest them by my American roaring. My cousin Ella Smith, however, very kindly consented to do what only the circumstances of the case prevented me from doing, and that was to transmit a letter by last Saturday's steamer. I have now seen pretty much all my relatives in this part of England, and I speak sincerely when I say that they not only answer but far exceed my most sanguine expectations. On Friday last I visited Doncaster, my mother's native town, taking Sheffield on my route. Arriving at the station, I found aunt Smith, uncle John, and his lady, in waiting for me. After a most cordial greeting we proceeded to Arthur Smith's, at Sunny Bar, where I partook of some refreshments, and then sallied forth with uncle John to see the place. We visited the old church where you worshipped in childhood, saw the house in which you were born, the residence of grandma from which you went when you were married, aunt Eleanor's former home, called upon her brother, Dr. Murray, and had some conversation with him, continued our walk as far as the celebrated Doncaster race-course, looked at the deaf and dumb institution in the immediate vicinity, and about six o'clock returned to Sunny Bar. Forgetting the copse of trees, or rather the name of the place which aunt mentioned, I plucked a few sprigs of grass from a plot in front of the old home, and also secured a few leaves from some shrubbery immediately before the house in which you were living at the time of your marriage.

"In the evening we had a family party at aunt Smith's. All the sons except Theophilus were present, and until two o'clock the following morning we remained together enjoying familiar conversation. They are a noble set, treated me like a prince, and would only part with me on Saturday morning with the promise that I would endeavour to visit them again. I was particularly pleased with uncle John : he is affable, gentlemanly, very intelligent, consistently pious, and exceedingly affectionate. * * * I shall have much to tell you about Doncaster upon my return—a town I have been better pleased with than any I have seen in England yet ; indeed, the road in the direction of the race-course, with its noble trees and splendid residences, is almost unsurpassed by anything I have ever seen.

"On Saturday I returned to Hull, and yesterday preached in Great Thornton Street to overflowing houses. In the evening I think there were at least 3,000 people in the chapel, and multitudes went away who could not even obtain a foothold. They had me the day before placarded upon the public corners and in the shop-windows, ' Rev. Alfred Cookman, of Philadelphia, Sir,' etc., will preach at such a time. * * * In the morning they wept all over the house. Some shouted. I was blessed, and indeed we had a gracious waiting together. I am sure I never preached better than at night ; much feeling was evinced, and I trust that the great day will reveal the result of my yesterday's labours. As I pass through the streets, they point at me and say, ' There he goes ; that is Mr. Cookman's American grandson.' Aunt Holmes, who you know is exceedingly prudent, said to me that I ought to come to England, for at the present juncture they needed some like me. You can have no idea of the respect which is paid and the affection which is manifested toward me. Grandfather heard me twice yesterday, and appeared highly delighted. The old gentleman is in good spirits. His friends think that my visit at this time is a godsend, for it has had a most reviving influence upon him, who previously seemed quite depressed. He is a noble man. Every hour serves to increase my love and respect. This morning I visited the tomb of my grandma Cookman and uncle Alfred, under the Waltham Street Chapel. By-the-way, they (the authorities) wish me to re-open the chapel for them next Sabbath week. Do not know but I shall comply."

He was next to enjoy what, to every Anglo-American and to every American Methodist, is one of the richest treats which can possibly be afforded—the sight of London, and the sight of the British Wesleyan Conference. To a young man whose reading has been chiefly in the English classics, in the history and poetry of Britain, until the names of her authors and of the places of their resort have become household words, it is a source of inexpressible pleasure to look upon their very haunts—the streets where they walked, the inns they frequented, the favourite nooks where they loved to linger. And to one imbued with the spirit and traditions of John Wesley, nothing could be more inspiring than to touch the institutions, to see and hear the men to whom he had transmitted his wisdom and power. All this was the more enjoyable to Alfred Cookman because the teachings of his father and the presence of his father's friends imparted a realness to everything about him. These conditions, added to his own enthusiastic nature, transferred him into the very heart of all he saw and heard.

To his mother :—

"LONDON, *August* 16, 1850.

"I leave this populous city in a few minutes for Hull, and yet I cannot consent to quit its precincts without penning you a short note, especially as this will be the last opportunity of writing by to-morrow's steamer. I have now been spending one entire week in London, the heart of the world. I have seen and heard much which it will be in vain for me to attempt to detail at this time and under present circumstances. Grandfather met me here last Monday evening, and we have been spending our time together very pleasantly. I have been honoured with a seat on the platform of the British Conference, have been treated with the utmost respect and affection by the different preachers, have heard many of them in debate, and last Sabbath enjoyed the gratification of listening to Dr. Bunting in the morning and Dr. Dixon in the evening. Yesterday I saw the royal procession for the purpose of proroguing Parliament—Her Majesty Queen Victoria, His Highness Prince Albert, dukes, duchesses, etc., etc. All the public institutions, such as the British Museum, Bank of England, Tower of London, etc., I have visited. Oh, it will take me a week to tell you about my sojourn in this city of cities! On my way here I spent about a day and a half with aunt Townsend in Bristol. . . . She studied my happiness, and did all in her power to render my visit pleasant.

"Next Sabbath I preach at Kingston Chapel, Hull, in the morning, address the Sabbath School in the afternoon, and preach for grandfather at his church, viz., the Tabernacle, in the evening. You will say, 'Too bad—too bad! gone for rest, and yet performing usual labour.' Well, I will be careful, and spare myself as much as possible. You have no idea what a sensation I have produced in my father's native town.

"I shall not get to France. Grandfather seems anxious that I should be with him, and, as I have only a short time longer in England, I suppose I must forego the trip and gratify him. Perhaps at some future day I shall enjoy the opportunity. I should like to write more, but have not the time. We must now start for the cars. God bless you! I think of you all, morning, noon, and night. Oh, how much I have to tell you all! If you were with me, my pleasure would be complete."

To his mother :—

"STEPNEY LODGE, *August* 19, 1850.

"On Friday morning last, in company with my grandfather, I left great London, and set out for Hull. Early in the evening we reached our place of destination, and as we passed through the streets found that handbills had been printed and posted up, announcing that I would preach on the Sabbath. This is something so new to me, so different from our plan across the water, that I acknowledge it does not strike me favourably. At Stepney we found Cartwright, the housekeeper, quite well, and all things pretty much the same as when we left. On Saturday I of course began to think about my Sabbath duties and exercises. After determining on my subjects, I went down to uncle Holmes's, and spent an hour or two most delightfully with John, Annie, and aunt Smith, who is keeping house for them during the absence of her sister. I took with me your very beautiful and affectionate letter, and ventured to read the greater part of it to them, as I did also to grandfather. The reference to little John's success was most touching, and served to draw tears from many eyes. Let me most sincerely congratulate him on his

triumphant admission into the high-school, and at the same time express
the hope that his future course will be marked by as much devotion to
study, as much honourable and rapid advancement, as has his past career
in connection with Zane Street. The allusion in your letter was the
more interesting from the fact that we sometimes tease Annie Holmes
about John Emory. She is a pretty, amiable, affectionate girl of thirteen, quite large for her age, and I am sure that a sight of her would be
attended with danger to any of my susceptible brothers. From the
daguerreotype she seems to have taken quite a fancy to John ; hence the
tormenting she suffers.

"Well, to continue my narrative, Saturday passed away, Sunday
came. Arm-in-arm my grandfather and I proceeded to Kingston Chapel,
a most commodious, elegant, and comfortable place, capable of accom-
modating between three and four thousand people. We found it
crowded, and I proceeded in my old style (for any other suits me as
well as Saul's armour did David) to represent the Christian warrior, his
enemies, duties, and triumphs. God owned and blessed the word, and
notes of joy were heard in our camp. In the afternoon I addressed the
Sabbath School in the same church, and certainly I witnessed one of the
most beautiful and gratifying spectacles that I could possibly have looked
upon. The immense gallery, fifteen or sixteen pews deep, was filled all
around with well-behaved children ; the lower floor was crowded even
in the aisles with their parents, as well as the friends of the institution.
Oh, it was a glorious, a memorable occasion ! I did myself full justice,
and the people seemed more than gratified. In the evening I preached
in the Tabernacle. . . . I have in my short life seen dense crowds,
but I am sure that I never saw anything to equal the congregation last
night. It was one unwieldy mass of human beings, almost piled one on
top of another ; and hundreds, I am told, went away who could not
obtain even a foothold.

"I chose as my subject the Great Supper, and preached, I hope, in
demonstration of the Spirit and with power. I felt that my arm was
strong, and that by the help of God a blow must be struck. At the
close of the service a number came forward to the altar as penitents, and
I left with the soldiers of Christ in possession of the field. Will you
believe me if I tell you that I could scarce walk home ? I had let out
every link of my chain, and I had hardly strength left to stand. However, here I am this morning, a little Mondayish, it is true, but by
nightfall I expect to be as bright and vigorous as ever. Grandfather
seems quite delighted with my efforts, but tells me I will kill myself, and
that I must not be so lavish of my strength and voice.

"As I intimated in my letter written in London, I fear I will not get to Paris this time. Grandfather seems anxious to have me with him during the remainder of my stay in England, and I suppose that, in view of his advanced age, he must be gratified in this. Perhaps in a very few years another opportunity will offer, and then I can travel somewhat upon the Continent. I have been making some inquiries about the Southampton steamers, and I think that there is no one to start about the time I want to go home. I have seen England, talked with my grandfather and other relatives, and now I begin to feel as if it were my duty to get back to my field of labour again. I know exactly how they are situated, and am sure that the interests of both appointments would be subserved by my return. Early in September, then, I expect to turn my face homeward. So look out for me about the 20th or 25th. At every step in Hull I meet with the former friends and acquaintances of my beloved parents. Some of them weep when they see me, others manifest great pleasure, and refer with enthusiasm to their former acquaintance with my father and mother. One attended the same school with them, another went a-fishing, and a third was a bosom friend. Dr. McClintock and myself stayed at the same place in London, went to see the lions together, and enjoyed much pleasant intercourse.

"I preach to-night (Tuesday) at Kingston ; next Sabbath at Waltham and Thornton Streets."

To his mother :—

"STEPNEY LODGE, HULL, *August* 23, 1850.

"Thus far, I believe, every steamer which has left England for America since my arrival here has borne a letter to those at home. To-morrow is the regular day for the departure of one of the Cunard line, and although I have written once this week, yet I cannot consent to let this opportunity pass without dispatching you at least a few lines. My health since I have been in England has continued quite good, and my enjoyment has exceeded my most sanguine expectations. The comforts by which I have been surrounded, the exceedingly affectionate attentions of different friends, as well as the continual feast of vision with which I have been providentially favoured, all have conspired to render the last six weeks the happiest period of my life. The country presents the appearance of an extensive garden, separated for convenience sake into small fields by beautiful green hedges. Indeed, I know of no feature in the natural scenery of England which will sooner strike the traveller's eye than the neat and well-trimmed hedges which are everywhere to be seen. The foliage of the trees, too, as well as the verdure of the fields, is much richer and more elegant than anything we see in America. This is owing to the humidity of the atmosphere, as well as to the absence of that intense heat which so often with us exerts a blighting influence on all natural objects. Some of the landscapes here are surpassingly beautiful ; perhaps there is not that wildness in the scenery that we have with us, but there is a cultivation and variety, together with a picturesque appearance and classic interest, which never fails to please the eye and captivate the heart.

" In the distance, for instance, upon the summit of a noble hill, you discover, surrounded by towering trees, some old castle which has stood for centuries, and which, crumbling under the influence of time, occupied only by the owl and the bat, remains as a monument of former times. Not far off you perceive a comfortable-looking farmhouse ; a noble lawn in front, and a highly cultivated garden in the rear. Around you see the different fields. In one, perhaps, the cattle are quietly grazing ; in another labourers are diligently engaged in securing the golden harvest ; while in a third the little lambs skip in every direction, as if almost intoxicated with joy. Away in the horizon is a flourishing town (England abounds in towns), which always has its church built in the Gothic style, and whose glittering spire, like a golden finger, points toward heaven, as if it would direct the minds of the people thitherward. While gazing upon the scene, diversified with fields and forests, noblemen's mansions and labourers' cottages, gray and gloomy castles, as well as chaste and cheerful village churches, you are suddenly startled by the whiz of a locomotive, which, with its train, like a rushing comet, in the twinkling of an eye disappears in a damp and gloomy tunnel ; then emerging passes over the massy stone bridge of a quiet stream, and, after darting about among the hills for a moment, is lost to view. I did not know when I attempted this description that I should have covered so large a portion of my sheet, and yet I am sure that, if I had done the picture justice, it would require more space and time than I at the present could conveniently or possibly employ. Anything further of the same nature I will have to postpone until my return to your delightful society.

" On Tuesday evening, according to appointment, I preached in Kingston Chapel to at least three thousand people. God was pleased to own and bless His Word, delivered in an humble dependence upon the energizing influences of the Holy Spirit ; for at the close of the services, during a prayer-meeting which was held, about forty individuals presented themselves at the altar, desiring an interest in the prayers of God's people. Wednesday night I blew my trumpet in old George

Yard, where Wesley, Benson, and my beloved father have been heard, with pleasure and profit. Again our altar was more than crowded with those inquiring their way to Zion. Last night I preached in the Tabernacle to a congregation literally wedged together. The crowd, I think, was even greater than on last Sunday evening. I never saw a more attentive, solemn, and feeling auditory. We had seekers all around our altar as well as in the vestry. Not unto me, O Lord, but unto Thy name be all the glory. Who knows but that a kind Providence, who thus far has most delightfully opened my way before me, has determined to honour my visit by giving me souls for my hire and seals to my ministry? If there should be only one who, in the great day of final retribution, shall ascribe to my instrumentality his or her salvation, I shall be more than compensated for the time spent or money expended in my visit to the United Kingdom.

"On Sabbath I am to be at Waltham Street in the morning and at Thornton Street at night. Oh that the God of my father would be present to wound and to heal ! I fear I shall not see aunt Holmes before my return. She continues at Swanage, and uncle doubts whether they will get back before my departure. I have had many very, very pleasant interviews with aunt Smith. Yesterday she took me to see Mr. and Mrs. Morley, who now reside in Hull. They referred to you in the most affectionate manner."

From Mrs. Smith, of Hull, to Mrs. Mary Cookman :—

"HULL, *August* 28, 1850.

"MY DEAREST MARY,—Many of my correspondents complain, and not without just cause, that I have degenerated in regular correspondence. . . . And now, my beloved Mary, I congratulate you on being blessed with such a son. If he is a specimen of the other members of your family, those relatives who live to welcome them as they may come to visit England have a rich treat in store. I say I expected to see a nice, intelligent young man, but I had not raised my expectations to the reality. Not one of your family rejoices more that he has come over than myself. I have such a delightful picture in my mind of the union betwixt the families on this side and beyond the Atlantic as I cannot describe ; there was a break in the chain, but now we seem firmly linked together. I feel we are all one, and bound together by indissoluble ties. Oh ! we are sorry to let him leave us, and we are not alone. How many in Hull will have to praise God for his visit ! They have said, ' Can't you use influence for him to remain in Hull another month ? '

with much more. I could only silence them by assuring them it was impossible ; we had received that morning a schedule of his berth, which was taken in the steamer 'Asia.' He leaves behind him a name, but, what is of far more worth, many, many seals to his ministry. Any one but himself would be in danger from popularity ; when anything is said in his praise to his grandfather, he replies, 'Oh, he owes much to his mother ; I always had a very high opinion of her judgment, attention, and piety.' It gladdens my heart to hear him.

"I walked with Alfred one morning to introduce him to old Mr. Morley, who desired he would pray with him ere he left the manse. I stayed a little time after his departure to his grandfather. Mr. Morley was obliged to leave the room, and go into another to give vent to a flood of tears ere he could converse with me, and on his return every other subject was banished except you and yours, and the pleasure he had in your society when he lived in Fishergate. My dear sister Holmes mourns her absence from home at this time. I reap the benefit, for I might have been in another part of the country in ignorance of my loss. I do, indeed, praise God for my present privileges ; and I feel no doubt but that Mrs. H. is in her providential path, for, to use her own words, ' However dear Alfred is, Thomas is dearer, and has the first claim on my consideration.'

" As I have sat under Alfred's ministry, I have recalled the instrument in God's hand of leading me to Himself, and then was filled with praise that an insignificant being like myself should be the first link in the glorious chain ; and when I saw the altar rails crowded with penitents, my heart leaped with joy, my heart burned within me, and I thought what glorious results might arise from one of the least being savingly converted to God."

This letter very appropriately closes the correspondence touching the visit to England. His letters, written with so much frankness, the outpourings of· a faithful son's heart to his devoted mother, give ample incidental proof of the widespread, popular, and useful influence of his pulpit exercises. The testimonies of his cousin and aunt abundantly confirm this incidental revelation. The aunt acknowledges any one but himself would have been in danger from such popularity. Such unbounded enthusiasm over so young a man was well calculated to turn his head ; but it does not seem to have affected him, beyond exciting a devout recognition of God's goodness, and pleasure at the gratification he thought it would afford his loving mother. Then as always there was, to all appearances at least, a sweet absence of egotism, a simple unconsciousness of the incense of praise which was ever rising in his presence. His absorbing purpose was to win souls to Christ. For his success in "slaying sinners," in receiving the gratitude and applause of the people, he ascribed all the glory to God.

Three features crop out in these letters. The character of his preaching, already substantially formed, and which he calls "his own"—pictorial or dramatic representation—is seen in the account of some of his sermons ; the tireless zeal for work, unable to rest without work, and uniting with his recreations ceaseless preaching ; and also we hear of him for the first time before an audience of children—a direction in his ministry in which he was afterward to acquire such remarkable facility and success.

CHAPTER X.

HOME AGAIN.—MARRIAGE.—MINISTRY AT WEST CHESTER
AND HARRISBURG.

THE early autumn found him at his post in Kensington,
preaching to large congregations, and attending to all pastoral work with fresh delight and diligence. Of course the
little family group in Race Street was frequently visited.
He had come back filled with beautiful thoughts and recollections, which it was his joy to communicate to those who
were as dear to him as his own life. Much, however, as he
enjoyed the pastimes of home, he did not neglect the duties
of his charge—his hours were full of useful occupation.
Thus busily employed, the autumn and winter glided away,
and the session of the Conference approached.

A few extracts from his correspondence while stationed
at Kensington are sufficient to show the zealous spirit with
which he was animated :—

"*January* 14, 1850.

"On Sabbath I preached both morning and evening to excellent congregations. God was eminently with me on both occasions. At night
I was uncommonly assisted : an unusual seriousness pervaded the assembly, some came forward to the altar, and I trust that eternity will
alone reveal the extensive good done. Last evening I preached with
much liberty ; more knelt at our altar than on the previous night, numbers in the congregation wept freely, and we are encouraged to look for
better times. I do most earnestly desire to be a successful minister of
the New Testament. While I experience an unceasing love for my

honourable and responsible work, at the same time I would perceive a corresponding influence attending my labours. Oh that God would constitute me a chosen instrument of good to those among whom I may toil from time to time!"

"*January* 6, 1851.

"Last Sabbath, the first Sunday of the new year, I preached in Kensington morning and evening on the subject of the Judgment. I have rarely addressed more attentive and solemn congregations. God was eminently with me on both occasions. At the conclusion of the evening service we entered heartily into a prayer-meeting. In exhortation I felt as if I was only the speaking-trumpet of Jehovah. Almost immediately twelve approached our altar—all very interesting cases ; a number professed to experience peace, and before 10 p.m. we had the shout of the King in our camp. To God be all the glory !"

"*February*, 1851.

"In Philadelphia a good feeling seems to prevail at almost every appointment. Trinity, the church where our family worship, has been catching some of the descending drops. Little sister professes to have experienced peace, and has joined the Church ; she seems to be as firm as an ocean rock. There are only two now of our family who remain without the pale of the Church—viz., George and Will, and we are praying and confidently hoping that very soon they will become the subjects of saving grace. On Sunday I preached three times—twice to immense congregations in Kensington, and in the afternoon at Fifth Street to a very full house. This evening we renew the battle, and expect that our efforts will be more signally blessed in the salvation of priceless souls. My heart is in the work. I glory in being permitted to head the sacramental host in the assaults upon the strongholds of the wicked one."

On the 6th of March, 1851, Mr. Cookman was united in marriage to Miss Annie E., daughter of Mr. Abraham Bruner, of Columbia, by the Rev. William Urie, of the Methodist Episcopal Church.

As evidence of the happiness which crowned this union, and also of the pleasant and delicate way in which he ever manifested his affection for his wife, I anticipate by some

years the following effusion, written at the close of his
pastoral term at Union Church, Philadelphia, 1861 :—

"This day completes the first decade of my married life. On the
6th of March, 1851, I linked my fortunes with those of my dearly-
beloved wife, and now, on the tenth anniversary of our *blessed union*, I
would record my gratitude to Almighty God, whose kind providence
gave and hath preserved to me one so well deserving the name of ' helpmeet.'

"Our life, made up of fidelity and love, has been like a deepening and
widening stream, upon which we have floated together in delightful harmony. Our home, with its five little buds of beauty and promise, has
been an *Eden spot*, where our Infinite Father, who dwelt with the first
pair in Paradise, has vouchsafed us His constant presence. Oh how
much of pure love and true joy have been compressed within these ten
years—the happiest ten years of my life ! Accept, my precious Annie,
this humble but sincere testimony to your thoughtful care, constant
kindness, unsullied goodness, untiring fidelity, and uninterrupted, aye,
increasing devotion.

"We have lived and loved together thus long—and now on this
anniversary day let us, in token of our gratitude to God and our affection
for one another, build a pillar of witness. It shall be composed of these
ten stones, one for each year of our married life : LOVE—TRUTH—
PURITY—KINDNESS—FIDELITY—SINCERITY—CONSTANCY—THANK-
FULNESS—HOLINESS—CHRIST THE FOUNDATION STONE.

"This is the altar upon which we will renew our vows 'to love,
comfort, honour, and keep one another so long as we both shall live.'"

Within a few weeks after the marriage Mr. Cookman was
appointed to the charge of West Chester station. West
Chester is the county town of Chester County, about thirty
miles from Philadelphia, and beautifully situated in a rich
farming district, which was settled originally almost wholly
by Quakers. The town has long been noted for the thrift,
intelligence, and sobriety of its inhabitants. The Methodist
Church there was not strong either in wealth or numbers,
but the members, feeling themselves highly favoured by Mr.
Cookman's appointment, resolved to do the best they could
to render him and his bride comfortable and happy.

Mr. Cookman, accustomed hitherto to look up to a head
for direction and support, was now thrown wholly on his
own resources. He knew where was the source of power—
the Throne of Grace—and resorting to it, he obtained help
of God. His preaching from the opening Sunday attracted
general attention. His fame had preceded him, and very
soon his church was crowded, not only by the Methodists
and their immediate sympathizers, but also by the *élite* of the
neighbourhood. The "Friends" were charmed by the
spirituality of his sermons and the godly simplicity of his
manners. He became the central figure of the religious
community, and all eyes and hearts were turned toward him ;
his influence grew day by day, and his ascendency over the
minds of the people became in a short time such as no other
minister had attained in years.

With a laudable ambition for success, and an earnest zeal
for the Divine glory, he was a man full of work, spending
the forenoons of the day in the study and the afternoons in
pastoral visitation, and mingling socially with all classes of
the people and with all denominations of Christians. The
sociability and catholicity which so distinguished his father,
and which subsequently became so pre-eminent in him, began
already to be seen as traits of character. Effective and
popular as he was in the pulpit, he did not depend wholly
upon the efforts of the Sabbath to accomplish the work of
God, but was incessant in his attentions to the members of
the congregation in the private walks of life. There was no
element of power which he did not seek thus early to subordinate to the efficiency of his ministry. But while absorb-
ingly devoted to his own charge and to the work which lay
directly before him, it was not possible for one of such gifts,
whose family name was talismanic in all the churches, and
whose personal reputation was already wide-spread, to escape

constant appeals from far and near for special services in the way of sermons and addresses.

The following letters to his young friend, Andrew Longacre, give a faint idea of the intensity and extensiveness of his labours. As will be seen, his summer vacation in 1851 was spent in attendance upon various camp-meetings. He went rapidly from one to another of these gatherings, and preached to the delight and edification of the masses who frequented them. A strange way to take vacation! And yet the habit adopted thus early in his career continued uniformly through life; his month for relaxation, instead of being spent in the recreations of innocent pastimes, in absolute desistance from his customary home work and excitements, was usually absorbed in the most active and taxing exercises. The change of scene, the bodily movement, the forming of new acquaintances, the free, joyous mingling with his ministerial brethren, the ever-fresh inspirations which such associations evoked, but, above all, the opportunity of working for the Master on a wide-spread scale—these were considerations which controlled and sustained his choice.

To Mr. Andrew Longacre, of Philadelphia :—

"WEST CHESTER, *September* 5, 1851.

* * * "Believe me that my silence has not been occasioned by any diminution of any kindly or affectionate feeling, but purely by the force of circumstances. As you are aware, I have been away from my charge for the last few weeks, and during most of my absence have been so circumstanced as to render letter-writing a matter of absolute impossibility. In the providence of God, I have been permitted to return to my field of labour, and very gladly avail myself of a little leisure to communicate with one for whom I have entertained the sincerest regard. Your prosperity has always greatly interested me. Believing that God had endued you with very considerable talent, satisfied that you possessed in no small degree the grace of the Holy Spirit, I thought that in a more public sphere you might better promote the glory of God and subserve the interests of His Church ; hence my strong desire and earnest entreaty

that you should prayerfully consider the important work of the Christian ministry. The subsequent developments of Divine providence have, I think, most clearly proved that the impression which induced me to single you out for this sphere was directed from heaven. Perhaps you may be disposed to think that I am writing too plainly when I make allusion to your gifts and graces. Believe me, I am perfectly sincere, and express myself in this undisguised way from a firm conviction that many young men suffer more from depression than elation of spirits. From a fear of adding fuel to the flame of vanity, encouragement is often withheld, while the individual is writhing under the influence of despondency and despair. I believe in my soul this is wrong, and, as a general thing, I make it a rule to repeat to the person referred to anything commendatory which I may have heard. This is a privilege which becomes a feast for my own soul, while at the same time it is intended to stimulate and encourage the one addressed.

"Most sincerely do I rejoice in your success, and as earnestly do I pray that God may bless you with that measure of health and strength which shall fully fit you for the earnest and successful prosecution of your ministerial labours. During the summer I attended five camp-meetings, preaching frequently and labouring arduously. I greatly regretted my inability to reach Red Lion, which ground I have not visited for two years. My valise was packed and arrangements made to start, but at the last moment I concluded that I would yield to the solicitations of Peninsula friends, who positively insisted upon my tarrying longer in that region. God seemed to own and bless my feeble endeavours, so that I would fain believe my course was overruled for good. I trust that the meeting at Red Lion, like many which have preceded it in that forest, proved both pleasant and profitable. I enjoyed for a day or two its counterpart on the Shrewsbury Circuit, where there were upward of three hundred tents and any number of Baltimoreans. At present I am enjoying my happy and comfortable home—a very little paradise. When will you come and participate in its pleasures? I can promise you a cordial welcome and hospitable treatment. Next week I desire, if possible, to spend a day or two with mother, whom I have not seen for many weeks. Perhaps you may be in the city then, and I may enjoy a personal intervi w, which, after all, is infinitely preferable to pen-and-ink communication."

Among his excursions from home was one on a literary errand—probably the first of its kind—to Dickinson Seminary, located at Williamsport, Pennsylvania. The following letter to his wife discloses a little of the anxiety of the young orator, but more of the joy of the young father :—

"WILLIAMSPORT, *Monday noon.*

"I have a leisure moment which shall be devoted to a family correspondence. After bidding you farewell I returned to my lonely home, and proceeded to change and finish my address. This accomplished, I arranged my matters, and, joining Professor Wentworth, returned to the depôt. We dined with your friend H——, and started about one o'clock. A long, tedious ride in the canal-boat brought us to Williamsport about half-past twelve on Saturday. General Packer met me at the boat, and is entertaining Brother Myers and myself most elegantly. Our home is the head-quarters in the town. Yesterday we had three services, Professor Wentworth preaching in the morning and your humble servant in the evening. All went off satisfactorily. The officers of the institution and the people of the town are more than kind, offering me every attention. I deliver my address this evening. Cannot tell how it will take. The examinations are progressing, and will not be concluded before Wednesday. I find that I shall not be able to get home before Friday. How is my precious Bruner? Dear little duck! I have him and his mother in my mind almost constantly. Kiss him over and over and over again for his absent pa."

With all these engagements, the duties of his pastorate were not neglected. The protracted meeting at which he hints was soon begun, and resulted in a general and thorough revival of religion, the fruits of which remain to this day.

At the ensuing session of the Conference—spring of 1852 —he was elected to elders' orders, and ordained by Bishop Janes, and re-appointed to West Chester. His work this year was but a continuation of that of the preceding. The revival did not spend itself, but progressed through all the months, marked more by the universal quickening and growth of believers than by the multiplication of converts. But I will allow the Rev. W. C. Best, of West Chester, to testify of the permanent good accomplished during these years :—

" Mr. Cookman and his wife were received with open arms and warm hearts, for his reputation as a man of humble piety and a minister of uncommon ability had preceded him. He at once took a position in the community, and fully retained it until his removal, such as none of his predecessors had enjoyed. He found a church embarrassed with a debt of three thousand dollars of ten years' standing, very much in need of repairs, and with a small number of members, and they by no means wealthy. During his term of service he not only put the church in thorough repair, but paid off the entire debt. He found here but one hundred and fifty-two members. At the end of his first year he returned one hundred and seventy members and seventy-five probationers. At the end of his second year he reported two hundred and twenty-five full members and twenty-six probationers. The church was always full when Brother Cookman was to preach. He had larger regular congregations than any of our ministers have preached to here, either before or since, with perhaps a single exception, and that was during the war.

" He was as popular in other churches as in his own. Everybody loved him, and spoke of him as the lovely, eloquent Cookman. His popularity in the town may be judged of from the number of marriages he was called upon to perform. Though the town was small, and the society weak, he married almost as many in the two years as were married in the past five years, though the town and society have largely increased in numbers. Of those converted under his ministry there was much of stable material. One minister (Rev. Thomas Poulson), two of the members of the present board of trustees, and several others of the present efficient workers in our Church, were part of the fruit of his labour. This fruit, remaining after the lapse of twenty years, certainly speaks favourably of the character of the revivals had under his ministry. It is but fair to state that Brother Cookman gave an impulse and position to Methodism in West Chester such as it never had, and we still enjoy the benefits thereof. Though twenty years have rolled away since he laboured here, his name is still like ' precious oint- ment poured forth,' and his memory is deeply revered by all who knew him. He is still called the most popular preacher of any denomination that ever statedly ministered in West Chester. It is difficult to decide which was the stronger attraction for the people—his unassuming piety, and sweet, loving spirit, or his thrilling eloquence that so enchained the multitudes."

The session of the Philadelphia Conference in 1853 was held at Harrisburg, the capital of the State of Pennsylvania. Mr. Cookman's term had expired at West Chester, and in the course of the administration he must be sent to a new charge. He was undoubtedly the most popular young minister in the Conference. Several prominent churches within his Conference, and some from beyond it, applied for his services ; among them none pressed its claims with more persistence than the Locust Street Church, Harris- burg, the seat of the Conference. The members of this charge were on the spot ; they had generously opened their homes for the entertainment of the preachers. Their suit prevailed ; and when the appointments were announced, and Alfred Cookman was read out for Locust Street, the crowded audience burst into a tumult of applause.

There could have been no situation better suited to pro- mote Mr. Cookman's self-development and to extend his influence than this appointment. The borough of Harris- burg, containing about 8,000 inhabitants, was beautifully located on the east side of the Susquehanna River, and, as

the capital of the state, was a point where controlling business and political interests concentrated. In the winter
time the Legislature drew together not only the members of
the State Government, but also leading men having ends to
accomplish with the Government. The Locust Street Church
was conveniently located ; and very soon his zeal and eloquence attracted general attention. He was elected chaplain of the House of Delegates, was selected to offer the
prayer at the inauguration of Governor Bigler, and at this
early age obtained relatively as great an ascendency over
the prominent politicians and the community at Harrisburg
as his father had previously done over all classes at Washington. The following notice of his preaching, from one of
the Harrisburg papers, shows the estimation in which he
was held :—

"Rev. Mr. Cookman preached another eloquent sermon on Sunday
evening. . . . The whole discourse was replete with sublime thoughts
and beautiful illustrations, and made a salutary and, we trust, a lasting
impression upon the minds of the large and attentive auditory. One
secret of Mr. Cookman's popularity and success as a preacher is that his
sermons are *all* good, and that whatever emergency calls him forth, he
has a peculiar faculty of happily adapting his discourse to the occasion.
We have observed this in several instances, when Mr. Cookman has
delivered impromptu addresses in response to unexpected calls made
upon him. We like his sermons on account of their freshness and origi-
nality, and the thoroughness and earnestness with which they are delivered. For a young man he is a speaker of superior ability. He has
been thoroughly educated, and has all the finish which literary acquirements can bestow upon naturally fine powers of declamation. Mr.
Cookman bids fair to win for himself a reputation for pulpit eloquence
equal to that enjoyed by his eloquent and lamented father."

Toward the close of his first year Mr. Cookman was
strongly urged to go to Pittsburgh to take charge of a new
Church enterprise in that city, but a sense of duty to the
charge he already occupied prevailed over the urgent invita-

tion, and he remained and completed the full term of two
years. His ministry was highly successful in adding members to the Church. The multitudes who frequented the
sanctuary and listened to his beautiful imagery and forcible
appeals, did not go away merely enchanted with the witchery
of words and action ; they remained to weep for their sins,
and " to lay hold of the hope set before them in the Gospel."
If the preacher culled flowers with which to please the fancy,
he did not the less forge and shoot sharp arrows which
pierced the consciences of his hearers. At the end of two
years the Church had gained ninety members and seventy
probationers, and increased equally in its financial and social
standing.

Through these years the devoted pastor was also an active
itinerant, going hither and thither throughout the state and
in adjoining states, on all possible errands of evangelistic
and literary labour. Traces of him appear among his Baltimore friends.

Mr. Cookman had entered the field as a lecturer, and,
judging from the comments of the press, obtained no mean
success :—

" The first of a series of lectures in the Methodist Episcopal Church,
Fourth Street, of this city (Philadelphia), was delivered on Thursday
evening of last week by the Rev. Mr. Cookman, of Harrisburg. The
subject was The Bible. He is a very eloquent man. He delivered it
without 'notes' ; and on this account it was very impressive. There
was a peculiarity in it which we think worthy of remark, although it
may have been noticed by few of the audience. It was this : he availed
himself of ' apt alliterations' artful aid,' said that the Bible was the *basis*,
the *bond*, the *bulwark*, and the *boast* of free institutions. It was the basis,
because we derive from the Bible the best principles of government, and
that from it alone we learn the lesson of self-government. Other books
take up the subject from the circumference, and proceed thence to the
centre ; this begins at the centre, and works out to the circumference. In
other words, those begin with society at large, and this with the individual.

8

" He showed that the Bible was the bond of our institutions, because it taught the universal brotherhood of Man, and knew no North, no South, no East, no West. He showed it to be the bulwark of our Republic by comparisons with other governments in other days, which have passed away, because they had not the principles of the Bible to protect them from vice and its destructive tendencies. And he concluded by showing that the Bible was the boast of our free institutions, because it was designed for universal acceptance, and was universally circulated among us by Protestant Christianity ; and on this branch of his subject he was *very* eloquent. He compared the different denominations, when met together to promote the distribution of the Bible in our happy land, and from thence throughout the world, to a rainbow—all the colours in the bow being distinctly visible, and yet happily harmonizing in one beautiful whole ! And then concluded by calling upon us as *American citizens* to protect the Bible as the sheet-anchor of our liberties, and to act out the pretty sentiment, '' We won't give up the Bible.' ''

A year later he lectured again in Philadelphia, and received from another paper the following appreciative notice :—

"On Monday evening we had the pleasure of hearing the fifth lecture of the course before the Young Men's Christian Association by the Rev. Alfred Cookman, of Pittsburgh. The Presbyterian Church, capacious as it is, was well filled with a cultivated and intelligent audience. The lecturer's theme was Concentrated Energy, and his remarks were mainly addressed to the young, urging upon them, in language at once argumentative, forcible, and eloquent, the necessity of a fixed purpose, pursued with untiring effort, or, in a word, of *concentrated energy*, as a prerequisite to success and distinction in any pursuit, and in *all* the pursuits of life. Mr. Cookman's style is clear and perspicuous, while it is at the same time brilliant and ornate. His voice, which is perfectly under his control, is remarkably distinct, musical, and sonorous, and his manner of delivery is highly oratorical and effective. His lecture gave unbounded satisfaction, and placed him high in the opinion of our people as a finished scholar and a popular speaker. Mr. Cookman, although quite a young man, has already won for himself an enviable reputation, and, if his life and health are spared, he will undoubtedly before many years stand in the very front rank of the ministry of the Methodist Episcopal Church."

While stationed at Harrisburg, he was invited to deliver

the annual ˙sermon before "The Society of Evangelical
Inquiry of Dickinson College." The sermon was well received, and established for its author a high reputation with
the students. In the evening of the same day on which this
sermon was delivered, he preached at the Methodist Church
in the town. It was the first time he had been in the old
church since he was a boy in his father's household. Vivid
and tender were the memories which rushed upon his heart,
and he could not do otherwise than refer to his father and
the occasion of his own conversion. We are so fortunate
as to have a description of the effects of his preaching from
an eye-witness, the Rev. J. Duey Moore, of the Baltimore
Conference, who was then a youth resident in Carlisle.
Writing to the Rev. John E. Cookman, he says :—

"I remember, when I was a boy, your brother was invited
to preach in Carlisle. In the morning he preached in the
College Chapel, and at night in the old church, Main Street,
the same church which your father had the charge of in
other days. His theme was 'The Vision of Dry Bones.'
The church was crowded. In concluding his sermon, he
referred to his sainted father in a most touching manner ; the
effect was beyond all human description. I remember hearing an old minister of our church, who had sat under your
father's ministry, say, 'The form of George Cookman came
before me while his son was preaching, to such an extent
that I was carried back to the days when the crowds gathered
to hear what I regarded the best pulpit orator I ever listened
to.'

"After concluding his sermon, he gave an account of his
conversion, which took place in that church when he was
quite young. Speaking of it he said, 'Kneeling there
(pointing to a bench at the right of the pulpit), a poor, dis-
tressed penitent, a brother in Christ, a member of the Pres-

byterian Church, by the name of Mr. Hamilton, came to me amid my sorrow, and, placing his hand upon my head, told me to "look fully to Christ, and He would save me "; and as I tried to do as he told me, the darkness gave way, and, kneeling there with this dear brother by the Cross, great light and peace rested upon me. I was forgiven.' As your brother had not heard from Mr. Hamilton for years, he thought he had passed to his reward ; but he (Mr. Hamilton) was in the church, and just as soon as the congregation was dismissed he walked to the altar and introduced himself to your brother. I will never forget their meeting. As the people were retiring from their pews, their eyes caught the venerable form of Mr. James Hamilton advancing toward the pulpit, and, as all eyes followed him until he came before your brother, they waited to see the result. Oh, how the people did weep as they looked upon two who had not met since they met amid the light of the Cross—one as a penitent, then crying 'Save me !' the other saying, 'Christ can save !' As I write I think I can see myself as I was then, holding my dear sainted father's hand (he was an intimate friend of your father and brother), and, looking up into his face, saw the tears flowing down his cheeks while he looked upon this meeting.''

CHAPTER XI.

THE Methodists of Pittsburgh having completed their new
and beautiful church, renewed their invitation to Mr. Cookman to consent to be transferred to take the charge of it.
Nothwithstanding Mr. Cookman's love for his Conference,
in view of the advice of the bishops and the noble enterprise at Pittsburg, he accepted the invitation, and was transferred by Bishop Morris in the spring of 1855. It was not
without regret that the people of Harrisburg parted with
him. As evidence of the universal respect and affection
with which he was regarded, I quote from one of the news-
papers of the day :—

"Rev. Mr. Cookman preached his farewell sermon on Sabbath
evening. So great was the anxiety to hear it that the church was
crowded to its utmost capacity at an early hour, and a large number of
persons were unable to obtain seats at all. Mr. Cookman preached a
discourse eminently appropriate to the occasion, and was more than
ordinarily eloquent and impressive. He spoke with much apparent sincerity and feeling, and a large portion of the congregation were affected
to tears. Mr. Cookman has laboured in this community for two years
with great success, and was respected and beloved not only by his own
congregation, but by the people of our town generally. He was popular with all classes and all denominations, and his departure is universally regretted. He left Harrisburg yesterday afternoon for Pittsburgh,
the scene of his future ministerial labours, carrying with him the heart-
warm blessings of hundreds of true friends. May the largest prosperity
attend him."

How Mr. Cookman was impressed with Pittsburgh before his transfer, may be gathered from the following letter to his wife :—

"Pittsburgh, *Tuesday afternoon, June* 14, 1854.

... "About three o'clock the train came thundering along. Finding seats we hurried off, and until day-dawn dozed away the tedious moments. Then the scenery, wild and majestic, opened upon us, which of course we enjoyed richly and to the end of our journey. Some of the views in crossing the mountain transcend anything I have ever beheld. Without accident we reached Pittsburgh in good time, not near as much fatigued as I frequently am after riding to Philadelphia. You will feel anxious to know what I think of Pittsburgh. Well, I must say I rather like it. True, there is a good deal of smoke, and the houses generally look cloudy, but it is not near as bad as I anticipated. The buildings are good, some of the residences quite elegant, and everything seems to exhibit the spirit of energy and enterprise. The place strongly reminds me of many English cities which I have visited. It is not unlike New York, more like it certainly than Philadelphia. I fancy that like myself you would be agreeably disappointed in Pittsburgh. I have already traversed the city pretty thoroughly; among other places I have visited the new Christ M. E. Church, and do not think me enthusiastic or extravagant when I say that it is far, *far* ahead of anything in the form of a Methodist Church I have ever seen. They are about finishing the basement, which is very handsomely frescoed and fitted up in elegant style. The audience-room will be most magnificent. I wandered through, as I desired, entirely *incognito*. If I can I will procure a lithographic representation of the edifice, that you may have some idea. Well, now, I hear you say, 'Just as I expected and prophesied. He had no business to go to Pittsburgh; a convert already.' No, dear, I would prefer to remain in the Philadelphia Conference than to assume the responsibility which would devolve upon the pastor of such a charge. Very much would be expected, and I do not want to be obliged to meet such expectations. Worse things, though, you may rest assured, might happen to us than being sent to Pittsburgh. So far as I am concerned, with my beloved Annie and charming boys, I could be perfectly happy in a cabin on the tallest peak of the Alleghanies. It is your presence and enthusiastic love which covers my path with sunshine and makes me a happy home anywhere. You need not fear, I think, a transfer to Pittsburgh. I am staying at the *City Hotel*, kept by Messrs. Glass and Chase, gentlemen who have treated me already with very marked attention and favour. I wonder how you all are this evening. I think of you almost constantly, and am the happiest when I can bask in the refreshing radiance of your sunny faces. Well, I believe I have written all that I have to communicate just now. It is, I fear, an illegible scrawl, penned in the midst of noise and confusion. Puzzle it out, however, and when you have done kiss yourself over and over again for one who loves you better than all the world beside. Then take up Bruner, and give him a dozen for his papa; then *petty Kenney*, and let her have an equal number."

Mr. Cookman was twenty-seven years of age when appointed to Christ Church. The new edifice, of the Gothic order of architecture, situated in Penn Street, was then the costliest church building in American Methodism, and was about the first decided advance in the movement in architectural beauty in Methodist houses of worship. The number of members that brought this laudable undertaking to completion was small. They were, however, men of means, courage, and prayer. They felt that the right man in the pulpit would secure success. No higher mark of confidence could have been placed on Mr. Cookman than that he should be selected for so important a position.

The sequel proved the wisdom of the choice. Under his control, the enterprise moved off prosperously from the beginning, and the most sanguine expectations of its originators were fulfilled. Though young in years, he was a man of experience; courageous, and at the same time cautious, he showed both the ardour which prepared him to enter fully into the advanced views of his official men, and also the judgment to direct their earnestness with the steadiness and tact which insured the best results. His power to attract the people by his preaching was to be tested as never before. Heretofore his churches had been "free," and this was "pewed"; but his ability was at once recognized, and his church was speedily filled. His faculty as an organizer was

to be promptly and fully proved, and that, too, under circumstances peculiar and trying—but here, as in the pulpit,
he showed himself eminently capable.　　It is doubtful if
there be any surer test of the ability of a minister for administration as well as preaching and pastoral work than the
successful guidance of a great and powerful Church, especially in the forming periods of its existence.　　To balance
all conflicting claims, to keep all the forces in accord, to
incorporate new elements with the old without violence, to
evoke and start enterprises into safe and effective channels,
to impress all the workers and all the methods with a
thoroughly spiritual stamp—all this requires talents of a high
order, and talents well poised.　　The native sense and the
admirable discernment of Mr. Cookman were never more
displayed, before or since, than in the management of the
affairs of Christ Church.

But while busy with his new charge in the first months of
his pastorate, he does not forget the fond mother from whom
he was so far separated.　　Could there be a more affectionate
expression, alike creditable to him and to her, than this
letter?　　I give it with its italicizing retained :—

"PITTSBURGH, *May* 25, 1855.

"Will's letter reached us this week, bringing the unwelcome intelligence that you have been seriously ill.　At such a time we feel it to be
a duty and a privilege to take up our pen and express our sympathy and
undying love.　Your children may sometimes exhibit a censurable care-
lessness and indifference, but believe me there underlies their conduct as
enthusiastic affection for their *mother* as ever found a place in a human
heart.　The effect of your instructions, and the influence of your kind,
gentle nature, have been to win every noble feeling of which they are
capable, and if they were to-day severally interrogated who is the best
and purest among human kind, they would unhesitatingly answer, ' *Our
mother !*'　I have no greater happiness than to sit down and, in connection with the eventful past, dwell upon those *virtues* which you so beautifully developed in the midst of your family, and think of that ceaseless

and *self-denying love* which always shed sunshine on our home. It was and is *a happy home!* the remembrance of which shall be dear to our hearts through the entire period of our earthly pilgrimage. *Thank you, dear mother, a thousand times over,* for your gushing sympathy, your faithful instructions, your consistent and beautiful example, your jealous care and unremitting efforts for the happiness and welfare of your children. You have been not only a good mother, but the *best of mothers.* Our appreciation of your character and services increases with our age ; and when you are safely housed in glory, we will often come together and wonder that one so pure and lovely was so long lent to us and the world. *My burning tears attest the sincerity* of the feelings I express—feelings which are largely shared by every member of your beloved family. Even Will, whom you occasionally deem a little headstrong and unmanageable, tells me in his *letter* that requirements which once seemed irksome to his independent nature are now regarded in an entirely different light. It is his *highest delight* to serve and gratify her whom he feels to be his *best and truest friend.* The loss of his mother, he states, would blot out every earthly joy, and make him almost wish for the oblivion of the death-slumber. Shall I ask you to excuse this spontaneous burst of filial feeling? This, I am sure, will not be necessary, for while it has relieved my overflowing heart, it may, perhaps, kindle a pleasurable feeling in the bosom of one whom I *would be proud to make happy.* I hope by this time your sickness has been arrested, and you are able to attend to your domestic duties. When you feel that you can conveniently and comfortably take up your pen, we shall be most happy to receive one of your thrice-welcome letters. In the meanwhile charge one of the fraternity to act as your amanuensis, and let us at least know the state of your health and the course of domestic affairs. The children exhibit every day some new charm, some fresh attraction. Next week the Western Virginia Conference meets in Wheeling. If nothing should prevent, I think I shall join a company of preachers and go down for a day or two. The Pittsburgh Conference meets in Johnstown on the 13th of June."

Mr. Cookman had been transferred, and had entered upon his work in advance of the session of the Pittsburgh Conference. The transfer to a new Conference involved a trial to him, as it would to any man of like refined nature, and it was with no little misgiving that he looked forward to the session. A transfer for the express purpose of being appointed to the grandest and wealthiest Church of the Conference, would be likely to render him an object of a somewhat careful and cool attention. His fame had preceded him—would he measure up to it? His praise was in all the churches—was he proud and reserved? These and such questions would occur to brethren and to him. Methodist preachers are but men, and, like other men, they do not relish being dispossessed by strangers of the fields which their own hard toil has made to bud and bloom.

But it was impossible for a body of good men to have hard feelings toward Alfred Cookman. He had only to show himself among his brethren, and all prejudice was disarmed. From youth there was that in him which transfused the hearts of all with love and confidence. The Pittsburgh preachers were won by his first looks and words. He impressed them as a faithful preacher, with a single aim, with all the instincts and habits of his brethren, and that he had come to Pittsburgh not for the sake of position, but for the good of souls. His honours seemed to sit so lightly upon him, his whole demeanour in public and private was so savoury of genuine modesty and deep piety, that, with a quickness and generosity so distinctive of their class, the ministers immediately extended to him the *entente cordiale*, which henceforth made him happy among them.

The demands on Mr. Cookman for outside work increased, as from this prominent point the circle of his reputation constantly widened. From all directions the calls for special services flooded his table—requests for dedicating churches, for addresses, lectures, and all kinds of efforts in aid of old and new causes.

An address delivered during this period in Philadelphia, at Music Fund Hall, on behalf of the Bedford Street Mission of the Methodist Episcopal Church, was probably one

of the most effective of his life. It was elaborately prepared, and was delivered in his happiest style. The impression was deep, immediate, and abiding. His vehement
oratory swept the vast audience whithersoever he listed. He
and the cause he pleaded were from that evening, if they
they had not been previously, thoroughly intrenched in the
hearts of the hearers. Back again among his early friends
a visitor, he came freighted with the best thoughts he could
command ; his soul in closest sympathy with missions among
the destitute, and his nature fired by old associations and
glowing with the love of Jesus, he rose with the hour, the
place, the audience, and it was thought by many that they
had rarely, if ever, listened to a more powerful popular
address.

The letter which follows, written to his youngest brother,
John, now the Rev. John E. Cookman, a member of the
New York Conference, will be read with interest. His
views on Biblical schools may be regarded by some as
behind the times. Yet the ground of his objections were
felt to be weighty by many minds as recently as fifteen years
ago. Even now there are a few in other denominations
besides the Methodist who have grave questionings as to
the positive benefit of the training of theological schools.
It is feared by them that it tends to make men machines,
to quench native fire, to create generations of preachers
who will carry from the seminary too much the tone and
manner of a "faculty"; that, while it may produce theolo-
gians, it will educate the students too far away from the
people to fit them as preachers for the masses, and so raise
up ministers for this and coming ages who will not be, in
all respects, as effective and successful as those hitherto
known in Methodism.

Although it is now conceded that theological schools

have become a necessity of the Church, yet I regard it as no discredit to our friend that he cherished and expressed the feelings contained in this letter. It is for those who have the charge of these schools to see to it that his fears and the fears of thousands as sincerely devoted to the Church are not realized. Said Robert Hall of the learned Kippis, " He might be a very clever man by nature, for aught I know, but he laid so many books upon his head that his brains could not move." Vital force, springing from the heart as the motor—the one indispensable condition of effective preaching—was what our friend believed more and more with each succeeding year of his ministry. Goethe says :—

> " What you don't feel, you'll never catch by hunting ;
> It must gush out spontaneously from the soul ;
> And with a fresh delight enchanting
> The hearts of all that hear, control."

To his brother, Mr. John E. Cookman, he wrote :—

" PITTSBURGH, July 22, 1856.

" To say that your letter afforded me great pleasure, expresses but feebly the real feelings of my heart. While I know that you had always associated with your future the work of the ministry, still I began to fear that business and the world were becoming so attractive and absorbing that you would be diverted from a nobler and more useful sphere. What was my joy, then, to hear from yourself that your present employments failed to satisfy the desires and ambition of your nature, and, in obedience to conscientious convictions, you felt like preparing yourself to do the work of an evangelist.

" From personal experience I know the importance—aye, the necessity of *Divine help and strength* in a situation similar to that in which you are placed. Therefore, while I will most cheerfully render you such advice and assistance as may be in my power, at the same time I would impress you with the propriety and advantage of fleeing to the strong for strength. Hide yourself in God. Trust for providential direction, and you shall not stray or stumble. The God of the fatherless, in so important a step as that which you contemplate, will certainly and satisfactorily exhibit a superintending agency, and in future you will review the whole with gratitude and joy. My first and most fervent counsel, therefore, would be that you yield yourself up *fully* unto God. Let no idle, no secret sin, no unwillingness to toil or sacrifice or suffer, debar you from the full realization of your privileges in the Gospel of God's dear Son. However imperfect your mental and physical developments may seem to yourself, there is no reason why, as a Christian, you should not rival a Fletcher, a McCheyne, a Summerfield, in their almost seraphic purity and zeal and devotion. Attend, then, to the all-important subject of personal piety in the first instance, and I have no fear for the rest. God will overrule all for your benefit and His glory.

"With respect to the importance or advantage of a college course, I am not entirely clear or satisfied. Had you not spent four years in the Philadelphia High-School, I should not be in so much doubt. I remember, however, that you have acquired, to a considerable extent, habits of study ; you have obtained pretty general information on the different branches of science, which will serve as a foundation on which to build in the future ; you have received regularly and legitimately the degree of A.B., which of course will be followed in due time with an A.M. In these respects you are very far in advance of a large majority of those who are admitted to our Methodist itinerancy. Then, when I think of the associations and influences which are found in most colleges, I tremble lest my cherished brother, for whose success I am so deeply concerned, should be moved off the sure foundation. A Biblical institute, as a substitute for a college, has been presented to my mind, but here again I have my difficulties. I should fear that its influence would be to subdue that enthusiasm which I believe will prove in the future your charm and your power.

"The truth is, I am only about half-persuaded in my mind respecting the advantages of such schools. I compare the genuine Methodist preacher, whose soul is one blaze of holy zeal—whose mind, self-disciplined, is filled with practical and profitable truth—whose aim is so single that his whole life is a striking commentary upon the sentiment, 'This one thing I do'—who goes through the world like fire through the prairie ; I say I compare such a one with a critical, metaphysical, Germanized student of divinity, who, perhaps, looks as blue and feels as cold as if he had been shivering in an ice-house, and who preaches as stiffly as if his lips and heart and arms had all been literally frozen. There is no kind of doubt but I can find self-made men in the Methodist Episcopal Church who are not only equal but superior to others of our own and sister denominations who can boast the advantages of literary and theological training. With respect, however, to this matter, I would not determine for you. If you feel that college studies would increase your mental discipline as no other exercise could, I would not utter a word of discouragement, but rather a hearty '*God-speed!*' I am rather inclined to the conclusion that Brush College, after all, will prove the best school for the development of your physical and intellectual powers. If you could spend the autumn and winter in reading, composing, and exercising as opportunity might offer, and in the spring take an easy circuit, as for instance Village Green, or Springfield, I believe that you would accomplish as much for yourself and the Church as you would by conjugating Latin verbs and studying heathen mythology. If you feel inclined to this latter course, my home and humble services are at your disposal. I appreciate the peculiarity and perplexities of your situation, and, while I scarcely feel prepared to advise, would earnestly counsel that you seek wisdom from God, who giveth liberally and upbraideth not."

Mr. Cookman was able to go up to the session of the Pittsburgh Conference in 1856 with a good showing for the year. The number of members had increased from ninety to one hundred and thirty-two, and twenty-six probationers. At the seat of the Conference he was called upon to speak, in connection with the Rev. Dr. Durbin and others, on the occasion of the anniversary of the Conference Missionary Society. A correspondent of the Pittsburgh *Christian Advocate* wrote of the speeches :—

"The Rev. Alfred Cookman, of Penn Street Church, Pittsburgh, and Dr. John P. Durbin electrified the audience with two of the most powerful speeches to which it has been our privilege to listen. Cookman is a gifted son of eloquence, and nature has given him a most exuberant fancy. His speeches abound in the most gorgeous imagery, and in this respect he is said to resemble his distinguished father. Of Durbin, as a great thinker and a great orator, it is scarcely necessary to speak. He presented some most striking thoughts on the subject of missions. Cookman's speech might be said to abound with the lightning-flashes of genius, while Durbin followed in one continued thunder-roll of ponderous thought."

The same correspondent noticed Mr. Cookman's sermon on the Sabbath, in the Presbyterian Church, in these terms:—

" We would as soon think of daguerreotyping the storm, or with our feeble voice of imitating the roar of the thunder, as to undertake to convey to our readers the impression made by Cookman's sermon. Certain we are that of all who heard it, no one will forget it."

Writing, also, of a Bible speech he made at the same session, he said it was "a speech such as no man but one of his peculiar gifts could make."

These descriptions, while due allowance may be made for the enthusiasm excited by the youth of Mr. Cookman, give proof of the high appreciation in which his gifts were held by one who was probably a member of the Conference. They also show the tireless energy of the young minister in thus standing forward on three important occasions to plead in causes of the first magnitude. Neither then nor afterward did the thought of saving himself or his *capital* ever seem to enter his mind. What he could do for the Master was done to the best of his ability, and there the matter rested.

The following letter to his brother, Mr. William Wilberforce Cookman, on receiving the news of his conversion reveals the depth of his religious affection :—

" PITTSBURGH, *February* 19, 1857.

" Tuesday's mail brought the most delightful letter I have received for a very long time. It was a letter from dear mother, filled with the details of your conversion. Like our precious parent, I have been specially concerned for your religious welfare. Two or three times this winter I have been on the point of addressing you a few lines. As my protracted meeting has progressed, I have not only thought of you, but in prayer have wrestled for your salvation. How *rejoiced,* then, was I to learn that you had resolutely espoused the cause of the Saviour, and were triumphing in a consciousness of sins forgiven. Indeed, when I read mother's letter, the fountains of my nature broke open, and I poured forth copious tears of thankfulness and joy. This morning your fraternal epistle came to hand, and, as I glanced over its lines in returning from the post-office, I found that my cup was again running over. Bless the Lord, O my soul, and all that is within me, bless and praise

His holy name! I am delighted that your experience is of so definite and satisfactory a character. This is desirable, not only because it adds to the sum of our peace at the present, but because it constitutes our conversion a great *landmark* in our life, to which, in future years, we can revert with special pleasure and profit. You may expect in the future to suffer through manifold and powerful temptations; still, if in the midst of the trial you will only maintain your integrity and Christian profession, the temptation or temptations shall really answer a good purpose in establishing your faith and strengthening your godly virtues. It is in the storm or tempest that the sailor learns what he never could have learned if all around had continued calm and prosperous; then, of all times, he is becoming the practised and thorough seaman. When tempted or tried, remember the Rock that is higher than thou. Go to God; with the simplicity of a son or a child, tell Him all your doubts and fears and desires; plead the promises of His Word; and, as in thousands of instances, so in your case, He will surely make a way for your escape. I need not represent the advantage and importance of a *daily* reading of the Holy Scriptures. This is an exercise which you appreciate and will observe. Neither will I dwell upon the necessity of frequent prayer. *Morning, noon,* and *night* you will be found before God, pouring your wants and requests into His ever-attentive ear. Have you *joined the Church?* Remember that this is not only a great privilege, but a Scriptural duty. You will find within the pale of the Christian Church sympathy and assistance as they cannot be found elsewhere. Uniting yourself with a *class,* lay it down as a *principle* or *rule* of your life always to attend when it is possible to go. A man who regularly attends his class-meeting cannot very well backslide. Associate with your experience and profession increasing religious *activity.* This sustains the same relation to our *spiritual* life that stated physical exercise does to our natural life. Enter *every avenue of usefulness.* Do all the good in your power. Resolve that the world shall be better for your having lived in it. *My precious brother, my heart goes out after you in sincerest and strongest affection.* You were always *dear* to me because of the noble elements which constitute your nature, but you are *doubly dear* since your regeneration. I feel now that

> " ' Our hopes and aims are one,
>   Our comforts and our cares ! '

"We may warrantably indulge the delightful hope that *our fraternal love,* overleaping the river of death, will be perpetuated coeval with the existence of the soul.

"I still feel the deepest and liveliest interest in your *secular* affairs.

With the blessing of God, which you can now confidently implore and expect, all will be well. Can we not persuade George to give God his heart? If he would yield, then we should be an undivided family in the Church of Jesus Christ. Let us agree to pray for him."

At the close of Mr. Cookman's second year in Pittsburgh, spring of 1857, his return to the Philadelphia Conference was requested and granted. Before dismissing this important term of his ministry, I insert an estimate of his services at Christ Church from the pen of Dr. Wright, a member of its official board :—

" For a young man of comparatively little experience as a preacher in charge, to be called to the pastorate of an undertaking from which so much was expected on the one hand, and so much disaster to the cause of Methodism prophesied on the other, gave rise to much discussion as to the propriety of the appointment, many urging that a preacher of more experience would be better.

" Under these somewhat embarrassing circumstances, which were known to our young brother, he came doubting, but *firmly trusting*. When I first met him, one cold, dreary, Pittsburgh March morning, he looked anything but joyful. I introduced him to my family as our expected young preacher of whom they had heard me speak so often, and was disposed to be cheerful over his coming ; but the young preacher was not so disposed, and looked sad, and with a grave expression said: 'I am here to obey orders, but my opinion is that the officiary of your Church have made a mistake in asking my transfer to this important charge. I hope it has been ordered through your prayers, for I feel greatly the need of aid from on high to enter upon the discharge of the duties.' He then spoke of the magnitude of the enterprise, and his belief that the success of such efforts for the future would be determined in a great measure by

the first years of their history.   Thus believing, he said he
felt the weight of the responsibility all the more, that its
organization should be a success in every way, especially in
the salvation of sinners and the upbuilding of the Church
for good.

   " He entered upon his duties as the first pastor of Christ
Methodist Episcopal Church the following Sabbath, and
preached to a crowded house from the 6th chapter and 14th
verse of Galatians,—'God forbid,' etc.   The cross of Christ
and the atoning blood of the Lamb, ever beautiful and
powerful to save, was the burden of his theme on that day.
The timid young man of the day before was now as bold in
the annunciation of the truths that centre around the cross
as Paul, whom he so much loved, and upon whose character
he loved to dwell.   If there had been any doubts about
the propriety of calling the young brother to the new charge,
they were all dispelled by the impression produced upon the
minds and hearts of his first congregation.   A good, happy
brother was asked, on coming out of church, what he
thought of the sermon : 'Ah !' he replied, 'there is no
German silver about that—it has the true ring of the genuine
metal.'

   " In the organization of Christ Church membership from
the various Methodist congregations in Pittsburgh, Brother
Alfred Cookman performed a delicate task, in which he
acted with the good sense and judgment of more mature
years and experience.   Under the inspiration of his consecration to the work of the salvation of sinners, Alfred Cookman developed while at Christ Church some of the noblest
traits of his manhood, and showed what was possible when
the man is devoted to his Master's work.   The fervour of his
longings for the conversion of sinners was always marked
by a deep and loving pathos, expressed with singular

beauty and propriety of language, that rarely failed in making a deep and lasting impression. The congregations that waited upon his ministry while in Pittsburgh were large—often so crowded that persons had to leave for want of room.

" One of the elements of his great success in Pittsburgh was his love and devotion to the Sabbath-school interests of the Church. He organized a large school, and never did he seem more in his element than when working among the children; and never was there a body of children who seemed to be happier and gave more attention than when he was talking to them—either in examining them in their catechism, illustrating their Scriptural lesson, or in telling some story that pointed a moral which was always fixed in their minds by some appropriate illustration.

" Many of the children of the school came early under the influence of religion, gave their names to the Church, and Brother Alfred lived long enough to see several of the boys thus brought to Christ preachers, two of whom are now in the Baltimore Conference.

" In his devotion to the Sabbath-school interests of Christ Church he was ably assisted by his excellent wife, who had charge of the infant class-room. In all of his responsible duties and relations to Christ Church he was ever faithful to the great trust imposed upon him, and his Master abundantly blessed and honoured him with great success in bringing a large and influential membership to-gether, and establishing an objective point for Methodism in Pittsburgh.

" He impressed the large and wealthy congregation with the importance and duty of contributing generously of their means. The after-history of this Church shows that they have not forgotten his injunction, but have gone on increas-

ing their gifts, till now Christ Church stands among the
first in the Methodist Episcopal Church as a contributor to
all the interests of the Church."

The Rev. W. M. Paxton, D.D., now of New York, who
was the pastor of the First Presbyterian Church in Pittsburgh when Mr. Cookman was at Christ Church, has furnished a very pleasing testimony to the excellence of his
character and the usefulness of his ministry. After referring
to some of the difficulties which Mr. Cookman had to meet,
he says :—

" He, however, proved himself fully equal to the emergency. I now look back with admiration upon the masterly
manner in which he met all these difficulties, and turned
hostility into friendship. His humble, unpretending manner
disarmed prejudice ; his sincere, honest heart inspired confidence ; his loving, gentle spirit won the affection of the
people ; and his able and eloquent preaching gave him a
high place in the estimation of the public. His success
became apparent upon the first day the church was opened,
and before the close of the first year he had dissipated all
opposition, gathered around him a large and influential congregation, and established himself in the regard of the whole
community. At the end of one year, when his first term
of service expired, such was the desire, not only of his own
congregation but of the whole community, to retain his
services, that the bishops were constrained to renew his
appointment.

" His whole work in Pittsburgh was admirable in every
way. He organized his congregation well, preached well,
and was instrumental in the conversion of many souls.
But, beyond all this, he had a large catholic spirit, which
brought him into useful fellowship with his brethren of other
denominations, and enlisted him in every good work. He was

in every sense a Methodist, but he was not a narrow denominationalist; and, above all, he had nothing in his heart to keep him from rejoicing in the success of another's work.

" His residence in Pittsburgh being within two doors of my own, an intimacy sprang up between us, which soon ripened into a warm and lasting friendship. The more I knew of him the more I loved him. He had an honest heart that inspired trust, and made me feel that all his expressions, either of opinion or friendship, could be relied upon. His religion was deep, earnest, and controlling. He believed in heart-religion because he had an experience of it, and out of the abundance of his heart his mouth spoke. With him religion was a pervading principle, controlling all thought and action. ' He walked with God.' He realized more than most Christians the personal presence of the Saviour, and had many blessed seasons of high and holy communion as on the Mount. It was upon this rich treasury of heart-experience that he drew largely for his sermons. His spontaneous conversation was upon religion; it was in his heart, and he delighted to talk of it. I have many precious recollections of such conversations. He was in all his views and convictions a Methodist, and yet in his experience he was so much of a Calvinist that we had many ' good times together.' "

The subjoined characterization of Mr. Cookman and his work appeared at the time of his leaving Pittsburgh, in one of the daily papers of the city :—

" Rev. Alfred Cookman has been with us but two years, yet in that short time he has indelibly impressed us with his sincerity as a Christian,. his worth as a gentleman, and his ability as a pulpit orator. To his value as a Christian, his life and zeal in the cause he assumes testifies. Of his worth as a gentleman, the many and warm attachments formed during his short residence with us are the assurances. Of his ability as an orator, the large and discriminating audiences which have attended him are the very best evidences.

"Viewing the tenets of his Church in a spirit of liberality, austerity has not characterized his teaching; inspired with the social value of courtesy, his etiquette has not been based upon an exclusive code. Carefully regarding the end in view, he has not perverted the gifts of oratory to the gratification of vanity; but subordinating everything to the objects of his ministry, he has worthily maintained the dignity of the Christian teacher. Ignoring fanaticism in religion, he has not failed to discharge his duties as a citizen. Marking the nice distinction between Christian morality and political ethics, he has saved his congregation the scandal too many have suffered where the sanctuary has been desecrated by the introduction of party issues. Yet, with an ardent patriotism that finds a fitting response within the hearts of all who love their country, and which rises too far above mere party to be subjected to its criticism, he has pointed out the breakers which threaten our noble Ship of State, and conjured us by his eloquence to cling to the Bible as the only compass by which she may be safely directed.

"For all this we regret his loss. Succumbing to its necessity, we can only, with the poet, bid him

> "'Go, speed the stars of thought
>   On to their shining goals;
> The sower scatters broad his seed,
>   *The wheat thou strewest be souls!*'"

He and his family took their final leave of Pittsburgh at the midnight hour. So intense was the feeling at parting with them, that large numbers of their friends formed a procession and accompanied them to the depôt, where they took the train for Philadelphia.

CHAPTER XII.

MR. COOKMAN's return to Philadelphia was heartily received
by his brethren of the Conference and the laymen of the
city. The Green Street charge was especially favoured in
securing his services as their pastor. His fame as a preacher
and his efficiency as a worker had greatly augmented since
he had left Kensington Station, and his advent to the city
was adapted to awaken much delight and expectation. The
Green Street Church was a new, tasteful, and commodious
building, with free seats, situated among a dense population,
and offered every advantage for the popular talents of the
zealous pastor. He was now perfectly in his element. With
loving kindred and genial friends about him, a comfortable,
though not pretentious home, a large and enthusiastic society
of helpers, a crowded and sympathizing congregation, he
entered upon a career of popularity and usefulness which
may be regarded as an epoch in his ministry.

It is doubtful if Philadelphia Methodism has known in its
whole history a pastoral term of two years more signally
fraught with proofs of the Divine favour and the stable
results of evangelical ministrations than these of our friend
at Green Street. The scenes under his preaching—the perpetual blaze of revival, the marked cases of conversion and

sanctification—were more like the occurrences of primitive Methodism, and showed conclusively that the ancient glory had not departed from the sons of the fathers. At the close of his second year he reported seven hundred members and one hundred and fourteen probationers—a net gain of two hundred and thirty-five persons—with large advances in all the collections for benevolent objects, especially in that for the missionary cause.

As an explanation in part of the eminent success of Mr. Cookman at Green Street, it may be said that it took place during the great religious revival of 1857 and 1858. An awakening seldom paralleled pervaded all classes of society and churches of every communion, extending from the cities to the country districts, until there was not a hamlet, however remote, which did not feel its power. Waves of Divine blessing, in rapid succession, rolled over the land ; religion was at the flood—it was the theme on every lip ; men turned aside from the busy mart at the hour of noon, and thronged the places of prayer ; the workshop, the drinking-saloon, the theatre, the highway, became consecrated places, where the voice of singing and of supplication from earnest penitents and exultant converts was heard ; the sanctuaries were crowded with men and women, asking what they must do to be saved ; not alone the women and children, but men— strong, wicked men, who hitherto had neither regarded man nor feared God—mourned for their sins, and rejoiced in the freedom of forgiveness ; ministers whose popularity had declined were invested with new favour, and the different denominations, that had been until recently either antagonistic or indifferent, were suddenly fused into a thorough union and co-operation.

Mr. Cookman knew enough to put himself abreast this Divine flood, and to move with it. Neither the general spirit of revival nor his tact can wholly explain his success.

It is proper to call attention to an important fact of personal experience, which rendered his ministry at Green Street, in his own opinion, the most pregnant period of his history. It will be remembered that within a few months after obtaining the evidence of "perfect love," through inadvertency he lost it. Through these years his position on this great subject had not been at all satisfactory to himself. It had been hesitating. Doubts, questionings had disturbed his mind; and though he was mainly in sympathy with the doctrine of "full salvation," still there was neither a definite view nor a settled experience. His ministry was acceptable and useful; he was truly devoted to God and His cause, but yet he was ill at ease, and his soul, under a deep sense of unrealized power, was often sorrowful. The war of contending feelings marred his peace and frittered his strength; something he needed to lift him out of this conflict, and to develop all the resources of his spiritual nature into the utmost unity and force. The Spirit of God was gently but surely leading him backward and forward at the same time —backward to the simple, child-like faith in which he stood at Newtown, and forward to the same faith, re-enforced by an experience which could more fully guard it, through a knowledge of the errors that caused its forfeiture, and the memory of the bitterness which that forfeiture had entailed.

Whatever had been lost during these ten years of comparative failure, all was not lost. I do not mean that simply a saved, justified condition had been maintained; this no one can question; but I mean that there had been progress in the deeper knowledge of God's Word, in the more thorough insight into his own heart, in the increased confidence in the agencies of the Gospel, acquired by a longer and broader

observation—all of which constituted preparations for that
subsequent experience which in its marks and results became
so signal and abiding.   To one who has gained some great
height by untrodden and devious paths, there may seem a
much straighter course when he looks back over the broad
sweep through which he has passed ; but he cannot say that
any step, much less which step, has been useless in the
successive steps that have brought him to the eminence on
which he stands.

There is a certain positiveness in a knowledge which is
worked out for one's self, to which the soul comes through
its own provings amid doubts, fears, temptations, that im-
parts a conviction of truthfulness, a tenacity of purpose,
which is an indispensable element in him who in any sense
is to be a leader in God's advanced hosts.   The stand which
Alfred Cookman was about to take at Green Street for the
doctrine of " perfect love " would be quite a different stand
from that which he took on Attleboro Circuit in the first
inexperienced months of his ministry ; not different in the
nature of the work accomplished, nor in the evidences accompanying it, but in the increased capacity which he would
have to understand, to hold, and to propagate it.   Thence-
forth neither the jokes of his brethren nor the arguments of
those who, either for cavil or conscience, saw fit to differ
with him, would be able to move him.

It was not a necessity that he should have lost the witness
of entire sanctification, much less that he should have
continued so long a time without its restoration, but it is a
significant fact in the history of many of those who have
received this witness, that they seldom remain from the
beginning uninterruptedly in its possession and enjoyment.
From want of a full perception of the conditions of the
higher order of life, from a defect of judgment which can be

corrected only by experience, the soul which has rejoiced in the evidence of love made perfect not unfrequently comes under a darkness which is more or less protracted. One of the most merciful provisions of Christianity is that all believers, of whatever stage of attainment or degree of faith, may so long as they live learn by the things which they suffer, and be corrected by their very mistakes. It is of God's infinite wisdom and goodness so to sanctify to the good man even his errors, that by them he shall rise into a corrected and purer life.

As joints to stalks, condensing their substance and giving firmness for the support of further growth ; as knots in the threads, binding them into unity and strength as hither and thither they cross each other in weaving the fisher's net, so the covenants of good men gather up their otherwise scattered resources, and compact them into the higher forms of spiritual efficiency.

I give in his own words the account of his restoration to this great Scriptural blessing :—

" Oh, how many precious years I wasted in quibbling and debating respecting the great differences, not seeing that I was antagonizing a doctrine which must be spiritually discerned, and the tendency of which is to bring people nearer God. Meanwhile I had foolishly fallen into the habit of using tobacco, an indulgence which, while it afforded, palatably, gratification, at the same time seemed to satisfy both my nervous and social nature. Years elapsed. When I would confront the obligation of entire consecration, the sacrifice of my foolish habit would be presented as a test of obedience ; I would consent. Light, strength, and blessing were the result. Afterward temptation would be presented. I would listen to suggestions like this : ' This is one of the good things of God ; your religion does not require a course of asceticism ; this indulgence 'is not specifically forbidden in the New Testament ; some good people whom you know are addicted to this practice,' thus seeking to quiet an uneasy conscience. I would draw back into the old habit again. After a while I began to see that the indulgence at best was *doubtful for me*, and that I was giving my carnality rather than my Christian experience the benefit of the doubt. It could not harm me to give it up, while to persist in the practice was costing me too much in my religious enjoyment.

" I found that after all my objections to sanctification as a distinct work of grace, there was nevertheless a conscious lack in my own religious experience—it was not strong, round, full, abiding. I frequently asked myself, ' What is that I need and desire in comparison with what I have and profess ?' I looked at the three steps insisted upon by the friends of holiness,—namely, ' First, entire consecration ; second, acceptance of Jesus moment by moment as a perfect Saviour ; third, a meek and definite profession of the grace received ' ; and I said, ' These are Scriptural and reasonable duties.'

" The remembrance of my experience in Newtown supplied an overwhelming confirmation of all this, and at the same time a powerful stimulant in the direction of duty. What then ? ' I will cast aside all preconceived theories, doubtful indulgences, and culpable unbelief, and retrace my steps.' Alas, that I should have wandered from the light at all, and afterward wasted so many years in vacillating between self and God ! Can I ever forgive myself? Oh, what bitter, bitter memories ! The acknowledgment I make is constrained by candour and a concern for others. It is the greatest humiliation of my life. If I had the ear of those who have entered into the clearer light of Christian purity, I would beseech and charge them with a brother's interest and earnestness that they be warned by my folly. Oh, let such consent to die, if it were possible, ten deaths before they wilfully depart from the path of holiness; for, if they retrace their steps, there will still be the remembrance of original purity tarnished, and that will prove a drop of bitterness in the cup of their sweetest comfort.

"Eternal praise to my long-suffering Lord, nearly ten years have elapsed since, as the pastor of Green Street Church in the city of Philadelphia, I again carefully and fully dedicated my all to God, the consecration of course including the doubtful indulgence. I said, 'I will try to abstain for Christ's sake; I trust I would do anything for His sake, and certainly I can consent to this self-denial that Jesus may be glorified.' I again accepted Christ as my Saviour from all sin, realized the witness of the same Spirit, and since then have been walking in the light as God is in the light, realizing that experimental doctrine of the fellowship and communion with saints, and humbly and gratefully testify that the blood of Jesus cleanseth me from all sin. 'As ye have received Christ Jesus the Lord, so walk ye in Him'; that is, as I understand, 'Maintain the same attitude before God you assumed when you accepted Christ as your all-sufficient Saviour.' I received Him in a spirit of entire consecration, implicit faith, and humble confession. The constant repetition of these three steps, I find, enables me to walk in Him. I cannot afford for a single moment ever to remove my offering, to fail in looking unto Jesus, or to part with the spirit of confession.

"Thus I have honestly unfolded some personal experience in connection with the higher life; the recital humbles me in the dust, as it calls up the memory of years of vacillating and unsatisfactory religious life, but it also fills me with the profoundest gratitude for that abounding grace which not only bore with me, but brought me to see again my privilege in the Gospel, and now for ten years has been preserving me in the experience and blessing, and in the profession of this great grace. Precious reader, I now offer you the testimony ; but mark, before it meets your eye it has been carefully placed upon the Altar that sanctifieth the gift, and an earnest prayer offered that it may be blessed to your spiritual profit. As you lay down this humble article, will you not, for your own sake and for the Church's sake, resolve to be entirely and eternally the Lord's ?   God help and bless you ! "

The candour, directness, and fervour which pervade this statement must commend it to every one.   The " Tobacco Test " was for himself alone ; the use of tobacco was in *his* way, in the full consecration which he sought to make to God ; he did not pretend to raise it as a question for any one else.   With him whatsoever is not of faith is sin; what he could not do conscientiously, he could not do at all ; but he would have others to think and act for themselves in doubt-ful matters, believing that every man should be fully per-suaded in his own mind.   Mr. Cookman, in the presentation of the Christian life, was the farthest removed from a narrow and censorious spirit ; he never raised artificial conditions ; was not given to the specifying of isolated acts either of self-denial or performance, but rather inculcated a broad, deep, thorough devotion, under whose enlightened impulse he was sure the new-born, or the wholly sanctified soul, would adjust itself to the Divine requirements.   It was of little consequence to him whether a brother accepted liter-ally his methods or opinions on minor points of personal habit, so he had the root of holiness, and showed in his life its essential fruits.   Here was a point which aided not a little to give him influence over all classes of minds.

Nothing can possibly exceed the emphasis with which our

friend was henceforth committed to the doctrine of "perfect love." "Heart purity"—a favourite expression with him— was from this time to the close of his life the distinctive theme of his ministry; not, however, to the exclusion of other topics, but as comprehending all phases of Christian truth, penetrating and vivifying them with its light. It absorbed his best thoughts; it was the burden of his ablest sermons; it was that which was best in him as a man; his whole being was permeated with its unction; at home or abroad, in the pulpit or the social circle, in the study or by the seashore, at the altar of prayer or by the sick-bed, the instinct of his soul, the atmosphere of his life, was "Holiness to the Lord."

In connection with his preaching talents, his skill as an administrator of Church affairs, his aptitude with the Sunday School, and his engaging manners, this re-baptism with the Spirit of power at Green Street was most opportune. It fully equipped him as a good soldier of Christ for the arduous and eventful campaign which lay before him. What a pity it is that the details of a pastorate so replete with incident and instruction are almost wholly lost for the want of any proper record! The words spoken, the deeds done, are bearing fruit in souls, and their only transcript is the holy and happy lives they helped to form.

The revival spoken of began during the first winter (1857-8) of Mr. Cookman's ministry at Green Street.

I have at hand a report of one of his sermons preached during this great revival. Its insertion is in point, as tending to illustrate the style of his extemporaneous discourses, and the character of those thrilling home-thrust appeals by which he roused the consciences of his hearers :—

"'*Thou fool, this night thy soul shall be required of thee.*'
"These words, contained in St. Luke's Gospel, twelfth chapter, and

twentieth verse, constitute the subject of a sermon preached last Sabbath evening in the Methodist Church, Green Street, below Eleventh,
by the pastor, Rev. Alfred Cookman.

"Mr. Cookman is among the youngest members of the ministry of
Philadelphia, and so too among the most promising of their number.
His genius seems to be eagle-winged, soaring aloof from either notes or
manuscript, and pouring itself out in an easy-flowing stream of eloquence, as sublime in its flights as it is forcible in argument.

"The popular appreciation of this promising young preacher is well
expressed in the immense audiences which usually throng the church in
which he is stationed.   On the present occasion the house was literally
crowded.   In attempting a synopsis of his able discourse, however, we
shall endeavour rather to preserve the chain of his argument than to
give a faithful transcript on paper of his style of oratory. . .

"The speaker here announced that the special point of inquiry to
which he desired to call the attention of his hearers was,

"'IN WHAT DID THIS MAN'S FOLLY CONSIST?'

"'The most degrading epithet to be found in the vocabulary of
language had been applied to the subject referred to in the parable.

"'Such an expression ("thou fool"), coming from the source it did,
must have had sufficient reason to sustain it.   But here arose the difficulty.   The great principle intended to be taught by this parable the
reasoning of the *world* was not prepared to receive.   Here, indeed, was
the issue.   The judgment of God was arrayed against the judgment of
unconverted man.

"'To proceed, however, with the investigation into the folly of this
rich owner of certain lands, we should be told, *first*—in vindication of
his course—that he had been a *rich man ;* and it was an indisputable
fact that *riches covered a multitude of sins !*   He knew, from the fact that
rich men were almost universally lauded for their wisdom, that the process of fastening the charge of folly upon so distinguished a one of
their number was no idle undertaking.   Again, it would be pleaded in
his behalf that he had been industrious and persevering, and had, as a
consequence, reaped an abundant harvest as his reward ; but the question here arose, "Do enterprise and wisdom, in all cases, constitute
synonymous terms?"   He thought not.   Moreover, he would probably
be accounted a wise man because he had *taken thought*, within himself,
as to "what he should do."

"'Yes, he had taken thought, and the conclusion of his thoughts
had been that he would build new barns, and on announcing this resolution he did not doubt but that he had been regarded as the very wisest
man in all that region.   But, again, the world would give him credit for

acting *wisely*, in that he had resolved to enjoy himself with the good things he had accumulated all the rest of his days—for having taken a resolution, probably, of associating with him in his enjoyments a few select boon companions, who should revel with him in the delight he was then picturing to his soul.'

" Here the speaker saw pictured before his imagination the phantom of this prince reclining upon his silken couch at the dead hour of night, revolving in his mind the glorious future that awaited him. This delineation was at once artistic, eloquent, and thrilling. ' It was at the dead hour of night : the labourers of his fields were soundly slumbering in other apartments of his splendid dwelling ; but sleep on her airy pinions came not to woo his wakeful soul to regions of repose. No, no—his mind was too much engaged in counting over the vastness of his wealth ; picturing before his excited vision the full-grown proportions of his newly-conceived barns ; devising the magnificent entertainments with which he meant to regale his admiring friends. So his soul was wandering into the treacherous regions of the undiscovered future, counting up the years of pleasure yet to come, when lo ! suddenly as the lightning's flash—a voice aroused him—a voice from a quarter least expected and most dreaded thundered in his ear the terrible doom—" THIS NIGHT !—*thy soul shall be required of thee!*"

" ' Never had Belshazzar been more terrified when the miraculous hand had written his doom upon the wall of his banqueting-chamber than had the rich man been at this midnight announcement. Never had Saul of Tarsus been more awe-struck when at the gates of Damascus he had been stricken sightless from his horse by a light from heaven, than had this man been on hearing his unlooked-for doom at this silent hour of the night. And well it might be so. His transition from the regions of his vision into the vestibule of eternity, in a single instant, and the certainty that before the rosy dawn of morn he should appear in the presence of a sin-judging Jehovah, were enough to have wrung from his lips the burning confession—" 'Tis true, I am a FOOL indeed !"

" ' But he would ask again, " Wherein did his folly most particularly appear ?"

" ' His answer to this would be, first, " *Because he had forgotten the claims of God !*" He had undertaken to arrange for himself a train of future happiness—had begun the work of hewing out for himself " broken cisterns that could hold no water "—had lost sight of the *living* pleasures of the future—was indeed basking in pleasures to some extent of which God does not wish to deprive His children ; but the matter which pre-eminently stamped him as a fool was *that he had forgotten the Author of all his mercies.*

10

"'When he had retired at night, good angels had long watched around his couch, but they heard no voice of thankfulness offered to their Father in Heaven. Others had mourned in penitence over their transgressions, but he had no tears to shed over his sins; others had pleaded for favours from the Divine hand, but he had no prayer to offer; others had prayed for light to see the truth, but he had no such desire, for "he loved darkness rather than light, because his deeds were evil"; and from all this it was that the appellation of "fool" had been justly applied to him.

"'But his folly was apparent, in the *second place*, because *he had forgotten the claims of his soul.*

"'He had said, "Soul, take thine ease," and herein had been committed his capital mistake. What an insult to the soul was this!—to undertake to satisfy the future longings of the soul by offering it a species of gratification that would be equally tempting to a brute!

"'"A fool!" exclaims the objector, with perfect astonishment, "and did he not assiduously employ his thinking faculties? did he not ask within himself what he should do?" Yes, he admitted that he had asked this question; and had it been in his (the speaker's) province to reply, he should have answered him, "Feed the hungry and clothe the naked"; but his inquiry had not been what he should do *to be saved*, but what he should do for his body. All his inquiries had been concerning matters confined to this world, entirely forgetting the capacities and duration of the soul.' Here the speaker inserted an emphatic pause, and then continued, that he 'hoped all his hearers would duly consider the value of an immortal soul—and withal consider well the uncertain character of its earthly pilgrimage. Poised, as it were, upon a little point of time, with heaven above, hell beneath, and eternity beyond, requiring but the slightest vibration of Jehovah's breath to blow it away for ever!

"'To neglect this, no matter what might be our earthly achievements, we should gain nothing. "For what shall it profit a man (he prayed to God that this inquiry might sink deep into our hearts) if he gain the whole world and lose his own soul?"

"'But again: He had not only forgotten the claims of the soul, but also the *claims of death.* "Soul, thou hast laid up for *many years,*" had been his declaration. And what a declaration this for a being whose breath was in his nostrils! It was well to bear in mind that of all known uncertainties, *life* was the most uncertain. Wealth, by means of strong walls and iron chests, might be safely secured; reputation, by preserving a strict correctness in all our walks and actions, might be retained; but see! how is it with human life? Mark yonder railroad-train flying along the iron way with lightning speed—there is a sudden crash! It was the work of an instant; and now we may pass around among the dead, the dying, and the wounded of that mass of living, happy beings but a moment before! Yes, even to-day the realization of a scene like this had been echoed through our streets, and his hearers had doubtless heard of it.

"'Die we must, be our circumstances whatever they may. We could not tell what would become of us, yet heaven or hell *must* be our destiny.

"'Death had come to the rich man in the text, and at the dead hour of night laid his skeleton hand upon him, and thundered into his ears, "This night thy soul shall be required!" Then probably the first prayer had been wrung from those ungrateful lips, as he implored the fell messenger to spare him but till morning, that he might take leave of his family, or that he might execute his will, or, above all, that he might have if it were but an hour to make his peace with God. But no! the decree of the avenger had gone forth, and was inexorable in its demands. Now was the time—now he must die!

"'Oh! how great had been the folly of this man—and yet there were many of us quite as foolish as he: like fools we were living, and, like the arch-infidel Voltaire, when we came to die it would be to "take a leap in the dark."

"'But *lastly:* He had not only forgotten the claims of God, of his soul, and of death, but he had forgotten the claims of judgment. The evidences of Scripture were most explicit that "what a man soweth, that shall he also reap." Another rule was, that in proportion as we had received it would be required of us in the end. And in view of this, he would ask of the soul that had never been washed in the laver of regeneration—that had never responded to the noble impulses of a god-like charity, but whose whole existence had been devoted to the circumscribed limits of self-aggrandizement—of what value was it all? for in the hour of death all would have to be given up. And then that awful future! where, instead of drinking of the pure, delightful waters that flow from beneath the Father's throne, the lost soul must drink the bitter cup of the Father's wrath, even to its dregs; and, instead of basking amid the melodies of heavenly anthems, must for ever dwell amid the desponding echoes of the groans of the tormented.'

"The above sermon was an extemporaneous effort entirely, and elicited the most marked attention throughout its delivery."

The services of Mr. Cookman at the dedication of

Waugh Chapel, produced at Washington the impression which the advent of a "Cookman" was adapted to make in the national capital. A correspondent of one of our *Advocates* wrote of the occasion :—

"I will allude to but one more point, and that is the dedication of the Waugh Chapel last Sabbath. The services were extremely interesting. The sermons, in the morning and afternoon, were preached by the Revs. Alfred Cookman and John Emory Cookman, both sons of the late lamented George Cookman, who was lost on the ill-fated "President." Both of these young men partake in a remarkable degree of the spirit and eloquence which characterized their father, especially as seen in his little volume of published speeches and sermons. The sermon in the morning was a beautiful exposition of the reasons why the apostle 'gloried in the Cross,' in which the youthful speaker held an overflowing audience, among whom were many members of Congress and judges of the Supreme Court, in almost breathless attention for more than an hour. In the afternoon there was another great crowd to hear John Emory Cookman, who is, I learn, only nineteen years of age, and who has been a member of the Church but one year. Both of these young men are destined ere long, if their lives are spared, to rank among the most popular pulpit orators in our country."

Among the conversions with which God honoured the ministry of Mr. Cookman during this period was that of his brother George, who, though next oldest to himself, had never before professed saving faith in Christ. On the first Sabbath evening of January, 1859, Mr. Cookman preached a most solemn and earnest sermon on the word "Now" to an immense congregation, and at its close invited penitents to the altar. He was feeling that night an especial solicitude for the conversion of his brother. The brother was seated in the rear of the choir (front) gallery, and, though the obstacles were apparently great, he deliberately arose, descended to the lower floor, and came forward to the altar and was converted. Nothing could exceed the joy of the pastor at this result, in which the brother who had been the companion of his boyhood was given to him in the fellow- ..hip of Jesus. The two became inseparable workers for the Master—George rivalling in the ranks of the laity the zeal and usefulness of Alfred in the ranks of the ministry. If Alfred's ministry at Green Street had done nothing more than to give to Methodism and to Christianity at large in Philadelphia, George Cookman, as an example of piety and earnest work, it would have been enough. His career was destined to be short, but full of good fruits, and such as only few young laymen in America have lived.

As evincing the manifold character of Mr. Cookman's ministry at this time, his adaptation to all classes, the attractiveness of his singularly pure and persuasive influence, there was a young Friend taken into the Church by him who has since filled no small place in the public estimation. This thoughtful, ardent young woman found in Mr. Cook- man's spirit and instructions what her nature needed. She came out from the Society of Friends, and united with the Methodist Episcopal Church. She showed a genuine piety, an inquiring temper, and promise of marked usefulness. What her precise relations to the Christian Church may be at present, I do not know ; but there is not a loyal heart in all America that has not beaten responsively to the truthful, brave, and eloquent words which she afterward uttered in the nation's darkest trials. Her scathing rebukes of treason and her searching exposures of wrong, her animated, cheer- ful eulogies of liberty, heroism, and the flag, have roused to hatred of violence and to love of right even where the arguments of men had failed. I refer to Miss Annie E. Dickinson. The tribute which she has kindly written to the memory of him who was for so brief a time her pastor abundantly attests the depth of her attachment for him, and proves that her heart must be in sympathy with the great truths which it was his single joy to advance. Her words are :—

"It is not an easy task you mark me. . . . Years have gone by since I sat down by your brother, looked into a face that warmed like the sun, and listened to a voice that called me away from all things poor and mean and earthly, as a strain of celestial music might call.

"Long years full of strife and care and toil—yet face and voice seem and sound as clear as though they shone and spoke but yesterday.

"A love of humanity wide as humanity, a charity inexhaustible, an earnestness that stirred the most careless, a hungering and thirsting after righteousness—not for its rewards—a tireless effort in season and out of season, with tender, yet powerful touch to mould and fashion others into the likeness of the Master ; a longing so boundless to *be* like his Master, as to wear through flesh and blood full early, and carry the sanctified soul to know Him 'face to face.'

"This was Alfred Cookman.

"Sad hearts out of count has he left behind ; eyes will grow dim and voices choked for years to come, when they think of or speak his name. For he was one of those rare souls so exalted as to breathe the atmosphere of heaven, yet so gently human as to draw love and tenderness from whoso approached him.

"So his life seems to me, and, so seeming, I would that my pen were gifted with some of his subtle power to show it forth to others.

"As it is, I speak from my heart."

Only one letter of Mr. Cookman of this particular period has come into my possession. It was written on his birthday to his wife at her parental home in Columbia, and breathes the child-like, playful spirit, the earnest, constant zeal which so uniformly and beautifully blended in his daily life. I can imagine the air of conscious dignity with which the presents of the little brothers were ac-

cepted, as though they had conferred upon their papa a
real benefaction :—

"PHILADELPHIA, *Tuesday afternoon, January* 4, 1859.

"Certainly you will expect me to act the correspondent on my *birthday*. Thirty-one years ago I struck Columbia in my descent to this
sorrow-smitten planet. From that starting-point I have prosecuted an
eventful and, in most respects, a delightful pilgrimage. To-day I erect
my Ebenezer again, and gratefully acknowledge 'hitherto hath the Lord
helped me.' Our meeting is progressing with considerable interest and
success. Last night, despite the snow-storm, the body of the church
was quite well filled. Brother E. J. Way preached an excellent sermon.
Ten presented themselves for prayers, and four were happily converted.
George is proceeding most prosperously in his Christian course ; he says
he is perfectly satisfied. Saidie tells us that last night he went to bed
joyously singing, 'I will believe, I now believe, that Jesus died for me.'
Nothing, she estimates, could exceed his tenderness and kindness to her.
He was always faithful and affectionate, but now, she states, there is an
expression and exhibition of this feeling she has never seen before. It
will inaugurate a new epoch in their domestic history. Saidie is resolved
that George shall not go to heaven without her. Her mind, I think, is
made up to walk with him in the narrow way. She talks about nothing
else, and weeps almost constantly. Oh that her night may soon end in
joyous day ! The children are both well. Just now they came into my
study and placed on my table their porte-monnaies, saying, 'Pa, this is
your birthday present from us.' Dear little fellows ! they did it of their
own accord, and in perfect good faith. I put their present in my pocket,
and thanked them very sincerely. They will not be separated. George
asks a great many questions about his sister Annie ; wants to know if
she will live after the doctor cuts her with his lancet. When I speak of
ma's return, their little eyes dance with delight."

I close the Green Street pastorate with a brief testimony
from J. F. Bird, M.D., a member of the charge :—

"He got behind the 'Cross' on the occasion of his first sermon, and
there remained until his term, which continued for two years, was ended.
The young people crowded to hear him, and very many became *earnest*
members of the Church through his instrumentality, and are now doing
good service in 'every good word and work.' Among them was his
brother George. At one of the most interesting services ever held in

this or any other church, this dearly beloved brother presented himself at the altar, and very soon was happily converted. In writing to an absent friend, giving an account of this conversion, he said, ' I shout with my pen and with my soul over the auspicious event.' He had laboured for it and prayed for it incessantly by night and by day, and therefore could not but ' shout' when his desire was realized.

" Mr. Cookman always regarded this appointment as one of the happiest, as it was one of the most successful, of his ministerial career. He laboured for the *good* of the *people*. He lost sight of self. This was the secret of his success. An intelligent member of the Church was asked by a member of the Conference what was ' the secret of Cookman's success.' The answer was, ' His evident desire to do the people good.' "

CHAPTER XIII.

THE next turn of the itinerant wheel did not take Mr. Cookman far. He was appointed to the Union Church in Fourth Street, in March, 1859. The Union charge is the next oldest to St. George's in the city, and is surrounded by business houses, which have from year to year pressed out the resident population to remoter sections. It is still a strong station ; but at the time Mr. Cookman was sent to it, before other charges had been created, either wholly or partially from its membership, it was a powerful organization, including some of the most influential families of Methodism. Many of these families came from a distance, preferring to continue in connection with a Church with which they had been so long in close fellowship to joining those which were nearer their residences. The Union was consequently not so favourably located for a large congregation ; but its proximity to the hotels and its free seats were advantageous conditions, and Mr. Cookman's popularity began immediately to produce an increased attendance upon the public services.

As indicative of the high estimate in which Mr. Cookman's ministry was held, I make a brief extract from a letter of Mr. Thomas L. Mason, a well-known member of

Union Church. Writing to the Rev. John E. Cookman, he says :—

"When Alfred was in Pittsburgh he promised me that, if the appoint-ing power would agree to it, he would be pleased to be pastor of Union. When Conference met, Green Street (being heavily in debt) insisted upon having him, and to accommodate our Green Street friends we gave in, with the understanding that at the expiration of two years he would be sent to Union—and so he was. Our parsonage was in Eighth Street, above Race, but, to accommodate his little children, we removed it to 224. North Fifth Street, and partially refurnished it. He was received at Union with open arms and open hearts. Our congregations were good, our finances much improved. He was particularly successful with the young."

Mr. Cookman had the happiness of having many choice friends in the congregation. There were those under his ministry who had long held him in the highest personal esteem. His whole nature found scope for its gratification. Around genial hearth-stones his sanctified affections enjoyed agreeable companionship, while in the Church his hands were strengthened by judicious counsels and tender sympathies. The Rev. Andrew Longacre, laid aside by feeble health from the active work of the ministry, was a member of the congregation, and ministered, by his calm and gentle friendship, to his comfort and usefulness. His brother George, in the first flush of spiritual grace, with uncommon endowments of speech and song, was at his elbow. His own mother, also, was one of his flock. She who had so often fed him with the Word of life, must now be fed by him. But now, as before and since, she gave, if possible, more than she received. To lean on the support of a wisdom which, in his opinion, had become almost oracular, a faith which knew no abatement, a zeal which no waters could quench, was to him no slight privilege, a rich blessing in so arduous a position. There, too, was the sanctuary in the private house of Mr. J. B. Longacre, in Spring Garden Street, which the pastor could regard as very much his own, and to which, as to a quiet haven, he habitually resorted. The eldest daughter of Mr. Longacre, Mrs. John Keen, upon the decease of her devout mother, still maintained the meetings for "holiness" which her mother had founded. These meetings had been from their commencement a gathering-point for the friends of the higher Christian life in Philadelphia. Here Mr. Cookman's heart was often refreshed; and issuing thence with deeper, calmer thoughts of God, he entered upon the recurring duties of his large and laborious pastorate with perceptibly increased vigour and success.

More than ever before, the earnest pastor, thus beloved at home, was in demand abroad. Whether announced in his own city or in any other place, on special occasions, he was sure to be greeted by a throng of people. His preaching at times was with overwhelming effect. The Rev. Mr. Longacre gives an account of the popular influence of a sermon preached about this time at Penn's Grove camp-meeting in New Jersey :—

"I recall a sermon he preached at a camp-meeting in New Jersey, on the text 'Thy will be done.' The collection preceded the sermon, and it left the congregation a good deal unsettled. But at the first sound of his voice all was hushed into attention. As he preached and passed on into the appeal of his discourse, the whole vast throng was bowed in tears. People wept aloud, the preachers crowding the stand, and the passers-by on the edge of the circle. Near me was seated a travelling preacher of the Hicksite Friends. He had been restless at first, but gradually seemed subdued by the power of the preacher, until at the conclusion he stood up and cried with a loud voice, as if yielding to the constraining influence of the Spirit, 'We have heard the Gospel preached in the demonstration of the Spirit and with power.' We went to the tables right after the service, but for many minutes those at our table could not eat. We sat looking at each other, and weeping tears that could not be controlled."

During the autumn of 1859, Mr. Cookman was invited
to Baltimore to preach at Monument Street Church.   This
was one of the churches comprised in the Baltimore City
Station when his father was one of the pastors.   His coming
was a signal for an outpouring of his devoted friends and
the public generally.   He wrote to his wife :—

"I seize a moment to drop you a line.   These Baltimore friends are
so incessant in their attentions and so abundant in their kindness that I
have scarce opportunity to think of anything but what is passing around
me.

"Yesterday I preached to overflowing congregations.   Although the
North Baltimore friends had concluded *not* to advertise the service,
fearing an unmanageable crowd, yet both morning and evening *hundreds*
went away who could not be accommodated with standing-room.

"I preached ' Power ' in the morning, and the ' New Birth ' at night ;
in the afternoon made three addresses ; spent a sleepless night.   To-day
am hardly able to stagger about.   This morning at ten we had a *most
precious meeting* for an hour and a half.   My soul is kept in perfect
peace.   Oh the strong consolation there is in Christ !   How delightful
to labour when we realize the presence of the Master !

" Invitations for dinner and tea are more numerous than I can possibly
accept.   The friends vie with each other in their kind attentions.   Look
out for me on Wednesday.   Love to all friends.   Many kisses for the
children.   Tell them to be very good."

Again he wrote to his wife :—

"I am sure you will not object to receiving a few lines from a lonely
husband.   An exceedingly pleasant ride on the cars brought us to Philadelphia about five p.m.   On my way to the parsonage I, of course,
dropped in at the Race Street homestead.   Mother and Mary were
making their arrangements to sup with Mrs. W. W. Cookman.   All
were very well, and full of inquiries respecting yourself and the children.

"Arriving at the ' Fifth Street house,' I was welcomed by Lizzie
P——, who had everything very clean and comfortable.   Taking up my
letters and papers, I felt such a sense of loneliness as cannot be described.
I remembered this would not do, and as I bowed my knee in prayer
sweetly realized that I was in the best of company.   My compassionate
Saviour came quickly to my relief, and the room was transformed into
the audience-chamber of Deity.   Oh how unutterably sweet—how in-

describably valuable, is the religion of the Lord Jesus! My appreciation and enjoyment of its sacred influences are increasing day by day.

" My letters were from Rev. H. Slicer, enclosing an invitation and a free pass to the Shrewsbury camp-meeting ; and another from the Rev. Mr. Thomas, urging me to serve him on the occasion of a church dedication. The former I will avail myself of; the latter I must decline."

The Shrewsbury camp-meeting was a favourite resort of Mr. Cookman. He loved to meet the Baltimore Methodists. whenever he could, and nowhere were his labours more acceptable and useful than among them at the camp-meetings. He will be heard of again at Shrewsbury.

Mr. Cookman's pastoral term at Union, happy as it was in most of its aspects, was not wholly without trials. It covered a period which was one of great anxiety and perplexity both in the State and the Church. The " irrepressible conflict" between slavery and freedom was fast approaching a crisis. The elements of dissatisfaction and discord which had been rising and gathering, had assumed such intensity as to forebode the most violent and destructive storm. The whole nation trembled with uncontrollable agitation; every ecclesiastical organization, and more especially the Methodist Episcopal Church, was shaking to its centre with a controversy, the sharpness of which had precipitated the most equable men into bitter hostility. Hatred was fast taking the place of love, distrust of confidence ; lifetime friends were becoming alienated ; section was arraying itself against section; Northern opinion was divided ; men stood side by side on 'Change, or sat side by side in the pew, or ate together, members of the same family, who differed almost wholly in their judgment of the causes and the cure of national and ecclesiastical troubles.

It was one of those times of decision in which Almighty God brings nations and individuals to the bar of judgment, and to which destiny holds them with an inexorable grasp. The wisest men stood bewildered in counsel ; Conservatives were wringing their hands in despair or clinching their fists in fury ; and even Radicals, while not doubting the correctness of their principles, were alarmed at the consequences which their success threatened to entail. "Conscience," exclaimed Mr. Hunter, of Virginia, in the United States Senate, "has done this. Sir, there is no hope of reconciliation or of the Union ; the *conscience* of the North is against us." It was so ; the enlightened conscience of the free states had reached a point when it could no longer tolerate the extension of slavery.

This conscience, however, was not yet prepared to demand its abolition in the slave states. Very few of the most pronounced anti-slavery men felt themselves to be a party to the wrong where it was protected by municipal law, and was beyond any possible constitutional process except by the concurrence of those who framed these municipal laws. Yet there were men in the Church whose conscience compelled them to exert themselves to abate slavery in the Church by requiring all slave-holding members to emancipate their slaves. They wished thus to leaven the State through the Church ; to assist in creating, by a clear testimony and by such ecclesiastical pressure as they could command, a public sentiment in favour of "abolition." There were differences of opinion as to the power of the General Conference of the Methodist Episcopal Church to expel members for slave-holding, and also as to the expediency of exercising this power if it existed. The differences of opinion were not confined to any locality of the Church, though those who held an opinion adverse to such a power were massed mostly along the "Border Conferences," embracing the Baltimore, Philadelphia, Pittsburgh, West

Virginia, and Missouri Conferences, with contiguous Conferences lying north.

The whole question has since been consigned by the " logic of events " to a dead past, and is of interest chiefly as one of the teachings of history. No issues which have since transpired can throw the shadow of a suspicion on the honesty of the men who, in so great a debate, stood and acted apart. Time has healed—no, victory, in the happiest fruits of righteousness and peace, has healed—the breaches of the angry strife. But it was an ordeal for many souls which cannot soon be forgotten—a fiery trial ; and though it only consumed the straw, that the gold might shine with the richer splendour, it was not the less painful in its endurance.

Mr. Cookman was among those who believed that a law should be enacted excluding slave-holders from the Church. When measures were introduced to effect this change, through what was deemed the proper constitutional process, he gave them his prompt and uniform support by voting for them. He stood almost alone in his Conference. There was a small knot of six of seven men out of about three hundred, and these were most of them men of advanced years. He was young, bright, popular,—the idol of his brethren and of the people ; his early education had been in the South ; his principal friends were either slave-holders or their sympathizers ; his opinions seemed to impugn the piety of people who nourished him in infancy and youth ; his vote seemed to fasten sin on those who were regarded as above reproach ; the measure he supported must exclude many from the Church whom he hoped to meet in heaven, and even apparently blot with a stain the memory of many who had died in the faith. But Alfred Cookman felt that he must do his duty. He would not follow his principles to all their logical results; he could only see principles, and to them he must stand.

He did not question the piety and virtue of thousands hitherto and then involved in slave-holding; but of two evils he must accept the least. The opportunity had come for him to act, and it was for him to say whether he should spare the feelings of friends, or do what he could to liberate five millions of slaves; whether he should pander to a spirit of oppression, even though softened by religion, or strike a blow for universal freedom. He rose to the crisis of the hour. Cutting away from all social and personal entanglements, the man stood forth in an act of moral heroism seldom surpassed in the history of Methodism. When the resolutions initiating the change were pending before his Conference, he got down on his knees in the pew, and, bathed in tears, poured out his soul to God for light and strength, and arose and voted "*Aye!*" Here was the iron in his nature.

Let those who think Alfred Cookman was not a man of the truest and highest courage mark this. His forbearance for the weaknesses of men, his indisposition to insist upon points in which men differed with him, his great charity, which folded in its arms earnest souls and dropped out of sight their accidental disagreements, have been construed into a want of courage. Mr. Cookman never wasted his force on men of straw, but when real giants were to be crushed, he had the power to do it.

In keeping with the vote thus given was the sermon he preached in his own church about the same period, called by one his "*grand, grand* anti-slavery sermon," from Isaiah viii. 12, 13. As might be expected, some of his nearest friends and principal supporters were wounded, and did not hesitate to express their displeasure. His only answer to all such was, " I can afford to forgive them." Under an oppressive sense of the responsibility which a declaration of his views would involve, he had made the sermon on his knees. He delivered it with the greatest fearlessness, and at the same time with an evident sincerity and tenderness, which convinced all who heard him that nothing short of the most thorough loyalty to the great Master animated his soul. At the close of the service his face shone with a spiritual light that showed how closely he had communed with the Holy Spirit, and how triumphantly the Spirit had vindicated him in the discharge of a most painful duty.

We have before seen the fatherly interest Mr. Cookman manifested when his youngest brother was first meditating the ministry ; now that his brother was fairly engaged in the direct and indirect duties which it brought, he could not do otherwise than afford him all possible counsel and sympathy. His brother John had only recently become a pastor at New Brunswick, New Jersey, and was to visit Philadelphia, to address the Young Men's Christian Association. He wrote to his brother :—

" PHILADELPHIA, *November* 16, 1860.

" Perhaps you are ready to chide my delay in replying to your letter. The reason of my procrastination was that the information you desired had to be sought, and could not be had until after a meeting of the managers of the Young Men's Christian Association. That meeting was held on Wednesday evening, when it was resolved to postpone the anniversary until the evening of the 3rd of December, when it will come off at Concert Hall. Had it been held before, some one of the churches must have been the place selected. A very general and earnest wish was expressed that you might be one of the speakers. Dr. Tyng has declined. Mr. Crowell and Dr. Newton are spoken of as your colleagues. Respecting a theme, I scarcely know what to say. The relation of Christian young men to the times, or the responsibility and duties in the present crisis of our national and world's history, would, I think, be suitable.

11

"The value of a powerful illustration can scarcely be estimated. I say this as an offset to the claim you set up, '*Pay what thou owest.*' I could do this in a fortnight of sermons, and, retaining '*the figure,*' be decidedly the gainer. You know, however, that I love to act generously. No one is more interested for your success than myself. It is my triumph to see you triumph. '*Cookman*' is the name which, with the blessing of God, I desire to float aloft, commanding the respect, confidence, and affection of the world. Family pride (I trust it is sanctified) has a wonderful development in my experience. My beloved brother, never do anything or say anything that would lower that name one iota in public estimation. If we desire our name to remain unimpeached and be increasingly honoured, then, struggling up above the infected atmosphere of this lower world, let us stand in the clear, broad, beautiful sunlight of God's immediate presence. Men will recognise us as Christ's; honour our principles, respect our character, and yield to our influence. John, take my advice, and be satisfied with nothing less than a heart constantly filled with God. It is a grand idea and a grander experience to be co-workers with God; infinite wisdom and illimitable power enlisted in our behalf. It helps us to think, to study, to pray, to preach, and to labour; it becomes the guarantee of inevitable and glorious success. I mean all I write, and hope that you will immediately put this matter to an experimental test.

"But to the illustration. I have been turning it over in my thoughts, and cannot call up anything that I think could be rendered more effective than Tennyson's 'Charge of the Light Brigade' at Balaklava. I enclose a copy, which you will please preserve, and return when you have done with it. Its application to this light brigade of young soldiers for Jesus, charging upon the flanked batteries of hell, would, I think, be very thrilling. *Forward the light brigade;* ring the changes just here.

"How are dear mother and Mary? We have many inquiries respecting their welfare. Will you not all come to spend the Christmas holidays in Philadelphia? I think you might excuse Mary *at once*, and allow her Philadelphia friends a chance. The festival at Sansom Street Hall passed off splendidly. Among the rest, Mr. Reese Alsop was present. He scanned our crowd as if he would find a cherished one. Dr. Kennaday is preaching this week at Trinity. No special interest is reported. The services are held in the lecture-room. The Tuesday afternoon meeting is largely attended, and I think increasingly interesting. The children's class is getting on nicely under the auspices of M—— W——. She is vindicating the wisdom of our selection. Take good care of yourself, or rather commit yourself, body, soul, and all, to Christ, and let *Him* take care of you."

It could hardly be otherwise than that Mr. Cookman's reputation should attract attention in New York. We accordingly find him invited thither on different occasions to speak at public meetings, and to represent the Philadelphia churches. In the autumn of 1860 he spoke at the anniversary of " Five Points' Mission," under the care of the ladies of the Methodist Episcopal Church. The anniversary was held at the Academy of Music. The audience was very large and enthusiastic. " His address," said a gentleman, recently, " I can never forget. The three principal figures—the child and the Bible, the woman and her diamond ring, the sinking ship—are as vivid as if I had heard them only yesterday." A visit to New York, in company with Mr. George H. Stuart and other prominent Philadelphia gentlemen, to wait on a delegation of Irish Christians, was noticed by him in the following pleasant way to his wife :—

" METROPOLITAN HOTEL, NEW YORK, *Friday morning.*

" How very gladly do I seize a moment this morning to add to your pleasure, for I am sure you will be delighted to hear from your *itinerant* husband. In company with Revs. Westbrook, Taylor, Wylie, and other gentlemen, I enjoyed exceedingly the journey from Philadelphia to New York. Mr. Taylor and I, seated side by side, engaged in a decidedly religious conversation, which proved a very feast to my soul. Indeed, ever since my departure, my blessed Father has kept my mind in perfect peace. I very sweetly realize that He is around and within and all about me. Oh the unutterable joy of uninterrupted communion with God ! Mr. Stuart was at the hotel to give us one of his warm-hearted welcomes. After some ablutions, etc., we proceeded to the Cooper Institute. Owing to the storm, there was no crowd, but a very respectable attendance—certainly one thousand people. The exercises throughout were unusually spirited and interesting.

" The honoured representatives of Ireland acquitted themselves very creditably. Your unworthy husband was called out. I said what was in my heart at the moment, and was kindly received. I feel it such a privilege to plead, under such circumstances, the promise, ' Lo, I am

with you *alway*,' and find the presence of my Master on the platform
as in the pulpit.   About midnight we went to Mr. Stuart's room, and
enjoyed together a season of prayer; after which, at peace with God and
men, I placed my head on the pillow, and was soon lost in the oblivion
of sweet sleep.   This morning I am very well, and feel my heart overflowing with love to God.   At noon I must be present at the Fulton
Street prayer-meeting.   My friends around are very polite and affectionate.   How much I love, and how grateful I feel for Christian companions ! How are my darling wife and precious children this morning ?
I need not tell you how dear you all are to me.   Many kisses for the
boys and little sister.   Tell them that pa hopes they will be very
obedient to ma, and very kind to each other."

This letter suggests a marked feature in the character and
ministry of Mr. Cookman during these four years, which
has not yet been as distinctly noticed as its importance and
the full representation of his career require.   I refer to his
position as a representative man before the evangelical
churches of Philadelphia.   While there never was a more
pronounced Methodist than he, I doubt if there ever was
one freer from bigotry.   He dwelt in a high serene atmosphere of love, whence he could look down and see all the
bounds and fences of sectarianism dissolve in the unbroken
sweep of Christian unity.   He loved all Christ's followers,
and was ready at all times to act with them in those un-
denominational movements which contemplate the glory of
His kingdom in the salvation of men.   The churches were
not slow to perceive his mind and to feel the kindle of his
spirit; and hence both for his piety and his talents he
became by common consent the leading man of his Methodist brethren as a mover in those stirring days of revival to
which allusion has already been made.   He was closely
identified with such men as the Rev. Messrs. Newton,
Brainard, Taylor, Dudley Tyng, Reuben Jeffrey, and Mr.
George H. Stuart, in promoting the general work of religion.
A young man, he was in full sympathy with the Young Men's

Christian Association, as an institution providentially raised up to afford not only a beautiful expression of Christian union, but also a common ground for the most effective labours of all believers for the temporal and spiritual welfare of young men. He and other pastors were glad to labour under the leadership of the layman whose name is a synonym for pure philanthropy throughout our country. The work accomplished in those early days of the Association of Philadelphia can hardly be too highly estimated, and has only been paralleled by that of the Christian Commission during the late civil war.

Mr. Stuart has not ceased to value the services and to cherish the memory of his friend Mr. Cookman. He has kindly furnished to the Rev. John E. Cookman a brief estimate of his character and work as they impressed him at this time :—

" I have been privileged to know many faithful and gifted servants o Christ, and to know them a second time in the perusal of their biographies—Dr. Murray, of Elizabeth ; Drs. Edgar and Cooke, of Ireland ; and Dr. Hamilton, of London, among them—but I can say that a more fervent and devoted minister of the Cross than *Alfred Cookman* I never knew. In him the old fire that burned in the hearts of Whitefield and Summerfield glowed with all the fervour of the first and Pentecostal days of Methodism ; and no one could come within the sphere of his influence without feeling that he was one for whom to live was Christ, and to die was gain.

" Mr. Cookman's coming to this city was not long previous to the beginning of the great revival of 1857 and 1858. Through its precious scenes of awakening, of conversion, he laboured with all the fervour of his nature and of grace. When I recall him in connection with that time of revival, his name seems voluntarily to associate itself with that of the eloquent and devoted young servant of Christ, the sorely lamented *Dudley Tyng.* Mr. Cookman preached several times with great unction and power in the Union Tabernacle, which was moved about the city during that time. A single sermon of his on the prophet's vision of the valley of dry bones was blessed to the conversion of several persons, one of whom heard him as she stood without the tent.

"Never shall I forget a 'noonday prayer-meeting' held during the revival, at which your brother presided. With deep feeling he asked for special prayer for the only son of his father who remained still without an interest in the great salvation. You may judge with what fervour that request was responded to. A few days later word came that the prayer had been heard and answered, and that *George Cookman* was rejoicing in the hope of the glory of God. He too has gone to the upper sanctuary ; but permit me to recall the fact that when, by age, I was called to lay down the office of President of our Young Men's Christian Association, its duties devolved upon this beloved brother, who was chosen as my successor. Very precious still to me is the memory of George Cookman, the second President of the Young Men's Christian Association.

"Alfred Cookman was one of those who represented in the mind of the Christian public the brotherly *unity* of the *whole* Church of Christ. His light-hearted catholicity, and his unqualified love for all who held by the Head, were what gave him his place among us. On any public occasion when the churches of Christ were called on to unite in utterance or in action, he was always expected, and never in vain.

"How faithful he was to all the interests committed to him inside his own denomination, you can testify of. I can say that he was one of those who made us feel that all these divisions were but regiments and brigades of the *one great army*, the hosts of the living God.

"My own personal relation to him was one of pleasure and of profit always. He was a brother in sympathy, a friend in help.

"When a sentence,* at which our Christian world has not ceased to wonder, cut me off from my place in the Reformed Presbyterian General Synod, he was among the first to give utterance to his Christian confidence and sympathy, in a letter which I highly prize as a memento of our Christian friendship."

Here also are words of the same import to Mr. John E.
Cookman, from the distinguished and venerated Rev.
Richard Newton, D.D., rector of the Church of the Epiphany, Philadelphia :—

"No argument in support of the reality and truth of the religion of

---

* Mr. Stuart was suspended by the General Synod of the Reformed Presbyterian Church for singing such hymns as " Rock of Ages," and communing with Christians like Alfred Cookman.

the Gospel is worth half so much as that which is furnished by the example of one so blameless, so consistent, so holy as was your loved and
lamented brother.

" I had not the pleasure of an intimate personal acquaintance with him.
But during the years of his ministry in Philadelphia we often met together in various union services. On different platforms, where those
who love the cause of Jesus take sweet fellowship together, we often
stood side by side in striving to promote the honour of our Master's
name and the welfare of His blood-bought Church. And now that he
is gone, the recollection of those seasons is very dear and precious to
me. His large-hearted love for the friends of Jesus ; the singleness of
his aims ; the earnestness of his zeal ; the fervency of his spirit ; the
untiring devotion, the unction and power that appeared in all he did
and said, were the points about him that always most strikingly impressed those who came in contact with him. These were the broad
seals upon his character that stamped him as one of God's own anointed
ministers, and won for him a warm place in the hearts of all to whom
the living image of Jesus is dearer than everything else. I feel that it
was a privilege to have known him here on earth, and I look forward
with kindling hope to the higher privilege of meeting him in that bright
world to which he has gone, and where the union of Christ's people,
whom he so loved to cultivate here, will be perfected for ever.

" May God graciously send down on all the ministers of Jesus still on
earth a double portion of that sweet spirit of purity, humility, zeal, and
charity, which shone so brightly and so beautifully in all the life and
character of your lamented brother ! "

Mr. Cookman completed his term at Union Church in
the spring of 1861. His pastorate here, though not marked
by a general and continuous revival, was nevertheless
eminently useful. Mr. Mason says :—

" His Saturday-afternoon meetings were a grand success. All the
Sunday-school children loved him very much. We had constant accessions to the Church in small numbers. We held two protracted meetings in the body of the church. There was no great excitement, but
many were converted and added to the Church, and some remain to
this day. During one of these meetings a lady boarding at the Union
Hotel said to some friends, ' Let's go over to the Methodist meeting and
have some fun.' They occupied the fourth pew on the south middle
aisle. *Before the fun commenced*, Alfred asked all that felt they were

sinners to stand up, and, to the great amazement of her friends, Mrs. C. stood up. She was converted, was a useful member of Union Church many years, and removing to Camden, New Jersey, took a card and joined the Church there, where she lets her light shine still.

"Alfred's life, his character, and influence in the city was all for good. He was one of the purest ministers we ever had—the true minister in the market, the home, and in the house of God. One of his most effective sermons was preached on the steps of my house—to my son, Thomas T. Mason, jun., who was just leaving for the army of the Cumberland. Taking him by the hand, he said, ' Tom, take God with you, and all will be well.' After the terrible battle of Stone River, in Tennessee, my son was cut down with typhoid fever, and just before he died he turned to his comrade, Thomas C. Moore, and said, ' Tom, I am taking God with me.' "

CHAPTER XIV.

SUCH was the influence which Mr. Cookman had gained at
Philadelphia, both in and out of the Methodist Church, that
it would have seemed wise to retain him in that city. There
came now a demand for his removal to New York. His
fame as a preacher had become so wide-spread as to cause
his services to be in request in many places, both for special
occasions and for the pastorate. He had been four years
in Philadelphia, and he must make a change—" Why not go
to New York? " The application of the Central Church in
New York was successful, and Mr. Cookman was accordingly transferred to the New York Conference in May,
1861, and stationed at that Church. The same society,
which had originally worshipped in Vestry Street, had
secured the services of the father, and he was to have
entered upon his duties with them immediately upon his
return from Europe ; they were now equally fortunate to be
able to command the son in their new and more commanding position in Seventh Avenue.

Some letters, written to his wife while he was in process
of transfer and settlement are indicative of the mingled sense
of responsibility and pleasure with which he contemplated
the change :—

"NEWARK, N. J.; *May* 14, 1861.

"You must not think for a moment that you are forgotten. Never were you dearer to my heart than now ; indeed, I am sick to see my wife and children. The days drag their weary length along until I sit down in my domestic circle again. Last Thursday afternoon, in company with my friend Ridgaway, I started for Poughkeepsie, the seat of the New York Conference. The sail up the Hudson (seventy-five miles) was magnificent. The half had not been told me. It must be seen and enjoyed to be understood. Oh how much I longed for your presence, to make my joy complete ! It will be a delightful trip for us some day during the approaching summer. Poughkeepsie is a beautiful city. My home was with a family by the name of Van K——, members of the Dutch Reformed Church. They live in elegant style, and did everything possible to promote our comfort. On Friday morning I was introduced to the New York Conference, a body of nearly three hundred members, fine-looking and intelligent. They were very cordial—came forward and assured me of a most hearty welcome. John is on the spot, solicitous respecting his reception into the Conference, of which there is some little doubt. The doubt grows out of the fact that the Conference is already crowded with men, and, as at Philadelphia, they talk of postponing the reception of young men until next spring. Ridgaway preached on Friday night. . . .

"Saturday afternoon I returned to New York ; preached at Eighteenth Street on Sabbath morning, and in Union Square at three o'clock p. m. Had large audiences and great freedom. In the evening I crossed the East River and worshipped in Henry Ward Beecher's Church. It was a great treat !—a wonderful congregation, splendid singing, superior prayers, and a timely, pointed, practical, and popular sermon on camp-life. There is but one such man in this world. Instead of returning to Poughkeepsie yesterday I rambled about with Ridgaway, visiting the Book-room and office of the *Methodist*, and gazing at the 'Great Eastern,' which arrived on Saturday last. In the afternoon I accompanied him to Newark, and am spending a few hours at the palatial residence of my friend W——. It is only a stern sense of duty which detains me in this region, for, as I intimated before, I am restless to see my dearly beloved family. To-day I will write to James W—— to ship my goods. Probably they will reach New York by Saturday. I will have them stored at the parsonage ; will preach on Sabbath, and, if at all possible, start for Columbia either Monday or Tuesday. I have met quite a number of the Seventh Avenue friends. They are extremely cordial, expressing the greatest pleasure in the prospect of my appointment. They strike me as a sincere, warm-hearted congregation, with whom I can labour pleasantly and profitably."

These letters recall very vividly to my mind the interview to which Mr. Cookman refers. I had been invited to make one of the addresses at the anniversary of the American Bible Society, and I remember that no one greeted me more cordially at the close of the exercises than our friend. We planned—as I wished to visit the New York Conference then in session at Poughkeepsie—to go up the Hudson by steamboat the same afternoon. Neither of us had seen the famous river, and so we anticipated much. It was our good luck to have a charming afternoon, and also to meet on board the Rev. A. K. Sanford, a member of the Conference, whose familiarity with the route greatly heightened our pleasure. It was one of those delightful occasions when all the senses were open. The first buds of green were tinting the landscape, lending great freshness to scenes which otherwise would have been remarkable only for fidelity and boldness of outline. Mr. Cookman, with that keen perception of the beautiful for which he was so remarkable, seemed quite ravished with the ever-shifting views, which in their rapid succession kept alive a perpetual feeling of surprise and admiration. At the Conference he was, as a transferred man, the object of interest, and a desire was generally expressed to hear him preach ; but, with instinctive modesty, he waived the request, and sent the committee for his unsuspecting companion.

Just so soon as Mr. Cookman got settled in his new home, which had been put in order for his family, he began to unfold those methods of usefulness in the observance of which he had been everywhere successful. He now found himself placed in a comparatively untried field. He was but one of hundreds of pastors of first-rate ability brought

to the great centre from all parts of the country.   The congregations of the Central Church were devout, refined, and
intelligent, but not large and overflowing, such as he had been
accustomed to.   They thus lacked an important element
of effective oratory in a popular preacher, and also the conditions so necessary to the extensive revivals which had so
often attended his ministrations.

Mr. Cookman speedily adapted himself to the altered
circumstances, went quietly to work, and in the absence of
all parade, addressed himself to the proper vocation of a
faithful pastor.   His diligence, zest, and wisdom soon began
to be manifest in the growth of the congregation, in the
deepening piety of the members, and in the general and harmonious advancement of all the institutions of the charge.
The Sunday School instantly felt his magical touch, and the
young men came around him as if drawn by an irresistible
spell ; the whole people were warmed into an intenser glow
by his benignant spirit.

The following letter to his wife, touching the prospective
removal into the new home, will be appreciated by all
Methodist ministers and their families.   One must go
and another come ; the parsonage must be refitted for
the incoming family.   It is a hard time for sick children
and invalid wives ; but the wheels roll on, and around
must go wives and children with the wheels.   The
Methodist Church is a militant Church, and not only
the ministers, but their families, must be regarded as part
of the army, and must feel it no hardship to be always
ready at the appointed signal to break camp and march.
The reference in this letter to the preacher's class suggests one of Mr. Cookman's strongest points.   No man
ever possessed greater facility in the difficult and useful
exercise of class-leading.   The class of six soon grew to be

a room full, and became a rallying ground in the work of
the station :—

"NEW YORK, *Friday morning, May,* 1861.

"I am in the midst of a vast population, and surrounded by many
kind friends ; nevertheless, I suffer a sense of isolation. My precious
family are absent, and none can serve as their substitutes. Were it not
for the presence of my blessed Saviour, which has been a delightful and
continued realization, I could scarcely have borne the deprivation I have
been suffering. My Heavenly Father has been specially gracious to me
within the last week or two ; accompanying me in my walks, visiting
me in my night seasons, strengthening and blessing me in the society of
friends, keeping my mind in perfect peace. Yesterday afternoon I entered on the duties of my pastorate by leading the preacher's class. It
was very small, only six being present ; among the rest my hostess,
Mrs. Skidmore. I cast myself on Christ, and enjoyed the service very
much. After the class, I visited, in company with Mrs. S., the parsonage. Rev. Mr. Hare kindly conducted me through the house. It is a
very comfortable establishment. I think you will like it quite as well
as any of your former homes. A detailed description I will reserve
until we meet. The former pastor, Brother Hare, will not get out till
next Monday. Then the trustees will commence vigorously the work of
repair and improvement. They will paper some of the rooms, and paint
the house throughout. This cannot be finished next week. Hence I
propose to get my pulpit supplied for the following Sabbath (the 26th of
May), and bring on my family the latter part of the next week. I am
so thoroughly home-sick that I cannot readily consent to remain here
another week. My goods will probably arrive to-morrow ; but, as
Brother Hare will not take up his bed and walk before next Monday, I
may have to remain until Tuesday, that I may superintend the transfer
of my boxes to our new home. In that case I shall not see you before
Tuesday evening or Wednesday next.

"John left this morning for Lennox, his appointment. He is in good
spirits, and thinks he will be pleased. We shall hear more on his return
next week. This evening is the occasion of our regular weekly prayer-
meeting. I am looking forward to it with considerable interest. On
Sabbath I expect to preach morning and evening. This is a prospective
trial, but I shall look to and depend upon Him who has said, 'I will
never leave thee—no ! I will never forsake thee.' Pray for me. If I
should complete my arrangements, we shall spend the following Sabbath
together quietly in Columbia. This will be for me a great treat after
the excitement of the last fortnight."

The first year of the pastorate at Central passed usefully
and pleasantly, affording every indication that the new
minister had taken a strong hold upon the affections of his
people.   It was the year of the outbreak of the Rebellion ;
and, perhaps, one of the most trying periods for all the
ordinary methods of ministerial work which the American
Church has known.   It was a time when the pruning-hook
was beaten into the spear, and the ploughshare into the
sword.   The war spirit had possessed the populations ; the
great masses had risen as one man for the vindication and
safety of the Union ; and from one end of the land to
the other the strange noise of drum and fife called the
young men to arms, and the highways and streets were
thronged with troops marching southward for battle.   New
York was in a ferment of excitement — her streets were
drill-grounds, her public squares barracks, her Sabbaths
fallen under the stern exigency of preparation for instant
conflict.

Amid such scenes it was no wonder if the congregations
of the churches were decimated, and the spirit of religious
revival repressed.   After the first blaze of patriotic fire had
spent itself, and the people had become used to matter-of-
fact war—found themselves humbled with disappointment,
and settled down to the hard tug of persistent efforts—
there came a reaction in the religious feeling, and an increased attendance of the multitudes upon public worship.
Through this season of discouragement Mr. Cookman, like
other faithful ministers, stood his ground, worked how,
where, and when he could.   We have seen that even before
his settlement in New York he preached to the soldiers at
Union Square.   It was a stirring sermon, full of patriotism,
but, if possible, fuller of Christ.   That service was but the
first of many that followed—sermons and speeches which

helped to keep alive in the country both faith in God and faith in the Republic.

In New York, as in Philadelphia, we hear of him at the Union prayer-meetings. He who had borne such an active part in the one city could not remain idle in the other. At the anniversary of the Fulton Street prayer-meeting he was heard to utter these clear and ringing words :—

" It may not be uninteresting or inappropriate for me to state that while I lived in the city of Philadelphia I had the honour to be the pastor of the Church which stands upon the site of the ' Old Academy,' as it was designated, the favourite preaching-place of the illustrious Whitefield.

" In the lecture-room of that Church was organized the first noonday prayer-meeting for the city of Philadelphia. It was commenced by a young man who had resided in the city of New York, and who had frequently availed himself of the privileges of this Fulton Street noonday service. After his removal to Philadelphia, he felt that a similar meeting would be profitable in his own experience and for the community at large, and was resolved to assume the responsibility of its establishment. It is but proper to say that, in the first instance, the effort was feeble and unpromising ; and many times have I passed by the door of that lecture-room, and, glancing in when I ought to have gone in, observed three or four prostrate before God, importuning an outpouring of Divine influence upon themselves and upon others. Those prayers, however, were effectual ; they reached the ear and they influenced the heart of an almighty Saviour ; and before long the number attending the service in that lecture-room was very considerably increased. It was then resolved to remove to Jayne's Hall, of which doubtless you have all heard very frequently ; and after the removal to Jayne's Hall, the interest so rapidly extended that before the lapse of a week four thousand persons might have been seen associated together for the purpose of public prayer.

"If these humble efforts were followed by such special results in that case, what may we not hope for after the patient and the persistent prayers that have been going up from this Fulton Street meeting, and from similar services, during a succession of years? I have the impression that when these terrible providences which are associated with our present war shall have mellowed the great national heart, the results of these prayers will appear in a mighty and un‾precedented Pentecostal baptism, when there shall not be four thousand or forty thousand only, but millions prostrate beneath the mighty power of God. And oh! in the prospect of such an outpouring, may we not to-day linger in the midst of our great country, desolated not only by civil but spiritual rebellion, covered all over with moral death, and may we not imitate the example of the prophet, as with the voice of one man, and pray, 'Come, come from the four winds, O breath! and breath upon these souls that they may live'?

"As an encouragement to prayer for individuals, will you excuse me if I introduce a passage from personal experience? I was the eldest of six children, five sons and one daughter. The mysterious hand of God's providence buried my precious father while I was still young in yon broad, deep ocean. My widowed mother—for whom I will even in this public way praise the Father of the fatherless—was greatly concerned, of course, for the salvation of all her children. Her prayers, which were importunate and constant, were heard in heaven, and soon they began to be answered, as one after the other of her sons was brought into the kingdom of our Lord Jesus Christ. Four years ago we were, as I trust, a united family in Christ, with one exception, and that exception was a beloved brother, a noble, affectionate young man, twenty-seven years of age. He had been my associate during life; we had played together as boys; we had slept in the same bed; we had attended the academy together; we had bowed at the same maternal knee, and had joined in repeating the petition, 'Our Father which art in heaven.'

" I cannot tell this audience how I agonized for the salvation of that brother, and how anxious I was that we might be a united family in the Saviour in time, and then an undivided household in paradise. Morning, noon, and night I brought this interest to a throne of heavenly grace; and one day I rose in the Philadelphia noon prayer-meeting and asked them to pray for that brother. Oh how they prayed! I shall never forget their interest and earnestness, and if I am so happy as to reach the glory-land, I think I shall find out some of those Christians, and will thank them for their united and importunate prayers upon the occasion of that noonday service. Only a short time elapsed when that brother, who was unaware that united prayer had been offered in his behalf, was found prostrate penitently before God, and became a subject of regenerating grace. He joined the Church, and has subsequently come to be one of the most earnest, consistent young Christians I ever knew.

" Before I sit down, allow me to speak of a circumstance which transpired in the neighbourhood of Boston. A few years since, two gentlemen entered a car in that city *en route* for the interior, and, seated side by side, they very naturally fell into conversation, when it transpired that they were both travelling to the same place; and soon, to their mutual surprise, they discovered that they bore the same name. Then they ascertained that they were both going to see an elder brother, one whom they had not met for many, many years; and then the almost overpowering truth burst upon them that they were literal, natural brothers, who in the providence of God had met in this most extraordinary way. They had been separated from early childhood, and now, after the lapse of thirty long years, they had been most surprisingly brought together. As I have been sitting here and listening to allusions about heaven, I have said in my heart, 'That is my place of destination, and I hope, through grace, to stand triumphantly upon Canaan's shining shore.' And then, as you have used the term Christian, I have said inwardly, ' That is pre-eminently my name.' I am a Methodist Christian. I do not attach a very great deal of importance to the Methodist, but I would place very strong emphasis upon the designation Christian. Just as my name is Alfred _Cookman_. I care not for the Alfred : I would just as soon it was George or Joseph or John ; but I cling tenaciously to my family name. As you have made very touching and beautiful reference to Jesus, I can say He is my Elder Brother, and I hope after a while to be associated with Him in heaven. It is a delightful truth that we are associated to-day, brothers and sisters in Christ Jesus, hastening onward as rapidly as time can bear us,—

> " ' To the house of our Father above,
> The palace of angels and God.' "

The delight which Mr. Cookman found in his family is manifest in all his letters. Those who knew him most intimately will recall that he never seemed so perfectly happy as when in the bosom of his home. The letters which he wrote to his children when absent on their summer vacations were full of sweetness. They did not lack good advice ; but were rather characterized by parental tenderness and familiarity. He could be a child among his children. Up to this time there had been no alloy in his domestic bliss—the children, his wife, and himself had been favoured with uninterrupted health; but now it pleased God to allow sickness to enter the circle. His eldest son and first-born, Bruner, was affected with a painful disease, which finally, after some years of suspense, terminated his life. A few letters of this date happily illustrate the feelings which animated his soul under the chequered dispensations of Providence. Happy in the sunshine, he was not despondent in the shade. The first touches of sorrow were borne with resignation, and served but to mellow his rapidly growing experience.

The following are some of the letters to his children:—

"NEW YORK, *June* 21, 1862.

"This is Saturday night, when pa, you know, usually studies his sermons. Bruner is asleep, Will is asleep, little Beck Evans is asleep, ma is getting ready for bed, and I am writing a letter to my dear George and precious Frank and sweet little sister Puss. Well, how have you been getting along this week? I hope you have been very good, making as little noise as possible; obeying all that aunt B—— or grandma has said, remembering your prayers every night and morning, asking your blessing, and behaving well at the table, and acting like little New York gentlemen. On Tuesday I watched you waving your hats and handkerchiefs and flags until I could see you no longer; then I sat down until I reached Lancaster. There I waited an hour, and took another train of cars, and got to Philadelphia in time for tea, stayed at uncle George's all night, and the next day started for New York.

"When I got home little Prince danced for joy, he was so glad to see me. Then I started for Nyack, where I found ma and Brune and Will and little baby-sister. They were almost as much delighted as Prince, and asked me a hundred questions about George and Frank and sister. I told ma you were magnificent boys; that Frank did not cry; that sister was growing to be a large and lovely girl. We talk about you every day, and want the weeks to go by right fast until we shall all sit down together in Columbia. Thursday afternoon we returned from Mr. T.'s. Yesterday ma and Brune had a long, pleasant ride in Mr. R.'s carriage. Brune drove nearly all the way. To-day ma and Brune and Will and Betty and the baby went with Mr. P—— to the Central Park, and heard the music. It was splendid !

"Now I most close my letter. On Monday we have our Sabbath-school excursion. Next week, perhaps, I will write and tell you all about it. Be very good boys. We send kisses. George must kiss Frank and Sis for ma ; Frank must kiss George and Sis for ma ; Sis must kiss George and Frank for Brune. Do not forget. Good-night."

"My dear, darling Little Puss,—This is *your* letter, written by your precious papa. Every day he thinks about you, and wants the time to come when he may take you in his arms again. If you were here to-night he would not be satisfied with one less than a dozen kisses. Your dear brother Bruner has been very sick. He often talks about his little pet sister in Columbia. You ought to see his dog. The dog's name is Prince—a happy little fellow that barks at Willie, and plays with Frank, and jumps up on George, and follows Brune wherever he goes. I know he would love you dearly ; he could not help it. Everybody loves my little darling Puss, but nobody better than her devoted pa. Be a very good girl ; learn to jump rope ; help grandma to water the flowers ; mind everything aunt B—— says to you ; kiss Mozie and little Alfred for me : don't eat all the currants and gooseberries before I come, but keep ever so many for your dear pa. Would you not like me to send you a pretty picture-book ? Keep a look-out, and some of these days Kate will find one in the post-office for Miss Annie Cookman. Won't that be nice ? Now give me a good-bye kiss."

"New York, *June* 24, 1862.

"My dear George and Frank and Little Sister,—We received George's letter this afternoon, and were glad to know that you are all well and enjoying yourselves. Be very good children, and in a few weeks you will see your dear ma and Bruner and Willie and the baby. Did I not promise to tell you about the Sunday-school excursion ? Well, yesterday morning we rose early, got ready, and went down to the wharf, where we found a large number of the boys and girls, with their parents and teachers. At about eight o'clock we started, and sailed down the bay. It was a beautiful morning, the sun was shining brightly, the air was cool, the boat was large and comfortable. Bruney, Willie, baby, Betty, Julia, and mamma, with the little carriage, were all on board. Brune ate cakes and drank mineral water. About eleven o'clock we got to Biddle's Grove, on Staten Island. This was a beautiful place, with swings and tables and a great many nice things. We had an excellent dinner, some charming walks, a game of ball, and then we started for home, where we arrived in the evening about seven o'clock. It was one of the happiest days I ever spent. Now I have bad news to tell you. Little Prince is dead. He died to-day. Instead of getting better, as we hoped, he got worse, until he could not walk or stand, and then the poor little fellow died. Bruner sat down and took a good cry. Some persons think he was so pretty that he ought to be stuffed, like those animals you saw at Barnum's Museum. But this is not worth while. He will either be buried or thrown into the river. Your little brother Willie told me this afternoon he was going to take ' me da—da in the 'team·boat.' When he takes me, I reckon we will go to Columbia. Now remember to be very good ; say no bad words ; go with no bad boys ; be kind to grandma and grandpa ; obey all aunt B—— says, and do not get sick or hurt yourselves.

 · " Now I must give you a good-night kiss—one for George, one for Frank, and one for dear little sister Puss. Ma says I must send ever so many for her, and Bruney for him, and Willie for him."

The following letter to Mr. Thomas W. Price, of Philadelphia, on the loss of an infant child, named for Mrs. Cookman, evinces the facility and heartiness with which Mr. Cookman could enter into the feelings of his friends. No wonder such a nature should have touched depths and drawn to it affections which lie quite unmoved by ordinary men :—

"COLUMBIA, *August* 5, 1862.

" Glancing through the columns of yesterday's *Inquirer*, my eye fell on a notice of the death of your dear little Annie Cookman. It shocked us not a little, for when we last saw her she was the very picture of health. How often is it the case that our cherished ones, whose promise for long life is the most flattering, are the first to be smitten by death's relentless hand !

" You will believe me when I assure you that this bereavement has awakened in our hearts the liveliest sympathy and sorrow.

" We recognised in this little namesake a living and breathing bond, to bind even more closely that special affection which subsists between our families. We remember the interest and love with which you regarded this last-born, we are reminded of the unusual sweetness and loveliness of the babe herself, and then feel that you have sustained a sad loss. Another breach is occasioned in your affections.

"In circumstances like these, how consolatory are the truths of our holy religion! The unseen hand of God's providence has taken from your family nest this little immortal, and, lifting her up, constituted her an angel in the paradise above. Thus the attractiveness of heaven is increased. As we pass on in life, meeting such afflictions, earth becomes more and more a strange land, while heaven wears more and more of a home-like aspect. Associated with the little brother who some years since was wrested from your parental embrace, the two now, as I doubt not, stand on 'the shining shore' to welcome the family into everlasting habitations.

"When you sing in the future that line of the long-metre doxology, viz., '*Praise Him above*, ye heavenly host,' it will possess a deeper meaning, awaken more tender feelings, and enkindle more heavenly aspirations.

"So far as I am aware, this is the first Annie Cookman that has entered those realms of light ; and if spirits can know one another, then I am sure *her name* in that world will immediately introduce her to the fellowship of some dearly beloved ones who have gone before.

"God bless you abundantly, my cherished brother and sister! My heart has always been full of love for you both, and now in your affliction I want to say something or do something that may lighten the burden which this bereavement has laid upon your tender and deeply affectionate hearts. May I not pray that our covenant-keeping God will sanctify this dispensation to your good, vouchsafe you special consolation and grace, and make you eventually an undivided family in the skies? I should have been at the funeral but for the illness of our babe. For about ten days she has been hovering between life and death. Her condition is still very critical. I shall not be astonished if these precious children (*little Annie and Rebecca*), of about the same age, should both be in a better world about the same time."

Before following Mr. Cookman to his next charge, I must present an example of the patriotic speeches which he delivered, and also of the firm and advanced opinions which he expressed on national affairs, in the great crisis of the country. In the summer of 1862, while on a visit with his family at Columbia, an immense war meeting was held at Lancaster, and he was one of the speakers. I quote from a report of it which appeared in one of the daily papers :—

"FELLOW-CITIZENS,—This is to me a somewhat unexpected call, but I should feel myself recreant to every great principle of patriotism and of truth if I refused or even hesitated in this my native county—for it may not be known to many of you that I first opened my eyes upon God's world within the limits of old Lancaster ; it gave me a being, and it gave me one of the best of wives, so that I feel under immense obligations to it. (Cheers.) I say that I should feel myself recreant to every principle of truth and right if I hesitated to seize this opportunity to say, in the language of old John Adams, ' Sink or swim, live or die, survive or perish, I give my heart and my hand' to these Union measures. It is my living sentiment, and with the blessing of God it will be my dying sentiment—liberty and the Union now, liberty and the Union for ever. (Great applause.)

" It is useless for any of us to disguise the fact—the stern and startling fact—that this Union, which is so unutterably dear to our hearts, is at the present time in imminent peril. Thousands—yea, hundreds of thousands—of our fellow-citizens, organized and armed, are intent upon the overthrow of this, I dare to say, the very best government that yonder sun ever looked down upon ; a government which ought to be just as dear to them as to ourselves ; a government with which our own hopes and the hopes of our children and children's children are intimately bound up to the very latest generation ; a government closely connected, as we think, with the cause of liberty throughout the world, —for if our experiment of self-government should prove a failure, we are satisfied that it must put back the hand of freedom on the dial-plate of time at least fifty or one hundred years ; a government which, so far as we may judge, is one of Jehovah's right hands of power for the overthrow of despotism, error, ignorance, and everything which could hinder the coming of His kingdom. Thousands and hundreds of thousands of our fellow-citizens, with worse than Vandal-like violence, are rushing forward to destroy the superstructure of that government. Now the practical inquiry occurs, What is to be done ? The answer, it appears to me, is an easy one.

" My fellow-citizens, what would you do if to-night at twelve o'clock you were to find an assassin in your bed-chamber, fully resolved upon your life ? I make no question but that you would spring from your slumbers and grapple with him, and not even hesitate to put him to death in order to save your own life. Parent, what would you do if a rebellion were to arise in your domestic circle? Would you not stretch forward the hand of authority and quickly quell it? Citizens of Lancaster, what would you do if an infamous mob should rise up in these streets to destroy valuable property and imperil precious life? I make no doubt that you would take down the muskets and rifles still remaining among you, and with the point of the bayonet or with the use of ammunition drive back and put down such a mob. And you would do right. Self-protection would demand such a course. And in this case it is a stern duty. As Luther remarked on one occasion, ' May God help us !— we cannot do otherwise.' That flag yonder must float ; our government must be maintained. (Cheers.) Our Union must be preserved and perpetuated in all its purity and integrity. (Cheers.) Millions may be spent, hundreds of thousands of lives may be sacrificed, a whole generation may be blotted out, and still we insist that it is of the very first consequence that our nationality be vindicated. (' Good,' and cheers.) Now I apprehend that it is with this great principle in view we are assembled and associated this afternoon.

"A remark of Colonel Forney's brought to my mind a circumstance which transpired many years ago. It is said that in a military engagement which occurred somewhere near the boundary-line which separates England and Scotland, a young chieftain fell just at the moment when, at the head of his troop, he was furiously and successfully charging the foe. His comrades in arms, seeing him fall, were immediately seized with consternation, and began to retire in confusion. Witnessing this, his soul immediately filled with sorrow, and, although he was feeble, he managed with some effort to raise himself upon his elbow, and while the life-blood was fast gushing from the gaping wound, while eternity was opening before him, he seized his sword, and, waving it over his head, shouted at the top of his voice, 'My boys, I am not dead ! I am not dead, but I am looking to see that every man does his duty.' (Cheers.) So I am here this afternoon to say that our Union is not dead. She has been wounded, foully and fearfully wounded ; and, observe, too, in the house of her friends. Still she is not dead. Hear it, you daughters and sons of Lancaster !—she is not dead—never dead ; but, sword in hand, she is looking to see that every citizen does his duty. (Great applause.) She is looking to ascertain whether, in this time of exigency, we will rally to the rescue ; whether in this, the darkest hour of the Republic, we will come up united to the help of freedom and the help of God. For, remember, this is the cause of truth ; this is the cause of justice ; this is the cause of freedom ; this is the cause of the Union ; this is the cause of God. (Cheers.) I insist that God is always on the side of truth and justice and freedom. Will you not, then—will you not—will not all these young men and citizens, esteem it at once an obligation and a privilege and a joy to consecrate their energies, their substance, their time, their lives, and their all upon the altar of our country's cause? (Cheers.)

" Allusion has been made to the patriot daughters of Lancaster. God bless them ! I see them in these windows, and assembled in the vicinity of this stand. God bless them ! Mothers, wives, daughters, sisters collected here, we have some faint idea of the sacrifices you are called upon to make, and of the sufferings which you, in the providence of God, must still undergo. Still I trust that at least an overwhelming majority of you have the spirit of that mother in the city of Philadelphia, who said the other day, 'What are sons worth without a country?' (Cheers.) I trust you have the spirit of a friend and former parishioner of mine in the borough of Harrisburg, who has sent six stalwart sons to the scene of strife. Just before they left home and their mother's presence, they assembled in a photographic gallery and had their pictures taken, the eldest son standing in the midst of his other brothers, and grasping the flag of the stars and stripes ; and that picture left with the mother is an evidence of undying affection. I think, too, in this connexion, of a mother in the State of New York, whose son the other day proceeded to the seat of war. He was connected with the Sheppard Rifles, Colonel Fareim commanding. It so occurred that the young man's position was at the end of the platoon, near the curbstone, and the mother, anxious to be with him as long as he remained in New York, took her place at his side. As the regiment moved along Fourteenth Street and down Broadway, that heroic old American mother walked with her boy, keeping step with him. To relieve him while she could, she took his musket from his hand, and stuck it over her old shoulder, and so she marched with him, side by side, carrying his musket ; and the boy was so much moved by her devotion that the tears literally ran down his cheeks. ' Don't cry—don't cry, my boy !' she said ; ' be brave, and then, with God's blessing, all must and will be well.' (Cheers.) So, mothers and wives and sisters and daughters of Lancaster, say to your cherished ones, 'Go, go !' It is like tearing the heart out of our living and breathing bodies ; it is like enshrouding our present and future with a gloom that must all the time be felt ; nevertheless, go and fight these battles of truth and justice and liberty, and God's blessing must be upon you and yours. (Applause.)

" As the last speaker remarked, it is a gloomy hour in our country's history ; but I apprehend, my fellow-citizens, that if we look over the events of the last fifteen months we will still find reason for thankful-ness. Is it nothing that that effeminacy which was beginning to curse

our citizens has met so powerful and sufficient an antidote ?   Is it nothing
that that spirit of insubordination which has been so painfully rife in our
happy land, and which is, perhaps, one of the very causes of our present
troubles, is receiving so effectual a check ?   Is it nothing that our
patriotism, which seemed almost cold, is to-day burning with a brilliant
flame,—that that sentiment, which had almost died out, has become a
principal passion in the nation's heart ?   I take it upon myself to say
that there have been more acts of moral heroism in this land within the
last fifteen months than in all our history previously.   (Cheers.)   And
is all this nothing ?   Is it nothing that success from time to time has
crowned our arms ?   Is it nothing that Nashville is ours ?   Is it nothing
that Memphis is ours, and New Orleans is ours, and Norfolk is ours,
and Winchester is ours, and the Shenandoah Valley is ours, and that
Richmond is, we trust and think, soon to be ours ?   (Cheers.)   Is it
nothing that that flag which we all love so much——and, by the way, I
am just here reminded of a sentiment of a rebel prisoner, who said to a
friend of mine, that when they came within sight of the old flag they
were very likely to feel weak in the knees (Laughter and applause)——
I say, is it nothing that that grand old flag on the last Fourth of July
floated in every one of the thirty-four states ?   (Cheers.)   Is all that
nothing ?   (Great applause.)

"Some of you, perhaps, have heard of a very remarkable iron egg,
said to be still preserved in the city of Dresden.   There is a legend connected with this egg, which runs somewhat to this effect : On a certain
occasion a prince sent the iron egg to his betrothed.   When she received the gift she looked at it, and, becoming entirely disgusted with so
rude a present, she flung it in disgust upon the ground.   As it struck
the earth, a secret spring was touched, and lo ! a silver yolk rolled forth
from the egg.   As she gathered up the yolk, she touched another secret
spring, and lo ! a golden chicken was evolved.   She took the chicken
in both hands, and in doing so she touched a secret spring, and lo ! a
ruby crown appeared.   She touched a secret spring in the ruby crown,
and lo ! her eyes were blessed with the sight of a magnificent marriage
diamond ring.   So let me remind you that this nation from the hand of
God's providence seemed to have received an iron egg—an egg all
crusted with tears and clotted with blood ; but lo ! with the dismantling
of Sumter a secret spring was touched, and a silver yolk appeared,
which, like a shield of patriotism, spread over all the Northern States
of this great and glorious Union.   A secret spring in this silver yolk of
patriotism was touched, and instead of one golden chicken we have a
brood—McClellan (cheers), Halleck, Banks, Burnside, Hunter, Foote,
Farragut, Grant, and Buell, and many others whom I might, and per-

haps ought to name. (Cheers.) Now these golden chickens are each one bringing a ruby crown of victory. McClellan, Yorktown ; Halleck, Corinth ; Banks, Winchester ; Burnside, Roanoke and Newbern ; Grant, Forts Henry and Donelson ; Buell, Shiloh ; Foote, Island No 10 ; and Farragut—not a very pretty name, but certainly a very pretty deed—has given us New Orleans. Each one has contributed his ruby to make up a great crown of victory, and when the secret spring in that crown shall be touched, the ring of the Union will appear still un-broken, and rendered more beautiful and valuable than ever before by the addition of the sparkling diamond of universal liberty. (Tremen-dous applause.)

> " ' The cloud is vanishing from the day ;
> Lo ! the right is about to conquer—
> Clear the way ! '

"Men of thought, men of action, clear the way—clear the way ! Our army at Harrison's Landing, our country dismembered and bleed-ing, the cause of freedom throughout the world, and God sitting upon the circle of yonder firmament, are making powerful and resistless calls upon us to do our duty, and our whole duty, to our country." (Cheers.)

The session of the New York Conference held in the Washington Square Church, New York, was one of marked interest and solemnity, especially on account of the Report which was adopted on the state of the country. One of the members of the Conference, Captain Pelatiah Ward, who had volunteered early in the war, had been killed in battle during the past summer. He was a generous, valiant man, and much loved by his brethren. The President of the United States had issued the proclamation of emancipation, the justice and policy of which were yet much debated ; and the unanimity which at the outbreak of the rebellion univer-sally prevailed had become much disturbed by factious opposition. Mr. Cookman felt it was no time for Methodist preachers to mince words, to stickle over questions of con-stitutional nicety, but that the trumpet from them, as leaders of public opinion, must give a certain sound. He drew up the report. Its reading excited the deepest emotion ; thrilling speeches were made by leading members of the Conference, and with but slight opposition it was adopted amid great applause. I give the resolutions :—

"*Resolved*—1. That as members and ministers of the Methodist Episcopal Church within the bounds of the New York Annual Conference, we cheerfully renew our vows of uncompromising and unconditional loyalty to the United States of America—a nationality we are proud to acknowledge, and resolved, with the blessing of Heaven, to maintain.

"2. That it is our duty, enforced alike by the Word of God and our Book of Discipline, to submit to and to co-operate with the regularly constituted civil authorities, and to enjoin the same upon our people.

"3. That while we do not deny, but rather recognise and defend, the right of our people to discuss the measures and policy of the Government, at the same time we would counsel that, in the present critical condition of public affairs, this right is to be exercised with great forbearance, caution, and prudence.

"4. That the conduct of those who, influenced by political affinities or Southern sympathies, and under the pretext of discriminating between the Administration and the Government, throw themselves in the path of almost every warlike measure, is in our view covert treason, which has the malignity without the manliness of those who have arrayed themselves in open hostility to our liberties, and is deserving of our sternest denunciation and our most determined opposition.

"5. That slavery is an evil, incompatible in its spirit and practice with the principles of Christianity, with republican institutions, with the peace and prosperity of our country, and with the traditions, doctrines, and discipline of our Church ; and that our long and anxious inquiry, ' What shall be done for its extirpation ?' has been singularly answered by Divine Providence, which has given to Abraham Lincoln, President of the United States, the power and the disposition to issue a proclamation guaranteeing the boon of freedom to millions of Southern bondmen.

"6. That we heartily concur in this proclamation as indicating the righteousness of our cause, securing the sympathies of the liberty-loving the world over, and, above all, insuring the approbation of the Universal Father, who is invariably on the side of justice and freedom.

"7. That we find abundant reason for gratitude and encouragement in the recent revival of the nation's patriotism ; in the maintenance of our public credit ; in the change of public opinion abroad, especially in England ; and in the gradual, but we trust sure, progress of our arms.

"8. That we cordially accept the President's recommendation to observe the thirtieth day of the present month as a season of solemn fasting and prayer ; and that, assembling in our various places of worship, we will humble ourselves, and earnestly supplicate the great Ruler of nations to forgive our national offences ; to guide, sustain, and bless our public rulers ; to look upon our army and navy mercifully, giving success to our arms, so that this infamous rebellion may be speedily crushed, and peace, at once righteous and permanent, may return to and smile upon our American heritage.

"9. That our interest in and sympathy for those who represent us in the field continues unabated, and that to all those who are suffering in consequence of the havoc or desolations of this terrible war, we offer our sincerest sympathies and Christian condolence.

" 10. That a copy of these resolutions be transmitted to the President of the United States, and that they be published in the *Christian Advocate and Journal.*"

It was such action as this on the part of the Methodist ministers, sustained by the laymen for whom and to whom they spoke, both at the ballot-box and on the battle-field, that led Mr. Lincoln to say that no Church had done so much to support the Government in its efforts to maintain the Union as the Methodist ministers and people. It was not a little due to Mr. Cookman that the declaration of the New York Conference, representing a large popular sentiment in the commercial heart of the nation, assumed a shape so positive and incisive. It was but the emanation of his own convictions.

The pastorate of Mr. Cookman closed at the Central Church with the universal regret of its members. The young people had become ardently attached to him. He had taken especial pains to draw together and render efficient the young men of the congregation, and for this purpose had organised among them a society called the " Christian Brotherhood," which held regular meetings for business, religious, social, and literary exercises, and also took general supervision of the young men who attended the Church services. This society was pleased to express their appreciation of their retiring pastor by passing resolutions which are valuable as a tribute to him and as a hint to other ministers :—

" *Whereas* Rev. Alfred Cookman, our late pastor, has, in the economy of our Church, been transferred to another field of labour—

" *Resolved*, That we remember with great pleasure our relations during the term of his pastorate, and that we deem his unusual interest in our Association, and continued efforts to promote its prosperity, as worthy of particular mention and record.

" *Resolved*, That to his regular attendance upon our meetings, his courteous yet earnest participation in our discussions, his evident anxiety that our organization should prove of the highest benefit to the Church, and his constant endeavour for this result, is due much of its prosperity and usefulness.

" *Resolved*, That upon retrospect of the term of Brother Cookman's service, we are led to believe that the pastors of our churches would add greatly to the effectiveness of their labours by more fully interesting themselves in the established meetings and organizations of their charges ; as an active sympathy in concerns already enlisting the sympathies of their people must afford opportunity not otherwise enjoyed of learning their dispositions and peculiarities, of securing a place in their affections, and of gaining confidence, respect, and influence—as also, by counsel and co-operation, of promoting wiser action and developing wider results.

" *Resolved*, That the name of Rev. Alfred Cookman be placed upon the list of honorary members of this Brotherhood."

CHAPTER XV.

MR. COOKMAN was next appointed, in the spring of 1863, to the Trinity Methodist Episcopal Church in West Thirty-fourth Street. Here his ministry proved highly acceptable and useful. The congregations were never larger than while he was pastor, and there were many valuable accessions to the Church. There are some persons still connected with Trinity, and some belonging to other churches in the city, who were the fruits of his fidelity at this time, and who are among the most useful and active Christians in New York. The savour· of his piety diffused itself rapidly through all the departments of the station. He established a service on Friday afternoons, under his personal control, for the advancement of Christian purity, and succeeded in gathering to it many of the earnest lovers of holiness within his own charge, and some beyond it. These meetings were very helpful to the piety of the Church, and were instrumental in bringing not a few into the clearer light of perfect love. In their use his personal religious experience was also greatly enriched, and his ministry correspondingly nourished.

The most marked event of this pastoral term was Mr. Cookman's visit to the Army of the Potomac on special service under the direction of the Christian Commission. He showed himself ready not only to talk sacrifice, but to go to the front, that he might cheer, in the capacity of minister and brother, the hearts of the valiant and exposed soldiers. The best epitome of his thoughts and doings while thus engaged is furnished in his letters written to friends at home. The Sanitary and Christian Commissions, organized for the relief of the soldiers of the United States, in addition to what was done for them directly by the Government, were sustained wholly by the voluntary offerings of the people, and constituted in their work one of the brightest features of the war. Never before was stern suffering so alleviated by the tenderer aspects of Christian and humane sentiment. The benevolence of the country rose in a majesty and beauty which signally contrasted with the dark clouds of fratricidal conflict. The Christian Commission aimed not only to extend to the fainting warrior the delicacies which the body and mind so much needed, but also, and chiefly, the Word of Life—in the shape of Bibles, good books, tracts, preaching, and pastoral visitation. It drafted for its occasional services ministers and laymen of the first talents; and the good it accomplished, while abundantly attested in the records of its history, cannot be fully known until all earthly accounts are written up.

The following letters to his wife and children will be found interesting :—

"WASHINGTON, *Saturday night*, 10 *o'clock*.

"You will not object to a short note, I am sure. I am finishing my first Sabbath in the service of the Christian Commission. This morning I proceeded, according to arrangement, to the camp or barracks of the First New Hampshire. To our surprise and disappointment, we found that they had suddenly left the night before. Part of another regiment, however, had come in, and the proposition was for us to preach to them in the afternoon. Thereupon I hastened to Wesley Chapel, and heard a masterly sermon on the subject of the Transfiguration from my friend B. Peyton Brown ; met any number of old friends ; yielded to the pressing invitation of Mrs. T——, and accompanied her home to dinner.

"After dinner Brother Scott called, and we proceeded again to the camp of the First Maine. The men were drawn up in a hollow square. It was a magnificent spectacle. They appeared in full dress uniform and under arms, accompanied by a brass band. Surrounded by a large company of Washingtonians, I held forth the Word of Life. It was an open-air service, and consequently very exhausting. Nevertheless I got through comfortably. The men were solemn and attentive, and I trust good was done. After the service I distributed some papers and hymn-books, and seized the opportunity to converse religiously with a number of the soldiers. With Brother Charles Lane, my first class-leader, I then went home to tea. Oh how very, very cordial he was ! I praise my Heavenly Father for his friendship and love. At seven I went to the Armoury Square Hospital, and preached to a chapel full of soldiers. Never have I addressed a more attentive or apparently interested company of men. They hung on every syllable. At the close about twenty rose for prayers. The power of the Highest rested upon the assemblage. We sang 'Going home,' 'Marching along,' 'Rest for the weary' : oh how the noble boys poured out the tide of song ! I thought while I was preaching to them, many a faithful mother and sister are pouring out their souls in earnest prayers for their absent sons and brothers. God gave me their hearts, and the chaplain is clamorous for me to remain and labour among them during the present week. I leave the determination of this to that faithful God whose I am and whom I serve.

"This ends my first day of labour. Glory to God to-night for His mercy shown the very feeblest of all His messengers ! Oh how my soul trusts and rejoices in the God and Rock of my salvation ! To-morrow I move, as a good soldier of Jesus, just where my Captain directs. My foot has been very sore, obliging me to limp in walking ; still I have not been hindered in any department of work. Remember me to all friends. Ask my people to pray for their absent pastor, that God will own and bless his humble labours in behalf of our brave soldiers. Kiss my children for papa. Tell dear mother and sister Mary, and John and sister M——, to remember me specially before God, and believe me yours devotedly."

"BRANDY STATION, AT THE FRONT, *February* 29, 1864.

"Here I am at the front, within a few miles of General Lee's army,

13

and yet as calm as a summer's eve. We left Washington this morning about ten o'clock, and, after a most interesting ride of seventy miles, reached our place of destination at half-past two this afternoon. The country through which we passed wears an air of desolation which was dismal to contemplate : no fences, no houses, no cultivation whatever,— only the *débris* of destroyed property and continuous camps of soldiers. By my side in the car sat a Captain C——, of Camden, New Jersey, who has been connected with the army since the commencement of the war. He was very kind and communicative, pointing out the scenes of several battles, and calling attention to various points of interest.

"My companions in the service of the Commission, Brothers Hatfield and Watkins, were very fraternal and pleasant. Arriving at Brandy Station, we found our head-quarters quite near,—an ordinary camp-meeting tent, with a front and rear apartment. Here we have our bunks for sleeping ; rather rough, but better almost than I had expected. Our commissary prepared our dinner. When we sat down we could not restrain immoderate laughter. It was primitive truly. Tin cups for chocolate, tin plates, the brownest sugar, and no butter. However, we got along gloriously. My precious little George would have enjoyed it, for there was plenty of good molasses to eat with our bread. The meal dispatched, we sallied forth and spent an hour very pleasantly in the contraband camp, which is quite near. As the Commission cannot give us work until to-morrow, we arranged for a meeting to-night among the coloured people. There is an Uncle Ben and an Uncle Dick, who are represented as most interesting characters. We have just dispatched our supper—tin cups and plates, of course, but some butter and beef-steak—a right good meal. I have made up my mind to my circumstances, and hope to enjoy and profit by them.

"My friend Scott was very kind in completing my outfit. I think I have everything needful for one in my circumstances. My only trial now is my absence from my family. I think of you very frequently, and ask my Heavenly Father to watch over and preserve you all. My mind is still kept in perfect peace. God opens my way, and strengthens and comforts me as I walk in that way. Blessed be His name ! The brethren are hurrying me to accompany them to the negro meeting. Tell the Friday afternoon meeting to pray for me specially."

"CAMP SIXTH N. Y. HEAVY ARTILLERY, *March* 2, 1864.

"Will you not confess that I am a faithful army correspondent ? I believe that I have written every day since we parted. Yesterday we were confined at Brandy Station by the storm. It was one of the most dismal days I ever witnessed. Shut up in our tent, letter-writing was an agreeable pastime. This morning I rose after a good night's rest to look forth upon a cloudless sky ; but the mud—oh, the mud ! I now better understand the difficulty of army movements. The passage of army waggons (of which there is no end) and heavy artillery is almost entirely interrupted by the condition of the soil.

" This morning I visited head-quarters, and had a most agreeable interview with General Meade. He received us very politely, invited us into his tent, bade us be seated, and chatted very familiarly and kindly. His photographs are very good ; perhaps they give the impression of a larger and more rugged man than the original. His recent illness has left him thin, but he professes to be enjoying excellent health at the present. A careworn expression lingers round his face ; but is this wonderful when we consider the burden of care which rests upon his patriotic heart ? He impressed me with his gentlemanly bearing and kind spirit, rather than with his superior soldierly appearance. We called at the same time on General Patrick, who is one of the notabilities here, occupying the position of Provost Marshal of this division of the army. He is an intelligent, affable, and interesting man.' I have reached my field of labour. The N. Y. Sixth Heavy Artillery numbers about 1,300 men. Besides these there are New York, Connecticut, and Massachusetts batteries, and the ammunition trains, all around us, numbering together 3,000 or 4,000 men. Here, then, I am to toil for their advantage. It is not exactly the place I would have chosen for myself, nevertheless it may be the right place. When it was mentioned to me, I did not dare to murmur or remonstrate, for I have put myself in God's hands, and, without any agency of my own, want to see what He proposes to do with me during my sojourn at the front.

" The soldiers are in winter-quarters—log huts covered with canvas. The officers' quarters are exceedingly tasty and comfortable : little homes that would not disfigure Central Park. Many of them have their wives here, and seem disposed to enjoy life while it lasts. To visit the men in their tents, converse with them, etc., etc., will occupy most of my time. A little while ago I walked over to look at the battery of the N. Y. Fifth Heavy Artillery. A young lieutenant whom I providentially met was singularly polite and kind—escorting me to various points of interest, showing me all the appurtenances of their heavy Parrot guns, etc. I was careful to introduce the subject of religion, and was delighted to find him respectful and tender. How is my dear wife this afternoon ? I have not as yet heard a word from home. I suppose that my correspondence will almost necessarily be a good deal interrupted. Our quarters here are considerably rougher than they were at Brandy Station ; but, never mind, they are better than I deserve."

"HEAD-QUARTERS OF RESERVE ARTILLERY, *March* 3, 1864.

"I am sitting in our chapel tent, which is used by the soldiers during the day as a kind of reading-room. They find here books, papers, with all the necessary articles for penning letters, etc. It is very thoughtful and kind in the Christian Commission to furnish them with these conveniences.

"Last night I commenced operations in this vicinity, preaching to a company of soldiers who crowded our chapel tent. They were very attentive, and thirteen rose for prayers. I have appointed an inquiry and experience meeting for this afternoon, and expect to preach again to-night. I say 'expect,' for everything in an army is very uncertain. Owing to the soft condition of the soil, the corps of heavy artillery, especially, will hardly be able to move for a number of weeks, and yet as I write the roar of cannon fills my ears. It may be only target-practice, or it may be the commencement of an engagement ; most probably the former. Do not at any time be alarmed about me. I am led by Infinite Wisdom, defended by Infinite Power, comforted by Infinite Love. I do not allow myself to live in the future—for three weeks would seem long —but a day at a time I try to do my work, looking unto Jesus.

"Our accommodations are not even what we had at Brandy Station. Our tent is about ten feet square. In that little space we do our cooking and sleeping. The former is supervised by a superannuated soldier, who does the best he can. The sleeping was decidedly cold last night. I had to withdraw my nose from the air, which was full of frost, and roll myself up in a coil or bundle, to make all the animal heat available. Even then I spent some sleepless hours through chilliness. I do not repeat these things by way of complaint—nay, I am too good a soldier for that. This is only a reference to the seasoning process I am undergoing. I feel very well to-day, and hope, with the blessing of God, to endure hardness, and then return to you in the fulness of the blessing of the Gospel of peace. Give my love to my dear people. Tell them to pray for me very specially."

"RESERVE ARTILLERY, *March* 4, 1864.

"A few moments before dinner will afford me an opportunity to pen you a short letter. This, I am sure, will not be unwelcome. It is now one week since I left you. I am not sorry the week is gone, for, Providence favouring, I am that much nearer my loved home. To-day it is blustering, raw, disagreeable ; most probably the herald of another storm. Last evening we had even a larger crowd of soldiers than the night previous. They were deeply serious. Six or seven rose for prayers. I trust that good influences are at work. We followed the sermon with a prayer-meeting. Four prayers were offered ; two of them by lieutenants of the regiment—noble fellows. Tattoo sounds at eight o'clock, at which time the roll is called, and the soldiers are required to go to their tents. This, of course, limits our services. If we had another hour, say till nine, I have no doubt it would be for the advantage of all concerned.

" Another disadvantage is the godlessness of the officers ; that is, most of them, for there are a few honourable exceptions. Last night they had a regular ball in the camp, which was attended by their wives and sisters. The festivities were protracted until a late hour, for one of my last remembrances was the strains of music. I slept very comfortably last night, piled on the coats and shawls, made myself warm, and got through the night in a refreshing way. This afternoon I propose to ride on horseback over to Brandy Station and find my correspondence, for up to this hour I have not heard a word from home.

" Tell sister M—— that I am waiting upon God ; sitting with a teachable spirit at the feet of Him who has said, 'Learn of me.' I want to be instructed in the deep things of God, and furnished unto every good word and every good work. I surrender myself into the care of my infinitely wise and powerful Father, trusting that He will lead me into usefulness and truth, plenty and peace. I am sure He will ; but it is sometimes a trial to walk blindly, not knowing the how or the wherefore. Bless His holy name, there is nothing, so far as I am aware, between Him and myself, and I trust momentarily and sweetly in the merit of Jesus Christ my Lord. Kiss my children for their absent papa. I shall be delighted to clasp them in my arms again. Love to all. They are calling me for dinner."

" HEAD-QUARTERS RESERVE ARTILLERY, *March* 5, 1864.

" After writing to you yesterday, I borrowed the horse of one of the captains, and had a delightful ride over to Brandy Station. I thought of my boys, and wished that they might be here for a little while to enjoy the privilege of galloping over the Virginia fields. At Brandy Station I found a letter in waiting—the one you sent by the hand of sister M—— to Philadelphia, and while I tarried the cars arrived, bringing another written on Tuesday evening. Thank you kindly for these affectionate epistles. They come like angel visitants. I need not say that they were read and re-read. I was sorry to hear of the continued illness of the children ; perhaps by this time they are all better. Leaving them in the care of our faithful Heavenly Father, I feel assured that He will order all things well. Remember that if their illness is serious or dangerous, you must at once telegraph for me. Parting with sister and little 'Streak of Sunshine' must have been another trial for you. That boy Will would be the life and light of any home.

"Last night I preached again to a company of soldiers that entirely crowded the tent. I trust that seed was sown in their hearts which will speedily appear in the form of fruit. After the service was over, and all were gone, I sat in my tent reading ; while thus engaged the curtain was drawn aside, and a soldier entering, glided to my side. 'Chaplain,' said he, 'I cannot rest—cannot sleep—I must have relief. Won't you pray for me?' 'Oh yes, soldier,' said I, 'most gladly;' and after preaching unto him Jesus, we kneeled down together, and I poured out my soul in prayer for his speedy salvation. These facts are my inspiration and encouragement during this time of exile from home.

"Last night I rested rather comfortably ; my shawl makes a good pillow, and my overcoat, thrown over my blanket, contributes to the warmth of my bed. To-day it is raining again ; most probably this will prove a repetition of last Tuesday's storm. Softening this Virginia soil, these rains will oblige the army to remain where it is. In my experience I am panting for more of God, more of His truth, more of His holiness, more of His power ; 'hungering and thirsting' expresses my feelings at this time. Oh ! I want to return home in the fulness of the blessing of the Gospel of peace."

"ARTILLERY RESERVE, *March* 7, 1864.

"My last letter was written on Saturday. In the evening of that day we had an experience-meeting ; I would have given almost anything to have had you present. The testimonies of Christian soldiers melted my heart to tenderness, and my head was literally a fountain of tears. One and another spoke affectionately of pious and praying mothers. A noble Ohio soldier said, 'When I left my home, a dear, kind sister gave me that little Testament,' drawing the book from his side-pocket and holding it up. 'I had not been a member of the army long, before I realized I must have a friend. Who should be my friend? I opened my little Testament and read of JESUS. Oh what a Friend He has been to me ! This book has been a great comfort to me in my absence from home. It is full of sweet promises. One is, " In my Father's house are many mansions," etc. If I fall on the battle-field, I believe I shall go to occupy my mansion in the everlasting kingdom of God.'

"But I cannot begin to tell you all. It was one of *the* hours of my life. Twelve or fifteen rose for prayers, and all testified 'It is good to be here.' Yesterday I preached in the afternoon, and again in the evening. The interest is constantly on the increase. Last night the tent was packed, and numbers went away unable to get in. Men rose in every direction asking our prayers. Some came to me after the meeting, and with unrestrained tears said, 'Chaplain, pray for me.' The Christian men of the regiment and batteries are in the best of spirits, while the outsiders are evidently interested and impressed. Some are insisting that I shall accept the chaplaincy of the regiment, and march with them during the approaching summer ; but this is not practicable. I am sitting at the Master's feet, anxious to know His will concerning me. 'Lord ! teach me and lead me,' is my constant prayer. I enjoy the Divine presence more in preaching than at any other time. I am waiting for revelations of God beyond anything I have ever experienced.

"The discomforts of my present situation will make me appreciate and enjoy the advantages of my home when I return. For the last two days we have been smoked out. The wind has driven the smoke down the pipe of our little stove, making it almost impossible to breathe. When I would rest upon the bed, I have been obliged to cover my face with my handkerchief, and breathe through the linen. This morning the wind has shifted again, and we get along better. My foot is still pretty sore, preventing me from walking far ; but I do not suffer much, and get along very well. To-day we are to have a grand review of this division of the army. The weather is pleasant, and I suppose it will be a grand affair. I wish my boys could witness it."

" SIXTH NEW YORK HEAVY ARTILLERY, *March* 9, 1864.

"Yesterday, I believe, is the first week-day that I have failed to write to you since our separation. The reason was a jaunt to Culpepper Court-house, distant about ten or twelve miles. I started in the morning about ten o'clock, called at Brandy Station (but found no letters), pushed on to Culpepper, which I reached a little after twelve. This has been quite an important Virginia town. Some of the houses are respectable, but, like all Southern villages, and especially those that have been ravaged by war, it has an untasteful and dilapidated look. The soldiers have been very rude. Only one of a number of churches is fit for occupancy. I met with some friends, and enjoyed my visit. About half-past two I started back, making a little détour from the road, and calling at the house of Hon. John Minor Botts. He is faithful among the faithless. A member of Congress when father was chaplain, he remembered father, and this fact secured me a warm welcome. Leaving his comfortable mansion (the only one I have seen in the Old Dominion), I reached my present quarters about half-past four.

" The horseback ride of twenty-two miles left me wretchedly stiff and sore. Nevertheless I preached in the evening. The Spirit of the Lord seemed to rest upon the soldiers. Upwards of twelve rose for prayers, and the meeting which followed was spirited and profitable. The night before we had an experience-meeting. It was glorious. One old soldier said, 'I was converted in 1843 ; ran well until I joined the army. Then I began to lose ground. Like *Peter*, I denied my Lord, and, soldiers, I do not know but in some instances, like Peter, I blasphemed. I said bad words. I came to this meeting. In this tent God found me, as He found *Adam* in the garden. He said, "Soldier, where art thou ?" Like Adam, I thought to hide myself. I tried to get away. No use. Now I stand up, make this humble confession, and ask you to pray for me.' A number profess to have experienced religion within the last few days, and still the work goes on. The Christian Commission is the *Church in the army*. And though it may be attended with sacrifice, all patriotic parties ought to be willing to take their turn in serving the Church."

"SIXTH NEW YORK HEAVY ARTILLERY,
Friday morning, March 11, 1864.

" I have been writing this morning a letter to a wife who resides at Garrison Station, on the line of the Hudson River Railroad. Last night her husband was converted. The case is a thrillingly interesting one. Two weeks since he tore himself from a dear, pious, and faithful wife and three beloved children. His companion remonstrated with tears in her eyes. Still he enlisted.

" After great hardship he reached this camp on Wednesday morning. In the evening he came to the tent. The preached Word affected his heart, and he rose for prayer. All day yesterday he was a subject of powerful awakening. Last evening, during our experience-meeting, he rose up (a noble-looking man), and, with tears raining down his cheeks, said, ' Oh fellow-soldiers, how much I want to be saved ! All day I have been wrestling with conviction. Now I yield—I yield ; I can hold out no more. I am resolved to seek and serve God. Oh, won't you please to pray for me?' I dropped on my knees, and poured out my soul in importunate pleading. All the soldiers were wonderfully interested and engaged. Prayer finished, the soldier rose again, and said, ' Fellow-soldiers, I must tell you ; I believe God has heard and answered prayer. The love of Jesus is shed abroad in my heart. I am happy in God. I came to be a soldier of the nation—now I am in addition a soldier of Jesus. When we were coming here, very many of our company were sorry that they had enlisted ; but oh ! if you will enlist in the service of Jesus you will never be sorry.' Thereupon another soldier sprang upon his feet and said, 'I will enlist to-night. Two of my children are in Heaven. I want to meet them there, and I intend to march with that dear man. Hear, fellow-soldiers, I enlist to-night.' I can give you no idea of the meeting. It was wonderful—glorious ; surpassed anything I ever witnessed. My own soul was richly baptized. I lay down on my bed with a heart melting in gratitude before God.

" Yesterday was one of the stormiest I ever saw. It rained violently and blew fearfully. I thought again and again our tent must be prostrated. God, however, watched over us, and at the close of the day we were living to praise Him. This morning it is foggy and misty. The wind still lingers in the north-east. I am sustained by the conviction that I am in the line of duty, and God strengthens and blesses me. When the time comes to return home, I shall feel great joy in turning my face and directing my steps to the dearest spot on earth to me. How are you this morning, my darling Annie ? and how are my beloved children? If I had the 'wishing-cap' or the 'seven-league boots,' I should know all about you in a little while. Our omnipresent and omnipotent Father watches between us while we are absent one from another. Blessed be His name ! Give the children three kisses apiece for papa. Remember me affectionately to all relatives and friends. Tell sister M—— to pray on. God hears and is answering her prayers. Ask all friends to remember me at a throne of grace."

" SIXTH N. Y. HEAVY ARTILLERY, *Saturday, March* 12, 1864.

" We have had a long, dismal rain-storm. Yesterday we had in the morning a regular north-east drizzle ; in the afternoon and evening most violent thunder-showers. This weather has shut us up in our tents, and left the country around in a most terrible condition. The streams are swollen to twice or thrice their original size, while the soil is stirred in its depths. I think there is a good deal of solicitude at Washington respecting an advance of the army ; but while the roads are in their present condition the troops must almost necessarily continue stationary. This will harmonize with the views of the soldiers, who, from previous experience, seem to dread exposure, especially lying out, at this uncertain season of the year. If they remain in winter quarters ten days longer, it will include my term of service, and leave me free to return home without the necessity of accompanying them in their proposed marches. I think, however, any movement of the army now would be a sufficient reason why I, with only a few days of furlough* remaining, should retire from the front.

"This morning the sun shines brightly, and the air is as balmy as the breath of May. I am quite well, barring a little rheumatism in my shoulders, which makes it difficult to get my coat off and on. My foot has been giving me a good deal of trouble.

"Our meetings yesterday were delightful. In the afternoon it was a prayer and experience meeting ; at night I preached on the subject of forgiveness of sins. The attendance was large and the interest unabated. Large numbers rose for prayers. One new convert got up last night and exhorted his fellow-soldiers powerfully. After this he prayed with great tenderness and unction. I realize in my own experience great nearness to the Saviour. Oh, what should I do without the love and fellowship of Jesus ! Just now an old soldier brings into our little tent a box he has received from home. Opening it for pa—apples, chickens, preserves, eggs, cakes, etc. Noble fellow ! he is insisting that we shall help ourselves. He would be glad if we would take half that he has. Perfectly delighted, he says, 'Ain't it nice ?' 'How thoughtful and kind are my family at home !' Oh what a glorious thing it is to be kind and generous and noble ! So I have filled up my daily epistle. To-morrow is the Sabbath of the Lord. Oh that it may prove the best day of my life ! "

"ARTILLERY RESERVE, *March* 19, 1864.

" This is your letter from your papa. A little rough stool is my table, but it does almost as well as my study desks. How very often I think about you, my dear boys ! When I see the soldiers drawn up in their evening parade, and hear the drums beat, then I think about you, and wish you were here to look upon these stirring scenes. When I get astride of a nice horse I think about you, and wish you were here to have a ride. When I lie upon my blanket at night I think about you, and pray our kind Heavenly Father to take good care of you during my absence.

" Yesterday afternoon we had a great '*scare.*' Word came that the rebels were advancing upon us. Sure enough, they were crossing the Rapidan River, the dividing line between the two armies. Orders came from head-quarters to be ready to march at a moment's notice. Accordingly the soldiers packed their knapsacks, filled their haversacks with three days' rations, and for a while all was excitement. Pa thought he

---

* From his Church.

was in for it, but in God was his trust. About seven o'clock the order to march was recalled. This morning the regiment is all ready. While I write fighting is going on. We can distinctly hear the cannons roar in the distance. Pa had almost made up his mind to leave this morning for Washington, but he thought, 'No, Monday is my time, and I will wait and trust in my Heavenly Father, who has always taken such good care of me.' How blessed it is, my boys, to love God, and feel that He loves us! Then we are safe anywhere. I want you all to be good, and then all will be well."

It was always a great trial to Mr. Cookman to be separated from his family. He had scarcely got settled upon his return from the army, when the physical condition of his children required that some of them, at least, should be taken to the homestead on the banks of the Susquehanna, and the others with the mother soon followed. We are indebted, however, to these separations for those familiar and tender letters to his wife and children which reveal so charmingly the family side of his character.

"NEW YORK, *June* 24, 1864.

" You must not think that pa has forgotten you because he has neglected to write you a letter. Every day he thinks about his little George and Frank, and wonders how they are getting along. I hope that you are very obedient and kind to aunt Beckie and grandma, and all the rest. I trust that you never quarrel with one another. Remember, little brothers should be always full of love. You must not forget your prayers morning and evening. Never say bad words or associate with bad boys. If you hear a boy swear, turn your back upon him, and say, he cannot be my playmate or companion any longer. Always go to Sunday School, and remember to behave well in church. People around are looking at you, and expect good conduct from the sons of a minister. I am pleased to know that you go to school every day, and go so cheerfully. Give attention to your lessons, and learn as much and as fast as you can. Be very attentive and kind to uncle Cyrus. Do not climb up on him as you used to do, for that might give him pain in his wound. Run his errands. Do everything you can to make him happy, for you know he is your noble, brave soldier uncle. When you are large boys or big men you will refer with pride to your patriot uncle, who was wounded in the service of his country.

"Yesterday *we*—that is, ma, Brune, Sis, Will, and myself—accompanied the Seventh Avenue Sabbath School on their excursion to Staten Island. The day was warm, but we had a real nice time. Swings, football, copenhagen, and other sports interested the little folks. No accident occurred, and we returned to the city about seven o'clock in the evening. I suppose you would like to know about your little brothers and sisters. Well, *Brune* is still very pale and thin, but I think a little better than he was. He is very anxious for the time to come when we shall go to Columbia, for he wants very much to see his little brothers again. *Sister* has been sick, but is better again. She has had her large doll fixed up, and is quite proud of it. She is a dear little girl. *Will* is still a little 'streak of sunshine'—is as fond of papa's study as ever. Both he and Sis have new portemonnaies. Will has about twelve cents, and Sis six. He is perfectly delighted with his treasure. Now, Frank, don't your mouth water for a kiss? On the second Sabbath of July (10th) I expect to be in Harrisburg. Perhaps some time the week before I will bring ma and the rest to Columbia. Will you be glad to see us? Now my letter is full. Good-bye. Give our love to all. Be good boys."

"NEW YORK, *July* 19, 1864.

"Did you ever receive a letter before? Now remember that this is all yours, so that when mamma has read it to you, you can fold it up and put it in the envelope again, and carry it about in your pocket, and say, 'This is papa's letter to "Little Sunshine."' Won't that be splendid? How papa misses his little boy! The *study* is so quiet now; the chairs keep in their places; the old valise stays in the cupboard; no *whoop* to tell that the locomotive is coming; no *invitation* to go in the cars to Columbia; nobody asks for my *lead-pencil* now; or for a sheet of *white paper* now; or for a *book with pictures in* now. When papa sits down at the table he is all alone. No little darling Will to sit close alongside and wait for his buttered bread, or perhaps for a little sip of papa's coffee, which you know is particularly nice. Don't you pity poor papa? Never mind. It won't be long. Two or three weeks, and then pa will get in the steam-cars again. The old '*locomoshs*' will go 'chu! chu! chu!' and after a while he will come to Columbia. Then he will look out of the car window, and there will be bright-eyed little Willie on the fence waving his white handkerchief, shouting, 'Hurrah, boys! hurrah! here comes my precious papa!' Won't that be splendid? But I hear my little boy say, 'What will you bring me?' *Kisses*—ever so many sugar-candy kisses. Don't you love my kisses? I am sure I love yours. I wish you were here to give me one of those real, ripe, sweet, juicy kisses that grow on your little red lips. Tell mamma that papa is right well. He has just been writing letters to uncle Frank and Edmund Y——. This afternoon he expects to attend Dr. Palmer's meeting, and perhaps afterward ride out to Harlem and see grandma. Now, if little 'Streak of Sunshine' was along, we would go on board the 'Tiger Lily,' and sail as far as High Bridge. Wouldn't that be splendid? I hope that while I am away you will be a first-rate boy. Never strike your dear little sister—no, indeed! Never quarrel with your little brothers, or pout or be disobedient to your precious mamma. At the table do you eat with your fingers?—no, indeed, but with your fork. Did you know it? William Wilberforce Cookman is a perfect little gentleman. When I get back to Columbia, I will ask mamma and aunt Beckie and grandma, and if they say you have been a good boy, then you shall have one of those nice, new, beautiful two-cent pieces. Now don't you laugh—it is so. I will put it in that fat little hand, and you shall feel—'it is *mine.*' Now I must close Willie's letter. When mamma gets through reading it, then give her a splendid kiss, and tell her that is from papa ; and then go all around and give every one one of your best, and tell them all it is from your dear pa Good-bye,· my little darling."

Before leaving Trinity, Mr. and Mrs. Cookman suffered a deep affliction in the death of little Rebecca, a child three years and six months old. She was absent from home when she died. This was the first time the Destroyer had invaded their family circle. The father thus touchingly alludes to their bereavement :—

" We have just been placing in the cold grave another beautiful gem, to develop and re-appear in the promised resurrection. Our sweet little Rebecca is now in the special keeping of Him who looks down and watches all her dust till He shall bid it rise. I have many times sought to comfort bereaved parents. God, by this providence, has been better preparing me for this part of my ministerial duty. Our precious darling was incomparably more beautiful in death than during life. Losing all her baby-like look, she presented the appearance of a lovely little girl —her features regular and perfect, her face little wasted, and indescrib- ably sweet in its expression ; indeed, her exceeding beauty in death was a matter of universal remark.   I felt to-day what a trial it is to bury one who is ' bone of your bone and flesh of your flesh.'

"Returning from the grave, the heart-stricken mother could not restrain the audible ' Farewell, my precious darling !'   I thought, ' Yes, until we meet again in a tearless and deathless realm.'   Oh how precious the word 'Comforter' is to me this afternoon !   The blessed Third Person comes unusually near, and comforts me with the comfort of God. I have no doubt that this experience is in answer to the prayers of those who are very dear to me."

Thus closed the pastorate at Trinity, and with it Mr. Cookman's ministry in New York.   The General Conference, at its session of 1864, in Philadelphia, had extended the time that a minister could be appointed to any one charge from two to three successive years ; but, for reasons which seemed sufficient to all concerned, he declined a re-appointment for the third year, and accepted a pressing invitation to return to Philadelphia.   He and the Trinity people parted on the most agreeable terms, and among them to this day no name is more revered for the fragrant memories which cluster about it than his.

CHAPTER XVI.

THE immediate cause of the transfer of Mr. Cookman
again (1865) to the Philadelphia Conference, so soon after
leaving it for New York, was that his services were
earnestly sought for the new church which had been erected
in Philadelphia in Spring Garden Street. Several of his
former parishioners at Green Street were active men in
erecting the new church, and they felt that no one was so
well qualified to build up the new charge, to give it consistency and stability, as their former beloved pastor.

The authorities having determined upon Mr. Cookman's
transfer to Philadelphia, he hastened to the session of his
old Conference at Harrisburg. Thence he wrote to his
wife :

"HARRISBURG, *March*, 1865.

"I should have written yesterday, but duties multiplied, engrossing
all my time ; among the rest the responsibility and trial of preaching
last night. Oh ! it was a heavy burden, but I took it up in the name
of my Master, *and was helped.* I feel very humble and quiet and
grateful this morning. We have commenced an eight o'clock prayer-
meeting this morning ; the season was very blessed. You will be
interested in every step of my progress, and so I will go back. On
Tuesday night I left Philadelphia with quite a number of ministerial
brethren. Comfortably ensconced in a berth of the sleeping-car, I

dozed until Harrisburg was announced ; proceeding to our friend C.'s, I met a most affectionate reception. The brethren at Conference were very cordial ; business was rapidly dispatched, and a place assigned me on one or two committees, and at the close of the morning session my appointment for evening was announced. During the day I met friends in every direction ; they were as cordial as though I had been their pastor last year. God has given us a strong hold upon the hearts of this people.

"The duty of preaching last night involved a terrible trial. I would rather have taken severe lashings ; *but I dared* not refuse—it seemed to me that it might be in the order of God ; and what is my will in comparison with the Divine will? My Heavenly Father knows how simple and pure was my motive. I *had a good time*—the brethren say great good was accomplished ; but this morning I feel like a whipped child, indisposed to look anybody in the face. My soul, however, is full of tender love for Jesus ; I cling to Him with increasing affection and devotion. ' Happy, if Thou, my Lord, approve.' Pray for me : I want that this Conference time may be a Pentecostal *season for us all.*"

Mr. Cookman's welcome was, if possible, even heartier than on the occasion of his return from Pittsburgh. It is doubtful if any friends are like the heart's first friends. His early associates were now more deeply attached to him than ever before. His re-entrance into their ranks was hailed with delight ; and he, as was natural, felt again the tranquillizing sense of home, which gave him a new spring for his chosen work. The reception which the people would give him could not be questioned, in view of his popularity when stationed in the city and the enthusiastic greetings which always met him on his occasional visits. His brother George wrote in the winter of 1863 to his mother after one of these brief sojourns :

"We enjoyed Alfred's visit hugely. He is a prime fellow, and his trip over here was productive of great good. I never saw such a sight as the Monday evening he preached at Green Street—altar crowded, and some thirty or forty in the congregation rose for prayers. We are going to have him back to Philadelphia some of these days."

The Spring Garden charge presented the most favourable conditions for Mr. Cookman's resumption of the Christian ministry as a pastor in the great city of the Keystone State. The new, capacious, and elegant church, with every modern facility for effective church work, was admirably located to accommodate the growing population in the north-west section of the city. It was thoroughly manned by official boards full of energy, zeal, and liberality. Its success was assured from the beginning. The new pastor's name was a tower of strength. The pews immediately after the dedication were rapidly taken, and it entered promptly upon a career of usefulness such as has been hardly surpassed by any charge in any of our great centres.

Among the features of the Church was its large and well-conducted Sunday School. No minister ever more highly appreciated the Sunday School as an arm of pastoral success than Mr. Cookman. He was in the truest sense in all places a part of his school, regarding himself as responsible for a close contact with it and a most intimate knowledge of its workings. He felt that the same heart must send its pulsations through the whole congregation, composed alike of adults and children. His habit was to know and to be known to teachers and scholars, to meet them on the most familiar terms, and so to inspire them with affection as to be able to utilize them as instruments and as materials for the incessant supply of workers in the Church and additions to its members. The secret of his great power with children was his love for them. This the children could always see and feel, and hence he invariably enlisted their sympathies. He was one of the most successful talkers to youth America has known. His tact in awakening and keeping attention,

14

by presenting truth under the drapery of description, or in the form of illustration, or by some apt question, or by the flash of gentle humour, or by a tone of solemn appeal, was really consummate. Who ever knew an audience of children to tire under him? Who has not seen congregations of them, wearied by some prosy homilist who had preceded him, suddenly electrified as he rose before them, and his look of familiar sweetness and voice of melody caught eye and ear? He was never happier than when before the upturned faces of his "little brothers and sisters," as he loved to call his youthful auditory, or when, surrounded by a throng of them, they plucked familiarly at his coat to catch his notice, or when, seated at the fireside of his own or some other Christian home, the boys and girls drew about him to listen to his naïve and simple stories.

It is said of the celebrated John Charlier Gerson, who was Chancellor of the University of Paris, and the theological leader of the reformatory councils of Pisa (1409) and Constance (1415), that, after taking a prominent part in all the great questions of his age, he retired to a convent at Lyons, and found his chief delight in the instruction of children.* Alfred Cookman was never greater than when in his humility he stooped to be the companion and friend of Christ's little ones. Talking one day with a lad of one of his charges, he said, "Willie, do you pray?" "Yes, Mr. Cookman," was the reply. "When you pray, what do you pray for? You know we must have an object when we pray." "Why, sir, I have a very bad temper, and I pray to God to help me to overcome it." "And does He help you?" "Yes, sir, I think He does." Such was the affection,

---

* Lange's Comm. on Matt., p. 323.

the directness, with which he approached the children and youth of his parishes.

It may not be amiss here to present at some length in his own words his views of the relation of " the pastor and the Sunday School." The report, though not full, is very suggestive :—

" A practical talk on the relation of the pastor to the Sunday-school was made by the Rev. Alfred Cookman.

" He did not design discussing the theory of this relation, but to give his views of what it should be, illustrating by his own experience in trying to carry out his convictions on this subject.

" 1. A pastor ought to spend a part of every Sabbath in the midst of his school ; be intimately interested and identified with it. He should, if possible, know the name, secure the confidence, and engage the affections of every child in his charge. To further this, he may pass around the school from time to time quietly, unostentatiously, taking the hand of the teacher, smiling upon or speaking to the class, or to members of it, by name, as, 'Brother Charley, I hope that you are very well to-day,' or, ' Harry, my little brother, I trust that you are enjoying your lesson—do you find it difficult ? ' or, ' Mary, my little sister, you must not fail to give God your heart ; ' or, ' Lizzie, I am hoping that, after a while, I shall have the pleasure of meeting you in heaven, as I now have the pleasure of meeting you in Sabbath-school.' Thus the presence of the pastor will be greeted as a living, moving blessing, and as he crosses the threshold of the room little eyes will brighten, and hearts overflow with loving gladness.

" The pastor should also recognise his scholars in the street and at their homes, as well as in the schoolroom. The speaker had charged his children to run up to him and take him by the hand in the street, and to make themselves known whenever and wherever they should meet him.

" 2. A second suggestion is that the pastor should preach steadily or regularly to the children of his Church, members of his Sabbath-school. This is not to say that he should monopolize the superintendent's time by remarks, but have fixed periods when, after due preparation, he shall speak a word of loving counsel, warning, or encouragement. ' After due preparation,' mark, for there can hardly be a greater mistake than to suppose that this exercise requires little or no preparation. Dr. Newton, that prince of children's preachers, had told him that he

devoted as much time and labour to his 'children's sermons' as to those
which he prepared for the great congregation. The reason why it has
come to be a received truth that so few are adapted to talk to children,
is because so few take the time and thought necessary to *prepare* themselves for the work. Then, after thorough preparation, they must put
themselves in sympathy with their youthful hearers, and should aim
rather to *talk* to them than 'address' them.

"In connection with the service called 'Children's Sermon,' Mr.
Cookman has found it advantageous to encourage the older scholars to
submit to him, the Sabbath after they have heard it, a report of his
sermon, which may be longer or shorter as they may please. He receives it, takes it home, carefully examines and corrects it, marks it
'very good,' 'excellent,' 'good,' according to its merits, and signs it
carefully, 'Your affectionate pastor,' appending his name. The report
is then returned to the scholar. The idea has proved useful in several
very obvious ways.

"3. As a third suggestion, a pastor would find it helpful to him and
his school to have a week-day meeting of a children's class, over which
he could have supervision in the matter of Christian duty and walk. In
most of his charges, Mr. Cookman had held such a class on Saturday
afternoon at three o'clock. Punctuality is insisted upon, the roll called,
and absentees marked. If a scholar is absent two or three weeks con-
secutively, without an excuse, his name is stricken from the roll. After
singing and prayer, and singing again, the pastor asks a few questions
bearing on practical religion—as, whether they have remembered to read
their Bibles daily, and pray to God morning and night since they last
met, the answers being given by raising the hand. In such an exercise
the speaker had been impressed with the fact that so few of his scholars
were accustomed to pray *twice* a day. They are then encouraged to
stand up in their place and recite a passage of Scripture on a topic
announced the week before, or one having the name of Jesus in it, or
one beginning with A, B, C, D, etc., going regularly through the
alphabet. An opportunity is then given to the pastor to reply personally to the scholars, giving a short word to each on the text they have
recited perhaps, and then general remarks to the class for fifteen or
twenty minutes, with the aid of the blackboard, concluded with singing.
These exercises last three-quarters of an hour, never exceed an hour.
Tracts and children's papers and reward-cards are then distributed, and
the class separates. Each child is taken by the hand on parting, and
some such sentiment expressed as, 'I hope you will be found obedient
at home, kind to little brothers and sisters during the week,' etc.

"4. As a last suggestion, the pastor should be concerned to organize a Bible-class, composed of his teachers and members of the larger classes who might choose to join it. This class may meet during the week to study their next Sunday's lesson. They had organized one in the speaker's charge, which promised most important results. It meets on Saturday evenings. The first hour is devoted to the lesson, in asking and answering questions, using the question-book as a guide, but not confining themselves to it. This exercise is made a free, familiar interchange of thought and inquiry. The next half-hour of one week is devoted to teachers' experiences, the relation of encouragements and discouragements, or to prayer over the work. On the next week this half-hour is given to reading by the pastor of short biographical or other sketches of religious interest, making it eminently practical. On the third meeting two or three short essays, written by scholars, are read. On the fourth, after the regular exercises, committees appointed by the pastor on various subjects—such as sick and delinquent members, on new members, the prayer-meetings (which the young men and young women conduct separately), on sick and afflicted church members, on tract distribution, etc.—all make their reports. Thus an interest is taken in all the work of the Church, and the pastor is training helpers all around him. The whole secret of his success lies in some such efforts, by which his flock, young and old, shall be kept employed in the Master's vineyard.

"For a pastor to neglect the command, 'Feed my lambs,' and thus to turn aside from a field 'white to the harvest,' is to indicate a strange unfitness for the very work to which he ought to believe himself Divinely called beyond any question."

Several letters of Mr. Cookman to his children have already been given. I insert others here, written about this date, as illustrative of his manner of dealing with his own children. His children were summering at or near Columbia.

"This letter is for 'Posse kin,' as ma sometimes calls you. I expect you are having an elegant time at grandpa's—rolling your hoop, flying your kite, playing with Rollo, and helping grandma to make garden. You must not eat up all the gooseberries and cherries and currants before pa comes to Columbia; if you do, pa will lay you down on the floor, and he will tickle you—oh, how he will tickle you! I hope that you are a very good boy, that you obey everything that aunt Beckie tells you, that you say your prayers every morning and evening, that you never quarrel with little Bruner, and that you keep away from the railroad and river. Would you not like to see the little sister? She is a bouncing, beautiful girl, and begins to crow like a chicken. Frank Simpson talks a great deal about Bruner and George : he says, 'Boys gone in the cars—gone to Columbia.' When pa and ma come they will bring Frank and the little sister. Then you will take Frank in the garden and show him the flowers, won't you? and you will put little Annie in a carriage, and take her riding. Then pa will get a big carriage and a live horse, and with his little boys he will drive out in the country. Won't we have a good time? Now remember to be a good, obedient boy, and pa will bring you a pretty present. Give a kiss to grandma, grandpa, and aunt Rebecca, and all the rest. When they will let you see that new baby at uncle Aby's, you must ask him to let you give it a kiss for pa, and let it be one of your very best kisses. Pa and ma send you a *locomotive* full of love."

"Bruner's letter came to hand this morning. We were glad to learn that you were quite well and enjoying yourselves. You must be very good boys during your stay in Columbia. Make as little noise and trouble as possible. Grandma and grandpa are both old, and therefore cannot bear as much as they once could. You must try and remember this, and when you are in the house talk in subdued tones and sit quietly in your chairs. I think you ought to take a part of every day for reading. If all study and no play makes Jack a dull boy, then all play and no study makes Jack a very good-for-nothing boy. Select some interesting book, read more or less every day, and when I come to Columbia you can each one report the number of pages you have read, for I shall certainly ask the question. Do not quarrel with one another ; such conduct is disgraceful, and especially between brothers. This spirit often leads to blows, and blows to serious injuries, and even death. Nothing could grieve me so much as to know that my boys did not feel kindly or affectionately toward each other. Always be gentle and patient and affectionate in your conversation and sports and intercourse.

"Another thing—never forget that you are young Christians, members of the Church. The eyes of others are upon you. I do not suppose that you would tell falsehoods or say bad words, or take what did not belong to you. But remember that angry tempers and angry words are inconsistent with the Christian character. You have not left your religion in Philadelphia, but taken it with you. Let it influence you to *read your Bible every day, to pray three times a day,* and to go to class-meeting every week. Ask aunt Beckie if she will not take you with her ; and though it may be a trial—a great trial—yet for the sake of your dear Saviour consent to the trial, and resolve to attend a class-meeting every week. In this matter take your father's advice. He knows what is best, for he has been through all your experiences. Read this letter over and over again, think of and remember the advice we have given. *Be quiet as possible, read a little every day, don't quarrel, act like little Christians, go to class-meeting.* About going down the country, we will see when I go to Columbia. This morning we are all pretty well. The baby, who was quite sick all day yesterday, seems better. This is probably owing to the agreeable change in the weather. Mamma says that when it suddenly becomes cool you must not forget to put on thicker clothing. Will scalded his foot this morning, and for a while was a lame and crying little soldier. But petroleum and flour have cured him so far that he is now out of doors playing. How is little sister Puss ? Let every brother give her two kisses for me. I am glad she was pleased with her book. Of course she will read it all through, and be able to tell us all about it when we meet."

A meeting for the promotion of holiness was promptly established at Spring Garden ; but for sufficient reasons Mr. Cookman allowed it to be removed to the Methodist Book-rooms, in Arch Street. He by general consent was continued the leader of the meeting while he remained in the city. This " Friday-afternoon meeting " has become an institution, and is resorted to by persons of all denominations from far and near. Mr. Cookman also frequented, as when previously in Philadelphia, the meetings under the conduct of Mrs. Keen.

The first year of the pastorate at Spring Garden was one of solid and abiding usefulness. There is no record which acquaints us with the details of the devoted pastor's labours, but the minutes of the Conference show increase in all departments.

As evidence of the high esteem in which the pastor and his wife were held, the congregation, on the 6th of March 1866, the fifteenth anniversary of their marriage, gave them a "crystal wedding." Their home in Wallace Street was crowded with the members of the congregation, who brought with them many tasteful articles as mementoes of the occasion. A presentation speech was made to the happy pair by Mr. Alexander Irwin, to which Mr. Cookman replied in his usually felicitous style. He was much moved while he spoke, and at the close called upon the company to sing, "Praise God, from whom all blessings flow," and then offered prayer.

Mr. Cookman never appeared to greater advantage than amid those scenes, when he was surrounded by the company of his friends, drawn together in honour of himself, or of some friend, or for the advancement of the social culture of the Church. He was commonly the central attraction of all such gatherings, not so much by his official station as by the charm of his person and character : handsome, dignified, and affable, he moved among the circles which he frequented with a modest grace, an instinctive recognition of the claims of others, a kindly salutation for every one, an evident appreciation of all that is best in his fellow-beings, which, while it showed him to be a man of

> "Cheerful yesterdays, and confident to-morrows,"

also made it manifest to all that the source of his cheerfulness and of his friendship was deep in the springs of a pure nature.

Mr. Cookman's close sympathy with the Young Men's Christian Association during his former residence in Philadelphia will be remembered. He shows himself again on their platform, and speaks in the following timely and earnest words :

"Ecclesiastical history tells us of one of the ancient Christians who, when summoned before the tribunal where he was to receive his sentence of death, was asked, 'What is thy name?' He immediately responded, 'I am a Christian.' 'What is thy occupation?' He answered, 'I am a Christian.' 'What is thy native country?' He answered, 'I am a Christian.' 'Who were thy ancestors?' He answered, 'I am a Christian.' And to all the inquiries he responded consistently in the words, 'I am a Christian.' Sir, it is with a feeling akin to this that I appear upon your platform to-night—not as an American, not as a Methodist, not as a sectarian, Mr. President—I am a Christian. I glory in this worthy distinction; and in the presence of men and angels I announce the fact, 'I am a Christian'—a humble member, an unworthy representative of the Young Men's Christian Association of the City of Philadelphia.

"Allow me, sir, to congratulate you and the friends of this worthy enterprise upon the brilliant and truly inspiring scene which greets our vision and crowns our anniversary. Certainly these Christian labourers are encompassed about with a great cloud of witnesses. Look at them sitting in these boxes, occupying this lower floor and yonder gallery —filling the entire house, making it appear almost like an ancient amphitheatre, which, during the progress of the Olympic games, would be crowded in every part, causing the place to look like a living, breathing structure. It shows how dear to the heart of every Christian is the cause of Christianity, and the welfare of every instrumentality intended to promote the interests of religion. These young men shall rise up like a race of young giants, showing themselves mighty in pulling down the strongholds of the wicked one. Now we have in the midst of us the Ark of the Covenant. Upon our banners are inscribed the words, 'Christ and Him crucified.' This is the motto under which we successfully battle. It is true, we still want the baptism of fire—that fire which shall constantly burn in our hearts, that shall glow in our countenances, kindle upon our tongues, and shine in our lives.

"Mr. President, I was greatly excited by the cordial welcome you extended to these delegates, hailing as they do from the North, South, East, and West. Only a week since I was in the city of Pittsburgh, and spent there one of the happiest evenings of my life. That such may be the case with you all to-night is my earnest wish. But a few years have elapsed since the veterans of 1812, hailing from almost every state in the Union, assembled in yonder hall in Chestnut Street, where more than eighty-three years ago there was prepared for publication to the world the memorable Declaration of American Independence. Finding the room too small for the number present, they adjourned to the Chinese Museum, which afforded them more spacious accommodations.

At the second organization it was ascertained that some of the delegates were absent. The New York delegation was every moment expected. Soon the stentorian voice of the door-keeper was heard, and the shout of the 'New York Delegation' resounded throughout the building. That vast audience sprang upon their feet, and made the edifice literally vocal with their shouts of enthusiastic welcome. The Baltimore veterans, coming in immediately after, were received with the wildest shouts of enthusiastic joy. And now, when the good soldiers of Jesus Christ are coming from the battles of our world to sit down in a convention that shall never adjourn *sine die*, an angel at one door, with shouts of joy, will announce the names of the Young Men's Christian Association of New York; another angel, at another door, will announce the Young Men's Christian Association of Troy; another the names of the associations of Baltimore, Germantown, and a thousand other places, all coming to mingle together in the Paradise of God. May God grant such may be the case, and that we may all be united in a bond of union that shall never know dissolution ! "

CHAPTER XVII.

THE session of this Conference of 1866 over, Mr. Cookman hastened to the help of his brother John, who was
stationed in Poughkeepsie, New York. He found him in
the midst of an extensive revival, but greatly prostrated in
health ; and although he was himself just out of an arduous
winter's work, he could not refrain from entering earnestly
into the work on his brother's hands.

To his wife :—

"POUGHKEEPSIE, *Monday, March* 26.

... "We found John in bed, a victim of diphtheria and great
nervous prostration. Last Wednesday the doctor was very much
alarmed. Yesterday morning early, and again in the afternoon, he had
very bad spells. This morning, however, he seems better, and we hope
will recover rapidly. His people are earnest and united in the prayers
for the preservation of his life, which seems to them exceedingly valuable. His labours have been singularly blessed. It is estimated that
nearly three hundred have professed to experience religion, among
whom are a large number of heads of families, and strong, stalwart
young men. The end is not yet.

"I preached yesterday morning on the cloud of witnesses. After the
sermon the altar was surrounded by gentlemen and ladies, who proposed to join the Church on probation. In the afternoon we had a
prayer-meeting, with an altar full of penitents. In the evening I
preached on 'Ye will not come,' etc. The altar was again filled with
mourners, and some occupied the front seats. This morning, and every

morning at nine o'clock, a meeting, largely attended, is held in the
lecture-room.   I preach to-night, to-morrow night, and perhaps on
Wednesday night. John has not been out of his bed since last Tuesday,
so that he is entirely laid aside.   The friends interpret my presence
as a providential interposition.   If you need me before Thursday,
telegraph, and I will be forthcoming at the earliest moment, but, unless
there should be some emergency demanding my presence, I reckon I
shall stay till Thursday.   I have the prospect of incessant labour while
I remain here, but this work shall make my heart rejoice, and 'spend
the remnant of my days.' "

The successful close of the late civil war, it will be remembered, entailed upon the nation problems of reconstruction second only in importance and difficulty to that of
maintaining the unbroken authority of the general Government. The chief problem was the settlement of the relations
of the freed coloured race to the new order of things. The
negro was free—he could not be again reduced to slavery.
Should he advance in the essential conditions of freedom to
the possession of those civil rights without the exercise of
which liberty is but a name?   Such was the question which
in 1866 forced itself upon the true lovers of the country and
of humanity for a speedy and practical solution.

It cannot be denied that the first stage of transition from
bondage to freedom was to the coloured people of the
South a period of fearful trial and suffering. " The reaction
which followed at the waters of strife, upon the exultation
of the passage of the Red Sea, has been fitly described
as the likeness of the reaction which, from the days of
Moses downward, has followed on every great national emancipation—one very just and beneficent revolution—when
the ' evils it caused are felt, and the evils which it removed
are felt no longer.' " *   Many of the worst results of emancipation, which the enemies of the slaves had predicted and

---

* Stanley's " History of the Jewish Church."

their friends had feared, fell upon them. They wandered about in multitudes, without food, clothing, or shelter. Their irresponsible and defenceless condition exposed them to sickness and immorality. They were tempted to drunkenness, theft, and murder. It is not surprising that they, like the Israelites, longed at the "bitter waters" for the "fleshpots of Egypt." When in bondage, they felt only the evils of their sad state, and anticipated in freedom naught but the sweets of liberty. In their recollections they dreamed of their snug quarters, their hoe-cakes, their merry evening songs and dances, but forgot the chains, the whip, the extinction of manhood and all its ties ; and thus, as they saw in the present only privation and peril, no wonder their hearts failed them and hope well-nigh died out.

Many of the advocates of freedom were also alarmed. The old, oft-repeated sophistry, that the negro is incapable of self-government, seemed too well supported by the abuses and shiftlessness which could not but follow upon the heels of a people suddenly liberated, without the least education in the habits of self-help. It again required the faith and nerve to insist upon the rights of citizenship for the black man that it had originally required to demand his liberation. Mr. Cookman was among the number who stood forward quite early in the reconstruction agitation for the bestowal of these rights in all their fulness.

"PHILADELPHIA, *June* 6, 1866.

" Last night I made a speech in the largest coloured church in Philadelphia. Two bishops, a book agent, a missionary, an editor, etc. (all black), on the platform. Justice to the negro and justice to the traitor was my political creed announced : duty to their brethren in the South, the exhortation urged. We had a glorious time. I thought of our honoured father, how he would have revelled and kindled and flamed on such an occasion or under such circumstances.

" This suggests your inquiry respecting colonization. My impression is that colonization belongs to some future providential development.

God is using the African race just now to teach us a lesson of justice and human brotherhood. We are not sufficiently instructed or disciplined yet, and cannot dispense with the lesson-book. When we are disposed to do justly in every particular, then I rather expect that Providence will open some gold mines or oil wells, or something else in the African coast, or in some other locality where black people can best live, and so we shall work out the problem of colonization. At the present time they are not only important for testing our integrity, but also for cultivating our soil. As labourers they are indispensable to our wealth and prosperity. I think colonization must be left to Providence and the coloured people themselves. We cannot force them away; it would be unwise, unkind, unchristian; and to colonize as we have been doing is like emptying a river by taking out a bucketful now and then. Let us live for the present, faithfully discharging the duty of the passing hour, which is to educate and elevate a people whose unrequited labours, multiplied wrongs, tedious bondage, and deep degradation give them a special claim upon us. Give them the spelling-book, the Bible, equal rights before the law, and the elective franchise as their weapon of defence, and then leave all the rest to God. In such a case I would implicitly trust the providence of One who is Himself infinitely just and holy and good.

"We were very grateful to learn of the improvement in dear mother's health. She does not know how unspeakably precious she is in the appreciation of her children. As time leaves its mark upon face and form, our love seems to be gentler, tenderer, and more sacred. We feel to say, 'Handle her carefully, speak to her lovingly; pour all the sunshine possible over the remaining years of her earthly sojourn.' Oh, we enjoyed beyond expression her presence in Philadelphia. She never before seemed so beautiful in my eyes. I felt as if I wanted to see her every day. My visits were always too short for myself. God bless her with the best of His blessings—and He does, for He gives her Himself, and next to this He gives her the enthusiastic love of her devoted children. We give her her vindication before she is taken from us, that she has always been true, tender, sympathizing, loving, faithful—yes, the best of mothers.

"I have written you a long letter, and yet I have not said nearly all that is in my heart. My soul still trusts and triumphs in God. Oh for a gust of praise to spread abroad the preciousness and power of full salvation!"

The summer of 1866 found Mr. Cookman, as usual, turned "evangelist." Instead of spending the vacation month as a holiday, he went from camp-meeting to camp-meeting, a herald of salvation. "What is the use of giving you vacation?" said one of his official brethren ; "you don't rest, you go to all the camp-meetings and preach more 'than if you were at home. I cannot favour it unless you will rest." He replied, "I cannot accept on such condition. I must preach. The Gospel is free."

A letter to a prominent citizen of Baltimore, and an active layman of the Methodist Episcopal Church in that city, indicates the extent to which his services were useful at the Shrewsbury meeting, and for which his advice was subsequently sought :—

"PHILADELPHIA, *September* 3, 1866.

"I thank you for your fraternal letter. Any tidings from Shrewsbury, *blessed Shrewsbury*, would be welcome, but *such tidings* were specially grateful and encouraging.

"Restoration to perfect health, or the reception of an ample fortune in the case of a dear friend, ought not to be as cheering intelligence as the fact that one we love has by faith appropriated a perfect Saviour, and is living in the enjoyment of sanctifying grace.

"'*Glory to the Lamb*,' that the young men of North Baltimore are putting on the whole panoply of God! Full of the Divinity, and valiant for the truth, may they prove themselves mighty in pulling down the strongholds of sin and hell. If I had their ear, I would say, with a brother's love and earnestness, *Hold fast to that whereunto ye have attained.*' Do not allow any temptations or influences to lure you from the experience and profession of Christian holiness. For *Christ's* sake, for the *Church's* sake, for the world's sake, for the sake of this precious doctrine, for the sake of that *virgin purity* which is now upon your souls—for all these reasons do, I beseech you, do continue steadfast and immovable, testifying humbly but definitely that 'the blood of Jesus cleanseth from all sin.'

"Let no one think for a moment that because God has answered his prayer, and granted him a deeper work of grace, that therefore he may hope for an exemption from trials, temptations, and difficulties. These will come, but if we are '*looking unto Jesus*' they will not *move us off the Rock*, and that is the important matter. In the time of conflict or darkness, be concerned about *two things*. First, *Is my consecration entire?*

Yes. Second, *Do I this moment accept and trust in Jesus as my perfect Saviour ?* Yes. Then 'all is well'—I am on the Rock. The Rock may be in the valley or on the hill-top, in the cloud or in the sunshine —it matters not ; if we are on that sure foundation, all is well. It is not darkness or temptation or trial that separates the soul from God—*it is only sin.* Let, then, our trusting souls adopt as their motto, 'ANY-THING BUT SIN.'

"The days I spent at the camp-meeting were among the happiest and best of my life. Can I ever forget some of those blessed scenes and seasons ? Sabbath morning—Sabbath evening ; Tuesday morning —Tuesday night in the preachers' tent ; Wednesday morning, when I so reluctantly withdrew myself from those hallowed privileges. *Oh ! I remember it all.* It supplies a rich feast of memory. It constrains at this moment a *heartfelt glory to the Lamb.* I shall never *cease to praise God for the Shrewsbury camp-meeting of* 1866. My Baltimore friends, always precious, never seemed so dear before. Oh ! I want to walk with them upon the King's highway of holiness, and after a while spend an eternity with them in the sweet groves of bliss. Convey to any whom you may meet, assurances of my Christian affection, and believe me, beloved brother, yours for *full salvation.*"

Another honoured layman* of Baltimore, alluding to Mr. Cookman's labours at the same camp-meeting, wrote subsequently :—

"I owe more, under God, to Brother Cookman than to any other being for the experience which I now enjoy. His sweet voice, ringing out so clearly, '*Be ye holy,*' was the first to awaken in my mind an anxious inquiry on the subject of Christian holiness. He led me into the higher life—into the possession of a brighter and deeper religious experience. Now that he has fallen, I feel more than ever like being true to the doctrine which it seemed his special mission so forcibly to proclaim."

A letter written to his sister, February 15th, 1867, will be read with interest because of its references to the deaths of cherished friends, especially that of the Rev. Dr. Monroe,

---

* Mr. John Hurst.

Secretary of the Church Extension Society of the Methodist
Episcopal Church. It is not too much to say that the whole
Church shared in the feeling of sorrow here expressed by
Mr. Cookman. The letter, which was written soon after
from the seat of the Conference at Harrisburg, will recall
to those who were present the tender fidelity which he
showed as chairman of the committee on memorial services
for deceased brethren. The beautiful service for rendering
the occasion impressive was due to his thoughtfulness.

> *"February* 15, 1867.

" We have had an unusually solemn week. The tribe of Levi, with
its immediate adherents, seem, in the providence of God, to have been
placed in the front of the battle. The arrows of death are flying
around us thick and fast. First the self-sacrificing Beckwith, of the
Bedford Street Mission, fell, with this sentiment upon his lips : ' I am
safe in Jesus—all is well.' Last Saturday a daughter of the Rev.
William Barnes went to Heaven ; her last words were, 'I have fought
a good fight.' Tuesday I made the address at the funeral of Helen
Batcheldor,* and accompanied the *cortège* to Trenton. Her dying
testimony was, ' I see Jesus.' On Wednesday we had the funeral
obsequies of the lamented Munroe, one of the most useful and
efficient ministers of American Methodism. It was one of the most
impressive occasions of the kind I ever witnessed. Hundreds of ministers, great multitudes of people, the deepest bereavement, the most undisguised affection, and the most tender and touching eulogies. Munroe
died gloriously. It was virtually a translation, while the character of
the man and the circumstances of his death make the event a sermon
addressed to a continent. Personally I am greatly bereaved. Dr.
Munroe was a great favourite of mine—one of my model ministers.
My estimate of him is expressed in the resolutions of the Philadelphia
Preachers' Meeting. Dr. Mattison's address on the occasion of the
funeral was especially beautiful. I wish you could have heard it. In
the midst of ' deaths oft ' I cling to that perfect love that casteth out all
fear, sweetly realizing that with my life hid with Christ in God, nothing
shall be able to separate the bond. All is well—all is well."

---

* Widow of the late Rev. Mr. Batcheldor, of the New Jersey Conference, and daughter of the Rev. Dr. Bartine.

15

CHAPTER XVIII.

THE unremitting pastor had hardly rested from the evangelistic labours of the summer, when one of the heaviest
calamities of his life fell upon him in the sudden death of
his brother George, which occurred October 1st, 1867.

The death of this Christian man, though sudden, was not
without premonitions. His health had been precarious
for some time, but immediate danger was not apprehended.
He lived, however, in constant preparation for death, by
living in constant devotion to God and duty. He was
almost literally translated from the scenes of his earthly
activity and joy.

Wide and deep as was the sorrow felt at the loss of a layman uniting so many qualities of the Christian, the gentleman, and the business man, it could do but little to conduct
from the heart of Alfred the ache which settled upon it.
Rarely had two brothers been so joined from boyhood ; and,
subsequent to George's conversion, their fellowship had
been of the most intimate and intense character. There
was the most perfect natural and spiritual kinship—they
thought, felt, and acted together ; and when the one fell it
was like tearing from the survivor his other half, the comple-
ment of himself.

Laurel Hill was within the next few months to become even more sacred and precious, by reason of others who should be gathered to its silent bosom. In the spring following he was called as the pastor of Bishop Simpson's family to stand by the dying bed of their son, Mr. Charles Simpson, and to administer to him and to them the consolations which now more than ever experience had taught him to understand. He had seen its embrace receive his ministerial friends Munroe, Heston, and Brainard, his young friend Simpson, his child Rebecca, his brother George ; but the grave was yet unsatisfied, and the demand soon came for one even nearer and dearer than all the rest. His eldest son, Bruner, who had so long struggled with disease, and who at times had given signs of improvement with the hope of ultimate recovery, at last succumbed to the destroyer. The brave boy died March 2nd, 1868. Thus the shadows thickened around the devout pastor and his family. Yet in the deepest darkness he retained his cheerfulness ; under all the suffering his spirit—as grapes when pressed give forth the invigorating juice—seemed to grow in saintliness both as to intrinsic depth and visible influence.

> " The darts of anguish fix not
> Where the seat of suffering is thoroughly fortified
> By acquiescence in the will supreme."

The following " BIOGRAPHY OF A GOOD BOY " was written by Mr. Cookman, and afterwards published by request in the *Methodist Home Journal*, and is so creditable alike to father and son, and so well adapted to benefit the youthful readers of this volume, that I insert it almost entire :—

" BIOGRAPHY OF A GOOD BOY.

" Our precious son, Alfred Bruner Cookman, brought to our home great joy, and for nearly sixteen years was a constant satisfaction and comfort. If there is such a thing as natural goodness, he seemed to be its fortunate possessor. His instincts were all in the direction of virtue and propriety. Strictly conscientious, we never heard of his uttering either a profane or an obscene word. No one ever suspected him of anything like falsehood. As our memory serves us now, we cannot recall a single act of disobedience to his parents. In the family circle he stood as a faithful little monitor, constantly careful respecting the morals, habits, manners, and appearance of his brothers and sisters. Naturally dignified and thoughtful, he impressed all by his quiet movements, his perfect politeness, and his singular sense of propriety.

" With these superior qualities of character he associated fine intellectual characteristics. His feeble health, extending through a number of years, had hindered somewhat his literary culture, nevertheless few boys of his age had read so much. He was a voracious reader. Sometimes we would chide him for his application to his book, and had literally to drive him into other exercises.

"In the use of the pencil he evinced great taste and skill. An amateur artist of Philadelphia, after looking at some of his productions, congratulated us on his superior talent, suggesting that it furnished promise of future fame.

" In his recitations on the occasions of anniversaries and public meetings (exercises that he always enjoyed), he was graceful, impressive, and popular. It is a significant fact in this connexion that his last, and one of his happiest declamations, was 'The Burial of Sir John Moore.'

" His thoughtfulness revealed itself in his attention to and remembrance of sermons, the numerous questions he would ask on Scriptural, theological, and general subjects, and his interest on the vital question of his personal salvation.

" Five years since, when we expected him to die, he professed to experience on his bed of sickness the forgiveness of his sins. When he partially recovered, one of his first wishes expressed was to unite himself with the Church. Accordingly, on the first Sabbath of 1863, when he was ten years of age, his dear mother led him to the altar, while his father had the exceeding joy of welcoming him as a probationer in the Central Methodist Episcopal Church, in the city of New York.

" His Christian life was marked by consistency of conduct and strict attention to religious duty. His prayers were never forgotten. His Bible was read every day. His class-meeting was regularly attended. Fond of his Sabbath School, he was always in his place, and for his teacher and classmates cherished a special love. Those classmates had

its large rooms and efficient control, grew to great proportions, and in all the elements of strength and self-propaga-
ting power. It soon projected a mission-school, known as
the Epworth Chapel.

The customary meeting for the promotion of holiness
was established. Such a meeting was now with him a
necessity, not only of his ministry, but of his personal
religious life. He must gather some of his flock and of the
Christian community, however few, into the closest fellowship, for the distinct purpose of conference and prayer upon
the great object which he believed to lie at the very foundation of individual and Church growth. When a little dissent from his opinions and plans was expressed—though
feeling sometimes that he was misunderstood—he would
simply reply to the suggestion of friends that he should
explain himself, " Oh ! the Lord Jesus has my reputation in His keeping ; I have committed it all to Him,
and He will take care of it." There were those in the
charge who were not prepared to accept his teachings on
Christian purity ; but who as time wore on espoused them,
and became the strongest supporters of his ministry and his
warmest personal friends. The Wednesday-afternoon meeting was soon an institution of the Church and of the city,
and comprised among its habitual attendants members
of all the orthodox churches, of whom none were more
constant and prominent than many of the Society of
Friends.

Mr. Cookman's ministry had always had a charm for these
godly, thoughtful people—probably on account of its exceeding simplicity and spirituality—but never before did he
obtain among them such marked influence as in Wilmington.
They feasted on his words with as much regularity and zest
as his own members. They took him to their hearts and

homes—a partaker of their quiet, unostentatious hospitality, breathing the pure atmosphere of their simple piety, he returned their kindness and confidence with the benefactions of a spiritual prince.

The pleasant impressions received by Mr. Cookman on his first appearance in his new charge, as told a letter to his wife, were more than confirmed by succeeding results.

" GRACE PARSONAGE, WILMINGTON, DEL., *April* 9, 1868.

" At my study table again ! in one of the nicest, coziest studies I have had for many years. You want a detail of proceedings, and, as I am a systematic man, it will be better to commence with Sunday. Preached twice ; in the morning on ' Old Paths,' in the evening on the ' One thing needful ' ; administered the Sacrament and made an address. It was a glorious day ; congregation magnificent ; Sacrament the most blessed service of that kind I have enjoyed for years. Friends seemed in highest spirits, and my soul praised God. Monday our goods were delivered at the parsonage. I unwrapped the furniture, unpacked the piano, my pictures, and a part of my books. Monday night and Tuesday it rained like a young deluge, and as some of the goods were getting wet, and I was almost alone, I concluded it was better for me to unpack a little more. The house began to look like home when I started on Tuesday in the rain for Philadelphia.

" At half-past one or a quarter to two R—— and the children arrived. I intended to have taken them in the steam-boat at four p.m., but they had ordered their carriage to the depôt, and so, after lunching in the city, we left again in the half-past three train. The friends had carriages, expecting us by the steam-boat, but we anticipated them. Proceeding to the parsonage, we took the ladies a little by surprise. It did not, however, make the slightest difference. The children are delighted with their new home. Frank says it is delightful, and thinks his ma will enjoy it very much, and indeed, everything is very pretty and very comfortable. It suits me. The trustees and their wives gave us a most affectionate welcome. Supper was provided and served— fried oysters, chicken salad, ham, rolls, Maryland biscuits, sliced. oranges, cakes, tea, coffee, etc. The evening was spent most delightfully. About half-past ten, when they would leave, I proposed some singing, and then knelt down and offered our new home to God. It was a season of interest and comfort.

" This morning I have been arranging my books, while Rebecca is here, there, and everywhere—the best sister-in-law that the Lord ever made. The boys behaved beautifully last evening. I was proud of them. This morning they have been helping me with my books, but now they are out in the field enjoying a game of ball. This evening they are all invited to a birthday-party at Brother B.'s. If the weather is favourable I think Rebecca and the children will make a little excursion to Philadelphia to-morrow in the steam-boat. Going at seven a.m., they can have nearly seven hours in the city. Rebecca says I must tell you there are mattresses on every bed, blankets on every bed, pillows for every bed, sheets for every bed, etc. Providence permitting, I wish to start for Columbia on Monday, and bring you to the city on Tuesday. Then you must decide where you will stay, for all want you. Wednesday, after interring our dear boy, we will leave for Columbia."

The summer of 1868 opened auspiciously, and Mr. Cookman entered, about the middle of July, upon the customary religious campaign. The first camp-meeting was that of the National Association, held at Manheim, Lancaster County. The location had been selected by himself. The attendance from north, east, west, and south exceeded all expectations—the friends of the cause came together from the remotest parts of the country.

Mr. Cookman, as might be expected, was everywhere present and active throughout the meeting. He was selected to preach the sermon on Sunday evening. The responsibility he felt to be well-nigh insupportable, but after unusual time spent in prayer and meditation, he chose his subject and went to the pulpit, when to his surprise the conviction was forcibly made upon his mind—" You must abandon your sermon and tell your experience." He yielded reluctantly to what seemed to be the Spirit's guidance. As he proceeded to narrate the manner in which God had led him, particularly into the blessing of full salvation, the impression upon the congregation deepened with every word, until the effect was overwhelming. The immense audience was

entirely subdued, notes of victory rang over the whole
ground, and throughout the night from every tent might be
heard the songs of spiritual joy.

The ensuing autumn and winter found him steadily devoted to his pastoral work, with such occasional outside
engagements as claimed him throughout his career. Very
soon a gracious influence began to pervade the congregation. All the means of grace increased in the numbers who
frequented them. The meeting for holiness grew not only in
numbers but in unction, and worked like leaven through the
whole religious community. The ordinary prayer-meetings
were thronged, and awakenings and conversions were of
common occurrence. Before the winter had passed a deep
and thorough revival of religion took place, and many accessions were made to the Church. The revival thus begun
continued with more or less power during the entire term,
resulting from year to year in the salvation of penitent
sinners and in the purification of believers—in view of the
results of which one has said, "I believe eternity alone
will reveal the good he accomplished at Grace." While the
congregation and Sunday School generally shared in the
blessed fruits, the students of the Wesleyan Female College
participated largely in them—very many of the young ladies
were converted and established in the principles and habits
of a Christian life.

The Fiftieth Anniversary (Jubilee) of the Missionary
Society of the Methodist Episcopal Church was held in the
city of Washington, on Sabbath and Monday, the 10th and
11th of January, 1869, and Mr. Cookman was invited to
take part. He preached on Sunday morning at Wesley
Chapel, spoke at a platform meeting at the Foundry in the
evening, and on Monday evening delivered one of the addresses at the continuance of the anniversary proper. There

had been four or five able addresses in the morning, and three or four equally able had been delivered in the evening before Mr. Cookman was introduced to the audience. For two long days the people had heard of nothing but "missions," and it seemed as though both they and the subject had been exhausted—that there was nothing left for him to say, or, if he found anything to say, that he would have to say it to a worn-out and retreating audience. With peculiar adroitness in his first sentences he conciliated the congregation, and was heard to the last with unflagging attention.

A correspondent of *The Christian Advocate* wrote : " The address was pervaded with the blessed Spirit of the Master, and at times in rapt delight the audience wept and rejoiced ; and when the speaker closed his remarks, all present must have felt that they had been with him at the feet of Jesus receiving instruction and comfort for further effort."

Another correspondent said of it.: " His theme was the true missionary spirit. His melting pathos and indescribable sweetness of tone won every heart to the missionary cause. It is impossible to express the power of his address upon the audience gathered on the occasion, and the limits of our paper forbid any attempt to reproduce the words or thoughts presented."

It may not be amiss, as the missionary cause lay near Mr. Cookman's heart, and enlisted—as it had done with his father—his deepest sympathies and strongest efforts, to give extracts from this address as published in the Annual Report of the Missionary Society.

After introducing himself in his hard-pressed position as a gleaner, he said :—

" And now, sir, looking round upon the field, I do not seem to see a standing stalk of truth. These brethren, with their bright blades or their keen sickles, have been gathering the harvest—they have even carried it to the mill. They have ground it out in their close, clear, vigorous thinking; they have manufactured it into nourishing and delightful food, and it has been dealt out among the people ; you have been enjoying it in the morning and in the evening, and are now entirely satisfied. It seems to me that it only remains to return thanks and go home. Or, sir, if I may change the figure, I have thought during the evening, while occupying my seat, that we have been engaged during the day in the inspection of our great missionary ship : its keel, its timbers, its planking, its deck, its machinery—a most magnificent piece of machinery,—its pilotage, and its larder. Our flags are flying, our officers are in their places, and all that we are needing, as it would seem, is the missionary spirit, which might be entitled the motive power."

After showing that liberal contributions of money might be made in the absence of the real power necessary to success, he continued :—

" What is the missionary spirit ? Is it an ordinary interest in, or a kind of general concern for, the heathen abroad, or the heathen at home?—a cold and calculating love for those millions that have so long, too long, lingered in the shadow of sin and of death ? Nay, sir, such a spirit as that would never convert the world—has never illustrated itself as the secret spring or motive power of self-sacrificing and successful endeavour in this world. There must be love, it is true, but then let us remember it must be love on fire ; it must be love in a paroxysm ; it must be love intensified, absorbing, all-controlling. Observe, if you please, the missionary quitting his home, kindred, native land, and accustomed comforts. He is willing to abide in the ends of the earth, encompassed by heart-sickening idolatrous superstition and crime. Wherefore ? Is it because of a simple concern respecting the temporal, or even spiritual, welfare of those by whom he may be encompassed ? Nay, I insist it is rather because of the Christ-given and Christ-like love that burns in his heart and literally consumes his life. Oh, sir ! it is the missionary spirit that crosses broad seas, that clambers cloud-crowned mountains, that traverses far-distant regions, that sails around the world if it may save but a single soul. It is the missionary spirit that breathes miasmas, that bears heavy burdens, that challenges adversaries, that imperils precious life, that laughs at impossibilities, and cries, 'This must, and this shall be done !' It is the missionary spirit that gives and bears sacrifices, and dies, if it were necessary, and if it were possible, a hundred thousand deaths, if, like its Divine Exemplar, it might be going about doing good. Now, as I have said, there may be liberality, but there cannot be the missionary spirit where there is not a conscientious, Christ-like liberality."

Inquiring, then, how this missionary spirit shall be excited and maintained, he replied—"First, by the careful contemplation of the spiritual necessities of the unregenerate around us." With a few brief touches he illustrated the power of the eye to report to and sensibly affect the heart, and proceeded further to discuss a more vital condition :—

"Again, it might be asked, 'Are there not many of our own community who are familiar with temporal and spiritual wretchedness, who are acquainted with the necessities of the heathen world, who hear of this subject not only from year to year, but more frequently, and yet they have none of those exercises or experiences of missionary zeal?' That is true—that is undeniable ; and so we are constrained to the conclusion that something more is indispensable than this simple consideration. What is that something? I answer that it is a union and a living sympathy with the blessed Lord Jesus Christ. And now, sir, at the close of these anniversary exercises, this thought brings me where I joy to come, and where I should like to lead this little company—that is, to Calvary. I throw the arms of my affection around the consecrated cross of Jésus ; I drink in, in constantly increasing measure, His tender, sympathizing, self-sacrificing spirit. Now from this standpoint of the cross—from the measure of that feeling which influences the heart and life of the Divine Redeemer—I look out again upon the world; but now with what different feelings ! Now I hear with Christ's ears, I feel with Christ's heart, I see with His eyes ; now I am ready to labour with Christ's energies ; now I am disposed to give or go, or do or dare, or sacrifice or die—anything and everything—if I may but help in lifting our sin-cursed world up to God. This experience of which I am speaking is a vitalizing principle ; it is a Divine force. It is Jesus reigning, not (as my brother would say) simply in the skies ; there is something better than that. We can have heaven on the way to heaven. It is Jesus reigning in personal consciousness in the individual heart ; it is Christ living, breathing, dwelling, and triumphing in personal life. Philosophy is contemplative and studious, fond and full of plans and of theories; infidelity, as we all know, is given to boasting and to detraction; both of them laying spécial stress upon the human rather than upon the Divine.

"But, Mr. President and Christian friends, after all their proud vaunting, pray tell me what heathen shores they have ever visited. for purposes of mercy? What funeral pyre have they ever extinguished? What dumb idol have they ever cast down from its pedestal? What nation have they ever lifted up from its barbarism and degradation? What profligate have they ever reclaimed? What sorrowful heart have they ever cheered? Where to-night are their earnest, self-sacrificing missionaries? Where are their organizations for the amelioration of human suffering and the extension of wholesome and blessed truth in the world? Where are their Pauls, their Barnabases, their Wesleys, Wilberforces, Thomas Cokes, Asburys, Howards, Phebes, Dorcases, Nightingales, and Elizabeth Frys? I ask it with confidence and with Christian exultation. In vain I wait for an answer—there cometh none. Sir, we must come to Christ; we must drink in His spirit; for it is there, and there only, we will find the source and the fountain of this missionary spirit, which is so needful and so indispensable. The theory and practice of missions, as I take it, can be expressed almost in a single sentence. It is love to the blessed Lord Jesus Christ, who has bought us with His blood, drawing forth the stream of human sympathy, human affection, and human endeavour—a stream which, by an invariable law of nature and of God, seeks the lowest place—for, let me say to you, that Christian compassion, like Christ's compassion, always flows downward, and fixes upon those who need it the most. Was it not so with Paul? The love of Christ constrained him, and he counted not his life dear unto him so that he might but glorify his Saviour, propagate His Gospel, save immortal souls, and finish his course with joy.

"Mr. President, that great man had been to Calvary. . . . As we heard remarked this morning, with him it was a master-passion in death. I lingered in the dungeon, I looked over the shoulder of that great servant of Jesus Christ as he wrote his last epistle that he indicted to a faithful apostle, and I read with the speaker this morning these words: 'I am ready to be offered, and the time of my departure is at hand. I have fought a good fight, I have finished my course, I have kept the faith. Henceforth there is laid up for me a crown of righteousness, which the Lord, the righteous Judge, shall give me at that day.' Here my brother stopped; but I read on a little farther, 'And not for me only.' There came out his missionary spirit. That would have been too narrow, circumscribed, and selfish for that great heart. 'Not for me only.' Oh! Paul at that hour took in the hundreds of millions

of the world's population—' Not for me only, but for all those that love
His appearing.' . . .

" Mr. President, I am not by any means despondent or discouraged ;
but, on the contrary, I am full of cheerful hope and of Christian confidence. I believe the clouds above will vanish. I believe the right
is about to conquer.

> " ' Clear the way !
> A brazen wrong is crumbling into clay.
> With that right
> Shall many more enter, smiling, at the door.
> With that wrong
> Shall follow many others, great and small,
> That for ages long have held us as their prey.
> Men of thought and men of action,
> Clear the way ! '

I believe in the future. . . . . I believe in the government of the future,
and in the Church of the future. I think there is a day not very far
distant when from the watch-towers of Asia, once the land of lords
many, there shall roll out the exultant chorus, ' One Lord ! ' when from
the watch-towers of Europe, distracted by divisions in the faith, there
shall roll up the grateful chorus, ' One faith ! ' when from the watch-
towers of our own America, torn by controversies respecting the initia-
tory rite into the visible Church of our Lord Jesus, there shall roll
forth the inspiring chorus, ' One baptism ! ' when from the watch-
towers of Africa—as though the God of all the race were not her God,
as if the Father of the entire human family were not her Father—when
from the watch-towers of neglected and despised Africa there shall. roll
forth the chorus, ' One God and Father of all ! " when the sacramental
host, scattered all over the face of this lower creation, shall spring upon
their feet, and, seizing the harp of thanksgiving, they shall join in the
chorus that shall be responded to by the angels : ' One Lord, one faith
one baptism, one God and Father of all, who is above all, and through
all, and in you all ; ' ' to whom be glory, dominion, and majesty, and
blessing for ever ! '

" Mr. President, these eyes of mine may not see that day of rapture ;
but if not, then I expect with the great cloud of witnesses to stand
yonder upon the glory-illumined battlements of immortality, and looking
down, I shall surely enjoy the feast of vision. I may not be associated
with those who shall send up from the earth the shout that ' Jesus reigns ! '
if not, it seems to me I shall crowd a little closer to the throne with all

the glorified company, and I will join with them in singing that the kingdoms of yonder world have become the kingdoms of our Lord and of His Christ. Oh, sir ! at the close of this anniversary day, as the result of what I have seen and heard and enjoyed, I resolve to be a better man, and to be a more devoted friend to the missionary cause."

Ah ! how little it was thought, as the noble, healthful-looking orator took his seat amid shouts and tears, that these concluding references to himself were so painfully prophetic ! Three brief years—and yonder he is on the battlements, crying to Christ's hosts still in the conflict, " Forward ! and I will be looking down upon you."

By an act of the General Conference of 1868 the Philadelphia Conference had been divided. All that portion of its territory in Delaware, Maryland, and Virginia lying between the Delaware and Chesapeake Bays, and known as the Peninsula, had been set off to itself, and denominated the Wilmington Conference. The new Conference held its first session in Wilmington. Mr. Cookman remained in the Conference, and was re-appointed to Grace Church for the second year. He thus found himself a leading member in a leading charge of a forming Conference, and, with a loyalty to Methodism exceeded by none, he addressed himself vigorously to the development and conservation of the elements of progress within its bounds.

The National Committee had appointed their annual camp-meeting for July 6th, at Round Lake, near Saratoga, New York. The success of the two previous meetings at Vineland and Manheim, the eligibleness of the location at Round Lake, the increasing attention awakened on the subject of Christian holiness, drew together a vast concourse of people. Representatives were there from well-nigh all the states, the Canadas, and even from England.

On returning home from Round Lake, he barely took

time to brush from his feet the dust of one field before he
was off to another. He attended at least four camp-meetings in the Peninsula—hastening from the Camden Union
to Talbot Union, near Easton, Maryland, and thence to
Ennall's Springs, and thence homeward to Brandywine Summit. His labours at any one of these meetings would have
been enough to exhaust most men, but he went through
them all with an unflagging interest. His zeal and strength
seemed to know no abatement. Everywhere his presence
excited the utmost enthusiasm, and both preachers and
people rallied under his leadership with a unanimity and
intentness which rendered his services during this season
ever memorable for the marvellous victories achieved for the
cross of Christ. The like had not been known in this time-
honoured region for many years—the old battle-grounds of
Asbury, Garrettson, Smith, Laurenson, Cooper, and others
of the fathers, resounded with songs of triumph, which
carried the "oldest inhabitants living" back to the former
days, and made them feel that modern Methodism was still
instinct with apostolic fire.

As evidence of Mr. Cookman's power in prayer, an incident which occurred at this meeting is given by the Rev.
John Field, of Philadelphia, who was with him at the time :
"Captain D—— had presented himself repeatedly at the
altar of prayer. One day at the close of the morning service the Captain came out of the woods, where he had been
engaged in private prayer, and bowed again at the altar.
Brother Cookman noticed him, and immediately called
attention to him. 'Now,' said he, 'God has promised to
answer the united prayers of two or three : let us put Him
to the test.' Turning to Brother A——, he inquired, 'Do
you believe this ?' Brother A—— answered in the affirmative. He asked Brother B—— the same question, and he

also answered in the affirmative. Brother Cookman said, 'I also believe God's Word and His promise.' Amid profound silence the company bowed in prayer. Brother A—— prayed, then Brother B——. Brother Cookman followed. He carried the case of the poor penitent right to the Cross, and just as he closed his earnest prayer,—

> " ' Heaven came down our souls to greet,
> While glory crowned the mercy-seat.'

God's blessed Spirit witnessed with Captain D——'s that he was born of God. The Captain put his hand into his side-pocket, and, taking therefrom his pocket Bible, said, ' Now I understand it '—the passage still marked and pointing to it. ' I went out alone, bowed beneath the shade of a friendly tree, and opened my Bible ; my eye rested on this passage, " But thou, when thou prayest, enter into thy closet, and when thou hast shut thy door, pray to thy Father which is in secret ; and thy Father which seeth in secret shall reward thee openly." I was to be rewarded openly, and I am, amid this vast assembly—Glory be to the Lamb ! ' Brother Cookman took the Bible, and wrote in it, ' McNeil's Woods, August, noon, A.D. 1869, the happiest day of my life,' and the Captain signed it."

During the progress of the meeting he preached frequently and with great power. On one occasion he remained up the whole night, going from tent to tent, instructing penitents, and praying with them.

Nowhere was Mr. Cookman more at home than at Ennall's Springs, Dorchester County, Maryland. He had been accustomed from his early ministry to resort to that beautiful spot, honoured of God in the conversion of so many people. This year was the semi-centennial of its appropriation as a place for camp-meetings. The most delightful memories thronged about the place ; thousands on earth and thousands in heaven had been brought to God there, and it was proposed to observe the occasion by suitable services.

At Brandywine Summit, a few days later, he was preaching and working with equal power. It was not enough for him to deliver one of the sermons on Sunday, but he must occupy the pulpit the last evening of the meeting. He was found, too, among the children, lifting, by his tender, Christ-like spirit, the little ones to God.

" Rev. A. Cookman on the last night of the meeting preached a searching sermon, calling upon the people to estimate the value of the soul, and what is lost in losing it, and what profit it would be if all else in this life were gained but the soul lost. At midnight, in the greatest solemnity, the Sacrament of the Lord's Supper was administered to about thirteen hundred persons.

" The children's meetings, held during the progress of the camp, and under the management of Rev. Messrs. Cookman, Clymer, Gracey, and Pancoast, were of more than usual interest. They were not mere occasions of amusement in story-telling and pleasure in singing, but the most searching appeals were made to the children, and prayer-meetings followed, when scores presented themselves at the altar for prayers, and many were converted. Nothing during the meeting was more impressive than to see these little ones of the household arise and tell of the love of Jesus as they felt it in their hearts. In these meetings, little boys and girls, from ten to fourteen years of age, led in earnest prayer. While a sacred stillness prevailed in the immense tent in which the services were held, the voice of a boy or girl arose in sweetest tones to the throne of heavenly mercy ; aged veterans knelt before God with faces bathed in tears, and vast crowds looked on, while a little child should lead them. On the last day, the brethren above mentioned stood in the midst of this exceedingly large and interesting group of children, and, while many tears were shed, shook hands with each, and invoked on each the Divine blessing. Mothers came leading their little ones forward to be prayed for by Christian pastors."

In connection with the children's meetings referred to, a pleasing incident which occurred while Mr. Cookman was at Spring Garden may be appropriately mentioned. A gentleman from the far West, writing immediately after his death, said :—

" I attended his ministry at Spring Garden, Philadelphia, during the winter of 1866. I loved him then, but not as I have for the past five years. . . . I shall never forget one incident that occurred at that church—that was when a dear little son of his, of only eight years, presented himself as a candidate for probation. My heart melted then, as hundreds besides, when I saw the strong man bowed like a child, and heard him ask the Church if he should receive that lamb into the fold. I saw the loving father then as never before—also the spirit of Christ, when He said, ' Suffer little children to come unto me, and forbid them not, for of such is the kingdom of heaven.'

" When I saw Brother Cookman years afterwards, I asked him if he remembered that incident, and if that little boy had remained faithful. ' Oh, yes,' he said ; ' he is about twelve years old now, and is a sanctified boy.' "

While on this subject it will not be amiss to insert an extract from a short speech which fell from his lips on one occasion at a Sunday School convention :—

" The Rev. Alfred Cookman arose, and expressed his confidence in the conversion of children, declaring that he did not believe ' the way to heaven lay through the territory of sin,' but that children at an early age might be brought to a saving knowledge of redeeming love ; citing as an illustration the case of a boy who was converted at the age of ten, who was a pupil in the Sabbath School, became a teacher, a librarian, an exhorter, afterwards a minister of the Gospel, who then stood before them, to speak his faith in the power of regenerating grace in the hearts of the young.

" Mr. Cookman of course referred to his own history ; and those who are familiar with his love for children, and his rare power to interest them, cannot but feel grateful that he was so early called of God, since perhaps to this may be attributed that sympathy which he entertains for them ; a sympathy which has encouraged many youthful hearts to beat with holy aspirations for the favour of that Saviour who said, ' Suffer little children to come unto me.' "

CHAPTER XX.

THE camp-meetings over, the devoted pastor was once more quietly seated in the bosom of his family, and again engaged in those regular pastorial duties which to him were more congenial than all besides. It was in vain that he was invited to step aside from his chosen work into an educational institution : whatever might be the advantage of a settled home and school facilities for his children, his mission, to himself at least, was clear. The immediate care of souls was to him unspeakably precious ; to feed the flock of Christ, an employment beyond any other which the Church could offer him.

He was invited to Philadelphia to speak at the anniversary of the Young Men's Christian Association, held in the Academy of Music, November 30th. In the address which he delivered, one can but be struck with the great theme which seemed more and more to fill his mind, and which he deemed so important to Christian workers as hardly to be omitted without recognition upon all occasions—dependence upon the Holy Ghost.

. . . " The people heard Seneca, excellent man as he was ; they heard Seneca and the excellent truths he spoke, and deteriorated in their morals—they got worse and worse. The world has been listening to the teachings of Jesus—listening during all these centuries ; and, as these gentlemen will bear me witness, the world has been getting better and better in consequence of these truths.

"Mr. President, I know of no satisfactory answer that can be supplied, except that our Christianity has the Holy Ghost in it. It has the Word ; it has the truth which gives light ; but it has the Holy Spirit of God that gives life. And what we want is life ; for the world is dead, terribly dead, in trespasses and sins. In illustration of what I mean : I take it that there is not an individual in any of these galleries or under the sound of my voice, not one but is familiar with that fundamental truth, 'Thou shalt love the Lord thy God with all thy heart and soul and mind and strength.' We all hold that now ; but how many of this vast audience really do love God 'with all their heart and soul and mind and strength'? Perhaps, if appealed to personally or privately, many would say we have not the disposition ; some would confess that they were lacking in the ability. Now, mark, they have the truth ; they have it all their lives long ; but yet they do not love God with all their hearts. What then ? Let these come to God ; let them ask for the ability ; let them ask in the name of Christ and Him crucified ; let them plead with a humble reliance upon God's strength, His strength ; this is leading men in Christ Jesus. In answer to their prayer the Holy Ghost shall be given, and then they will not only know to love God, as they have during all these years, but they will love God with all their heart. It will not only be a fact in their minds, but it will be an experience in their hearts ; it will be a power, a blessed saving power in their lives.

"This, sir, I feel is just what our associations and churches and communities are now so much needing. We need this Divine power, this supernatural power ; it is necessary to accompany and apply the truth to the minds and hearts of those with whom we have to do. . . .

"In trying to do good in the world, the Infinite One fills us, inspires us, emboldens us, ennobles us, saves us, blesses us, makes us strong in nature and in the power of His might. Oh ! does not this quiet, thoughtful, attentive audience see the point I would make? Entirely consecrated to the service, and then filled with God ! A co-worker with Omnipotence ! I challenge the world to supply a more sublime ideal of character, of experience, of life !"

The Christmas festival was a delight to Mr. Cookman, and was always appropriately observed by suitable religious and social exercises. His house, with its interchange of gifts and salutations, was a scene of cheerful gaiety. With his own children and the children of the Sunday School he mingled freely, reminding them by his innocent mirthfulness that the religion which Jesus was born to establish is fitted to make everybody happy. The enthusiastic and tasteful celebrations of the season on its annual returns while he was at Grace Church were among the pleasantest occurrences of his pastorate, and cannot soon be blotted from the memories of his young parishioners.

In March, 1870, Mr. Cookman was re-appointed for the third year to Grace Church.

His delicate tact and tender thoughtfulness as a pastor were happily illustrated quite early in the year in connection with the last illness of one of the devout ladies of his Church, Mrs. Bates, the wife of Chancellor Bates. Mr. Bates's note, accompanying the letters written by Mr. Cookman to Mrs. Bates, afford the best explanation of the case, and also offer a very just tribute to the worth of the faithful pastor.

"The letter, of which the enclosed is a copy, was written by Mr. Cookman to Mrs. Bates during her last illness, at a period when a failure of voice precluded her from conversation with friends—hence the occasion for his giving her pastoral advice and sympathy *by letter*. It was most gratefully appreciated by her, and often read with expressions of great pleasure, and with much consolation and help under her feebleness. She held him in affectionate confidence and regard, and cordially received and rested upon his counsels ; and this letter, together with a subsequent one written from New England, of which also a copy is enclosed with this, did much toward inspiring her with a more cheerful and resigned spirit under her declining strength. It is a beautiful outflow of pastoral affection, breathing the very spirit of Christ Himself, and containing sentiments worthy to be written in letters of gold. It is a memorial of both the departed far more precious than rubies."

"You must not think that we have forgotten you in your affliction. A hundred times you have been in our thoughts, and very frequently, if it had been deemed practicable or best, we would have offered you in person the sympathy of a pastor's heart. It has occurred to me that a message of love through this medium might not be unwelcome, and hence I take a moment to communicate that there are some hearts outside of your happy home that are concerned for your welfare, and that do not fail or forget to present you in your feebleness to that Father who does not willingly afflict any of His dear children. The dispensation that withdraws you from the active duties of domestic life is profoundly mysterious. We will not presumptuously venture an explanation of this providence. At the same time, you will be comforted by the remembrance that our Father, if inscrutable, is *never wrong.* Clouds frequently cover His ways, but there is light on the other side of the cloud—light to reveal the fact of mystery—light with which we may meet the obligations and trials of the passing hour. We must 'trust where we cannot trace,' and remember that while living the life of faith we are moving as safely as though we understood everything. 'He that dwelleth in the secret place of the Most High shall abide under the shadow of the Almighty.'

"May I affectionately counsel that, with an implicit and steady reliance upon Jesus for the help of the Almighty Spirit, you accept all the will of God moment by moment—aye, *take that will into your heart, and love it* better than all beside ; for the difference between the unsaved and the fully saved is, that while the former find the will of God *without* them, and are obliged to submit to what they cannot change, the latter find that same will *within* them, and very cheerfully submit to what they would not change.

"Let this season of affliction be an epochal time in your earthly history—constituted such not only by a fuller, but by the *fullest* submission of yourself and family and all to the infinitely excellent will of your Father in heaven. You may safely trust that will, for it is never arbitrary, never wrong. It is always the expression of Divine wisdom and love.

"As you sometimes indulge in prospective vision, say that all the rest of your life shall be, in the fullest and strictest sense, a *consecrated* life—a life hid with Christ in God—a life blessed in its experiences and in its results, concerning itself principally for the spiritual welfare of those around you, and linking itself with the glory and triumph of the eternal future. Take this opportunity that the providence of God gives to write on all you have and are and hope for, ' Sacred to Jesus,' and spend the rest of your life in steadily '*looking only unto Jesus.*' These two sentences may be profitable mottoes for every useful and glorious life.

"Excuse the liberty I thus take in writing to you. My note may be a word in season. In any case, it will furnish assurance that you are remembered with sympathy and love and prayer by your tenderly attached pastor."

"HAMILTON CAMP-GROUND, MASSACHUSETTS, *June* 29, 1870.

"You will be surprised perhaps to receive this letter, but it will at least indicate that, although far away, still you are remembered by your affectionate pastor ; and not only have you a place in my thoughts, but also in my prayers. Many times in this consecrated forest I have been reminded of you in your feebleness, and lifted up my soul to God that He would be with you and bless you, and make your sickness a signal and glorious passage in your earthly history. We are having really a most wonderful time at our Hamilton camp-meeting, the first service of the kind I have ever attended in New England. The attendance is from all the surrounding states, and the interest and Divine power exceed, I think, anything I have ever witnessed. Hundreds of ministers and people are concerned to enjoy their full privilege in the Gospel. The community in this section is generally more intellectual and less demonstrative than that in the Middle and Southern States. They can and do meet mind with mind, but that still leaves the heart untouched. They want Holy Ghost power, and, asking, God is gloriously giving it to them. Unless I am greatly mistaken, the effects of this extraordinary meeting will be far-reaching and most blessed. Oh ! my dear sister, I do so much wish that your kind heart and whole being shall be entirely filled with God, submitting to His will in every particular, and tasting the joy of perfect love. Let us be altogether and eternally the Lord's.

"I thought that a breath of love from New England might bring a moment's refreshment to you in your sick-room. Give my tenderest love to the Judge, and to your sons and daughters."

Mr. Cookman's judgment in dealing with the sick was proved not alone in the feminine gentleness with which he could anticipate the needs of the cultured pious lady, but also in the force and skill with which he would approach the hardened and impenitent man. When he was stationed at Trinity, New York, a gentleman called upon him and requested him to visit a son, who was ill. The young man had been very wayward, was still obdurate, and refused all religious counsel and prayer. Mr. Cookman went, but the young man declined conversation—wished to have nothing to do with him; but instead of insisting, he immediately withdrew, with the quiet, loving remark, " Well, my friend, you may refuse to let me talk and pray with you, but you cannot prevent my praying *for* you." This kind word had its desired effect. He called again very soon to inquire for the invalid, and, to the surprise of all, was welcomed by him and invited to pray. The visits were repeated until the young man professed to be converted, and died confessing his faith in Christ.

From the last letter it will be seen that Mr. Cookman had already, thus early in the summer, entered upon his yearly camp-meeting tour.

The National Association had determined upon three camp-meetings for the year 1870—the first at Hamilton, Massachusetts, June 21st; the second at Oakington, Maryland, June 12th; and the third at Desplaines, Illinois, August 9th—all of which Mr. Cookman attended, preaching at them all, and labouring with the untiring zeal which had heretofore characterized him.

His impressions at the Hamilton meeting have been already partially presented. At the meeting alluded to in this letter he is reported to have said, " How I joy in that Divine declaration, ' Whatsoever ye shall ask in my name, that will I do, that the Father may be glorified in the Son.' This has been the very best Sabbath-day of all my earthly Sabbaths. An isolation from the world in the sense of non-conformity is the secret of spiritual power. I am able and I am willing to be a witness—and if alone, I would hold up this banner." The Sunday evening service was assigned to him, but, instead of preaching, he narrated his experience.

The camp-meeting at Oakington, July 12th, near Havre de Grace, Maryland, was very numerously attended. At one of the earlier prayer-meetings Mr. Cookman, addressing the friends, spoke in substance as follows :—

"We desire for your own sake, for the sake of your comfort, usefulness, but especially for Jesus' sake—we desire for you a rich, round, full, abiding, blessed religious experience and life. Oh how gladly and thankfully we would help you this morning if we could ! But we are reminded that there is a better Leader, a better Teacher, even the Holy Ghost. He guides into all truth. He takes of the things of Christ—the truth of Christ, the power of Christ, the blood of Christ, the grace of Christ—and shows them unto us. Let us put ourselves under His Divine tuition. Blessed Spirit, Third Person of the adorable Trinity, proceeding from the Father and the Son, we acknowledge Thee, we worship Thee, we praise Thee, we love Thee, we seek fellowship with Thee, we want to be filled this day, and every day, and constantly, with all this fulness. Oh, hear our prayer this morning service ! Come and direct our thoughts ; come and quicken our desires ; come and help our faith ; come and enable us in all the services this day to sing—

"'Come, Holy Ghost, for Thee we call ;
Spirit of power and blessing, come.'"

To accommodate the numerous friends of the national movement in the West, a camp-meeting was also held at Desplaines, Illinois, near Chicago, on the 9th of August.

Some estimate of Mr. Cookman's ministrations at this meeting may be formed from one or two facts communicated by John Emory Voak, M.D., of Bloomington, Ill., who was present at the time :

"While attending the meeting, having known Brother Cookman, I took particular pains to attend all his ministrations and every meeting that he led, and oh how my soul fed and feasted on the bread of life as dispensed by him !

17

"I never shall forget his sermon on the theme, 'Entire Sanctification.' Surely the Holy Spirit spoke through him to many hearts, and won them to Christ as a Saviour to the uttermost.

"I wish I could describe one of the most glorious meetings I ever attended, led by him. After answering the objection often urged against labouring for the promotion of holiness (instead of the conversion of sinners) most beautifully, he gave a sketch of his experience. He said that 'on these hands, these feet, these lips I have written, *Sacred to Jesus.*' After his enlarging on that beautiful motto, I am sure many in that meeting of preachers saw entire sanctification as a more comprehensive and sacred work than they had been wont to view it, and that they were then set apart as never before.

"One other incident which cannot be described occurred at the last service of that meeting. The time had come when we must part; all Christian hearts were solemn—some were sad—at the thought of leaving that hallowed ground. The leader felt he could not close without giving one more opportunity for sinners to come to Jesus, and for Christians to plunge anew into the fountain. To the surprise of perhaps every one, nearly two hundred arose for prayers. The scene seemed to inspire Brother Cookman, and he offered a prayer such as I never expect to hear equalled. The Holy Ghost made intercession in his soul with groanings that could not be uttered. He was in audience with Deity—aye, more, he had hold on God, and it literally raised him from his knees. I never heard such a fervent, effectual prayer, and it prevailed, as many will testify in the Day of Judgment."

This communication, together with Mr. Cookman's own account of the meeting, affords ample evidence that he never sought the entire sanctification of believers to the neglect of "calling sinners to repentance."

Besides attending the National camp-meetings, Mr. Cookman was present at the usual number of local camp-meetings through the summer, and performed at every one the same almost superhuman work. He could allow himself no respite, but flew like a herald of light from place to place. Ennall's Springs, Talbot County, Brandywine Summit, Camden Union, Ocean Grove, and possibly others, shared his ministrations.

He wrote from Ennall's Springs to Mrs. Cookman :—

"ENNALL'S, *Monday*, 1870.

"Sabbath is over; it was a bright, beautiful, blessed day—the atmosphere cool, pure, invigorating. We had good congregations. I preached both morning and evening, superintended the love-feast and two prayer-meetings, and at half-past ten went to bed pretty well worn out. This is vacation! Our services have all been very profitable, the prayer-meeting last night and this morning especially. There are a good many hungry souls here, and I have great joy in inviting and leading them to the blessed provisions of the Gospel. There are many tender, loving inquiries respecting your welfare. You would have met a most affectionate welcome at the hands of these Dorchester County people. Annie T—— is rather sad, occasioned by the change in her circumstances and the absence of her dear husband. Their tent, however, is just as attractive in its social circles and its bountifully spread table as ever.

"This afternoon we leave for Easton. Willie * seems to be very happy. The tables suit him. He has a wonderful weakness for the feathered creation—wings, legs, breast, and side-bones quickly disappear before his vigorous assaults. Thus far he behaves himself beautifully—keeps his clothes clean, and acts like a little gentleman. I feel proud of him. My own soul is strong in the Lord. I feel that in leading up the Church I am doing God's will, and am wonderfully blessed. The blessed Spirit shines upon my mind and seems to give efficiency to my feeble words. Pray for me. I do not forget you. Your unwavering love has not failed to make the deepest impression on my heart. May God have you ever in His special care and keeping ! "

"McNEILL'S WOODS.

"On another battle-field ! Arrived here last night about eight o'clock, after a four hours' ride from Ennall's. Will enjoyed the journey, especially the *driving*. This a delightful spot—a larger meeting decidedly than the one in Dorchester. Our reception was most enthusiastic. This morning I led the eight o'clock meeting. It was really one of the most precious and powerful services that I ever enjoyed. Brother Quigg, the presiding elder, preached this morning, and Brother John Field this afternoon. The meetings are increasing in interest, and presage victory. President Wilson and wife are here— arrived last evening. Will finds pleasant companions, and receives a great deal of attention. The friends here insist upon my staying until Friday morning. They think that the interest of souls and the Church are involved. I shall be better able to judge to-morrow."

---

* The fourth son, William Wilberforce.

CHAPTER XXI.

MR. COOKMAN was appointed chairman of a committee to arrange for a Peninsula Methodist Convention. Indeed, "the conception of the Convention," in the language of one, "was his. He was the presiding genius as well as the moving spirit." At the call of the committee the Convention assembled at Smyrna, Delaware, on November 15, 1870, and continued for three days.

The topics discussed were: The Methodist Episcopal Church—its active and relative growth, and its present position on the Peninsula; Education—its claims upon the Church; Working Forces of the Church—local ministry, women's work, young people's associations, etc.; Relation of the Church to the Moral Questions of the Day—Bible, Christian Sabbath, and Temperance cause; Family Religion; The Sabbath School; and The Spiritual Life of the Church. These themes were severally treated in one or more written papers and by open discussion. The first topic elicited many valuable facts concerning the past and present status of Methodism in one of its chosen fields.

This Peninsula Mr. Asbury was accustomed to call his garden for Methodist preachers. It still retains much of its original Methodist simplicity. To no one in the Convention was this statistical exhibit more gratifying than to Mr.

Cookman. On no field outside of his immediate parish work had he spent so much energy as on this; and as he contemplated the status of the Church, its numerical, social, financial capabilities, his mind was impressed with a sense of the great importance of a rebaptism of all these forces by the Holy Spirit, for the "consolidation, instruction, and inspiration of Peninsula Methodism."

It was therefore just to his taste that "The Spiritual Life of the Church" was assigned as his theme. I give the essay which he read entire, as containing some of his best thoughts on the relation of holiness to the Church :—

"THE SPIRITUAL LIFE OF THE CHURCH.

"The visible Church of Christ is a congregation of faithful men, in which the pure Word of God is preached and the sacraments duly administered.

" It stands above all other organizations ; the repository of the most valuable truth ; a fountain of light and life and love ; a blessing to the world.

" *The spiritual life of this Church*, that is, the life of God developing in the experience of its individual members, is its highest and best life —aye, and because of the important relations and the exalted position of the Church, it is the best life of the world ; the highest to which the race at large can possibly aspire. It links itself intimately and indissolubly with personal character, social order, family comfort, national prosperity, and our world's complete redemption.

" Now, will it not occur to any observant mind that this spiritual life, like our natural life, may exist in various stages of development?

" In a hospital, for illustration, may we not find a patient paralysed, unable to do anything, and yet life flickering in its socket? May we not find other invalids, feeble, complaining, scarcely able to stand up, not willing to communicate, knowing little of the joys of life, and yet not actually dying ? It may be they have brought this upon themselves as the consequence of their own folly or neglect. There has been some temptation, comparatively harmless to others, but injurious to them, and they have balanced the gratification it has afforded them against the fearful results that have developed, and so they have carnally and culpably clung to the doubtful indulgence until the effect is as we see.

Ah, brethren, do we not know by observation, and some of us by experience, that this is a sad picture of too many who profess to be the subjects of spiritual life ? Through neglect, or failure, or folly, or doubtful indulgence, or partial obedience, their religious life is feeble and sickly—some trust, but more of distressing doubt ; some hope, but more of torturing fear ; some joy, but more of spiritual joylessness ; little appetite for Divine things ; little disposition to exercise themselves in matters pertaining to godliness ; little interest in those means and measures that are intimately related to the salvation of the race and the glory of God.

"Oh how different from that spiritual life that hungers and thirsts after righteousness ; that runs in the way of obedience ; that works, and rejoices to work, in the vineyard ; that fights, aye, and endures hardness in the great battle with sin and Satan ! 'I am come,' said Christ, 'that they might have life, and that they *might have it more abundantly.*'

" Brethren, ought it not to be with us a matter of congratulation and thanksgiving that the home of our spiritual nature is in a Church that has always given so much attention to the development of the spiritual life ? For, observe, while some of the other denominations have arrayed themselves around their citadels of doctrine, waging occasion-ally an offensive, but more frequently a defensive warfare, Methodism, adventuring into the field of the wide, wide world, has employed her time and talents and energies in the culture and dissemination of spiritual life. Meanwhile her fundamental doctrines have remained in-tact and unchanged, proving that orthodoxy is much better conserved by the cultivation of the spiritual life than the spiritual life is promoted by an elaborate defence of orthodoxy. But, more than this, gaining constant accessions of this best life, growing stronger with the strength that the Divinity supplieth, our success, as a Christian denomination, has been almost without parallel or precedent. From a small class organized in the city of New York, with Philip Embury as the leader, the Methodist societies have grown until within their folds they enrol, upon this continent, more than two millions of members, and directly influence some seven or eight millions of our American population. . . .

"Nearly a century since, Thomas Coke, Francis Asbury, Benjamin Abbott, William Watters, Freeborn Garrettson, and others, whose names are as ointment poured forth, heralds of grace, filled with apostolic love and zeal and power, visited our Peninsula, unfurling the blood-stained banner, and preaching a salvation, free, full, present, conscious, and glorious. Their word was in demonstration of the Spirit : opposition gave way—prejudice vanished—hearts were opened

—spiritual life was accepted; and now for about a hundred years Methodism has had a home upon this Peninsula, much of the time the dominant religious denomination of the region.

"As we overlook the field to-day, can we not find occasion for encouragement and rejoicing in the fact that the spiritual life of Methodism all through this section retains very much of its original simplicity? We still hold fast and hold up the old distinctive doctrines of salvation for all through the mediation of Christ—justification by faith a personal necessity and a present privilege—the distinct and direct witness of the Holy Spirit with our spirit that we are children of God—entire sanctification, through the blood of Christ and by the power of the Holy Ghost, made available by an exercise of present trust in Jesus. We still retain, appreciate, and enjoy the class-meeting, the love-feast, the watch-night service, the quarterly-meeting, the camp-meeting, the protracted-meeting—means of grace that were originally the gift of God's providence, and which our fathers found to be so valuable and profitable. While in some other sections there is a disposition to lay aside or treat carelessly some of the old weapons, conforming to the spirit of an extravagant age and a fashionable world, Methodism on the Peninsula still satisfies herself with plain, free-seated churches; still experiences and shouts the joy of God's salvation; still goes in for earnestness of expression and of operations; still agrees that the people of God while '*in, must not be of the world,*' but must stand separate from and exalted above the world's littleness and vanities and falsities; still clings to and would battle in defence of the old and well-tried landmarks.

"But now, while we offer the language of congratulation and com-mendation, let us, still continuing our observation, ask, Is the spiritual life of our Church, within the limits of the Wilmington Conference, up to the New Testament standard? Let us 'examine ourselves.' Instead of offering God a *perfect love,* do we not yield Him a partial affection, allowing other objects to dispute in our hearts the sovereignty of His most holy and excellent will? Instead of *brotherly kindness,* is there not in our intercourse with fellow-Christians too frequently uncharitable-ness, backbiting, and even bitterness of spirit? Instead of self-denial and cross-bearing, conditions of Christian discipleship, is there not an acknowledged avoidance of the cross, and an inveterate disposition to self-pleasing? Instead of a *liberal spirit* and *systematic beneficence,* is there not an absence of settled principle that sometimes expresses itself in the language, 'I will give little or nothing, just as I please'? In-stead of *simplicity* in our attire and in our styles of living, so that we may have more to give to Christ's blessed work, is there not an aping

of the world's fashions and follies, a conformity that we know is prejudicial to a deep and growing spirituality? Instead of *words seasoned
with grace* and tending to edification, are not too many of our words
idle, gossipy, unkind, and unprofitable? Instead of a *burning and
abiding zeal* prompting to steady aggressions upon the kingdom of sin
and hell, are we not fitful in our efforts, soon wearying in well-
doing?

"These pointed inquiries suggest some of the delinquencies and
shortcomings of too many of our Church members, and constrain the
conclusion that there is a *higher spiritual life* for the Church—a life
whose exercise will reveal in personal consciousness to the believer, and
present to the world around more beautiful and valuable fruit. Now
the question arises, What is that higher and better life? We have no
hesitation in saying it is what in Methodist parlance we entitle 'Entire
Sanctification,' implying the specific, intelligent, complete, and everlasting consecration of all our regenerated powers to God—a consecration, of course, including the surrender of every doubtful indulgence,
and the willing acceptance of any and every test of Christian obedience
—and, in addition, implying the constant resting in Christ by faith
as our full and perfect Saviour, trusting Him not only to save us, *but
to keep us saved.* Let the Church accept this privilege, so exceeding
great and precious—let her perform this service, so reasonable and
Scriptural, and her spiritual life will be *more Divine, more practical, and
more enduring.*

"1. It will be more Divine. Consecrating ourselves without any
reservation or limitations to the service of God, and concerned to accept
of Christ in the fullest sense, we necessarily come nearer to God, and, in
a broader and deeper and fuller sense, become partakers of the Divine
nature—partakers of the Divine wisdom, and purity, and gentleness,
and patience, and loving-kindness, and power. But some one will ask,
Is this different from the grace received at conversion? We answer,
No! it is only more of that precious grace—as we sometimes hear, it is
a '*deeper work of grace.*' Christ comes in His spiritual presence to
abide in our soul, and while we trust in Him, He assumes the entire
responsibility of our complete salvation. Now, without wasting time
on disputed theories or theological distinctions, let us ask, Is not
this the great need of the spiritual life of the Church?—is not this
a conscious and confessed want in our experience as professing
Christians?

"We have life, but we do not have it abundantly. We love God,
but we do not love Him with a perfect love—for a perfect love is
necessarily dependent upon a perfect consecration; just at the point

that our consecration is imperfect our love is imperfect, for it is then a divided, which is an imperfect love. We walk in the path of obedience, but we do not always stand up and go steadily forward in that path. We have peace with God as the result of our justification and adoption, but we cannot testify to perfect rest—the rest of perfect order, perfect activity, perfect security, perfect faith, perfect love, and perfect peace in the soul. The spiritual life of the Church needs, beyond all cavil or controversy, the elevation, invigoration, and inspiration that this grace of Christian holiness would give it.

" 2. But again, the acceptance of our full Gospel privilege would make the spiritual life of the Church not only more pure and Divine, but *more practical.*

" Need we say that one of the greatest desiderata of the Church, and one of the most peremptory demands of the world around, is a more practical piety? Men will judge of our religion, not so much by what it is, as by what it does. Now you will be reminded that the higher Christian life for which we plead involves an entire consecration of ourselves to God, and this consecration implies the use of all we have and are in harmony with the Divine will, and for the promotion of the Divine glory. It writes on our hands, our feet, our senses, our bodies, ' All sacred to Jesus.' It uses our understanding, judgment, imagination, memory, conscience, will, and affections, all as belonging to Jesus. It holds the gifts of God's providence—such as time, health, energy, reputation, influence, home, kindred, friends, property—all as subordinate to the will of Jesus. It takes the entire man for Jesus. In his life it makes him temperate, gentle, careful, humble, earnest, honest, liberal, and loving. In his political relations it makes him as conscientious and pure as in the ordering of his private religious life. In his business it lifts him up from the mere drudgery of a respectable but debasing selfishness, and, filling him with Christian principles, and linking all his secular transactions with the Divine service, it makes him a co-worker with God in the world's elevation and salvation. In his family it erects the altar of domestic worship—supplies the inspiration of a Christian example, diffuses around the atmosphere of love, welcomes the presence of Jesus, and thus constitutes the home as the house of God and the very gate of heaven.

" 3. One other suggestion is, that the spiritual life of the Church needs to be *more enduring.*

" Confined at present too much to sacred places and special seasons, the tendency is to impulsive, spasmodic, irregular, and unreliable religious life. It glows in the summer amid the hallowed privileges of the consecrated forest. It burns in the fall or winter when revival fires

are blazing upon our Church altars. It emits fitful gleams on the
Sabbath Day, or in the class-room, or in the prayer-meeting : but a
strong, round, full, regular, satisfying, steadily increasing religious life
—a life that is as consistent at home as away from home, as faithful in
little things as in great matters, as careful in a transaction that the
world will never hear of as in one that shall be blazoned before the
Church and the world—ah! this is the pure and abiding life that the
Church needs and must have. Let Christ in His spiritual presence
abide in the heart, the life of our life, the soul of our soul, bringing all
our habits and practices into harmony with the Divine will, and the
spiritual life of the Church shall of necessity become more Divine—more
practical—more enduring.

"Brothers, is not this our need? Observe, we do not plead for
changes or improvements in our ecclesiastical machinery—we hold that
nearly all the main features of our working economy are the gifts of
God's providence, and cannot with advantage be substituted by
different arrangements. Again, we do not argue for or insist upon a
higher standard of piety. The standard, as we conceive, has been fixed
by Christ Himself, and is as old as the Apostolic age. Not able to
elevate it, and not willing to lower it one iota, we simply say to those
who are equally responsible and interested with ourselves, *Let us
measure up to it.* Let us be a holy people. Holiness is power. What
the Church needs, what the world around is looking and waiting for, is
more of power. We must have it for the fulfilment of our high and
holy mission, viz., the spiritual conquest of the world. Entire sanctification—says Dr. Abel Stevens, in his admirable history—was the great
potential idea of early Methodism. It made our first preachers mighty,
irresistible, a flame of fire. It made our fathers and mothers an aggres-
sive power and an almost unparalleled blessing in their day. It took
hold upon the consciences and hearts of the unsaved in great communities. 'Wherever,' said Mr. Wesley, 'the work of sanctification
revives, the work of God revives in its different branches.' 'This,' he
remarked, 'is the great depositum which God has given to the people
called Methodists. Their mission is to spread Scriptural holiness over
these lands.' Observe, not that *generic holiness* which, promoting
repentance, faith, justification, regeneration, and holy living, claims
that it is spreading Scriptural holiness. All the evangelical churches
join with us to do this. Our special mission, as we understand, is to
hold up entire sanctification as an experience to be obtained by faith,
and, because by faith, to be obtained now. *This, secured in a specific
sense, becomes our best preparation to spread it in both a specific and a
generic sense.*

" Oh brothers! successors to Coke and Asbury and Abbott and Garrettson, take up and carry forward the banner of holiness that they planted so faithfully in this region. Methodist people of the Peninsula who in the midst of fierce fires of opposition have demonstrated so undeniably your civil and ecclesiastical loyalty, clinging with a heroic devotion to your mother-nation and your mother-church, covenant that this historic ground, already glorious, shall be made more glorious still.

" Rekindle the old fires, rekindle them in every county, in every township, in every neighbourhood, in every home, in every heart. Take the entire region for God. Bring its warm hearts, its growing wealth, its multiplied comforts, its rich abundance, its acknowledged advantages, and lay all upon the Christian altar. Ask, believe, and wait for the promised baptism of the Holy Ghost, and, with an unprecedented endowment of spiritual life, the Church and territory within the limits of the Wilmington Conference shall vindicate the language of prophecy : ' Thou shalt also be a crown of glory in the hand of the Lord, and a royal diadem in the hand of thy God. Thou shalt no more be termed Forsaken, neither shall thy land be termed Desolate ; but thou shalt be called Hephzibah, and thy land Beulah ; for the Lord delighteth in thee, and thy land shall be married.' "

I quote from the published proceedings an account of the concluding service of the Convention :—

" The Communion service that followed formed a most beautiful, appropriate, and profitable finale of these days of privilege. Ministers and members from all parts of the Wilmington Conference gathered around the same hallowed altar. The pastors of the Presbyterian and Protestant Episcopal Churches of Smyrna, with many of their communicants, participated in this service. It was an hour never to be forgotten. Surely

" ' Heaven came down our souls to greet,
    And glory crowned the mercy-seat.' "

At the close of this memorable Communion, when the very atmosphere around seemed sacred with the Divine presence, Rev. Alfred Cookman, called upon, said :—

" Brethren, it is good for us to be here. As we look around and recognise these ministers and people of sister-churches uniting with us in commemorating the love of our common Lord, the sentiment instinctively leaps to our lips, 'Behold, how good and how pleasant it is for brethren to dwell together in unity.' Over this scene I fancy I see stretching a rainbow composed of the different evangelical churches ; for while, like the colours of the natural rainbow, each Church retains its identity, yet at the same time beautifully blending, sweetly harmonizing, we present altogether the advancing sign, the infallible pledge of our world's triumphant redemption. During these hallowed moments I have been reminded of the broken alabaster box of which mention is made on the New Testament page. It has occurred to me that each of the denominations may be supposed to have their fragment still redolent with the fragrance of truth. When we come together on these delightful occasions, is it not to unite our fragments, and so reconstruct the box? and oh, say, does not the great Head of the Church vouchsafe the unction of the Holy One? does not the precious perfume arising fill the house—aye, and does it not promise to fill earth and heaven too with love and joy and praise?

" Brethren, it is the moment of parting. We shall never all meet again under similar circumstances. How blessed the truth that *Christians never part for the last time!* We separate, but it is as the angels do, going forth for the performance of the Divine will, but with the assurance that our home is before the throne, and that

> " ' We shall meet again,
>   Meet ne'er to sever ;
>   Meet when love shall wreathe her chain
>   Round us for ever.'

" Thank God, we belong to a sky-born, sky-guided, sky-returning race, and sweetly the peace-march beats, ' Home, brothers, home ! ' "

The tide of feeling had now reached its highest point, and, overflowing, the entire congregation sprang to their feet, when Mr. Cookman, grasping the hand of the Episcopal clergyman on his left and the hand of the Presbyterian pastor on his right, proposed that members of the Convention and all the Christian people present should clasp hands and join to sing—

> " Say, brothers, will you meet me
>   On Canaan's happy shore?"

It was a beautiful scene. Tears were flowing, praises re-sounding all over the house, as, with thrilling tones, the large audience pledged themselves, singing again and again—

> " By the grace of God we'll meet you
> Where parting is no more."

A member of the Convention, the Rev. J. H. Lightbourn, in a letter, says, " Mr. Cookman's closing address, though impromptu, was one of the most beautiful and thrilling to which I ever listened."

The time drew nigh when Mr. Cookman's pastoral rela-tions with Grace Church must be dissolved. He probably had never been more useful for a single term. With a magnificent church building, a large congregation of thoughtful, sympathizing persons, in a city small enough to be easily compassed, and yet large and active enough to afford variety, surrounded by a community of generous hospitality, and assured by the most marked results of the usefulness of his ministry and his acceptability with the people generally, his days had glided along most delight-fully. No great sorrow had entered his home or his im-mediate family, except the death of the aged Mr. Bruner, which was in the course of nature ; and really the term at Grace seemed as a day in the lightness which love, joy, friendship, and success had imparted to every burden. He loved the people, and they loved him. The services he rendered to the cause of vital religion and good morals will not soon be forgotten by the citizens of Wilmington.

The Rev. George H. Smyth, late pastor of the West Presbyterian Church, Wilmington, Delaware, has kindly furnished some of his impressions of Mr. Cookman while they were neighbouring ministers in that city :—

" It was my privilege to labour in the city of Wilmington, Delaware, side by side with Brother Cookman for more than two years. The last year of his residence there we were often thrown together in devotional meetings, and met at social gatherings.

" The same unbroken uniformity of a calm, genial temperament ever rested upon him. Truly he looked like one that possessed a peace the world can neither give nor take away. Nor was it an acquired, stoical indifference that made him insensible to surrounding influences, for he had a most susceptible nature, that sympathized with everything that was innocent around him. He always appeared solemn and dignified in his bearing, and at the same time easy and unaffected in his manners.

" He had a keen sense of the ludicrous, and would laugh till he shook all over. I remember on one occasion we were in one of the Union prayer-meetings, held the first week of the new year, when an amusing incident occurred. . . . Mr. Cookman was seated on the platform, and, as a suppressed smile passed all over the meeting, I shall never forget the efforts he made to preserve his gravity, his hands over his face, and his whole body shaking with laughter. ' Oh,' said he afterward, ' I did want to get off the platform to some place where I could laugh ! '

" And yet, with all his pleasantry and readiness to contribute to the enjoyment of the social gathering, no man was freer from a spirit of levity or irreverence for sacred things than was Brother Cookman. He was a very spiritually-minded man, and seemed to breathe continually a devotional atmosphere.

" In no place did he seem more at home than in a prayer-meeting. He was a fine singer, and in his selection of appropriate and beautiful hymns, sung with his rich, mellow voice, and in his earnest pleadings with God, he would diffuse the sweetest devotional spirit into all present, and often melt the congregation to tears. While the people were kneeling sometimes at the close of a prayer, he would start a hymn, which contained a petition just as suited to the occasion as if it had been written for it, and all would sing it through on their knees before God, and then one and another would burst forth with earnest prayer.

" In this way, without calling on any one or urging any one to speak or pray, he would kindle the flame of devotion until no one could keep silent.

" The Orthodox Friends—than whom no more godly people are to be found in that city—were many of them attracted to his church, and associated with him in Christian work.

" Perhaps no man ever exerted a wider or better influence in that
community, in the same time, than did Alfred Cookman, and no man
was more highly esteemed or more tenderly loved.   And why should
he not ?   To very many his life and labours had proved, under God, an
unspeakable blessing.

" The moulding power of Brother Cookman's godly life over Grace
Church just at a most important period of its early history will continue,
I doubt not, to bless that Church to its latest day ; so it will many
outside of that Church who were brought in contact with his great,
catholic, Christ-like spirit.

" For, while a decided Methodist, Brother Cookman was a man of
large heart, expansive views, and a charity that cordially fellowshipped
with all true believers in the Lord Jesus Christ. Hence he was ever ready
for co-operation with any or all the other denominations in any movement for advancing the cause of Christ in the community or in the world.
I have heard it said by old men, that never before had there been such a
kind, fraternizing spirit among all denominations of Christians as there
was at that time in Wilmington."

The following tribute, in harmony with Mr. Smyth's
statement, appeared just before Mr. Cookman's removal, in
The Wilmington Commercial :—

"The Rev. Mr. Cookman closes the last three years of his ministry
in this city on next Sabbath.   They have been years of indefatigable
labour, of great acceptability, and distinguished success.   Being the
first pastor in the great Grace Methodist Episcopal Church—the most
beautiful church, we think, on this continent—it was his to settle its
spiritual foundations, and give tone and evangelical views to its wor-
shippers, and start the Church on in deeds of great enterprise.   He has
borne up the ark of testimony by his own personal piety, by his faithful
and eloquent preaching, his labours in Sabbath Schools, in the temperance cause, missionary operations, and, in fact, in every good word and
work among the sister churches and other denominations.   He truly
possesses a union and fraternal spirit, and wherever he goes he has a
hand and heart for everybody.

"It is with deep regret that his brethren of the Wilmington Conference part with him, and many of the laity will follow him with
tearful eyes, and prayerful wishes that they may meet again on this side
of the grave, and if not, they may meet in heaven.   The young, to
whom he has been peculiarly useful, and who are sincerely attached to
him, will be deeply affected.   May good angels go with him ! "

The parting interviews of the beloved pastor with his Church in all its departments—the general congregation, the Sunday School, the social meeting—were deeply affecting, but with none more so than with the chosen circle of persons who were in the habit of attending the Wednesday-afternoon meeting. Mr. W. S. Hillis, a minister of the Society of Friends, in opening the Wednesday-afternoon meeting at which Mr. Cookman was last present before leaving, felt impressed to select the account of St. Paul's last charge to the elders of the Church of Ephesus, Acts xx. 17, etc. ; and as he read the verses concluding, " And they all wept sore, and fell on Paul's neck, and kissed him ; sorrowing most of all for the words which he spake, that they should see his face no more," he was overcome by his emotions. Mr. Cookman and the whole audience wept, and for some time the sorrow was so uncontrollable as to make it impossible to proceed with the services. Alas ! how prophetic the selection of those words !

CHAPTER XXII.

CENTRAL CHURCH, NEWARK, N.J.—OCEAN GROVE CAMP-
GROUND.—NATIONAL CAMP-MEETINGS AT ROUND LAKE
AND URBANA.

FOR months prior to March, 1871, Mr. Cookman's mind
had been agitated with the question of his next appointment. He had been invited to Boston, Mass., Chicago, Ill.,
Cincinnati, Ohio, Washington, D.C., Philadelphia, Pa., and
Newark, N.J., and pressed earnestly in all these cases to
entertain the proposition for a transfer. He undoubtedly
meant, when he returned to the Philadelphia Conference, to
remain in it for life ; but the division of the Conference in
1868 had unexpectedly thrown him out of it into the Wilmington Conference, and now his Conference relations were
again unsettled. So imperative seemed the demand for his
services in certain important churches in the controlling
centres of population and influence, that he finally yielded,
though reluctantly, to higher convictions of duty—in regard
to the freest interchange of ministers throughout the whole
Church—and consented to be transferred to the Newark
Conference, and was stationed at the Central Church,
Market Street, Newark, N.J. This proved to be his last
transfer and his last appointment in the Church. At the next
roll-call, at the name of Alfred Cookman, instead of the
round, full, silvery " *here*," there would be silence and tears.

18

In view of the frequency of Mr. Cookman's transfers from one Conference to another, and of the class of churches which he generally served, a communication from Mr. John Thompson, of Philadelphia, will be found pertinent. A letter from himself to a lady friend reveals the same earnest desire that ever attended these changes, to know and follow the Divine will. An incident also occurred before he left Grace, while his mind was yet undetermined as to the course he should take.

There was a little prayer-meeting at which were present some of his closest friends. He prayed earnestly to be directed to go where God might will—to *suffer or to die* for Him; and requested his friends to make special prayer. The next morning they all said "Newark."

The Central Church, Newark, gave a cordial welcome to their new pastor. He found a large and handsome church edifice, well located, with a thrifty, active, and generous membership, disposed in every way to promote his comfort and usefulness. Within a few brief weeks he was ensconced' with his family in their pleasant home, and he was as deeply immersed in the duties of the pastorate as if no change had taken place from one charge to another. The facility with which pastors go from church to church, and with which the churches accept one pastor after another, is inexplicable to persons outside of Methodism. The only explanation is, it is law and usage—ministers and people have become accustomed to the system, and, content with its workings, they accept it as a matter of course, and as the wisest arrangement for the whole Church. The prompt and cheerful acquiescence in the plan does not, however, preclude the sharp pangs caused by the severance of pastoral relations—many times the pastor's heart aches for the absent flock, and the people's hearts yearn for the recent pastor—but soon the new pastor and the new people become so taken up with each other as to prevent undue pain, while the strong attachments of former relationships are silently cherished as the pure and tender memories of a past which is ever present.

As in every previous charge, so at Central, Mr. Cookman began very soon to see the effects of an earnest ministry in a quickened Church, an increasing congregation, and the general signs of the esteem of the people. There seemed to be every reasonable indication that in coming to Newark he was in the path of duty.

Far-reaching as was Mr. Cookman's ministerial influence, by reason not only of his fame, but his actual pastoral and occasional services in the Church, he never became too great for the little duties of the parish. Outside engagements, however numerous and clamorous, were not allowed to press aside the work which was due to his own people in their proper organization, visitation, and instruction. Here at Newark, as elsewhere, the spring and early summer were devoted to regular pastoral calls, to the formation of such helps as would facilitate his own usefulness and develop the talents and graces of the members of the Church and congregation. He believed in woman's work for the Church and for humanity; and as a minister was always successful in winning the affections and confidence of the ladies of the Church, and organizing them for high and beneficent ends. Ere midsummer the Central Church was alive with religious activity. The whole membership had caught a spark from the heart of the living, working pastor.

Reference has been already seen in Mr. Cookman's correspondence to Ocean Grove camp-ground. He had become so charmed with the spot as to buy a lot there, building a cottage upon it for the accommodation of his family. He was particularly fond of the sea-side. As with his father, so with him, the ocean possessed a great attraction—he could sit by the hour and look out upon its restless life, and commune with its never-ceasing music. His highest physical spirits were excited when he was laved by its waves or walked amid its breezes. He was only too glad to avail himself of the capital opportunity which the Ocean Grove Association afforded of uniting a summer residence with the facilities of religious culture upon the sea-side, under conditions which would be free from the objections of ordinary fashionable watering-places. The modern innovation of combining the social element of the family life and the devotional element of religious worship in the camp-meeting was pleasing to him, as meeting not only his own want, but also a want which he believed to be very generally felt among Christian people. Some such resorts had long been needed, where healthful air and innocent pastimes could be had, with cheapness, plainness, and sobriety, associated with such religious exercises as tend to keep alive the pious habits and sentiments of the home left behind; where the moral feelings of those who prefer the stricter virtues will not be constantly shocked with customs which are a violence to good taste, to say nothing of sound morality and vital religion ; and where people can be practically taught the union which should always subsist between social and spiritual enjoyments.

The first notable example of this peculiar feature of the camp-meeting was set by the company owning the Wesleyan Grove Camp-ground, on Martha's Vineyard Island, Massachusetts. From rude beginnings the Martha's Vineyard Camp-meeting has grown until it has become a vast watering-place, with additional grounds adjoining under different companies. Whole villages of cottages have been erected, many of them at much cost, with all the devices which necessity and taste can suggest. It is not an uncommon thing for families from remote parts of the country, and of all the different religious denominations, to go thither early in the warm season, and to remain till autumn. The success of Martha's Vineyard has caused similar efforts in various sections, both on the sea-coast and inland, within the past few years. Prominent among them is Ocean Grove, New Jersey. Mr. Cookman was greatly pleased with its success; he prized highly the moments he was able to spend there in the summer of 1871, and those persons who had the happiness to be with him through those brief days will long cherish the memory of his personal and ministerial influence as among the most pleasant of their lives.

The first trumpet of the summer's campaign summoned Mr. Cookman to the sixth National camp-meeting at Round Lake. Thither the hosts of the higher life were moving; the prospect was for an immense meeting, and the responsibility of the National Committee was correspondingly great; it was felt that none of the active members could be spared,— least of all the man whose modest presence, wise counsels, persuasive speech, and holy character constituted him to the cause a tower of strength. He was not well; to his rather enfeebled body and worn mind it would have been delicious to go at once to the sea-side—but no; among the promptest to start for and reach Round Lake was Mr. Cookman. Though young in years he was a veteran in service, and as the war-horse snuffeth the battle afar, and in the first noise of the tumult forgets his stiffened joints, so this our hero of a hundred victories, with the first step upon the field of contest, with the first notes of God's Israel preparing for the charge, forgot all his wounds and weariness, and from beginning to end was in the thickest of the fight, himself

farthest on to the front, where the battle raged the fiercest
—here, there, everywhere—personally contending, and by
his voice and example cheering on the soldiers of the cross.
When the conflict had closed, the smoke had rolled away,
the field was won, and the day pronounced glorious in the
annals of holiness, no heart was more serenely happy than
Mr. Cookman's. His wounds, however, were seen to bleed
afresh. His natural force had abated—the elastic spring,
the gay, buoyant carriage was perceptibly broken, and the
beginning of the end was at hand. But other battles were
still to be fought, and further victories to be won.

Immediately upon his return from Round Lake he took
his family to Ocean Grove. It was evident to all that his
health was much impaired, but it was hoped that the invigorating sea air and sea bathing, with the quiet of the place,
would soon restore him to his usual strength. In all likelihood this would have been the effect, had he remained
during the season thus in repose, desisting from the extreme
labours and excitements of successive camp-meetings. It
was expected by his friends that he would do so—some of
them urged its necessity upon him—but, despite all remon-
strances, the earnest persuasions of his wife and kindred,
he could not be constrained to rest. The fact is, he did
not know how to rest; it was a lesson he had never needed
to learn hitherto, and now it was exceedingly difficult for
him to begin it. If Mr. Cookman had foreseen the probable
consequences of unintermitted work through the summer,
it is doubtful if he would have persisted in his purpose—as
he had never had cause before to take care of himself, he
could not now feel the necessity of it, nor fully appreciate
the fears of his friends. The habit of "campaigning" was
strong upon him. The second National camp-meeting for
the season had begun at Urbana, Ohio; the brethren of

the committee were there, and how could he stay away in ease, while they were at work and needed him? " Oh, Alfred !" said his wife, in tears—and she knew better than any one else how sick he really was—" you will not go to Urbana ?" " My dear, " he replied, " it is God's will." When he arrived at Urbana, the members of the committee were surprised but extremely gratified to see him.

In addition to what has been already said of Mr. Cookman's preaching at this meeting, I give an account of it which appeared in one of the Cincinnati papers shortly afterwards :—

" At ten o'clock the clang of the bell called the congregation to Church Square, where Rev. Alfred Cookman delivered another of those grand sermons that are rapidly placing him in the front rank of the eloquent and effective pulpit orators of the Methodist Church. His text was read from Ephesians v. 18—'Be ye filled with the Spirit.' The preacher said, by way of introducing his subject, that on an occasion like this it would be superfluous to employ time to insist on the personality or individuality of the Holy Ghost, the Third Person of the Trinity. Unanimous assent to that doctrine may be taken for granted. He then referred briefly to the various offices of the Spirit, as contradistinguished from those of the other Persons of the Trinity, and quoted from various inspired writers to establish the fact that the promise of the Spirit's presence was one of the understood guarantees given to man in the Scriptures. When the Holy Spirit comes to man it is not to speak of Himself, but to take of the things of Christ and show them unto us. The Spirit does not reveal Himself, but reveals the personality and presence of Christ. This explains the prominence given to Christ in all effective preaching of the Gospel. I detract not an iota from the merits of Christ. I am not surprised to hear you sing, ' Oh, how I love Jesus !' but we must not fail to recognise that it is our glorious privilege and duty to speak of, pray to, live in, have fellowship with, be filled by the Holy Spirit.

" The effects of being filled with the Holy Spirit are developed in the consciousness, character, and life of man. Its effects on man's consciousness are : First, the soul will be hallowed in thought, feeling, and motive. Second, the soul will have a deep, full, and abiding experience of love—a valuable and beautiful fount of the very nature of the Spirit

Himself. Third, the soul will have the realization of real rest. Antago-
nisms will be allayed; antagonists transformed into servitors. The
soul where the Spirit makes His home will be made a perfect home.

"In character, religion aims to produce perfection. Character in its
highest form is not the product of merely human agencies; and a character developed by the Spirit's operation will involve: First, *holiness;*
freedom from littleness, lowness, or vileness. Second, *gentleness;* no
agent is comparable with the Spirit in this matter of gentleness—and
gentleness makes man great. Third, *wisdom;* this is pronounced in
God's Word; God's children shall be the happiest, best, and wisest on
His footstool. In personal life: first, a soul filled with the Spirit
supplies the impulse of an earnest, useful, and valuable life; second, it
will supply not only the motive power, but the ability to accomplish;
third, it associates with the words and labours of life the unction of the
Holy One.

"The speaker discussed at some length the question, What is
unction? He said: 'It is that subtle, intangible, irresistible influence
of the Holy Spirit that seals instruction upon the hearts to which it is
given. It is not the eloquent men of this world, the orators of great
occasions, whose words linger longest in their influence upon the hearts
of men. The unction may oftentimes be rather in the utterances of a
humble disciple than in the delivery of a powerful sermon. For this I
am more concerned than for anything else.' . . .

"His clear, ringing voice penetrated to the remotest bounds of
the great square, and under the influence of his eloquence men stood
motionless as statues. The hour of twelve came, and the gongs and
dinner-bells around the inclosure began an interruptive clangour. But
no person in that congregation could have been tempted away by an
epicurean feast. In that moment there was food for the moral and
religious nature being dispensed with all the liberality of eloquence, and
the wants of physical nature were unheeded in these appeals. An imperfect report would utterly mar the beauty of the speaker's utterances,
and a perfect report would fail to convey any idea of the glowing
eloquence of his style and the telling effect of his pathetic appeals to
men and women to 'be filled with the Holy Spirit.' Your types could
print the mere words, but no pen-power that I know of can clothe them
with the garb of oratory in which they trooped forth from the speaker's
lips, to take by storm the stubborn citadels of men's hearts and
minds."

CHAPTER XXIII.

WITH the camp-meeting at Urbana, Mr. Cookman's public services with the National Committee ceased. Some of the committee, during the season, moved farther westward, and held meetings in a large tent at Topeka, Kansas, Salt Lake City, and in different parts of California; but he was not able, for want of time and strength, to accompany them.

Mr. Cookman returned from Martha's Vineyard, spent two weeks at Ocean Grove, and then brought his family home, and early in September was at the regular work of his charge. The great spiritual preparation which he had earnestly desired for his fall and winter work had evidently been granted; his mind began promptly to unfold plans of increasing usefulness, and in all the public and social services there was an enlarged attendance and a manifest deepening of religious fervour. The special service for the promotion of holiness, not hitherto appointed, was now established, and from it the happiest results were anticipated.

There was, however, one drawback to the pastor's plans and expectations—a disturbing element had thrust itself forward and demanded recognition—a strange element,

which heretofore had never entered into his reckonings,
beset him : his health, always before so firm and reliable,
was now weak and treacherous. His physical constitution
had lost its elasticity; accustomed hitherto to recover its
vigour immediately with the suspension of hard work, it
now failed to show signs of recuperation. The bow, strung
too long, had lost its spring, and when the string was
loosed there was no rebound. Alfred Cookman had gone
too far for his strength : this last summer's campaign
had finished what former summers' work had begun and
hastened—the premature decay of his bodily powers.

It is impossible, as I now enter the shadows which begin
to gather about our friend, whom I have thus followed step
by step until this period of his life, to dismiss wholly from
sight a question which, despite the sanctity of his character,
the usefulness of his career, and the triumph of his death,
obtrudes itself upon me : Can his uniform course of attending and working at successive camp-meetings during the
summer seasons be wholly commended ? The difficulty of
seeing any mistake in a life so full of good fruits is very
great; and yet, when the loss to the Church and to the
world which the death of such a man entails is weighed,
those who feel it most deeply may be forgiven if they
suggest conditions which, humanly considered, may have
prevented it.

> " Oh, sir ! the good die first,
>   And they whose hearts are dry as summer dust
>   Burn to the socket,"

is an utterance which gratifies a sort of vengeful feeling
when we see the good stricken down in their prime and the
wicked living to old age ; but it is not such as Christianity
warrants. The earth needs the good. The cause of God
needs the wisdom of age as well as the zeal of youth. Life

is the order of God, and, except where it can be clearly
pointed out as a duty, it is not to be unduly exposed.
Times may come, calls may arise which demand its
jeopardy and even its sacrifice as the price of conscience,
liberty, humanity; but ordinarily God is most glorified
when, by a due observance of the law of health, it is
prolonged and preserved in cumulative perfection to
advanced years.

There is no reason why a holy man should not increase
in holiness and usefulness until old age, and present, though
in a different aspect, quite as beautiful an exemplification
of the force of religion in the aged as in the young. This is
a view of the subject quite necessary to be looked at,
especially by youth. There is something peculiarly fascinat-
ing to ardent natures in the halo which invests a rapid, fiery
course and an early, triumphant death; but to other minds
there is something repellent, as implying a logical connection between a life of the highest devotion and a premature
death. A devout man may conscientiously refuse incessant,
overtasking labour, and insist upon the hours and days of
relaxation, for the preservation of his health, in order that
he may thus offer to God a larger and more effective service.
St. Paul had a desire to depart and be with Christ, which he
felt to be far better for himself, because he would thus
sooner be free from suffering, and be present with the Lord;
but he yielded to the motive of usefulness to the Church
as a reason sufficiently strong to control his personal
preference, and consented to remain in the body.

The desire for the greatest usefulness may lead one man
to such intensity of action as to preclude intermission of
labour, under the impression that time thus spent is lost;
while the same desire may lead another to the strict observance of vacation, as more economical of time, because

regarded as indispensable to the maintenance of an equable
and steady strength. One man's motto is, "Labour here,
rest hereafter"; another's motto is, "Some rest and more
labour." Both may be equally religious, be alike governed
by the glory of God; but certainly if the human race,
before its universal death and resurrection, is to possess the
earth,—if in humanity as now constituted, only saved from
sin and immorality, God is to be glorified in what is ordinarily expected as the millennium,—then conservation of
physical health and the prolongation of human life must
be considered one of the first duties of practical religion.
God's greatest glory will be revealed in the highest perfection of the threefold man—soul, body, and spirit.

A doubt cannot be raised as to the thorough conscien-
tiousness of Mr. Cookman; nor, with the notions of individual liberty, which must be conceded in preference to
personal conduct, especially in view of the good sense and
the extreme care with which he canvassed all questions of
religion and morals, both for himself and others, is it easy
to say that *he* should have acted differently in the use of
his time and energies than he did. While he was in the
fulness of his vigour, fame, and usefulness, his friends used
to remonstrate with him against devoting his vacations in
the heats of summer to the same mental and bodily work to
which he was accustomed all the year round. He thought
the change of scene and place would be sufficient to prevent damage to his health. But the trouble was that, while
change of scene did bring a degree of relaxation, the mind
continued, only in an intenser degree, to be excited in the
same direction as in the ordinary work of the pastoral
charge. If, after the exhaustion of the camp-meetings, he
could have had freedom of care for a month each year, his
labours could have been continued, in all likelihood, for

many years, for his physical resources were truly remarkable; but it was not possible for a man, even of his bodily
powers, to go directly from the cares of a charge to the
herculean work of five or six camp-meetings every season,
and to return immediately to the exacting duties of the
pastorate, without detriment to his health, and probable
premature decay of his vital force. He did not realize his
danger in the beginning, and with each additional year his
zeal became so absorbing as to consume him; so that I
believe his course was finally one of deliberate choice, taken
with his eyes fully open to the worst consequences.

I cannot approve his election on general principles. I
may accept it as that which God's Spirit pointed out to him
as his proper path; and, in accepting it, I must be carried
away with admiration for so sublime an embodiment of that
ancient, heroic, self-sacrificing devotion which inspired the
apostles and confessors of the primitive ages, and which
still in these modern times impels scores and hundreds of
believers to brave the pestilence, the savage, and the deep
for the Cross of Christ. Surely no one can turn away from
the career of this saint of God, after contemplating his
self-sacrificing zeal for the salvation of his fellow-men, and
say "the age of heroes is past."

After all, it may be that one lesson, in addition to many
others, which Divine Providence meant to teach in the
history of His servant, is the greater moral beauty, the
richer blessedness of a zeal which consumes, in contradis-
tinction to the dwarfed religiousness which the thought of
self and the love of ease engender—low principles which,
alas! are too prevalent in our day. Sometimes extremes
can only be met by extremes; a low stoop is necessary to
reach a deep depression—so Alfred Cookman may have
been a sacrifice to an excessive zeal, whose force, all the

greater by its contrast, shall kindle the breasts of others, and arouse them from a too utilitarian and cold policy for the work of saving a selfish world.

But the day is passing—the sun nears the west—the shadows are lengthening : enough of my reflections. We will hear more from him. Some one remarked to him during his last illness, " Perhaps you have worked too hard, and have not been sufficiently careful of your health." " Well," he replied, " I do not know—I have enjoyed my work ; I have not been conscious of overtaxing myself. I had but one life to live here, and it was for the glory of Jesus ; and He has abundantly recompensed me."

The last article which came from Mr. Cookman's hand for publication, was a preface, written at the request of Mr. W. S. Hillis, of Wilmington, Delaware, for a little tract containing the account of Dr. Coan's labours in the island of Hilo. The tract was afterwards published. The article was conveyed in a letter to Mr. Hillis :—

"NEWARK, N.J., *October* 19, 1871.

" I ought perhaps to take a season of rest, but in my relations, both family and ecclesiastical, this seems impracticable. I am the child of the best of fathers, and He is pledged to the supervision of all my interests. What may be His design in my present condition I cannot know. Lying quietly and lovingly and confidently in His blessed embrace, I look up and say, ' Good is the will of the Lord.' I want to be entirely willing to do or not to do."

Mr. Cookman continued to fulfil all his ministerial duties during the weeks of September and October. But it was evident to his family and friends that his bodily strength was not adequate to the tasks he was performing. It was the opinion of medical men that his health was seriously impaired and needed absolute rest, and he was advised to take a tour to Europe. The way did not appear to be open,

and so he toiled on—hoping, though not without alternations
of fear, that with the cold frost of autumn his strength
would return. He would at this time, after being out through
the day making pastoral calls, come home and throw himself on the sofa utterly exhausted, and say, "Sometimes I
think my work is nearly done, and when I take my bed, it
may be my last sickness." Then again he would rally, and
talk of his plans for the future. He still moved quite freely
among his ministerial brethren. As late as the first of
October he was over to New York in attendance upon the
Preachers' Meeting, interchanging greetings and showing
all his wonted buoyancy of feeling. His hearty grasp
and glowing expressions on that occasion cannot soon be
forgotten.

While instant in labour in his own charge, he was ever
ready, sick as he was, to render outside help to the ministers
of neighbouring cities.

The Rev. L. R. Dunn writes :—

"After the summer campaign was over, he resumed his work with
great hopefulness. Having been a pastor for five years of the same
Church, and knowing intimately its official boards and its entire
membership, I can safely say that never before in all their history were
they labouring with greater unanimity, with loftier inspirations, and
with more assured promise and hope for their future enlargement and
prosperity. Every movement he made, every word he spoke, every
meeting he held, and every sermon he preached seemed to distil a fragrance not only in his own Church, but as far as he was known through
all the churches and all the community. . . . .

" As an illustration of this, an intelligent young man, who had been
brought to Christ during my ministry in the Central Church, although
afterwards connected with another of our churches in the city, was conversing with me after his death about his goodness and purity. So
impressed did he seem to be that I asked him if he had often heard him
preach. 'No,' said he, 'I have never heard him preach, *but I have
watched him as he was walking along the street.*' So that his very
shadow as he walked left its impress on the mind and heart of that

young man. . . . I had arranged to have a few days of extra services
in my charge, and he had promised to spend a day with me. He
came in during the afternoon meeting, and talked very sweetly and
impressively to all present of his experience of full salvation. After
service he went to my house with one of our dear mutual friends, and
remained until the evening service. When leaving the house he said
to me, ‘Let me take your arm : since my sickness this last summer I
have been a little lame, and my limbs sometimes seem to give way.’
Little did I think then, as he walked and talked of Jesus and His love,
that he was so near to his heavenly home. . . . He preached with
great power on ‘Put ye on the Lord Jesus,’ and his sermon seemed to
produce a deep impression.”

Nothing could exceed the spiritual-mindedness of Mr.
Cookman through these weeks. He was full of plans for
life, but a deep under-current of feeling bore all his thoughts
heavenward. He almost literally lived and moved in God.
His spirit was becoming so filled with the atmosphere of
the skies, that its tendency was upward ; and, imperceptibly
to himself and his friends, he was so ready for the ascent
that it was with difficulty he could be held to earth. Walking out one evening with his wife, as he looked up to the
heavens he said, “Those are my Father’s stars”—“That
is my Father’s moon.” A short time before he was taken
sick they visited a house where they saw an oil-painting of a
saint just entering heaven ; lingering by it, he said, “How
I covet her!—she is almost within the gate”; and then
requested his wife to sing—

> “Oh, the city ! oh, the glory !
> Far beyond the rapturous story
> Of the ages old and hoary—
> Oh ! ’tis heaven at last !”

He gazed in transport as he seemed to fancy her just
entering the heavenly city.

The month of October, with its keen, crisp breath, was
fast speeding away without reviving the flagging steps of the

weary invalid. He grew perceptibly weaker. While in attendance upon the National Committee in New York, about the middle of the month, he made a call at his brother's house in West Thirty-fourth Street. Though feeble, he was very bright and cheerful. His whole conversation was about Jesus and His cause. That visit proved the last. Two days before his final illness he attended a love-feast at the Halsey Street Methodist Episcopal Church, Newark. His ankles were then very weak, but such was his devotion to the Master's work that he could not refuse to go. At the close of the meeting he gave his experience from the commencement of his religious life, dwelling especially upon the holy influence and example of his mother. Returning home, two of his warm friends walked on either side of him to support his feeble steps. He said to them, " I know it is not popular to hold up the doctrine of holiness, but I thought I would do my whole duty then ; I feel this may be my last opportunity."

On Sunday, the 22nd of October, he performed his last public services. He had said many times when in health, " I would like to die, if it is God's will, with my armour on, and preach by my death as well as by my life." He often spoke of the Rev. Dudley Tyng, with whom he was intimately associated in Philadelphia, and said, " It was glorious to die as he did, for his dying testimony was yet echoing through the world." He even said he " would prefer to die in the pulpit." His wish, though not literally, was about to be substantially gratified. His work and his life were to end together. His death was to be the most effective sermon of his whole career—a fitting vindication and illustration of the power of the docrines he had preached and lived—a death which, for its singular spiritual glory, is destined to be spoken of while the annals of Christian saints

19

shall be read, and which for its wondrous force will be quoted and dwelt upon as a Divine inspiration while there shall be a Church to cherish the memory of the good, or a trembling believer who shall need cheer amid the stern struggles of life and death.

In the morning he preached from Mark iv. 25, "From him that hath not shall be taken away even that which he hath"—a very solemn and effective sermon. In the afternoon he visited the Sabbath School, as was his custom, and shook hands with every teacher and scholar. Toward evening he complained of not feeling well, and Mrs. Cookman was very anxious to get some one to fill his pulpit for the evening service. But he would not consent—saying, " I think I have a message from God for this people; I shall preach from 'the faded leaf.'" As he arose to announce his text, he held in his hand a faded leaf, saying, "This is my text : 'We all do fade as a leaf.'" Several persons remarked afterwards to his wife that " he looked like one transfigured." A lady said to her husband, "She did not think that Fletcher could have looked more seraphic." As he finished his sermon his feet gave way, and passing from the pulpit he handed the leaf to a friend, saying, " The leaf and the preacher are very much alike—*fading.*" He limped home, and when his wife received him in the parlour he was almost distracted with pain. As he was assisted to his chamber he remarked to her, " I have preached my own experience to-night,—'*Fading as a Leaf.*'"

The physician in attendance pronounced the disease *mialgia*, or acute inflammatory rheumatism, the pain being confined to the ankles and the soles of the feet. There was also a torpid condition of the liver, which added very much to his discomfort. The next few days were accompanied with intense suffering; but he was heard to say "that, while his whole lower nature was quivering with agony, his higher nature triumphed in God." At times he would be so filled with the Spirit as to burst out in the midst of his anguish into expressions of praise and love. I quote again from the Rev. Mr. Dunn: "In attempting to describe his sufferings to me he used the following language: ' If,' said he, ' the bones of my feet were all teeth, and each one had what we call the jumping toothache, it would give you some idea of what I suffer.' After conversation and prayer, when I rose to leave, he grasped my hand, and looking up so lovingly in my eyes, he said, ' My precious brother, how I love you ! I have always felt a special nearness to you ever since I have known you.' But, great as his sufferings were, he seemed then to have no idea he was so near his end, but talked freely of his plans for the future, and his hope of a speedy recovery."

After about one week of almost constant pain, approaching sometimes to convulsions, alleviated only by slight intervals of ease, he became apparently convalescent. When a lull in his sufferings took place he was very bright and cheerful, and he manifested the keenest interest in everything which occurred around him both beyond and within the house. Every little incident in the outer world was referred to with the liveliest appreciation; while the acts of kindness performed by those in attendance upon him, even of the most trivial kind, were received with the sweetest look of pleasure and gratitude. Always to the question, " How are you ?" he would reply, " I think I am a little better." After rallying from the first paroxysms of suffering, he had his books and paper brought to him, and employed his time as he was able in reading or being read to, and in writing notes to his friends. His Bible was daily by his side; when he was unable to read it, either the children or his wife would read it to him, and he would respond, "There is nothing like the Word of the Lord !" or "Oh, how precious !" At his request his daughter Annie read to him the sixteenth chapter of the Gospel of St. John —always a favourite chapter with him. She said to him one day, as he was suffering with pain in the back of his neck, " Pa, are you not afraid that it will go to your brain ?" " No, darling," he answered, "not unless the Lord Jesus would have it." October 29th, one week from the time of his prostration, a meeting being held by the members of his Church to pray especially for his recovery, he dictated for them the following note :—

" Mr. Cookman wishes me to say that he appreciates more than he can express the sympathy and love of his dear people. He loved you all very tenderly before his present illness ; he feels that he will love you much more in the future. This a Sabbath of great physical suffering, and yet it is proving, doubtless in answer to your prayers, the most precious of all his life. He says he is Christ's suffering little child ; and with every sharp, keen, excruciating pain, he feels that Jesus presses him even more closely to His great heart of love, and lets him realize the power of His Divine sympathy and tenderness. He says, ' God bless you all !—the kindest, dearest people that any pastor ever served.' "

CHAPTER XXIV.

It was after reviving from one of the severe paroxysms to which Mr. Cookman was subject, about one week from the first attack, that he had what may be regarded as a remarkable vision. He found himself just inside of heaven. He was first received by his grandfather Cookman, who said, " When you were in England, I took great pleasure in showing you the different places of interest ; now I welcome you to heaven, my grandson, washed in the blood of the Lamb !" He was next received by his father—whose features were as distinct as when he saw him in his boyhood days : he also said, " Welcome, my son, washed in the blood of the Lamb !" Then his brother George took him in his arms, and said, "Welcome, my brother, washed in the blood of the Lamb !" And lastly his son Bruner received him with the same salutation—" Welcome, father, washed in the blood of the Lamb !" Each one of these in turn presented him to the Throne. When he told his wife of what he had seen and heard, he remarked, "That was an abundant entrance." She asked him if it was a dream. He replied, " No, it was between sleeping and waking." Saint Stephen is not the last of God's suffering, dying servants who have seen heaven opened before their entrance into it.

He was often heard to repeat the simple words,—

> " I'm a poor sinner, and nothing at all,
> Jesus Christ is my all in all."

He now seemed to understand as never before the expression, "Perfect, or purified through suffering." "I have known for many years what it is to be washed in the blood of the Lamb; now I understand the full meaning of that verse, 'These are they which came out of *great tribulation*, and have washed their robes and made them white in the blood of the Lamb.' I used to maintain that the blood was sufficient, but I am coming to know that tribulation brings us to the blood that cleanseth." His mother, who visited him frequently, reminded him that the Saviour suffered in His feet, to which he afterwards often referred. "You know the nails pierced His precious feet, and He can sympathize with me in my sufferings. 'In all their afflictions He was afflicted.'" To his son Frank he said, "The effect of this sickness is to draw me closer and closer to the heart of Jesus."

The last letters he wrote will be read and cherished as well-nigh messages from heaven.

> " NEWARK, N.J., *November* 6, 1871.

" I am still the prisoner of the Lord—but oh, what an honour! what a privilege! what a joy! Infinite Love is my Keeper, and the Lord's prison-houses are incomparably more desirable than the gorgeous palaces of wickedness.

" This is now the third week of my affliction. Lying on my back, I am grateful to be able to use my *pencil* in communing with the dear friends whose tried affection is cherished among my heart's richest treasures, and the expression of whose sympathy is so soothing and welcome. When our Christian boy was wrested from us, no voice was more tender, no heart more sympathizing than your own. We have not forgotten it—and now that it pleases the best of fathers to afflict your unworthy brother, it is most encouraging and inspiring to know that the same true heart turns to the human in love and to the Divine in prayer.

" Precious sister, your prayers have reached the Throne, and the gracious answers have been blessing me both in my body and my soul. Two weeks since I was struck in my own pulpit, just at the close of the evening sermon. I felt my feet giving way ; I limped home, I scarcely know how. Lying down on my bed, the pain rapidly developed, until it was almost more than I could endure. Confined to the ankle and soles of the feet, it was as if that part were full of teeth, and all were quivering at the same moment with violent, jumping toothache. This, of course, made the feet so sore that I could not bear to have them touched. The pulsing pain in the sore feet, continuing day after day, involved my whole nervous system, until in the paroxysms I was almost like one the victim of convulsions. Oh the long, weary nights !—the throbbing pain beating the seconds of hours that seemed like little ages !

" Since Tuesday last I have had measurable relief, though prostrated beyond expression in my general system. Owing to the soreness of my feet, and the condition of my liver and other organs, the doctor insists on my remaining in bed a few days longer. I have thus entered into detail respecting myself, because I thought it might be what your kind, warm heart would desire to know.

" But now turning from the *sick* and *suffering* man, let me *humbly* acknowledge that the inward man, walking in the furnace, has been wonderfully sustained and enabled to triumph day after day. Oh, Sister Emily, how precious is full salvation in our times of extremity ! When every nerve was quivering with agony, the heart sent up its blessed testimony—' Washed in the blood of the Lamb.' I realized, too, that I would have some *little* claim to the other part of that blessed Scripture—' These are they that have come up through great tribulation,' etc. I could, if I were physically able, fill many pages with these experiences—*all of grace.* Join me to sing, ' Glory to the Lamb ! '

" All the rest are well, and send you and Brother Edward tenderest love. Do please write soon again—your letters are like so much light thrown into my sick room. God bless my Wilmington friends ! "

" NEWARK, *November* 8, 1871.

" To-day they are allowing me to sit up for a little while. Thank God for this indication of convalescence !—but I am still very much prostrated in my physical nature. To rest my weight on my feet or to take a single step would be quite out of question. As yet, there is no developing appetite whatever. I nibble a little, but it is a mere matter of form, or to make some contribution to the reduced strength of my system. The great concern on my mind has been to know exactly what is the will or design of my Heavenly Father in this dispensation. It has wonderfully increased my interest in and sympathy for suffering humanity. Oh, it seems to me I would most willingly rub or bathe the feet even of a suffering brute. It has realized to me the power and preciousness of many parts of Scripture bearing upon suffering— passages that previously had their exposition principally in my intellect. It has satisfied me of the independent action of the soul, for when my whole lower nature seemed to be quivering and quailing through excruciating pain, my higher being not only trusted, but triumphed in the God of my salvation. The best hours of my illness were when the fierce fires of suffering were kindling and scorching all around me. It has convinced me that full salvation is the only preparation for the ten thousand contingencies that belong to a mortal career. Oh, how sooth- ing to feel, hour by hour, that the soul has been washed in the blood of the Lamb, and to experience the inspiration of that perfect love that casteth out all fear that hath torment ! These, with other lessons, have been most precious and profitable ; and yet I cannot but think that my faithful Lord has some ulterior meaning in this affliction that is not as yet fully or satisfactorily revealed. I want to sit like little Samuel, and, with a humble and obedient heart, say, 'Speak, Lord, for Thy servant heareth.' God's will is so infinitely good, that without fear I would follow where it leads. Your allusions to the grassy hillocks in the Clyde Cemetery were most tender and touching. Truly, as you intimate, those sacred mounds become our earthly Pisgahs. They lift us above the world, and enable us to retrospect profitably the past and anticipate rapturously

> " ' Canaan, fair and happy land,
>   Where *our possessions* lie.'

" Let me thank you, my dear sister, for your gentle sympathy and strong and valued affection. 'A world in purchase for such a friend would not be too dear.' Your beautiful letter was read again and again in my sick room, and in every instance it lifted me up in my thoughts and feelings. Will you not remember me most affectionately to your beloved daughters? We shall still indulge the hope of sharing with them the hospitality of our itinerant home."

" *Saturday, November* 11, 1871.

" I am writing this note in my bed, to which I have been confined for three weeks. For some months past I have been far from well, but at the close of my sermon on the evening of October 22 I felt my feet giving away. I limped home, went to bed, and for about nine days was almost distracted with what my physicians entitled *mialgia*—an acute form of inflammatory rheumatism. The pain was confined to my ankles and the soles of my feet. It was just as if the back part of the feet were filled with teeth, and all at the same time affected with violent, jumping toothache. This, of course, made my feet so painful that I could scarcely bear to have them touched. Then the pulsing pain in the painful feet, continuing day after day, so involved my whole nervous system that towards the last it was almost like convulsions. The only relief that I got was through morphine and chloroform. For ten days I have been relieved of the pain, but still am very sick. Only once have I sat up, and then returned to bed with a raging fever. Fever, bloody expectorations, sore throat, torpid liver, disordered kidneys, absence of all appetite, hemorrhoids, and great weakness, are my symptoms at present. My physician, Dr. Nichols, a skilful and experienced practitioner of the old school, is very faithful in coming to see me twice a day. Then my precious wife (God bless her!) has been unremitting in her attentions. Day and night, like a loving angel, she has hovered over my pillow, studying my wants, anticipating my wishes. Oh, I can never repay her for her self-sacrificing and unwavering love! I fancy she looks thin through her constant nursing, but she would not permit any one to take her place, and I am sure I do not want any one else.

" Above all, dear mother, I have had the precious Jesus with me during every hour of my sickness. When my pains were most severe, He would let down on my soul such a weight of glory that I was obliged to break forth in strains of praise and joy. Oh, precious mother, how invaluable is full salvation in suffering and in the prospect of eternity! To feel that the soul is washed in the blood of the Lamb, and to realize the perfect love that casteth out all fear that hath torment ! Oh, this is more than all the world beside !

"But I am weary now. I can write no more."

Through all his sickness Mr. Cookman retained his fondness for singing, and sometimes would have his wife and his little Mary and Helen on his bed beside him, joining in such hymns as "Rock of Ages," "Oh, how I love Jesus !" " I shall be satisfied," " Jesus calls me." His voice never seemed fuller and sweeter. One day he was so much better as to be able to be out in the sitting-room. Lying on the sofa, or reclining in an easy chair, his face wore a most heavenly expression, and his remark upon everything around him was, "Oh, it is beautiful!" Seeing a gentleman walking fast in the street, he said, "That is the way I used to walk. I wonder if I ever shall walk that way again." His wife remarked "Certainly"; but he seemed to doubt it. On the last evening that he sat up, his sister Mary being present, he asked them to sing,—

"Oh, it was love, it was wondrous love!"

and other spiritual songs. He retired about nine o'clock, and that was the last time the family sung together.

One day he said to his wife, "Do you know what I have been doing? I have been *counting my friends.*" When told that it was impossible, he had so many, and that he could not have an enemy,—"No," he remarked, "I do not know that I have. God has been very good to me, but you know there are some very special friends."

Never was Mr. Cookman more devoted to his wife and children than now. Having consecrated his children to God from their birth, he confidently trusted them with the Heavenly Father. Every day he wished them all brought to his bedside ; especially the youngest, his baby-boy, Alfred, whom he called his sunshine, he would have on his bed and play with him by the hour. His little Willie said to him one day, "Papa, do you think you will ever bathe in the ocean again?" "No, darling, I reckon these feet will never touch that gravelled walk again." He even taught his boys to recite pieces, heard his daughter Annie recite a hymn, was so cheerful that all thought him convalescent, and, indeed, no one thought him critically ill until the day of his death.

On Saturday, the 11th of November, Dr. J. M. Ward, a member of the Presbyterian Church, visited and prayed with him. The Doctor afterward gave an account of the visit in *The Guide to Holiness.*

"I saw our dear Brother Alfred Cookman just two days before he left us. Committing to me at that time the care of his weekly meeting for the promotion of holiness, he added, ' I shall be out in a week or two, and will resume the care of it myself.' So he doubtless thought ; but the dear Lord had other service for him above. He was sitting in his chair by the bedside, his face glowing with heavenly brightness. To speak was painful to him, from soreness of the throat ; and yet so full, even to overflowing, was his heart with the love of Christ, that he could not refrain from talking. As truly might it have been said of him as of one of old, 'The love of Christ constraineth me ' ; for his utterances were such as the Holy Spirit only could give.

" In answer to a question as to his sufferings during the week, he said, 'They have been excruciating, and yet so gloriously has Jesus manifested Himself to me in them all that I have been immensely the gainer from them. Such views of Christ's presence with me—such views of His cleansing blood have I had as never before. Oh, the precious blood ! ' he exclaimed. Then, with an upward glancing of his eye, his head leaning backward upon the chair, he repeated, 'Oh, the precious blood, the precious cleansing blood of Jesus ! '

" No marvel that he was getting clearer views of the precious blood under clearer manifestations of Christ to him, for he was ripening most wonderfully, all unconscious to himself and us all, for his entrance upon his heavenly inheritance ; he was being ' made meet ' for the abundant entrance so soon to be administered to him into the heavenly Jerusalem. . . .

" The prayer was ended ; in a moment more the parting was said, while hand was pressing hand, and the interview closed. But the glory filling the chamber of the sainted one seemed still to encircle me all the way homeward, giving character to my first utterances to friends, as I said, ' Oh, what a blessed interview with Brother Cookman this afternoon ! ' "

During the Doctor's prayer he would frequently respond, " The sweet will of God." To his sister he said the same day, " If I could have life on earth by the lifting of my hand, I would not. If Jesus should ask me, 'Would I live or die?' I would answer, 'I refer it back to Thee.'" To the Rev. Mr. Dunn, in his last interview, he said, "I wish that I could tell you how precious Jesus has been to me during my sickness. I have had such views of Him as I never had before. Right in the midst of my intensest sufferings He has so manifested Himself to me that I have been lifted above them all."

He remarked to his wife, "God means something by this sickness; He is either fitting me for greater usefulness here or for heaven. I am lying passive in His hands, trying to learn the lessons He would teach me. I am sitting in the hands of the Heavenly Artist." To one of his official members he used substantially these words: "My Church is very dear to me ; my wife and children are very precious ; my friends are dear to me ; but *the sweet will of God* I love better than all else ; I have no choice to live or die. God has some design in this sickness—Jesus is very precious." Often he would repeat, "Lo! I am with you alway, even unto the end of the world." The same evening the Rev. William McDonald and two members of the Church visited him ; he enjoyed seeing them, and during prayer there was an extraordinary sense of the Divine presence.

Sunday, his last Sabbath on earth, was a beautiful day. He requested his wife to open the window and let the bright sunshine in the room, remarking, "The beams of the Sun of Righteousness are shining around me. Glory all around!" He requested to be sung—

> " Come, ye sinners, poor and needy,
> 　Weak and wounded, sick and sore ;"

and said, "That grand old hymn! Yes, I am weak and *wounded*, sick and *sore*."

He was very earnest all day in praying for the ministers and the preaching of the Word. In the afternoon Mr. McDonald visited him again, and they conversed closely and fully on the subject of holiness. He said among other things to this friend, " I have tried to preach holiness; I have honestly declared it; and oh, what a comfort it is to me now! I have been true to holiness; and now Jesus saves me—saves me fully. I am washed and made clean. Oh, I am so sweetly washed in the blood of the Lamb!" That evening he became extremely weak, and so sensitive to pain that he could not bear the least noise, and yet he was tender and quiet without the slightest manifestation of impatience, and so considerate that when he heard the voice of one of the brethren in an adjoining room he asked to see him. The friend remarked, "Why, my pastor, you are all ready—collar on and wrapper on." "Ah!" he replied, "your pastor has not much strength ; the outward is failing, but all is right within."

Quite early Monday morning he asked his wife the question, "Where will you live—in Columbia or Philadelphia?" Affected to tears, she replied, " Why do you ask me that question ?—I could not live anywhere without you." Seeing her feel thus, he sweetly said, " I thought I would like to know." This was the first morning he was unable to shave himself; he was very weak, and he evidently was impressed that his end was approaching. He asked his wife again, " My dear, if the Lord should take me away from you, could you say, 'The will of the Lord be done'?" She, startled at the question, replied, "I feel that you belong to the Lord ; I have always felt so, but I do not believe He is going to take you away from me." He responded, "God's will is always right and best, dear." "But," she said, "how can I live without you?" He replied, "Jesus can be everything to you;

He has been with us in the past, and He will never leave
nor forsake you. You know the Bible is full of promises
for the widow and fatherless. Live a moment at a time,
'looking unto Jesus'; and then, if *permitted*, I shall be with
you often ; I will be your *guardian angel*, and be the first
to meet you at the pearly gate."

His mother spent most of Monday with him. While she
was present he lost the use of his hand. He remarked, as
he looked at it, " This hand seems paralyzed, *but it belongs
to Jesus.*" He then repeated part of the hymn—

"God moves in a mysterious way."

His mother said, " I feel it a privilege, Alfred, to be in
this room, there is such a Divine influence ; it seems like
the gate of heaven." He responded, "Yes, there are
heavenly visitants here." About five o'clock p.m. she left
him to return to her home in New York, not supposing him
to be near death. As she was kissing him good-bye, he
held her hand, and, gazing into her eyes, he said, " Next
to Jesus, mother, I owe everything to you. Your holy influence, your godly example, your wise counsels have made
me the Christian and the minister that I am." To his brother
John he said, " John, you have been a mercy to me—mercy
is written on your brow. My friends are all a mercy to me.
I am not afraid to die. *Death is the gate to endless glory ;
I am washed in the blood of the Lamb.*" He desired to see
his sister-in-law, Miss Rebecca Bruner, who had just arrived
from Columbia, Pennsylvania, and after inquiring for the
loved ones at home, he said to her, " This is the sickest
day of my life, but all is well; I am so glad I have
preached full salvation : what should I do without it now ?
If you forget everything else, remember my testimony—
WASHED IN THE BLOOD OF THE LAMB ! Jesus is drawing

me closer and closer to His great heart of infinite love." To his wife he said, "I am Christ's little infant; just as you fold your little babe to your bosom, so I am nestling close to the heart of Jesus." Shortly afterwards his eldest son, George, returning from New York, came into the room; looking up to him, he said, "My son, your pa has been all day long *sweeping close by the gates of death.*" At his request he was removed to the other side of the bed, when he remarked, "How sweet and quiet everything seems !—I feel like resting now." Very soon he became sick, and immediately an effusion of the brain took place, when he became insensible to outward things, and within about four hours, at eleven o'clock p.m., surrounded by his family and the trustees of his Church, he died, sweeping through the gates of Paradise, washed in the blood of the Lamb.

Thus, on the 13th of November, 1871, passed to the bosom of God, in the prime of his life, one of the most saintly, earnest, and useful men of modern times. His dying testimony carries us back to the glowing record of St. Ignatius, when yearning for martyrdom : "Suffer me to imitate the passion of my God. My love is crucified ; there is no fire in me desiring earthly fuel ; that which lives and speaks within me says—'Home to the Father.'"

The intelligence of Mr. Cookman's death spread rapidly, and was everywhere received with astonishment and pain. His most intimate friends, even those who had seen him during his illness, were shocked at its suddenness. The thought of death had not been really associated with one who had moved so recently among men with a vigour which promised a long and healthful life. The shock at his sudden death was only exceeded by the universal grief which it caused. It was as though "one were dead in every house" where he was known or the odour of his sanctity had entered. It is a question if the mysterious loss of his father, though it may have gathered about it more romantic interest, excited a more general and profound grief. "When I heard of his death," writes a gentleman from Philadelphia, " I spent a week silently in tears." Exclaimed an old coloured woman in Wilmington when told of his death, " Dat man gone straight to glory." His family, his Church, the churches which he had previously served, were overwhelmed with sorrow. From private persons and public bodies, from both the secular and religious press, there teemed the most tender expressions of regret and condolence.

The funeral services took place in the Central Church, Market Street, Newark, at three p.m., on Thursday, the 16th. The following account appeared the next week in *The New York Christian Advocate :—*

" The parsonage was filled at the funeral with ministers, chiefly Methodist, but also of other denominations, who appeared subdued by the feeling that a very afflictive and mysterious dispensation had fallen upon the Church and the family in the unexpected removal of Brother Cookman. The plate on the beautiful coffin told the age of the deceased to be forty-four ; and pure, sweet flowers rested on either end, at the foot in the shape of a cross, at the head in that of a crown.

" At 2.30 p.m. the procession moved from the house, the family and bearers in carriages, followed by the officers of the Church, and perhaps a hundred clergymen from far and from near. One of the most affecting sights of the occasion was the little children of our departed brother about the coffin and in the procession, evidently not old enough to appreciate the fulness of their loss. The church—pulpit, altar, gallery, choir—was heavily draped in mourning, and crowded in every part, including the aisles, out into the street, by a deeply sympathizing congregation. In the pulpit were Bishop Simpson, Rev. De Witt Talmage, Dr. Porter, Dr. Crane, Rev. Mr. McDonald, and others ; the altar, also, and a considerable portion of the centre of the church, were occupied by brother clergymen. The opening anthem came soothingly, ' Cast thy burden on the Lord.'

"Rev. S. Van Benschoten read Psalm xc., and Mr. Talmage 1 Cor.

xv., when the venerable Dr. Porter led in a solemn and appropriate prayer. Rev. Bishop Simpson then addressed the hushed audience. Throughout, the bishop's manner was very subdued, as though struggling to repress the rising of a great sorrow.

"Rev. Mr. McDonald then rose and spoke of Brother Cookman in his relation to holiness and the National Camp-meeting Association. The choir sang 'White Robes,' and the deeply affected congregation took their last loving look at their beloved pastor and friend."

After the services the remains were carried to Philadelphia, accompanied by the family, members of the National Camp-meeting Committee, and a large delegation from the Central Church. They were deposited at the house of Mr. Frank Cookman, whence the next day they were escorted to the Union Methodist Episcopal Church in Fourth Street, where additional funeral services took place in presence of a densely crowded congregation. As the clergy walked slowly into the church, the strains of the "Dead March from Saul" helped to deepen the solemnity of the scene. An anthem was then sung by the choir, and the Rev. Dr. Nevin, of the Presbyterian Church, read the Scriptures. Rev. J. Dickerson announced the hymn, "Servant of God, well done," which was sung by the congregation; and the Rev. Dr. Pattison offered prayer. The Rev. Dr. Suddards, of the Protestant Episcopal Church, after reading another Scriptural lesson, addressed the audience, in which he made feeling allusion to his intimacy with the Rev. George G. Cookman, and paid a high tribute to the excellence and usefulness of both father and son. The Rev. Andrew Longacre next followed in an extended address, relating to the character, labours, and death of the deceased. The Rev. Mr. Alday, pastor of Union Church, then spoke more particularly of the last sickness of the departed. The closing address was by the Rev. Dr. (now Bishop) Foster, of Drew Theological Seminary, New Jersey, who spoke substantially as follows :—

"Alfred Cookman belonged to a royalty. There are many royalties of earth : there is the royalty of *genius*, but I should not class our brother with these—he was not a genius. There is a royalty of *intellect ;* of scientific research ; of the power to unfold great doctrines and grasp great principles. Though a man of a beautiful mind, a clear and strong intellect, the range and sweep of his observation was not his most wonderful gift. There is royalty of *eloquence :* our brother was not wanting in this ; he seemed to belong to a race whose lips were strangely touched.

" But he belonged to a royalty rarer by far than any of these—the *seraphic royalty* of earth. He was not Pauline, but he was Johannine. He was the brother of John, who leaned upon the Master's breast, from whom he drew his inspiration. He belonged to the race of Fletcher and of Payson—the best and rarest royalty God has ever permitted to grace the earth.

" When the brother prayed that the mantle of Alfred Cookman might fall on us, I said, ' Amen, Lord Jesus ! ' Not his mantle of eloquence or pulpit power, so much as his great, magnanimous, holy, and sacred character.

" As my little boy brought the message of the death of Alfred Cookman to my lecture-room, he knew how it would strike me : he knew he had ministered at the altar where his sainted mother and sister used to worship ; so he said in a whisper, ' Father, Brother Cookman is dead.' Oh, how it shocked me ! I thought at once that the most sacred man I knew had gone away from us ; and this is my testimony to-day. I have known the Church for thirty years ; I have known the men of the Church during that time through all the episcopacy and ministry ; and the most sacred man I have known is he who is enshrined in that casket."

The casket was then opened, and the large concourse present were permitted, moving up the central aisles and retiring by the rear doors, to see the face they shall look upon no more till resurrection morning. Many as they passed bent over and imprinted a kiss on the cold lips and marble brow, which wore the natural expression and sweetest smile, remembered so well by all who knew him in life. Tears fell freely as the scores whom he had led to Jesus bade him a last farewell. The preparations for burial followed; and Rev. Messrs. Gillingham, Turner, Dickerson, Major, and A. Wallace, surviving members of the class of 1848, Philadelphia Conference, of which Mr. Cookman was a member, carried the body of their classmate to the hearse in waiting, and also to the grave in Laurel Hill Cemetery, where the burial service was read by the Rev. W. L. Gray, Dr. Pattison, and Dr. J. H. Alday. The hymn "Rock of Ages" was sung—he having expressed when in health a liking for singing at Christians' graves—and just before sunset his body was committed to the earth. Laurel Hill, hitherto his Pisgah, was now his last resting-place.

Memorial services were held in many of the churches of Philadelphia; in Grace Church, Wilmington; in Central Church, Newark; and also in Trinity Methodist Episcopal Church, New York. The trustees of the Central Church, Newark, have had a Gothic tablet of Italian marble placed in the audience-room of their church, in the wall at the right of the pulpit, with this inscription :—

"En Memory of Reb. Alfred Cookman,

BORN JANUARY 4, 1828,

DIED NOVEMBER 13, 1871.

'*He walked with God and was not, for God took him.*'"

CHAPTER XXV.

WE have thus seen the earth close over all that was mortal
of Alfred Cookman. I have sought so to weave into the
narrative of his life the traits which distinguished him, as
they appeared not only to myself, but also to others, that
now there seems but little need from me for any special
characterization of the man or his work. Yet it may not
be amiss, before dismissing a subject which I have studied
with constantly increasing interest, to briefly sum up my
thoughts.

It has seldom fallen to any man to possess a nature in all
respects so admirably attempered as his was. He inherited
the physical and intellectual qualities of both his father and
mother, the distinctive type being possibly rather that of his
mother than his father—having much of the father's fiery
creative energy, he yet partook more largely of his mother's
strong common-sense. In body he was more robust than
his father; in intellect he was less bold and incisive, but
probably equally sure, and even more tenacious. From a
child he was healthful. When grown, in person he stood
about five feet nine inches, and was well proportioned, with
a full, round chest, a head of medium size, not a prominent
forehead, surmounted and surrounded by rich, glossy black

hair; his eyes were gray, large, and full, with a gentle, lustrous, rather than a piercing look; his nose was straight, with sufficiently distended nostrils; his mouth wide, lips moderately full, well set, but not too tightly compressed, showing an expression of mingled tenderness and firmness; a chin round, smoothly shaven, and massive enough for strength—the whole face just such as to make you say when you had the hastiest view of it, "There is a marked and trustworthy man." With a ruddy complexion, a sinewy form, a steady step, an erect carriage, he looked like one born to command; and he did command.

Mr. Cookman's fine physical fibre had much to do with the exquisite delicacy of his feelings. Truly natural, without the least artificiality, he responded healthfully to all the works of God about him, and was never more at home than when surrounded by primitive scenes and primitive people. He was very practical; the farthest removed from an affectation of superiority to common matter-of-fact life, he ever manifested a keen zest in all the ordinary occurrences of the family and the world. "There was nothing human which was foreign to him," in the sense that whatever interested his fellow-men interested him. He never fell into the mistake of a morbid sentimentalism which shuts itself away from men and things under the plea of contempt for mankind. He was truly modest, shrinking whenever possible from observation, and "wondering what the churches saw in him that they should desire his poor services." The lowest seat suited him best, and was invariably taken if the choice were left to him; and no man ever more surely fulfilled the apostolic injunction, "In honour preferring one another."

Generosity was strongly marked in his character. While

he was incapable of retaining a grudge against an enemy, to his friends he was unbounded in his devotion. He could not say too much in their praise or do too much for their advantage. This quality made him charming as a pastor— no matter if the circle of his friendship was constantly enlarging, he had capacity for its ever-widening increase— because he never seemed to forget or overlook any one he had ever loved; and into the circumstances of all people, whether of joy or grief, he could enter with an ease and directness which made all who were the recipients of his sympathy feel its genuineness. During his last sickness a gentleman called to tell him of the death of his boy. He entered promptly into the afflicted father's feelings, and in comforting him said, "Dear brother, the heart will ache. It is not wrong to weep. Jesus wept, and He does sympathize with us; but remember Jesus can dwell in an aching heart." A day or two afterwards the child was buried. It was a stormy day, and as Mr. Cookman lay upon his bed he was heard to pray that God would comfort the bereaved family, "for, Lord, it is hard to put away the little darling on such a stormy day."

This generosity of heart made him very kind to the poor. It was not an uncommon thing for him either to send or to take a basket of provisions to a destitute family, and oftener than otherwise a substantial sum of money accompanied the basket. Generosity, natural as it was, took shape under Christian principles, and was not allowed to spend itself impulsively. The one-tenth of his income was dedicated to strictly religious uses. The benevolent drawer as regularly received its *tithe deposit* as his pocket received the stated dues on account of salary or from other sources. Closely joined with this dedication of himself and a stated proportion of his income to God, was a firm faith in the care of Divine Providence. There were times when, with a large family, he was reduced to great straits; but he would always take his burden to the Lord Jesus, and somehow, often in a way wholly unexpected, relief would come. During these exigencies his liberality remained the same to others. "Their need," he would say, "may be greater than mine."

One of the most lovely features of Mr. Cookman's character was his filial affection. He revered the memory of his father, and loved his mother with a devotion which led him to sit at her feet as a little child. The recollections he retained of his father, which were sedulously cherished by the mother, invested the departed parent with a halo which, to the fervid imagination of the son, lifted him to a region ideally apart and unapproachable. The fame of the father was the son's natural inheritance, and as such he sought to preserve and improve upon it. And it is doubtful if Christian biography affords many instances where a guardianship has been more faithfully rendered, or an inheritance more legitimately and substantially enlarged. Alfred Cookman will live in the Church of the future as in all respects a worthy successor of his father, the Rev. George G. Cookman. That the son owed much to the father cannot be denied; but where has a son so well maintained himself on heights upon which his father's reputation placed him?

More, however, to the mother did he owe than to any other human being. I may repeat the thought of another and say, Mrs. Mary Cookman was mother of the body and *soul* of her son. What Wordsworth so justly and gratefully said of his sister, Alfred could have said of his mother:—

> " She gave me eyes, she gave me ears;
> And humble cares, delicate fears;

A heart, the fountain of sweet tears,
And love, and thought, and joy."

Her native sense, delicate tact, moral ascendency, firmness of discipline, religious fervour, feminine tenderness, and withal devotion to her son, which well-nigh inwardly consumed her with zeal for his welfare, afforded the happy combination of qualities which simultaneously and continuously stirred and guided the natural powers of her first-born. She never allowed him to outgrow her, and hence he never ceased to look up to her. In his middle age he could as confidently rely upon her understanding as upon her heart; and to the fact of this mother's influence may be largely traced not only the womanly grace of his mind and manner, but also the subtle force and reliable judgment which distinguished his career.

In seeking for the ultimate cause of Mr. Cookman's power, I am obliged to find it in his moral nature. Religion built upon a sound, natural basis was the real source of his influence. It is impossible to estimate the man without considering the joint and reciprocal effects of both his natural and spiritual constitution, for their interaction was marked from the beginning. This may be true of most men, but it was eminently so of him. These pages have certainly shown him to be a singularly godly person through his whole life; the testimony of many who knew him most intimately, and who were well qualified by their good sense and opportunities of observation to judge, is to the effect that he was one of the holiest of men—as free from moral taint as any among whom we walked. A factor so important in the make-up of his character cannot be disregarded in the determination of his intellectual calibre. That his religious condition did affect his intellectual condition cannot be questioned; nor do I pretend to doubt, but claim it rather as a glory, that the distinctive energy of Mr. Cookman was spiritual rather than intellectual.

But I am not willing to concede that this energy was so exclusively moral as some assert. He did not owe all he was to religion—no, not to that highest type of it, Christian holiness—in the sense that he could have been nothing, and would have had no marked power without it. He possessed by nature a very vigorous mind. Its structure was such that with the ordinary opportunities of education it would have put him in the foremost ranks in almost any profession he might have chosen. He was endowed with all the essential elements of success—a discriminating judgment, a retentive memory, a vivid fancy, a strong imagination, which saw things most clearly, a sympathizing heart, a power of application and adaptation ; these, united to a handsome person and a voice of wondrous compass and melody, must be accepted as the faculties which ordinarily warrant success. Genius, in the highest sense, seldom falls to mortals ; but if in its usual and lower sense it consists in the power which enables a man to see things as they are, and to transfuse them with a glow which makes other men see and feel them, then may we claim it for Mr. Cookman. What he talked about people saw and felt.

It is true that he has given no proofs of profound scholarship, and that he has left no evidence of fierce intellectual struggles and doubts. But it will be remembered that his career was thrust upon him, by a Providence he could not disregard, to be a preacher rather than a theologian. The work of the evangelist was definitively pointed out as his mission, and not the work of the student. His vocation was consequently to make history, not to write it. An actor in one of the most important crises of the American Church and nation, he has left to others, who may have the leisure and the taste, to record what he and his compeers have so nobly done. Had he resisted solicitations to so wide-spread a public service, and withdrawn to the seclusion of the study, he might have been as noted to-day for the depth and versatility of his attainments as for his popular and effective eloquence.

He did, I allow, accept calmly the doctrines of the Church. There is but little trace of dissent and disquiet in the history of his religious thought. But must spasms of disbelief, crises of fearful questioning, be regarded as the infallible signs of a strong mind? Shall it be regarded as an orthodox word among those who scoff at orthodox Christianity, that no man can be voted to the grade of able and original thinkers who has not passed through the throes of mortal doubt touching all the great fundamentals of truth which the wisdom of ages has sat in judgment upon and approved? If so, Mr. Cookman must be rejected. But it is a fact that many of the greatest minds of these and other times have never passed through any such phases of unrest. " So far from this, some of the finest spirits—those whose vision is most intuitive and penetrating—are the most exempt from such anxious soul travails. Indeed, I believe that there is no such safeguard against the worst consequences of such perplexities as a heart that is pure, humble, and ‘at leisure from itself.’ "

Such was the state of Alfred Cookman. His judgments were steadily, quietly reached; not that his intellect was less capable, but that a sound heart did the main work of the intellect.

The medium of Mr. Cookman's power was the office and work of the Christian pastor. By ruling, visiting, and preaching, this power was exerted upon the minds and hearts of the flock of Christ. For the threefold duty of his office he was fitted by the gifts and graces just discussed. This fitness made him ready and able to use, as circum-stances required, all the legitimate means of ministerial usefulness. He despised no means, neglected none, which could give him greater access to the hearts of the people. His invention was ever at work to impart freshness to old means, or, if necessary, to devise new expedients of exciting attention. He was among the first Methodist pastors to issue printed addresses to the congregation, or cards such as his " League of Prayer," to promote revivals of religion. He usually spent the forenoons of each day, except Monday, in his study, and the afternoons in pastoral calls. To the sick, the bereaved, and the penitent he was very attentive.

His visits were an effective instrument of his great suc-cess as a revivalist. He would follow up closely those who in the congregation manifested a desire for religion, and the result of his careful attention to persons thus exercised was that they seldom failed of obtaining comfort. Underlying his thoughtfulness and perseverance was his prayerfulness and faith. " I knew him," writes his wife, " when in Wilmington and other places, during a season of religious awakening, to stay up until near daybreak alone in his study, pleading with God for the conversion of the people ; and when I have goné to him in the night and entreated him to rest, he has said he 'could not, so great was his burden for souls.' He believed in intercessory prayer, and often remarked, ' Jesus spent whole nights in prayer ! '" The Rev. Mr. Inskip, speaking of him at the memorial service, Ocean Grove, said : " His great strength he got from God at the mercy-seat. . . . Perhaps on no other occasion was this more apparent than in that wonderful season of prayer at Vineland. A halo of glory was around him. He rose from his knees with his hands heavenward, his eyes closed; and the influence that was felt all over the ground told of his intimate relations with God." A gentleman of the Baptist Church spoke also of the same occasion: " I shall never forget the picture I saw at Vineland; it was under the arbour where Dr. and Mrs. Palmer were holding a meeting, and Brother Cookman led in prayer. He was on his knees, with his hands raised, asking God for blessings. Instinctively I opened my eyes. He rose from his knees, and reaching up as high as he could, seemed to grasp the blessings asked for; and then, falling on his knees again, he thanked God again for them. How much good it did me to see such faith that would just reach up and get what God was about to give ! "

Prayer and faith were never lost sight of in his prepara-tions for the pulpit. He sought direction of God in the selection and elaboration of his topics, and then depended upon God for their effectiveness. He was never happier than when preaching. While always pertinent and instruc-tive, he was at times borne away by a tide of holy feeling, which swept both preacher and audience upon its resistless strength. Mr. Cookman seldom attempted great profundity or metaphysical niceties, but mostly dealt in the plainer and more substantial facts of revelation—stating them usually in simple language, and enlivening them with a natural imagery, a lifelike or historical incident, so that they were appre-hended by all, even the most illiterate, and enjoyed also by the cultured among his hearers. The late Rev. Albert Barnes, of Philadelphia, was exceedingly fond of his preach-ing, as affording to his mind one of the best examples of pure Gospel sermonizing. A peculiarity of Mr. Cookman's preaching was the frequent recognition of the Three Persons in the Godhead. The cross of Christ, the blood of Jesus, was a constantly recurring theme; while he as repeatedly dwelt upon the person, office, and work of the Holy Ghost.

It was by no mere novelties he drew the masses—the common people heard him gladly, not as they rushed to see a show, but expecting from his lips the word of life ; and he gave them bread, the vital truth of God, to feed them, and did not mock them with a stone. His popularity in the pulpit was not due to meretricious ornaments, or to the low buffoonery that caters to a vicious taste, but to what he was as a holy man, and to what he said as the ambassador of Jesus Christ.

If his themes were few, they were chosen conscientiously, because he believed it was impossible for a man who preached to save men to stir from the cross of the Redeemer. He did, however, present these themes with great freshness and unction. "To me," said an eloquent minister, who knew him well and heard him often, "he was one of the freshest of speakers." Whatever of light from nature, art, or passing events could be shed on these topics for their more forcible illustration, he sought and diligently applied. Nothing was more apparent than that in the pulpit he was a thoughtful man in a thinking and active age. But, above all, did he make the invariable impression that his trust for the success of the Word was upon supernatural help. The hearer who did not gather this failed of the simplest teaching of the devout preacher. The whole effect of the man was, that whoever might be the instrument used, it is God who giveth the increase. The effect of his evident reliance upon Divine aid was also heightened by his free, natural, and forcible delivery. His voice and gestures were always suited to his subjects—now low, slow, and tender, and anon rising into vehemence of sound and action with the cumulation of thought and feeling. Ample preparation having been made,

generally with the pen in hand, he entered the pulpit un-
trammelled by manuscript, and in the delivery of the sermon
looked his audience directly in the eyes, and as he proceeded both gave and received inspiration.   It is doubtful
if, as a preacher, take him all in all, he had his superior
for effective popular discourse among the younger men of
the land.

As to his capacity as a ruler, one phrase will express the
whole—he ruled but little.   He trusted his people, and they
trusted him.   He was an ensample to the flock, a model of
purity in the minor as well as greater morals.   His speech
was always seasoned with grace, though not indifferent to
the flavour of humour ; he was the farthest removed from
bitterness, coarseness, and trifling.   He was temperate in all
things—totally so in things which might occasion offence—.
moderate in dress and in household expenditures.   With as
keen a relish for the refinements of life as any soul ever
attuned to the harmony of sweet sounds, he yet esteemed
saving men preferable to all the delights which art could
afford.   This thought is admirably pointed by the substance
of a conversation had with him by Mrs. Battershall, of New
York, while he was stationed at Spring Garden Street,
Philadelphia.

" Mr. Cookman, with that total absence of censoriousness
which characterizes a perfect Christian charity, and yet with
that earnestness we should expect from a faithful Christian
watchman, when Zion's best interests are imperilled, remarked to me on one occasion that ' the culture of the
beautiful within proper limit was all well and good, but he
considered the glory of God and the good of souls of
infinitely more value than the highest human culture.' "

Mr. Cookman's views of the ministerial vocation did not
shut him away from society or the nation.   He retained fully

his position as a citizen of the state. To him, as to one before him, "politics was the body of religion"; and he ever took the liveliest interest in the great social and political questions of his times, as closely related to the welfare of Christ's kingdom and the race. He was decided and active in the Temperance and other humane reforms, giving to them not only his countenance, but his cordial support. Much less did his calling as a Methodist pastor exclude him from the most intimate fellowship with all the people of God. He was incapable of narrowness. He loved the image of Jesus wherever he saw it, and was happy to count among his dearest friends and fellow-workers many ministers and laymen beyond the pale of his own denomination. In no slight degree did his truly catholic spirit help forward the deepening unity and spirituality which are now pervading the several branches of Christ's holy church. And it may be safely affirmed that there is no name of American Methodism of the present generation more ardently revered by Christians of all denominations than the name of Alfred Cookman.

In assigning him his place in the modern Church, the distinction which I claim for him is that of a *marked illustration* of the doctrine of Christian holiness. Whatever may have been originally in the mind of God concerning him, evidently the providential circumstances of his life tended to mould his character and to shape his mission for this end. He was not disobedient to the heavenly calling. He can in no sense be ranked with original men—such as found new systems of thought, new societies, or even new methods of activity; his rank is with the class who afford the material, furnish the facts out of which systems, societies, and methods are constructed. As a fact, Mr. Cookman's life is of incalculable value to the student of the great problem of Christian ethics. No mind, however critical, can contemplate so striking an exhibition of moral purity, in its direct relation to the Gospel as its efficient cause, and ignore the importance of the Divine element in the great process of elevating the human race. While to Christian inquirers with an animus to know what is the utmost that the Gospel of Christ can accomplish for a believer in Jesus, it is an instance which must excite the highest wonder and delight, as affording another example of the practicability and beauty of holiness in their own times and among their own circles. The grace of God purified the man while walking among fellows, lifted him up to shine as a clear, steady light by the very pathways of busy people.

And this, to show what Christianity can actually do for men as a purifying power, is what the world most needs to know. One clearly defined proof of this, such as is given in the case of our friend, is worth a thousand speculations. The danger of our age lies in the direction of sinking out of sight as a reality the agency of the Holy Ghost in the work of moral renovation. The tendency is to reduce the great First Cause of salvation to a series of subordinate and incidental causes whereby man is manipulated into a new life. The scientific spirit is reasoning God out of the process of saving the world. An idolatrous worship of intellect threatens to drown in an incense of thought, culture, ideas, the stronger part of human nature, the *heart*—out of which are the issues of life. It is sought in some localities to politely bow out of society the Gospel of the cleansing blood, of regenerating grace, for a new Gospel of "culture." Mr. Cookman's life is an attestation of the abiding strength and the spring-like freshness of the old Gospel. It is an example of moral and spiritual purity, made such not by the innovating process of the "schools," but by the power of the Holy Ghost, through the blood shed on Calvary.

"It is the old, old story of Jesus and His love."

As such I have sought to present it to men. It may be that greater men have died without any such extended record of their lives ; but I doubt if any one has lived among us more worthy of careful mention. He embodied in himself the attributes of humanity most necessary to be known, loved, and imitated. These attributes had their rise in the cross of Jesus Christ—a source accessible alike to all persons. He lived and died an example of the reality and power of Christian purity—one of the most beautiful specimens of a natural, simple, yet divinely spiritual manhood which it has fallen to this or any age to possess ; and as such he takes his position among the departed worthies of the Christian Church.

Mr. Cookman left seven children :—George Grimston, Frank Simpson, Annie Bruner, William Wilberforce, Mary, Helen Kier, and Alfred ; Alfred Bruner and Rebecca Evans having died before him. Mrs. Cookman, his widow, and the children, have their permanent residence in Philadelphia, Pa.

BY THE REV. ALFRED LONGACRE.

There can be no doubt that Mr. Cookman's personal character entered largely into the elements of his power. It was the substratum on which his ample influence securely rested. It is difficult, however, to distinguish in him the simple natural endowments from the precious gifts of Divine grace, since grace began its work so early in him. But it is not necessary to make the distinction. As we knew him, he was a thorough Christian gentleman, and the outward grace in him was but the gleam of the light of the gentle spirit and fine feelings within. To many of us he was what Tennyson calls his friend—

> " The sweetest soul
> That ever looked through human eyes."

He was magnanimous in every instinct, never little or mean, incapable of detraction himself and unsuspicious of it in others. His soul moved on the high plain where all is broad and liberal and unselfish.

He was honest to his convictions at every cost ; and there were votes in Conference that did cost him something in other days, as there were convictions as a teacher of the truth more recently that were not unattended with trial and alienation of friends. But nobody had ever to doubt where Alfred Cookman stood on a question of conscience. And this was with no shadow of bravado or self-assertion, but in the " meekness of wisdom," with the very "meekness and gentleness," the "sweet reasonableness of Christ."

His character was rounded and well poised, and there was with it also a deeper underlying wisdom than many who knew him well imagined, because it was always perfectly unobtrusive. Altogether he was peculiarly a man made to be loved. Unselfish in his friendship, his quick sympathies and warm interest were freely given in return for the love we gave him. Few men have ever been so widely or so greatly beloved. In the churches he had served—and I speak understandingly, for I have twice followed him at considerable intervals—his name is embalmed in a deep and peculiar affection, as one dearer and better than other men. .

Higher than all else was his character as a man of God. It was because he saw and felt the holiness of his life that his influence was so strong with us. His mind was drawn to the subject of entire sanctification in the very beginning of his ministry by Bishop and Mrs. Hamline, then visiting Newtown, one of his appointments. For a number of years, however, his views were undecided with respect to this doctrine. But about thirteen years ago his conscience was awakened to it again, and he entered into the clear enjoyment of it as a personal experience. His convictions on this subject became from that time the profoundest of his mind and heart ; and he never failed, on all fitting occasions, to let his belief and his experience be well understood. Yet I need scarce remind you that his confession had in it nothing of self-exaltation. He never failed to disclaim all goodness in or from himself; but he rejoiced always, and with exultant faith, in the power of the blood of Jesus to cleanse him from all sin.

His own faith and experience never seemed to separate him from others who did not think or feel as he did. No one felt at a distance from him by reason of his holiness. It was a holiness that attracted, not one that repelled.

He has supported this Scriptural teaching with all his consecrated abilities. To it he has given the most cogent of his arguments, and still more effectively his almost irresistible powers of persuasion.

But his life has been more powerful still. Men might, if they pleased, oppose his arguments with doubts and objections ; they might even turn away from his burning appeals; but no one could question the living purity of the man, the practical embodiment of holiness in his life. In the shadow of approaching death he expressed his joy and gratitude that he had been permitted to experience and to uphold this great salvation—the fulness of the power of Jesus Christ to save.

And he has gone. In the golden prime of his days, in the fresh maturity and plenitude of his beautiful life, he has gone from his work and from us, who have loved him so well.

Recollections of Alfred Cookman, as a preacher, by the Rev. James M. Lightbourn, of Baltimore, Md. :—

"Alfred Cookman was the best model of a Methodist preacher I ever knew. He was, in the highest and strictest sense of the word, a gentleman. True politeness springs from the heart—such was his. He was as gentle and respectful to the humble poor as he was graceful and polite to the most refined and cultured. With suavity of manners he united firmness of character. While his spirit was most loving, and his nature gentle and extremely sensitive, he was a hero in the cause of truth, both aggressively and defensively.

"As a camp-meeting preacher, Alfred Cookman was a prince among his brethren. An announcement that he would preach always insured a large congregation. A sermon preached by him at the Camden Camp, upon the subject of entire sanctification, will never be forgotten by those who heard it. It was the clearest exposition of the great doctrine I ever heard. His appeals were irresistible, and swept all hearts. The fire which he kindled that day he drew from heaven. The Spirit of the Lord God was upon him—his face was like that of an angel, and his voice rang over the vast audience, carrying conviction to many Laodicean hearts. Revivals have been known to follow his camp-meeting efforts."

A tribute from the Rev. T. De Witt Talmage, D.D. :—

" The Rev. Alfred Cookman's life comes back to me like the sound from a church-bell embowered in trees on a soft June day. It was nothing so much I ever heard him say, or anything I ever saw him do, that so impressed me as *himself*. He was the grace of the Gospel impersonated. I met him often on the platform of religious and philanthropic meetings. To be with him was to be blessed. The more I saw him the more I loved him. His preaching was not made up of ten grains of metaphysics and nine grains of German philosophy to one grain of Gospel, but with him Christ was *all and in all!* Sweep a circle of three feet around the cross of Jesus, and you take in all that there was of Alfred Cookman.

" It is not so much the Methodist Church that suffers from his departure as all Christendom. Oh that we all might have more of his spirit, and die at last his beautiful and triumphant death !"

The Rev. Dr. W. M. Paxton's estimate of Mr. Cookman's preaching :—

"As a preacher, I always regarded him as remarkable. His sermons were solid, able, experimental, instructive, and sometimes brilliant, glowing, eloquent. His pulpit power, as I estimated it, consisted largely in two things :—

" 1. In the happy faculty which he had of giving an experimental cast to all his thinking. Few men have been as successful as he was in imbuing all their preaching with their own rich experience.

" 2. In a singular capacity for pictorial illustration. This, I presume, was in a measure a natural gift, inherited from his distinguished father, who, I am told, was in his day unrivalled in this species of eloquence—but when his voice was silenced, the gift was reproduced in his son. I remember to have listened, or rather to have looked with great delight at his beautiful pictures, for they were so graphic that they passed like panoramic paintings before my view. I presume, of course, that a volume of his sermons will be published ; but permit me to suggest, also, that a small volume of pictorial illustrations, gathered from his sermons, might do great good. It occurs to me, however, that it is quite probable that many of his finest things were never written. The faculty being a gift, and not an acquirement, I can well understand that it would be fettered rather than assisted by the pen."

From the Rev. George S. Hare, D.D., the successor of Mr. Cookman at the Central Church, Newark, New Jersey :—

" I first met Alfred Cookman in Pittsburgh, Pennsylvania. He was very open and frank, and went at once to a warm place in my heart. The thing that struck me, outside of himself, at Pittsburgh, was that he was so entirely loved, and almost idolized by his people. I could easily tell why, from the impression he had made on myself. I met him again soon after in New York, where I was a pastor, and he had come to speak at an anniversary. I do not remember to have had any further intercourse with him until he succeeded me as pastor of the Central Church, in New York. I had removed to Trinity, in the same city, and of course we saw much of each other. I think the relations of an old pastor and his successor were never more delightful. Knowing the Church by heart, I had an opportunity to observe his influence upon it —to see how quickly he won all hearts, and how entirely they came to confide in him as a friend and teacher. He followed me also at Trinity, and our relations remained the same. We were true friends and brothers in our work, and Alfred Cookman never impressed me but in one way—as the gentlest, purest, and most sincere of men. I am again his successor, but never more will he succeed me. I came here under the shadow of his death to a broken-hearted people. It is doubtful if he ever accomplished more for a Church in any full term of service than for this Central Church of Newark in the few months of his pastorate here. He was ripe in his holiness, and his influence fell like a power of God on all around him. His triumphant death sealed it all, and left the Church so chastened in spirit, so in love with goodness, so aspirant toward purity, that it has been but an easy and joyful task to lead it on to good and noble works. His memory here is as sweet and precious as the memory of mortal man can be. I attempt no estimate of his character, but I give these few impressions of an influence which has fallen like sunshine on my way, with gratitude to God that He gave me Alfred Cookman for a friend and a brother."

I cannot more appropriately close these testimonials to the worth and usefulness of Mr. Cookman, nor the history of the life which it has been my pleasant task to record, than by quoting the reference made to his character and death by the Rev. W. M. Punshon, in the memorable address delivered by that gentleman before the late General Conference of the Methodist Episcopal Church in the city of Brooklyn. After eloquently characterizing Bishops Baker, Clark, Thompson, and Kingsley, the Rev. Drs. Mattison, Sewall, McClintock, and Nadal, all of whom had died since he came to America, he said :—

" And then I think of a later loss than these—a blameless and beautiful character, whose name had a hereditary charm for me, whose saintly spirit exhaled so sweet a fragrance that the perfume lingers with me yet, and who went home like a plumed warrior, for whom the everlasting doors were lifted, as he was stricken into victory in his prime, and who had nothing to do at the last but mount into the chariot of Israel, and go 'sweeping through the gates washed in the blood of the Lamb.' "

THE END.

Watson and Hazell, Printers, London and Aylesbury.